The Unshorn Thread

Tales Misforgotten

Book One

The Unshorn Thread

Colin P. Druce-McFadden

First Edition

To My Parents,
Who have always supported me,
Loved me,
And
Who introduced me to a world full of adventures.

Table of Contents:

Prologue: Page #

I	Reentry	9
II	What the Old Oak Saw	18

Chapters:

1	Wart	21
2	Castle Ektor	31
3	Exodus	48
4	Johnny Reb	59
5	Shadow and Regret	82
6	Upon a Summer's Day	85
7	Embers Amongst the Ashes	91
8	Points of Light and Dark	101
9	An Errand	112
10	Wicked Sir Bart	119
11	Parting Ways	127
12	The True American	130
13	The Dreamer Espied	151
14	Time and Tide	156
15	In the Beginning	171
16	Godfall	178
17	Revelation	184
18	Castle Tintagel	186
19	Dawn	192
20	Conrad	198
21	The Great Hunter	212
22	Prophecy and Peril	218
23	Eyes in the Dark	223
24	Hunter, Hunted	231
25	A Home No More	246
26	The Young Lord Pendragon	248
27	Blood and Ice	265
28	Kilkaenen Unseen	268
29	Reduced to Ashes	271
30	King of the Wild Frontier	275

Prologue

Reentry

The stars, my sky-borne comrades; my very component parts, fall from the heavens. My muscles ache and atrophy. The little blue marble grows before me. It is not the stars which are falling, I realize, but myself. How strange a feeling it is.

How strange it is to feel.

Sky lashes my face as it whips by, blisteringly hot yet sharp as a knife. I roll as I fall; the heat migrates across my shoulders, rests upon my spine. There it warms me, buffeting and massaging my immobile muscles back to life, coaxing the flow of blood back into my veins.
Staring up toward the stars, I find them distant. A blue-black curtain begins to draw between us.
Something tears, bursts and oozes down my side. An old wound, long forgotten but never dressed, never healed.
The heavens are blue now, the veil fully drawn. Wind, not sky, buffets me, blows into me through my wounded side, expanding in my flesh. I gasp with the pain and give rise to my chest for the first time in longer than I can possibly know. The pain overwhelms me and heaven and earth go black.

Points of light dance before me. For an instant I think myself to have been dreaming, that I remain amongst the heavens, fooled by hope and delirium once again. But no... these are not stars that dance before me; they are the lights that come to a waking mind as it fights against pain and disorientation; they are the harbingers of awareness and life, and so I cling to them. I stare at one point of light, willing it to open, to show me the waking world once more.

The sky, vast and cerulean leaps back into view before me. I have just enough time to realize that I am smiling before something cold and not quite solid slams into my spine and all is black once more.

No... not black, but very nearly so. Something presses against me. It squeezes me from all sides, forces the air from my lungs, crushes my injured flank. There is something else here as well, a frigid cold that is at once familiar and terrifying. Fear slides its wicked fingers along my neck, grasps me, pulls me deeper into the dark. I shudder in its grasp. The pressure mounts, clenching me ever tighter.

I wonder if this is what it is to die, to truly die. Have I so fleetingly tasted life again, merely to have it wrenched from me so soon?

Something deep in the recesses of the dark laughs to itself. Water creeps into my lungs.

A shiver of shock races along my spine. My muscles spasm, flexing and extending without need of my will. As I sink, the spasms grow more frequent, stronger. A leg kicks. An arm wheels. Without my aid my body struggles, lashing out at that which would snuff out the starlight of my heart.

An ironic mirth sparks to life in my belly. Try as I might, I cannot will my atrophied frame to obey me; it moves of its own accord, kicking out at the intangible grip of the sea. A thought bubbles up within me, as if pinned to the mirth in my belly: my frame is striking at that which I fear in the deep, and though I cannot control my motions, perhaps I can direct them.

I close my eyes in the dark, picture the grip of death rising from the seabed, rising to pull me down and bury me beneath the sand. My heart pounds all the harder. My left leg kicks out and down. Slowly, sporadically my other limbs follow suit and by spasm, by lunge, by flail, I rise. If I am awake or alive I cannot say, but still my carcass fights on, and so I rise. The pressure about me buckles. Pale light begins to bleed through my still-shut eyelids.

And then there is air about me.

It forces its way into me, raising me up farther still. My lungs rise, rise again and again, and at last I open my eyes.

I lie upon the sand, the spinning world about me both strange and familiar, like a dream mis-remembered.

The sound of footsteps greets my ear. Someone is walking along the water's edge, the sea lapping at his ankles. The footsteps stop beside me, and before I can get my head to stop spinning, there is a hand, small but firm, gripping me by the shoulder. I am pulled up from the beach until I am standing, looking down upon the face of a man. He is small in my reckoning, 'but then,' I recall, 'so are they all.' He wears a wry smile upon his lips.

"Just where I thought you would be," he says, half to himself. "I had half forgot how prompt it would be. I suppose there is nothing like eternity to make a man lax in his duty, eh?" He laughs, as if privy to some internal jest.

"Let us take you to the others," he says, beckoning me to follow him back along the shore. My eyes trace his path and fall upon a small islet. Finding me not beside him, he turns to me. "Yes," he says, "that is the place, though how you can know it already, I dare not guess."

"Was I..." I begin, the words feeling foreign upon my palate. "Was I not to meet someone there once?"

His smile returns.

"Whether you were or not, you shall today," he says. There is something between violence and fear in his smile as he turns from me. In silence, I follow him along the shore and across the shallow channel that separates the islet from the land.

My feet alight upon the narrow beach of the islet in silence, as if I am scarcely present in this place. My guide forges ahead into the dense brush that lines the shore. I linger a moment, turning to face the sea. A strange sort of recollection visits upon my mind: I stand now where once another did; I see the place now where once I fell.

From deep within me boils forth a keening wail, one which has festered within me for centuries. I scream my rage and pain at the lapping waves, scream until my knees buckle beneath me. Tears course down my cheeks as I kneel upon the land which once held my betrayer. I wipe them away but one teardrop, laden with salt, escapes, falls from my cheek and is dashed against the rocky earth. Renewed rage boils from my gut as I stare down upon the rock. I watch my teardrop be absorbed by the dry earth, watch the salt bleach the spot where it fell, and raise my fist in wrath.

"This earth, this rock has taken from me too much already," I cry out to none but myself. "I shall grant it no further boon!"

My fist comes crashing down, hard against the stone. I savor the sound and sensation of the crack as the stone is sundered beneath my blow. I scream my victorious grief to the heavens. I stand, raising the halves of the ruined stone above my head before hurling them into the sea. "Let them rest beneath the cold dark of the sea in my stead," I proclaim, gazing at the place where they have struck the surface until the ripples have faded away, until the sea has wiped even this final trace of them from its surface.

A hand rests upon my back. It is my guide, returned from the forest of the islet. I allow him to lead me within. We descend into the brush, into the gullet of the isle. As we do so a strange light begins to filter through the trees. It is a pale, unnatural color, though not uninviting. I feel myself hasten toward it, like an unknowing moth. A clearing presents itself before long, in which a coven of hooded figures stands, clearly awaiting our approach. The air is ambrosial and humid, as if the forest all about is sweating ichorous vapor.

Creatures glowing rusty red flit and gambol about the air. They are lank, scaly things — made of bone and hide alone. As we approach, one of the hooded figures raises a finger toward the floating creatures. Their cavort becomes more rapid, strained. Still in the air, they turn and bank about the clearing. Their thin frames stretch, long as ribbons. High-pitched cries spin about me. Whether these are cries of pain or are produced merely by wind-shear I cannot tell.

Another figure raises a finger into the air and the creatures' patterns become ever tighter. Fleetingly, I catch glimpses of something akin to writing in their motions, here and there a symbol familiar, but they are gone again before I can be sure.

My guide pushes me forward. Again I am surprised by his strength; I stagger forward into the empty space beneath the creatures. Cries, now unquestionably emanating from the creatures mouths, fill the air. As they arc close to me they bare their fangs, their jaws opening unnaturally wide. Wrath twinkles in their eyes. Their movements shift again, recognizable now as those of hunters cornering their prey. They charge one another, teeth sinking into scale and bone. Those struck first thrash about, impaling anything within their reach. Once each blow is dealt, there can be no escape. Tight, intricate knots of bone and blood form all about. Soon every fang has struck, every tail coiled, every claw grasped. The writhing slows. The screams die away. All that is left is an intricate knot of living sinew, at once ornate and wretched, beautiful and obscene.

My guide strides to my side. The instant he is beneath it, the writhing knot of flesh ceases moving. The only sound emanating from it now is a dull tugging, like a ship's rigging in the wind. My guide smiles, gazing upon me.

"You may wonder as to our intentions," he says. "Know that this knot, formed of flesh and bone, dredged from the deep places of this world is wrought for your protection. Without it, you might well be hurled beyond your now-vacant starry cell, beyond even our ability to retrieve you."

I gaze up at the knot. Hundreds of eyes, fixed and staring, meet my gaze from within the tangled mass. Instinctively I reach out to touch it, but a hand upon my flank stops me. My guide shakes his head.

"The knot-work is not yet finished," he says. "To truly safeguard you, we must bind you to something of this earth."

"Then let it be done," I say. "I would not return to that stretched, static existence for anything."

"Kneel and you shall hear, our star-borne refugee, the tale of the garden of Æthe and her charges four," says my guide, his voice ringing about the glade and through my very bones. "You knew, in your day, of Hephaestus the smith, whose weapons he forged of light and sky. You knew too, that he was not forever so skilled, had not forever been. Only after Zeus' light ascended atop the mount did Hephaestus find his fire. Look to the skies today; climb the mount... you shall find the forger of the lightning forever departed."

I find I cannot stand. My breathing labored in the thick air, I sink to my knees. My guide sits before me, and between us is set in the dirt a large and heavy object, wrapped in a sheaf of rusted maroon leather. The wrapped thing seems to shudder as its bearer's fingers release it. My guide retreats from it, nearly so faintly that one might not notice it. Nearly. His face is somber as I look from the thing upon the earth to him.

"Do you remember your gods?" he asks.

"How could I forget?"

He smiles his knowing smile.

"And what of those who came before?" he asks, a greedy twinkle in his eye.

"The Titans?" I ask, perplexed. "I can recall some of the tales. Perhaps I even met one once. It is all so long forgotten."

His expression turns grave.

"It is no great matter," he says. "Let it suffice then, to say that there was once a gardener, a woman of peerless horticulture. As a weaver crafts a basket, so she sowed the green. Life, death, prosper and ruin grew from her soil. This was the way of Æthe, the First Seed. Do you understand?"

Sleepily I nod. The ambrosia of the glade flows in my veins. My entranced heart pounds out a strange rhythm against my bones. I lean forward, yearning to hear more; and so my guide obliges.

"There came a time of great strife. It was then that the great lord Elatha, like your Zeus to his Hephaestus, came to Æthe in need. He told her that there was need of rending and the making of death.

"'Plant me the germ of our enemies' destruction, gardener,' he said. 'Sow me such devilries that they cannot but fall at my feet.'

"To this Æthe sighed and said: 'What you ask I will do, my lord. But be warned: With such a harvest comes always sacrifice, always loss.'

"But the great lord Elatha heeded not her warning, and so Æthe began her grim task. With her dagger she cleft four holes into the soil, and in each she dropped one of four seeds. Soil she then kicked atop each until it was buried in the earth. And from each grave she grew the four great portents of the ancient age."

I am suddenly aware of my guide's small, firm hand upon my chest. Looking down I find to my surprise how far forward I have leaned. Below me lies the leather-bound something, pulsing in my *spellbound sight. He presses me back to my seat, himself hovering above the thing only so long as he must. He holds my gaze a moment and then, against my every expectation, flicks open the leather wrappings. There, shining in the fell light of the glade lies an axe, the like of which I have never beheld. Its blade is at once heavy and æthereally sharp. The metal of it coils, fluid-like toward a knotted, rust-colored hardwood hilt. There the metal and wood twist about until one is indiscernible from the other. As I look upon the weapon, my guide begins to sing:*

"Planted in iron, and through it then grown
Our weapon was seeded in ages unknown
We formed it to sate the blood lust of our kin
His dark heart and vile mind, in payment to win

Its metal was forged beyond human skill
The need for which soon comprehend it you will
For our kinsman's name was Kilkaenen Unseen
Since always in darkness did wander the fiend

No love could find him; no parent could dote
So darkened his heart and ill feelings did bloat
Thus, by his hand, were struck father and dam
And through their meek hearts, his foretoken did ram

Of this early omen, we portentously noted
And within our ranks his evil promoted
Thus killer was born and our army amended
So toward our enemies, his baseness we bended

A means of control we set out to wreak
And channel his killings away from the meek
To do this, an elm tree Æthe watered with blood
Where deep in its roots it did mix with the mud

Thus thirsting, forever, for blood it would be
This sapling of iron and rancor and tree
For coiled 'round the trunk of the hoary old elm

15

Spun metal and blade from root to green helm

Now hunger and thirst the whetted thing did
For ichor as much as our champion's id
Carefully bound was this malcontent elm
So our true intentions it would not o'rwhelm

And quick grow it did, tight to its iron coil
Burling and curling from bloody base soil
When tall as the blade the sapling did creep
We chopped off its roots and the weapon did reap

Hungering now for its intake of gore
The fell blade we gave to Kilkaenen our whore
But, his hand on the weapon, we now know too well
Its thirst for fresh blood it never would quell

Too well and too hungry the blade had been wrought
For even Kilkaenen's rampages were naught
'Gainst the thirst for fresh blood which the blade it still sought
'Til finding no foe, it turned where it not ought

And thirsting for blood but not found, it did sink
Into Kilkaenen's chest for a final red drink

Now rumor has it, but no one dare knows
That through the ill axe his spirit still flows
Forget not his moniker, lest unaware
Kilkaenen the Unseen your sleeping breast tears

With this in our mind we hereby bequeath
His weapon on you sans scabbard or sheath
Your rage and your skill matches Kilkaenen's Will
Take him now with you, your comáte in the kill"

My guide stands behind me now. He plunges his hand into my injured flank and from it draws something small and violent. I hardly notice the blood that trickles down my side. He appears beside me, holding in his grasp a delicate and shiningly bright bit of metal, dripping with crimson. It is the head of an arrow. At the sight of it, the thought of dark ringlets alights upon my mind, the scent of perfumed breath upon my tongue. I blink and they are gone again.

My guide holds the bit of arrow aloft, making a show of it to the hooded figures gathered about. His movements are smooth; a sort of dance. He swings in low arcs above the axe, with each turn coming closer to its blade. The weapon does not move, yet I feel its yearning for the flesh that spins now so close to its edge.

My heart beats fiercely, in tandem with the blade. Images of my betrayal explode against my ribs with each pounding of my heart. There is blood in my mouth, its rusty taste mixing with my saliva, feeding my indignant rage.

My guide swings low again, too low this time. His hand slides across the axe, and there is blood upon the weapon in an instant. He moves his hand in small, exacting motions; churns the blood to ink; spatter into lettering. It is not a language I know, but I am sure that I can read the letters of my name in it before he is done. The glint of metal shines again between his fingers. It is not his own blood I realize, in which he has written, but mine.

The wound upon my flank burns blindingly, uncannily hot. The axe, Kilkaenen's Will, is in my grasp now. My guide lies dead at my feet, his small frame shrunken further still in death. He is akin to a child now, to my eyes.

Above me, the ring of knotted scale and eye and bone shivers apart. Freed, the creatures flail frantically about, but are soon caught in some unseen current. Unwittingly, they slap and thud against one another, drawn along the current to Kilkaenen's Will. Their bodies are cleft neatly as they break in waves against the blade, their blood spattering upon his hilt and my wrist. Like the wound in my side, their blood burns white-hot against my flesh. The glade begins to go dark about me. I land upon my back.

Before I succumb entirely to the black, I hear a voice, both strange and familiar:

"Their binding is done," it says. "Let us hope he keeps the vile thing fed well enough to be of some use."

What The Old Oak Saw

It was winter, and the house was barely visible through the storm. The stonework walls, laid together centuries prior by the hands of forgotten masons, were now veiled in ice and snow. The snow was falling at such an angle that there was hardly any of the original rock to be seen. In fact, the last real stonework that could be made out at all was that very last fraction of wall underneath the overhanging thatch of the roof. That too, was fading quickly into the growing drift that had encompassed the walkway and collapsed the hedges in its unyielding siege of the dwelling. A signpost, blasted by ice, stood at the edge of the buried road, its face indiscernible. So heavily had the snow amassed upon the sign that time and again dense chunks of ice had plummeted from their transitory home, only to be replaced moments later by their younger brethren. Only the old oak which stood beside the post, its roots covered by that which the sign could not carry, seemed able to bear the weight of what had arrived.

Usually at this time of year the storms would have subsided and the thawing would have begun in preparation for spring, but just as the sun had emerged from its hibernation and groggily crept out from under its thick blanket of clouds, that very morning there had been a shift in the winds. With a bellow that had shaken the very earth, a frigid gale had descended from the northern mountains and into the hills surrounding the poor little house. The wind brought with it an abomination of a cloud that tore across the sky, pressing against the borders of heaven itself for lack of room, darkening the earth below. Pregnant with snow, this grim tyrant of the skies thrust shards of ice down with such force that they cleft the flesh of those sluggish enough to be caught outdoors as the storm slammed through the borders of the town below. The chilling curtain had been drawn across town in an instant, creating out of the first bright morning in months a night as dark as could be remembered. The morning was now long forgotten, as the clouds had been in place for the entire day and well into that which was truly night. Still the storm raged on, as if angered that the sun had awakened at all.

Through it all, the walls of the cottage had stood, a final refuge from the maddening winds beyond the hinges of the door. Neither the hinges nor the latch had shaken when the storm had thrust its full force at the door. Though old, they had been well made and well cared for. It was not they that had caused the now silenced screams and the muffled calling out of names that had echoed down the hall.

No gust of wind, no matter how violent, could have shaken the house apart. The only aperture through which the wind had been allowed was a slight crack at the top of the door. Years of use and general age had hardened the wood, but had also shrunken the planks ever so slightly. There was just enough of a gap for the wind to howl through the house, and every now and again a flake of snow would shoot through the gap as if launched from its cloudy den for the express purpose of finding this one chink in the carefully tooled armor of the cottage. These few invaders had, over time, created a sort of murky puddle in the dust that had settled between the cracks in the stone flooring. Indeed, the door and walls had done their job well and had not yielded more than a bowlful of water to the interior of the house.

Yet no refuge was ever any stronger than its weakest point. It had been the thatch — that thick, insulating layer of grasses wrapped tightly and heaped upon the heavy beams of the roof which had failed its master and mistress. These grasses, usually very warm and comforting, had finally given in to the pressure exerted upon them by the four feet of snow and ice that had accumulated upon them throughout the day and collapsed, burying the elderly couple who had been tucked away in their bed for the night. They had closed their bedroom door as they always did before turning in, then climbed, ever so gently, into bed. It had been just as they lay their heads upon their pillows and just after their last goodnights and final I-love-yous were said that the thatch had rustled mournfully and given way. The man and wife were buried in an instant, entombed together in the ice. And still the storm raged on.

Chapter One

Wart

At the edge of the grounds of Castle Ektor, named after its self-titled lord, there sat a tiny shamble of a thatched cottage. This was the dwelling of Bedwyn, the groundskeeper of the tower house turned manor. It was also home to Bartholomew, Bedwyn's fat and fluffy feline friend, as well as a young whelp of a lad named Wart.

Late on the night of the spring snowstorm Wart lay in bed, his eyes arguing with his mind as to the value of sleep and, for that matter, bedtimes in general. He had just sat up and was about to go back beside the fire when the thing had come into his room. The air had gone solid and the room had filled with a gripping cold. Had Wart been brave enough he would have drawn the covers over his head, but the very presence of the warped thing at the foot of his bed stopped him. Wart stared into the dark in a vain attempt to fool both himself and whatever this creature was into believing that he knew exactly where it lurked and that he was not afraid. There was no seeing it. Only the deeper darkness at the foot of his bed and the sense of ice forming along his spine told him of the sudden danger in his room. A shambling, splintered figure had slipped through the crack under the door. It was a good foot taller than a man, but nowhere near as solid. A windy shadow of a thing, it hung there between him and his only escape. Wart could hear his heart pounding away against his ear drums. He knew they were red with blood as he felt the cold sweat beading upon his forehead. He thought of how he wanted desperately to run screaming past it and into Bedwyn's room. He would be safe there. Bedwyn would be able to stop it.

His eyes burned. He had been staring into the blackness, not blinking, for what seemed like forever. He had not dared move for fear of breaking whatever trance held the twisted figure in its place. Then it moved.

Wart's eyes were opening before he knew that they had closed. He must have been clamping his eyes shut as tight as they would go, for all Wart could see now was the shadowy after-image of eyes staring back at him in the darkened room. He was on his back, lying against his pillow. The thought that it had been a dream settled into his mind, starting his heart again, allowing him to breathe in. It was a strangely labored breath. Wart wondered if Bartholomew, the groundskeeper's cat, had slunk under the covers to fall asleep upon his chest.

His eyes were not focusing correctly. The clouds still hung there, just in front of his face. In fact they were getting darker, and if at all possible, deeper. Wart moved to sit up. His little arms did not budge. An icy hand was wrapped tightly around each of them. Cold sweat began once more to trickle down beside his ears. He choked. There had been no dream. The creature was sitting upon his chest, its crooked legs crouched in a spidery squat. They had not been images of his own eyes that Wart had seen, reflected through sleep; they had been those of the creature. The pressure on his chest had been its cold weight settling upon him, pushing him down. Wart felt as if the mere proximity of the thing was keeping his eyes heavy. It was as if he were fighting to wake from a deep slumber, but he now knew he had not slept a wink. He tried to scream. The sound trembled out of his lips as a shudder, too weak for Bedwyn to hear. The creature's eyes were fixed upon him. It did not move. Its face hung so closely to his that only his weakening breath could pass between them. Its eyes, those dark pits, hung in front of his, staring into him, burrowing into his heart with their icy gaze.

Wart's heart was trying to escape his chest. The beating was so forceful that he could feel the blood pumping along his veins and into his head and arms, the creature's grip too tight for the blood to pass his elbows. He felt as if he was going to pop from the dizzying pressure. The throbbing of his head seemed to be flowing through the air now, the pain and blood lifting out of his skull and into the caverns that hung before him. Focusing on the blood in his eyes, Wart could see the foul thing pulling at the strands of his life that flowed towards it. With every strained beat of his heart those winding funnels of ash were swelling, their edges pounding closer and closer to him. It was as if a part of him were being torn away from behind his stomach and being pulled out through his eyes, towards those swollen pits of dark. Wart knew he had only moments left before he could fight no longer. His lungs shook with the strain of rising, desperate to gather their last few scattered and shallow breaths. His head was so filled with blood that his vision had been tinted a dark maroon. Something beneath the skin under his left eye popped and a thin trickle of the vital fluid began a steady crawl down the pale surface of his upper lip.

As it all faded away, Wart thought of Bedwyn. He thought of how Bedwyn cared for him and of how Bedwyn would be left to keep the grounds of Castle Ektor alone without him. He thought of how old and weak Bedwyn was and how the poor man could hardly get through his share of the grounds-work without developing a severe case of the shakes. These thoughts made Wart's already overworked heart heavier still. *It wasn't right.* Bedwyn was a good man, and his was the only care Wart recieved from the world. The thought of Bedwyn alone was too much for Wart. *It just wasn't fair.* He struggled once more against the drain he felt in his stomach. Wart knew he was going to die, but he didn't care. It wasn't fair and it wasn't right. He may only have been a groundskeeper's apprentice for these first seven years of his life, but he was living on the grounds of a tower house and a defender thereof by default if not by right. He was young, yes, and weak, but Wart had to fight. He had to fight for Bedwyn and for Bartholomew and for himself, even if he *was* going to die. His heart told him so.

It was at that moment that something strange happened. Wart's vision cleared, but it was not the wraith that he saw before him, nor was it his room, but another place, and he saw it through different eyes:

Staring at the collapsed cottage through the bleak world surrounding him, the old man wondered how long he had been standing there. Standing across the lane, he was a good stone's throw from the shrunken cottage. Even with the blades of ice falling like sundered chandeliers between them, he saw every sad detail of it without even a squint of his weathered eyes. Every now and again a tattered wisp of gray flitted before his face. He did not raise a finger to pull the strands of hair back. He did not stir at all.

Had he been there to see it? He wondered. Had he watched in morbid fascination as the thatch had fallen and the cold death had slid in? Or was it merely too predictable a set of happenings not to have been guessed? The bedpost, barely visible now above the snow, seemed to shout out to him. "Horror! Death!" it cried, and from somewhere deep within him a sigh began to build. It bled out from his stomach and flooded up through his chest, churning the emptiness therein, giving it weight. Passing through his scarcely open lips the sigh hung in the air for a moment, solid and white, before it was carried away by the gale. For a moment he had forgotten the wild winds and the heaping icy siege. Watching his breath dissipate into the falling ice, he noticed that his face stung as if lashed by a thousand stinging nettles. The pain forced his eyes away from the sad, broken home. He wondered again how he had come to be in this place. There was no path to be seen in the snow, no telling dip in its level to discern how he had gotten to this place. The snow was so flat around him that he, buried up to his knees, tendrils of snow climbing the folds of his cloak, looked more like some warped old oak tree than a man. It seemed to him that the land had simply forgotten how he had gotten here, and in truth he was inclined to echo its sentiment on the matter. He hadn't the slightest idea how he had come to this place of frozen death. In truth, it seemed, he had no solid memories whatsoever. Only shadows and ghosts danced and faded through his mind.

'It must be this damnable storm,' he thought to himself. 'The cold and the discovery of this sad affair must have jilted me of my faculties,' he thought, glancing again at the tomb that stood in the darkness ahead of him. 'Best to take myself away from this place, find somewhere I can regain my senses.'

Turning his eyes away from the ruined home, however, yielded no such refuge. He closed his eyes and stooped his head, and for a moment seemed to admit defeat. His back hunched forward slightly, and masses of tangled, ice-encrusted hair fell beside his face. For a moment he was again motionless, a gnarled mass for the winds to beat against.

A thunderous burst of frozen air swept through the yard, toppling the ice from the signpost, as it had done many times over that night. The small lump of white plopped down upon the old man's foot. The old man's neck creaked as it swung slowly upward toward the sign. Glancing at the language thereupon, the old man's eyes inspected the single word carved into the wood: *Myrddin.*

A spark skittered across his mind. A small but definite flame appeared behind his eyes, and the man set off, down the hill towards town. The wind billowed across his back, sending icy tendrils of hair ahead of him. They seemed to strain in an attempt to hurry him along whatever path it was he had chosen. Try as they might, however, they could not speed him on his way. His progress was slow; every step seemed heavily weighted. His muscles felt as if they had shrunk with age and lack of use while they had been holding him, rooted to that spot before the cottage. Even so, it would have been hard to make him out a moment later from where the disemboweled cottage stood, a figure fading into the storm as it slunk down the hill.

Back in his room, Wart breathed deeply. His chest rose, despite the dark weight pressing down upon him. His eyes flew open, the fire of resolution burning behind them. He stared back into those black wells that had so nearly sucked the life from him.

Loosing a piercing scream that sounded like a thousand birds dying, the creature pitched backwards, bristling with rage. This sort of resistance to its witchery it had not known to be possible. One instant, the boy had been nearly dead, drawing his last breath, and the next he was fighting as a man possessed by some great beast. The creature's grip on Wart's arms loosened.

Knowing his only chance to free himself had arrived, Wart tugged with all his might at his right arm and, to his everlasting joy, it wrenched its way free. At his bedside there was a pewter goblet filled with water. Bedwyn had left it for Wart to drink when he got thirsty in the middle of the night. Wart's hand reached out desperately for the cup. With an earsplitting howl, the creature raised its left arm to crush Wart's skull, but the boy acted quicker, bringing the goblet down onto the creature's shoulder with all the force his young arm could give. Water sloshed over the bed. There was a sound like the crackling of leaves, and the creature's arm gave way, dissipating as it scattered across the bed.

The goblet burned cold in Wart's hand, forcing him to let it fall clattering to the floor. The creature's arm was beginning to rustle itself into clumps now. It was going to re-attach itself to the murky well from which it had fallen. Tugging his left arm free, Wart clasped his hands together. Years of torment from Sir Kaye had shown him how to fight those larger than himself. Clenching both his hands together, Wart swung his arms, slamming them into the right side of the creature's head. The sound of leaves came again and the creature lurched sideways off of the bed, unable to catch itself with its damaged arm.

Wart was up like a light and running to the closed door. The creature, now crumpled on the floor, threw its good arm toward him. It was too long a distance for the thing to have caught him, but just as the creature's fingers stopped short, Wart was gripped 'round the heart, fingers of cold piercing his chest. His pulse raced. He was slowing down, running through torrents of murk that rushed back towards the broken figure on the floor. The haze was thick around him, but Wart could still see the doorknob ahead. He reached out through the currents of black and grasped it. Turning the knob, Wart heard the creature issue a low and rumbling wail, a final attempt to keep him from escaping its grasp. Wart flung the door open and ran screaming into the hallway, slamming the door back against its hinges as he went.

The scene that met Wart's eyes was one of utter horror. The heavy oaken door that led into the cottage from the cold was dashed to smithereens. Splinters were all that hung from its iron hinges. It looked as if the door had slammed heavily into the chair that sat before the fire. Bedwyn's chair. Cloth and framework were scattered across the stone floor, mingled with traces of blood. Against the mason-work at the far end of the room was a large red mark. It was thick and wet, and little rivulets of blood were still winding their way down the canals of the rough stonework wall... winding towards a small, crumpled shape lying broken upon the floor. A shape almost too small to have been the old man. Yet it was. Bedwyn was gone. For a moment Wart's world stood still. There was no feeling left in the world. All was numb. It felt like it must be a wicked prank or some dream from which he would soon wake.

Then the cold returned. Cold from the shattered door, and cold from that which slouched ever closer to Wart from behind. Wart turned to see the thing forcing itself to its full height from beneath the door of his room. It grew in short bursts, emitting with each a creaking, splintering sound, like the snapping of tinder. The fight withdrew from Wart's heart. The man of which he had been so sure, his savior, was dead and gone; a battered corpse clotting upon the floor. Tears began to be drawn up from the well in his stomach. Tears of loss, of fear. Tears that told him he could do no more against this evil that had come into his world and destroyed his everything. Wart fell to his knees. What good was being a defender of the castle if there was no good left within it to save? Wart closed his eyes and waited for the thing to grasp him once again.

A ripple in the cold wind from the door told Wart that someone was in the room with him, someone already standing between him and the vile creature. He would not yet open his eyes, but Wart was sure it was the strange old man he had seen in his mind's eye. A voice heavy with age, but strong as that of a lord rebounded against the walls of the small cottage. "Your ilk have seen their last, creature! This child is now under the protection of something you cannot revoke with your darkness! Your hate and your hunger are now your own to bear. Sate them, now, as you have made so many others do in your time. Sate them and be undone!"

There was a hideous noise then, a scream like that of many dying birds mingled with the low moan of ancient despair. Then followed a strange and deep crack, as if some great breach had opened in a wall of ice. A ripple of air swept past Wart's ears and all was still.

"Child? You are safe now little one," came the voice again,

emanating from the world beyond Wart's shut eyelids — a world Wart was very much trying to deny existed. "Come now," it insisted, "what good is it to shut out the light after so nearly letting in the dark, eh?"

At this Wart began to sob, his chest heaving up and down violently with each breath. It was too much to be reprimanded now, too much by far. Trying to shut out every last inch of the world he now hated, Wart cupped his hands over his ears. If only he could find a way not to breathe, he might not have to take in any of it any longer.

"Haha, well this just won't do, now will it?" the man said. "Up we go." Wart felt two strong hands scoop him up from under his arms and into the air. A strange and not altogether comforting bristliness met his face, accompanied by a rough cloth, which Wart grabbed ahold of out of some instinct which all children share. They were moving now, out into the storm. Wart had thought the ice and snow would have frozen him to the core instantly, and just as he was about to utter a whimper to that effect, he opened his eyes. The flakes of snow and ice were, it seemed, whirling all about them and landing upon the ground. Few, no *none,* of them were striking either he or the old man he could now see carrying him. The bristliness he had felt turned out to be a long grey beard, stuck here and there with a small twig or a bit of bark.

Wart glanced over the old man's shoulder at his home, immediately regretting that he had. Thankfully, Bedwyn's cottage was already being gobbled up by the sheets of snow that still strangely refused to touch Wart or the old man. Wart shuddered and turned his head to rest on the chest of his unexpected guardian, making an even less expected realization as he did so. They were headed towards Castle Ektor! Surely the old man must be heading past the towerhouse. Even a weathered transient like him would have heard of the temper of the lord of this land. There was no mistaking it now. The path they were walking was a bee-line, its only possible destination the main gate of the castle. The *main* gate. Wart had never entered through the main gate before. A small door around and down the rocky foundation was reserved for the servants and grounds-folk.

"We mustn't," he blurted out. "Lord Ektor will throw us in the dungeons for it." Neither their pace nor their direction altered in the slightest. "Sir, please," Wart said, "I do not wish to see you imprisoned, sir. We mustn't —"

"Quiet now, child. All is well," came the quiet reply. Wart didn't know why this calmed him, only that it did. "What's your name, eh boy?" asked the old man.

"W-Wart," stammered the boy, "or least-wise that's what I've been called more often than anything else, far back as I can recall."

"Well Wart, you will soon be warm and safe again. You have my word," the old man said. Wart kept silent as they crossed the last few feet to the gate.

As they reached the castle there was a scuffling sound from behind the large wooden door. A small porthole opened and a pair of large eyes and an even larger pair of nostrils pressed themselves up to the opening. "What's this then?" the guard asked. "Are you expected? No one's told me of any arrivals after supper."

"We're coming in," The old man expounded. "It's cold and the child has had a terrible shock."

"Not expected?! Raggamuffings at the door? Oh you'd do well to remember whose manor this is, you rusted old plough-share!" the guard nearly screeched.

"I don't care one iota whose manor this is," retorted the old man, his grip tightening ever so slightly around Wart's middle-section. "I shall repeat the damn well obvious fact that it is frigid out here and that there is a child in need! If that is not reason enough, then let me tell you that I have just come from across what I assume you call a green in the summer-time and that the cottage just a stone's throw away has been broken in! Does the fool who lords over this land care at all for the safety of those who dwell in it? At the very least he should care for his own!"

The words were of such force that the guard shuddered back from the timbers of the door. He stood there a moment, a barely visible pair of eyes in the dim light of the entry hall. Then the eyes squinted and the porthole was slammed shut. An instant later there was a loud clanking and a rustling, the like of which was usually associated with a sword clattering against a metal sheath as it was drawn. The door began to swing heavily open, the guard behind it most likely about to yell something to the effect of "how dare you threaten the safety of our Lord Ektor," as he charged out the door at the old man. These words, however, never quite made it to the outside world, but were instead stuffed back down into the guard's stomach, just as the guard himself was stuffed back into the entry hall and pressed against the stone wall behind the main gate.

The instant the latch had been undone, the old man had swept forward and gripped the door by its edge and, one hand still carrying Wart, slammed it and the guard well and hard against the wall. In they went, man and child, to the warmth and refuge of Castle Ektor, the Main Gate thudding against its frame as the aged conqueror kicked it shut behind them.

Chapter Two

Castle Ektor

Slouched in his high-backed chair, Lord Ektor looked across the main hall of his castle. The serfs were bustling to and fro; setting a full feast upon the long and elegant table that was, at evenings, the center-piece of the hall. There had already been laid out turnips and potatoes, chestnuts and winter berries, smoked fish and all manner of pasties and pies. In reach of Ektor's right arm there was a stonework carafe from which came the scent of strong-smelling mead. An over-fed fire spread, belching and hiccupping, along the wall, too big for the chimney to contain. With help from candles set upon spikes that lined the walls, as well as their brothers set in silver upon the table, the vast glutton of flame made the room shine like the rivers of springtime.

The castle dogs slunk up the stairwell from the kitchens, following the feast. These were lean animals, but well versed in the art of scrap-snatching, and it was only due to their master's attentiveness to his table that they dined so meagerly. One of the serfs followed them up from the spit. A large duck, decorated with blackcurrant and wild thyme, sat upon a massive platter in his arms. As he was clearing the final step into the Hall, one of the hounds lingered in his path, hoping for an avalanche of supper. The serf stumbled, but caught himself. Only a small splash of brownish gravy dribbled from the platter and onto the back of the waiting dog. The poor beast was set upon in an instant by its kin, the other dogs pinning the yelping cur to the ground. Even this morsel was worth such ferocity. All three were now in a tussle upon the steps, slipping down a step now and again as the beleaguered animal fought to get to his feet. The serf, having stepped over the dogs watched them with a look of astonished glee. Turning toward the table, his mouth opened to remark upon the foolishness of animals. His grin faded quickly, an equal and opposite reaction to the bulging of his eyes, as he realized that Lord Ektor was not only standing, but glaring at him from across the long planks of the table.

"What vile nature is in you that you must further delay my table after ruining its main dish?!" roared the large and sagging man. The serf was taken aback, as to his reckoning he had just *saved* the duck rather than ruined it. His mouth opened and the words "It isn't all that bad, yer lordship," tumbled out. Instantly regretting them, the serf shook violently on his spindly legs as his lord rounded the edge of the table and came galumphing down the Great Hall towards him. "Not all that bad!? *Not all that...* do you realize that duck is my favorite dish?!" the lord near squealed. The serf recalled aloud, to his misfortune, that he had thought deer had been Lord Ektor's favorite, adding an "if you please, sir," in a vain attempt at softening the blow of contradicting his better.

"You'll do well never again to open that thick-wit mouth of yours, you punctured chamber pot!" Ektor exploded, grabbing the tray from the still shaking serf's hands, spilling twice the gravy the serf had upon the deer skins which lay upon the floor as he did so. "Now fetch someone capable of cleaning this up, you useless pustule!" he wretched, as he slammed the tray down upon the heavy timbers of the table. The serf only nodded as he went scrambling down the stairs to the relative safety of the kitchens.

"You know they only make further mistakes if you yell at them so, Father," came a strong voice full of pretense, emanating from the stairs that led to the sleeping quarters above.

"Kaye, my lad!" smiled Lord Ektor, the past moment's thundering all but forgotten. "What splendid timing you have! I was just about to have these useless lumps boxed at the ears for not summoning you in timely enough a manner as to sup with your old man!"

"Oh, come off it Father. I always know it's suppertime when the clatterings of the serfs and the yelpings of the dogs reach my ears. It isn't as if they have any other occasion to be allowed up here to the Great Hall!" said Kaye, slipping into the only other seat set at the table.

"Well, they'd best remember that it is their one allotted moment to bask in the glory that is the hall of their lord! I see more foolery and less decorum every day among the younger ones. Perhaps tomorrow we will have to make an example of that sack of waste that did nearly ruin my duck! What say you to that, eh my boy?"

Looking at his father, Kaye chuckled. Lord Ektor was leaning well over the table, his sizeable gut widening upon the cutlery as he leaned towards his son. A glint of frivolity twinkled in his eyes as he made reference to the beating and humiliation of his serf.

"Father, you do get in such a mood when you gain occasion to thrash something! Ha ha! We'll make a great spectacle of him, shall we? What shall we do to the poor fool? Lash him? Have him trudge around the curtain wall in naught but a loincloth? Hah! I rather like *that* idea!" Kaye snorted. It was one of the lord's favorite things to do, torture, and Kaye reveled in the way his father's face lit up at the very mention of the subject.

Ektor was, indeed, beaming at his son now. "You know, Kaye my lad, I do believe you're to be quite the tyrant after my days have passed! Ho-ho! Trudge around in his skivvies! Ho! Ho-ho! Yes we'll really have to see that! And we'll turn out the whole of the village to make sure the lesson is not lost upon them, eh? Ho-hoh!"

Lord Ektor and Kaye were just about to enter into hysterics and begin what would have surely been a night of gulping down drink, wasteful consumption of food and ever-elaborating ruminations concerning the humiliation of their poor mark. Glasses were raised to begin the first of what might have been many toasts when there echoed up the stair a thunderous boom, a cacophonous clattering following closely on its heels. Ears perked, both gentlemen turned their faces to stare blankly at the stairwell. A second rumbling thud found its way up to the Great Hall then, leaving no doubt that the first such sound had been the Main Gate slamming open. Whoever had opened the thing had just shut it tight again. There then followed a moment of frozen astonishment in the Great Hall. All was quiet. Even the fire seemed to forget its usual gassy and crumbly nature and burned silently in its nook. Kaye and Ektor were frozen, Ektor still leaning toward his son, one fat fist holding aloft a tankard of mead at an awkward angle, the mead beginning to dribble down the side of the tankard and down Ektor's fingers. Then came the faint but unmistakeable sound of steps coming up the spiral stair. Faint they were, but no doubt they had covered a floor of the tower house already and were now only two levels below the Great Hall.

"Kaye!" spat Ektor in a desperate whisper, lowering his tankard shakily back to its spot upon the table, "Kaye! We've interlopers in the Keep!"

"Oh, come Father. It isn't as if a war party will have chosen such a bleak night as this to raid our manor! Hah, the thought of it does make me laugh!" Kaye chortled. There was an uneasiness about the laugh, however, that gave away more than Kaye would have liked.

"Much the same, Son, where is your sword?" asked Lord Ektor, prying a sort of choked "hu-hah" from his straining vocal chords. "I'd be a touch more comfortable if you had brought it down to table with you, you know."

There was now a sound of far-off clanking and scuffling behind the now quite audible footsteps ascending the stair. It was as if whomever it was that was coming up the stair was being followed by an armored guard... or perhaps the first of many foot soldiers? Kaye looked at his father, his own worry beginning to show upon his features. "D-do you really think we might be being invaded?" he stammered.

"Hush, you gobshite!" shushed Ektor with a sneer. "You'll give away our positions to them!"

"It *is* a tower house, Father," blurted Kaye, "If they keep coming up the stair, they're bound to find us, no matter the room we are in."

Kaye was still talking at full volume, which caused Ektor's face to shudder, not only with indignation, but with the fear of their imminent discovery. Fearing that his father's head would unscrew itself entirely, Kaye opted for appeasement.

"Do you think I have time to go up to my bedchamber to fetch it, Father?" he asked, his lower jaw gaping stupidly. Lord Ektor's face turned red, his quick temper flaring at anything it could to release the pressure of his fear. "No, you damned fool! The stairwell you'd have to climb is the same stairwell that they're charging up now! They'd meet you at the door and you'd be cut to ribbons! Best to use what little brains you've been blessed with and arm yourself with what you can here!"

Both Ektor and Kaye set about the Hall, looking for anything that might be used as a weapon. Ektor tried to raise his chair off the ground, but found it too heavy to wield accurately and let it fall back to the floor. Kaye grabbed for a knife from the table, but saw that it was dull and good only for splitting cooked vegetables and butter. Ektor next hefted the carafe of mead, having it in his mind to throw it at whatever came through the doorway.

The footfalls were just beyond the doorframe now. At any moment the lord of the castle and his son would be assaulted by its unknown invaders. Ektor looked at the delicate thing he was wielding and, thinking of its sweet cargo, promptly laid it back upon the table, slopping some of the mead out of the carafe as he did so. Kaye had been struggling with an iron rod affixed to the wall. Upon it hung one of the many tapestries adorning and insulating the Hall. Succeeding only in scraping his knuckles and whitening his palms, Kaye surrendered the effort. Sneaking wayward glances at the door, Ektor and Kaye each made a final grab for whatever might be used to save his own skin.

Upon entering the Great Hall of Castle Ektor, Wart and his aged savior were witness to a sight that was far and away the battiest either could remember. There stood the lord of the land, Ektor, with one foot upon the feasting table and the other upon his own upturned chair. His clothes were stained with mead and in his hand there was an upturned silver candlestick, its candles still lit. His face was flushed with blood and there were what looked like tears in his half-squinted eyes. To his right stood Sir Kaye, disheveled and wielding a bellows above his head, both hands clenching it with all their might. His face too was hot with blood.

There followed a moment of silent reflection shared by all the Hall's strange inhabitants. The old man looked back and forth between Sir Kaye and Lord Ektor, as if trying to decipher what it was that had been going on during the moments before his arrival. Wart gaped in amazement. Was this how the lord of the land spent his evenings? Was the man at the fireplace really Sir Kaye? He looked so different without the constant decorum with which Wart was so accustomed to seeing him.

Kaye glared at the intruders. Was this some sort of ruse? Where were the soldiers, and who was this old heap of a man who carried what, by all accounts, looked to be the groundskeeper's page? Wax from the still-lit candlestick dribbled down Ektor's wrist, scalding him. "Fie! You vile, parasitic wax-waste!" yelped the lord, hurling his hapless weapon across the hall. Landing with its candles snuffed and broken, the dented candlestick perfectly mirrored its owner's lost sense of decorum.

At that moment there was heard again the sound of clattering from behind Wart and the old man. Turning, they found before them the very same guard who had so unsuccessfully barred their passage at the Main Gate. Out of breath and sporting a newly-formed bruise upon his cheekbone, the guard fell to one knee beside the old man, in full view of Lord Ektor and Sir Kaye.

"'Pologies, yer lordships," he wheezed, "they overpowered me, they did."

Ektor, still scratching at his wrist in an effort to free it from the cooling candle-wax, turned on his guard.

"You! You foul, beggarly tatter of a clapper-clawed nut-hook!" he roared. "Overpowered?! By the tickle-brained apprentice of our groundsman and this wisp-willow of a galoot?!"

"I beg your pardon..." began the old man.

"It would be only just for me to bash your bitty barnacled brains in with my fist for such outrage!" continued Ektor, paying no mind to the shabby time-worn man's words. He had closed upon the guard, and was about to give him the promised thrashing when something which felt like iron clamped down upon his shoulder. Turning, he found the offending article to be none other than the left hand of the old galoot himself. The force of the old man's grip had startled him to a stop, and now, as Ektor began to try and shake himself free, proved resolute in its task. Ektor looked the man in the eyes. The gaze that met his was not hostile, but rather calm and unwavering. It was as if the derelict was exerting no effort at all.

"I beg your pardon," resumed the old man, "but we have need of lodging for the night and noticed that your fires were lit," adding with a smile, "I see now that we are in time for supper as well."

Ektor wanted to explode with indignation, but could not yet peel his eyes from that of the ancient man, and thus merely flushed in response.

"Would you be so kind as to allow us to sit with you at table?" the old man asked.

It was Kaye, not Ektor, who responded first.

"Have you no sense of propriety, old man?" he said, lowering his bellows, but not yet surrendering them as he strode across the hall to join the assemblage at the door. "My father, Lord Ektor of the *province of Ektor*, is not the type of man to be asked for a seat at table! If you were of noble blood you would wait, biting your knuckles, for a courier to arrive with tidings from his lordship!"

Kaye would have continued, but the same eyes that had silenced Lord Ektor had now turned upon him. His feet stopped him a few feet before he meant them to, still paces away from the group at the door.

"It is not a wish to swap pleasantries with those of plenty that has drawn me to you this night," spoke the old man. "I am here of necessity. This child, whom I have borne hither, was in dire need. His blood has this very hour crept to the very brim of life's chalice. It was only my steady hand that stopped it from spilling upon the floor, which incidentally, is where you will find his prior keeper!"

Kaye began to open his mouth in protest, but was struck dumb as the old man continued. "If you desire proof of my tale, you need only step outside and inspect the remains of what was your groundskeeper's cottage," spoke the man. "Although, I dare say it may turn your stomachs away from such tender flesh as is set at your table."

At hearing this last detail, Wart turned and burrowed his face back into the old man's chest, his sobs rushing from the depths of his stomach once more.

"Kaye. Kaye, put a chair at table for our... guests," muttered Ektor in a strangely submissive voice. He excused the bewildered guard with a flick of the wrist and turned toward the table. Needing no further instruction, the guard clattered back down the stairs with near reckless abandon.

"Father? Can you be serious, or is this some bit of fun you're having?" Kaye asked as the old man, still carrying Wart, passed him and entered the Great Hall proper. Ektor was already setting right the upturned chair at the head of the table and adjusting the furs that lined it for warmth. The only response Kaye received for his question was the raising of an eyebrow and the telltale flushing of his father's cheeks. Whatever the reason for his actions, Ektor was assuredly not pleased by it. Kaye knew his father could hardly ever bring himself to act in any way that was against his will, and so followed suit righting the Hall. After a mere moment's work, Kaye became bored with this menial labor and sauntered to the stair. At the top of his lungs he bellowed for the servants, only to find two of them crowded close behind the door. They were the serf who had stumbled over the dogs, joined by the plump little servant girl from the kitchens. They had, evidently, been eavesdropping: wishing to know what it was that could reduce Lord Ektor to physical labor and quiet the snide remarks of Sir Kaye.

"Well then?!" roared Kaye, his delicate sense of entitlement offended, "What's this idleness, then?! Get to cleaning before I get to flogging!" At this, the servants dashed into the Hall and began setting right the chairs and furs, and even setting right a certain disgraced bit of silver and wax from its forlorn place upon the floor.

After the Hall had been set right and two new chairs had been arranged at table, the serfs were excused. "Don't you be huddling near that door again, mind!" shouted Kaye, escorting them to the stair. "I'll be down after supper to the kitchens, and if they aren't twice as clean as they were last night, there won't be reason for me *not* to strike the pair of you dumb!" Many a "yes, yer lordship," and "of course, your grace," were quietly uttered as the serfs made their way to the door of the Great Hall, shutting it as they went. Kaye remained by the door a moment, and then returned to the table, satisfied with himself.

Wart was wrapped tightly in the furs which adorned his seat at the end of the table, making no move toward the feast set before him. Ektor, returning his goblet of mead to his lips, stared at the child with thinly veiled rancor. As Kaye took his seat at his father's left hand, Ektor shifted his gaze from Wart to the old man sitting beside the boy. The man was slicing himself a healthy cut of the duck, and the sight of his favored dish being cut into by this unwanted guest caused Ektor's eyes to squint, his lips to purse shut, and a thin dribble of mead to crawl down to the tip of his chin. The thought of forcibly stuffing the entire duck down the old man's throat found its way into Ektor's brain. He restrained himself however, merely wiping the dribble of mead from his chin. Returning his goblet to the table, Ektor took his gaze from the old man and returned it to his plate, itself heaped with a very large portion of the duck. He was about to take his first bite when the old man spoke.

"Quite delicious, this sauce," he said, "although a bit heavily ladled, wouldn't you say?"

"Oy! Old man! You'll have decorum when at table with Lord Ektor, you will!" shouted Kaye, picking the grit from under his fingernails with his meat fork.

"Oh, indeed," replied the old man graciously. "I would not wish to breach the good etiquette being shown in this fine hall."

Despite himself, Wart gave a slight chuckle at this and then, catching himself, went right back to sitting silently. The old man reached over the table, grasping a honeyed roll from one of the platters. He plopped it down in front of the boy. "Welcome back to the land of the living, Wart!" he cheered, smiling. "Have a roll. A full stomach does wonders for the heart." Wart glanced first at the old man and then at Lord Ektor. Ektor was glaring at Wart once again. Chancing a rebuke from the corpulent lord, Wart quickly snatched the roll from his plate and buried himself deeper in the furs of his seat.

"Hah!" bellowed Lord Ektor. "He acts more rat than boy! Always scurrying about, that child is, hoarding and hiding in the shadows! It's why we call him Wart, you know!"

The old man raised an eyebrow at this, not understanding the implied connection between rodents and blotchy skin.

"He's a blemish on the good face of the castle, he is." Kaye chimed in. Ridicule, and that of Wart specifically, was a true joy and hobby of Kaye's. Chuckling at himself he stabbed at a potato with his meat fork.

"There doesn't seem anything wrong with the boy to me," said the old man. "He seems quite capable and intelligent, in fact."

"Hrmph," Ektor grumbled. "You can tell your lord that if you wish, codger, but he's an odd one at the very least, and mark that I said so."

"Tell my...?" questioned the old man, but Ektor cut him off.

"We take care of him best we can, of course. The child wants for nothing," he continued, shooting a glance of warning at Kaye. Kaye had been about to laugh at the words of his father but, in seeing the look on Ektor's face, went puzzledly back to carving his potato.

"I have no more knowledge of who you may mean by *my lord* than I do of why you are lying to me," the old man said, with such a manner of nonchalance that Lord Ektor stuttered in trying to find the proper reply.

"You... you mean to say that you are *not* the servant of Uther Pendragon?" Ektor was leaning close to the old man now, his chair on the verge of toppling to the ground. "Did you not say you were here of *necessity*? That you were here to take care of the boy's life? Who but the servant of Lord Pendragon would make such a claim?!" he demanded.

Kaye was now glancing back and forth between his father and the old man, his potato forgotten. "What, this old fool?" he chided. "He cannot be a herald of Lord Pendragon! Look at his garb! Look at the wretched state of his countenance!"

Ektor turned upon his son. "He arrived and made haste to the boy's lodging! Upon seeing the way the boy was living there, he immediately stormed my castle! Tell me you are certain that he is not some agent of Uther, disguised as a vagrant!"

"Who's Lord Uther?" asked Wart, peeking out from the furs.

Three responses assailed the boy before he'd even finished asking the question.

"You shut up!" called Kaye.

"None of your concern!" followed Ektor.

"I haven't the foggiest," smiled the old man.

"Oh come off it, man," exclaimed Ektor, at his meager wit's end. "You can claim not to be his servant; that I'll believe. To claim not to have *heard* of the closest personage these feral lands have to a king is quite another thing! You'll be saying you've never heard of Ambrosius either I suppose, may his grace be forever mourned." Ektor said this last bit as if in prayer. "No man upon this isle can say he owes not the Sibling Lords his fealty for their banishment of the vile Lord Vortigern and his Roman legions from our shores! What is your name so that I may send word of your impudence to Lord Pendragon?"

"Father, I maintain that this fool cannot be a herald of Lord

Pendragon," continued Kaye. "Uther, while a waning power, is still a great name and lord. The very thought that his herald would be so disheveled or so... odd a creature, sets alight my doubt."

Kaye and Ektor went on like this for a number of moments, each presenting his case to the other whilst taking less and less note of Wart and the old man. During this time, to Wart's ear, their conversation became naught but a buzz akin to that of a colony of bees. He was trying to remember what it was that Lord Ektor had said. A lord named Pendragon had sent the old man to visit him? What interest did the affairs of lords find in the ward of a groundsman? For a moment Wart entertained dreams of his being chosen for knighthood and of his being whisked away from the lands of Lord Ektor to those of a kinder master. But no — the old man had not even heard of such a man, nor did he seem near as dignified as had the other heralds Wart had seen visit Lord Ektor over the years. The old man spoke.

"A name. It is a funny thing, knowing of names and of their merits, while not having one of one's own," he mused.

"Of all the ham-headed... you've *got* to have a name, spindle-shanks!" Lord Ektor blared. Otherwise, what does your lord yell at you when you bungle up his affairs, eh? Old One? Smarmy Sallow-Jowls?!"

"I don't believe I have one of *those*, either," smiled the old man, digging once more into the steak and kidney pie.

"That's what you've just said! No one so intrusive can also be so mince-minded!" returned Ektor.

"I believe he means he is without a lord and master, Father," sniffed Kaye. "A funny thing to claim, as all lands that border your own are beholden to some house or another."

"As you lads were talking, I came to a conclusion," smirked the old man. "I haven't any recollection at all before what I assume is sometime after mid-day today." Smiling, he served himself a healthy portion of pudding, not in the least worried by his realization.

"What?! Prepostery! Pips and penny-feathers!" steamed Lord Ektor.

"Do you perchance remember a blow to the head?" asked Kaye. "I do hear that persons suffering a lack of memory often claim it to be due to such a thing. Further, I hear that such a loss of memory may be cured by a second blow upon the same spot. That, or possibly bloodletting."

"I'll oblige you by the administering of both!" bellowed Ektor.

This whole time Wart had been staring at the old man, his mouth hanging agape. It had been enough for the boy that he felt safe with his newfound guardian, but with this new revelation, that the old man *himself* did not know of his origins, the boy's curiosity crested.

"There's nothing, then? You don't remember your mother or home or anything?" the child piped up. Such things were central to Wart's understanding of the world and, whilst Wart could not recall his own mother, he felt it must be a horrible thing to suddenly realize you had forgotten her. "You must recall something. Please sir, think on your first memories and just go backwards!"

"My boy," said the old man, "my first memories are of the very storm which still, at this very moment, rampages about this castle. I haven't even the slightest inkling as to what it was that I was doing out in the wind and ice...." The old man trailed off, his eyes introspect. "Come to think of it, lad there *is* a name I recall, though I am not sure as to why or what significance it holds for me."

"Out with it man, so that I shall know to which end of the earth to throw you," growled Lord Ektor. The old man, lost in though, was entirely oblivious to the insult.

"Murd... Mired... Murm... Mum..." He mumbled. "Myrd... that's it... Myrd-something."

"*Myrddin*?!" gawked Kaye. "There's a settlement, for lack of a lesser term, by that name that lies at the northern border of my father's holdings."

"Ha! Ha Ha!" chortled Ektor. "A fine and fitting place for a lout such as yourself, man. We shall call you Myrddus, or hahah, Merdus rather, from the Latin! Hahahah!"

"Father, you are too full of wit!" exclaimed Kaye, shooting a conniving glance at Lord Ektor. "It is a name born to bear the *discharge* that is our strange guest's countenance."

"HA! Wonderful Kaye! Ha Ha!" mused Ektor, his cheeks reddening and his mouth widening so that he began to resemble a sort of squashed pomegranate.

Wart, confused, turned to look at the old man to see what his reaction to this sudden outburst of frivolity would be. The old man simply smiled and took a sip of mead, washing down his pudding.

"I rather think *Merlin* might suit better, if we are to Latinize the name," he said. "Merdus being the Latin for dung, and Merlin ringing a sight less vile. I further believe that such qualities as baseness and assumption do not befit men of your status, such as it is."

With this, the old man returned to the pudding, remarking offhandedly to Wart that it was "sumptuous" as he ladled some of the stuff into a saucer for the boy.

"Alright, *Merlin*, we have found for you a name. A name which has run out its welcome in these halls!" bellowed Kaye, upon his feet before he knew what had ahold of him. "My father and I have suffered you this long only because we thought that you might be a man of whose coming we had been forewarned. You have neither lived up to that belief nor have you shown any deference to your betters! Take your leave from this hall immediately or I shall hurl you from the windowsill myself!"

Kaye's outburst had stunned Ektor but, upon hearing his son's exclamatory demands, the feudal lord grinned from cheek to chubby cheek. His fist came down upon the tabletop, delivering a blow that shook its every timber. "Kaye, my lad! You've got more of my blood in your veins every day!" he beamed. Then, turning to the old man, he spoke in slow and venomous tones: "You are not welcome at my table again, Merlin. Take up what rags you have brought with you and exit my sight." To Ektor's reckoning this was a lenient dismissal, as he so very much wanted to have the old fool thrown into the castle dungeons and be forgotten altogether. A man without memory or land, however, was an anomaly, and anomalies were not to be trifled with in such superstitious times. It was only this sense of the unknown that held back Ektor's wrath.

Merlin did, in fact, rise from his seat at the table as commanded. Had he but bade a hasty farewell to those still seated, he would have been following every demand made upon his person by Ektor and Kaye. Yet Merlin did not retreat so hastily. He instead reached back down to the table and sipped the last of his mead, grinned, and pulled his tattered robes tighly about himself.

"Gentlemen, I thank you for the meal," he said in as calm a voice as ever. "I shall indeed retire for the evening. In one day's time I will call upon you again. Until then, some of what is mine shall remain in your care. Look after him well." Merlin smiled down at Wart, patting the child upon the head so that no one could mistake his meaning.

Ektor and Kaye began to object simultaneously, but neither's words found Merlin's ear, for he had already begun descending the stairway to the Main Gate. A moment later there could be heard the dull thud of the gate closing upon its frame. Upon hearing the gate bid its farewell to their strange visitor, both Ektor and Kaye shifted their grimaces from the stone doorway and down to the small frame of Wart. The child was not facing them, but was still peering toward the door somewhat absentmindedly, as he nibbled on a sizeable mince pie. A moment passed while the three sat, unmoving but for the bits of sweet falling from Wart's mouth and onto his lap. Ektor's eye twitched as he watched one particularly large crumb bounce off Wart's knee and go tumbling onto the floor.

The stillness in the room was palpable, such that even young Wart became aware if it. He'd just shoved and prodded the remainder of the pasty into his mouth and was labouredly working his jaw up and down around it when the tiny hairs on the tip tops of his ears raised themselves on end. Slowly he turned in his seat toward Ektor and Kaye, knowing that their eyes were on him. The expressions that met him as he gazed slack-jawed into the eyes of the men were so red, so contorted with silent rage, that Wart hardly recognized the men seated at the head of the table.

Ektor's forehead throbbed visibly with blood, his face a beet. Kaye's nose and lip were twisted up in so awful a sneer that Wart could see all the way up one of the man's nostrils. Ektor ground his teeth so terribly that Wart swore he could see the ivory flaking away.

"PAGE!" roared the big man, "Page, come and remove this PUSTULE from my sight!"

There was a clambering on the stairs then and a plump face peered first around the stonework doorway leading out from the Great Hall. Shortly, there followed the frame of a well-fed and rosy-cheeked girl.

"Beggin' yer pardon, sirs, but the boy's gone an' twisted his ankle runnin' up and down the stairs like he's been doin'," she explained.

"I'll have him horse-whipped!" yelled Kaye.

"I don't care one wit about that rawboned clod!" Ektor bellowed.

He pointed a fat finger at Wart, shouting: "Maggie, take this tick from off my thigh before it gorges itself so thoroughly that I go faint! Throw him back out into the groundskeeper's shack for all I care!"

At this Wart's eyes began to swell, and he would have bawled in protest had there not still been a sizeable portion of mince pie in his mouth. As it happened, however, there *was*, and all Wart could muster was a coughing, choking sound before Maggie was upon him.

Hefting her charge up and under one arm she made a hasty retreat from the Hall, swinging herself around for a hurried curtsy as she crossed the threshold of the stairwell. The voices of Ektor and Kaye picked up again once she and the choking boy were out the door. Both were loud and sounded incensed, but it was clear to those that inhabited the castle that the danger of the evening's events had passed.

Wart's legs swung to and fro as he was toted down the stairs. All that he could see were Maggie's billowing skirts and the stone steps as she trundled him down the stairwell. The jamb of a small wooden door came into sight then. Maggie swung her hip against the thing, forcing it open and hurling both Wart and herself inside. Wart had to duck to avoid hitting his head against the stone doorframe as he was slung unceremoniously through the entryway. In one smooth motion, Maggie kicked the door shut and plopped Wart jarringly back onto his feet. He coughed. A bit of the pasty had gone down the wrong flue during his trip down the stair, and his lungs were trying to expel it.

Whump came a strong palm against his back. The bit of pie shot out from his throat, sailing off into one of the dark corners of the room.

"Can't have you chokin' to death under my supervision, Artie," Maggie chuckled. "That wouldn't suit the lord's liking too much now would it?"

Wart smiled, his eyes tearing a bit from the exertion of loosing his erstwhile dessert. Maggie was a jovial young woman and tended to spread her general state of cheer to those whom she met during her duties at Castle Ektor. Sadly for Wart, that was seldom himself as she was head of the kitchens and, as apprentice to Bedwyn, he'd spent most of his time maintaining the castle grounds. Maybe it was this thought of his former caretaker and maybe it was the murderous pie, but Wart's little chest gave a great heave just then and he began to sob. Tears swelled like leavening bread from his bloodshot eyes.

"Ah, you have had a bit o' hardship today haven't you Artie?" said Maggie as she swept him up again, this time holding him against her profuse bosom. "Now let's see what we've got to calm your little nerves." Up from the floor she whisked a warm sheepskin and set it upon Wart's shoulders like an oversized cloak.

Maggie was alone in the use of the nickname 'Artie' for the boy, and it had always struck Wart odd that someone he saw so infrequently had such a pet name for him. There was something lovely in the separateness of the kitchens, he mused as he took hold of the sheepskin. It was as if he was alone on a sheltered island, away from the storm of the rest of existence; a haven encircled by cooking fires and sweet-smelling pots. It was a feeling that would only be aided by Sir Kaye's eventual forgetting to make good on his threat of inspecting the kitchens that night. A final sigh heaved its way out from his nose as Maggie plopped him down upon a small wooden stool. The seat, heated by the cooking fire that snapped and sparked in the chimney before him, warmed more than Wart's bottom as he breathed in the aromas of the kitchen.

"We're in luck, Artie!" smiled Maggie from behind a small pot set upon the hearth. "It seems that, in their infinite grace, the masters of the castle have again become agitated before we could set all of their dishes at table." With that she spooned a thick, dark substance from the pot and into an earthen bowl. "Nutmeg and cinnamon pudding," she said, placing the bowl onto Wart's lap along with a pewter spoon.

Staring at the pudding, Wart's thoughts turned to Merlin. "Do you think Merlin will really come back for me tomorrow?" he asked.

Maggie squinted a bit at the boy, a wry smile on her lips. "Is *that* the name o' the man that's been setting the masters off all night, then?" she replied. "I suppose he will so, if he says he will, but you've more important things than him to be mullin' over in that wee little head of yours." She then took up Wart's spoon and swept it into his mouth before he could question her more on the subject.

Sweet and warm, the pudding crept its way down Wart's throat. It was fantastically rich. "Fills the 'ole, eh Artie?" Maggie said, smiling. Wart smiled back, the spoon still in his mouth. The two of them sat beside the fire chuckling and giggling until the young lad's eyes began to droop. Maggie wrapped him up in the sheepskin then, laying him down to sleep along one of the broad kitchen tables amidst baskets of apples and sacks of flour.

Chapter Three
Exodus

Thick black fingers scratched at Wart's throat. The scent of smoldering branches shot once more in through his nostrils. The crackling and the dark were all around him. *It* had come for him again, come to complete the task it had set upon the night before. It had beset him quickly this time, far quicker than the last. A moment before, he'd been dozing sleepily. He had felt safe again, had remembered it being warmer than the night before — but could not recall why. Now the cold that embraced him was every bit as encompassing as had been that feeling of refuge; every bit so and more, for this embrace Wart knew all too horrifyingly well. The scraping, scratching chill of the claws stung like blades upon an open wound. Their embrace firmer now, harder to resist. Wart's heart pounded and faltered, beating in irregular rhythms. The tips of his fingers seized uncontrollably. The skin of his neck beneath the thing's claws felt brittle and numb. He feared that at any moment his neck would shatter like some fleshy icicle, sending his head rolling down along his bedsheets.

His bedsheets — something seemed off about them, but Wart's addled mind could not place what it was. Those pits, those endless depths which served as eyes to the creature hung before him once again. Again he felt the dizziness creep over him. Wart knew he'd have to fight it off again somehow, but the creature seemed so much more powerful than it had before, so much more prepared for his resistance. Struggling, Wart was hardly able to shift his frame. He'd have to do much better to free himself. Again his heart missed a beat. Worry and fear clutched it as tightly as the creature held him. Tears brimmed in eyes. He would not be strong enough this time. There were too many invisible hands helping to hold him down. The creature had won. As if on cue, those pits of dark that had been boring into him from their dry-socketed frames lurched forward. The creature's head splintered and shattered against Wart's, sending flashes of light through his brain and encasing him entirely in the crackling black of the creature's being.

With a crack and a moan, Wart was awake. For a moment his young, groggy brain could register nothing. Then, as the gradual advance of wakefulness began, Wart became aware of the world again. Pressed against his nose and throbbing forehead were the cool flagstones of the floor. Wrapped and twisted about him was a heavy sheepskin blanket. He could feel his right arm pinned beneath him against the floor, his left bound to his side by wool and leather. Just within the edge of his view a number of shiny green spheres wobbled about upon the floor. His ears tingled in the warmth of the surrounding room. They also informed him of the sound of footsteps hastily approaching him.

"Mercy be, Artie! Ye sleep until midday an' then go wakin' like a banshee! I've never seen someone flail about so in their sleep!" said Maggie as she hurried over from a large mixing pot on the fire. "You went and lifted your entire self off the table! I could've sworn you'd hung there a moment, too... but enough of that nonsense, now. Let's have a look at you." She quickly unraveled the knot of sheepskin from about Wart's body and stood him up, checking him over. He winced a bit as she was examining the arm he'd landed upon. "Tsk," she said, "It does look like ye've gone and sprained this a biteen. Best not try and use it for a while, but it'll heal up just fine, it will so." Brushing her stout hand lightly against Wart's face, she stood up and headed back to her cooking pot, a touch of whimsy on her face. "Now be a good lad and get to pickin' up those apples you've gone and dashed against the floor, will you Artie?" Wart looked around, his eyes finally coming into focus. Sure enough, the strange little green baubles that he'd seen all about him on the floor were Maggie's apples. Wart leaned over to right the basket from which the apples had been upset. His right wrist shot with pain. Surprised at how much it hurt, Wart gave a yelp and released the basket. Those few apples which had not yet fallen to the floor bounced and rolled about, ultimately joining their brethren upon the flagstones.

"Now, Artie!" chuckled Maggie. "Do try to keep from bruisin' at least *one* of them apples, so, and do mind that right hand of yours as well. Try just usin' the left, sure."

Wart grumbled something that sounded suspiciously like "who puts a sleeping child on the table anyhow?" and received a swift ladle to the behind. "Ouch, Maggie! What was that for?" he said, a perfect look of innocence on his face.

There was a look of imitated outrage on Maggie's face. "You'll be sure to do a nice job of pickin' up those apples now, Artie," said Maggie, her ladle aimed mock-menacingly at the boy. "Ye've already gone and turned my recipe for spit-roasted apples into one for apple pies!"

Wart giggled at this and resumed his task, using only his left arm. Once he had finished placing all the apples into the basket, Maggie helped him set it back upon the table. She then ladled a portion of the stew she'd been mixing in her large pot into a wooden bowl and set it before him. "Cottontail stew," she said, "as preferred by their lordships on the days they go out hunting... even if they *aren't* able to catch a single hare!" Wart laughed so hard that he snorted, setting Maggie herself off into barrelous chortlings.

Much of the afternoon was spent in this very manner: Wart helping Maggie with the duties of the kitchen and the two keeping each other in general merriment until the evening hours. Only when the haphazard serf from the previous evening limped into the kitchens in preparation for dinner did Wart have cause to dwell upon the happenings of the day before. Specifically, he thought of the words of Merlin as he had left Castle Ektor the night prior. 'In one day's time I will call upon you again,' he'd said. 'Until then some of what is mine shall remain in your care. Look after him well.' Wart knew this meant himself and knew he had mere hours left before Merlin's promised return. Trepidation gripped Wart, his heart sinking. Merlin had seemed a kindly and wonderfully strange visitor, but the prospect of being taken away to lands unknown by the wizened man was something very different.

"Maggie," asked the boy, "do you think I might just stay with you from now on? Here in the kitchens?"

Maggie turned to look upon the lad. Her eyes were heavy and her voice sorrowful as she replied. "It would be a lovely thing, that, wouldn't it, Artie?" she said. "But I rather think it's best we try and weather what the storm brings rather than change her course, lad." With this she returned to garnishing the plates as they were carried out to the Great Hall, the glint of a tear in her eye.

Then came a clamorous pounding from down the stairwell. So loud was it that it seemed to Wart that the wooden door must have rent its iron bucklings to go scattering across the floor as bare lumber. Maggie, startled at the booming sounds, dropped a whole braid of garlic into the gravy she'd been preparing. The boomings were followed by a swift clattering, not from the bottom of the stair, but rather the top. The castle guard, sword in hand, came careening down the steps to answer what could only be the assault of a battering ram against the entrance to his sworn protectorate. He practically whizzed as he flew past the open door to the castle kitchens. "That'd better not be who I think it is!" Wart heard the guard declare as his footsteps came to a halt at the bottom of the stair. There was the sound of the spy-hole swinging open after which followed a short conversation. Wart predominantly missed the particulars of this, due to both parties talking — or rather shouting — over each other. Their cacophonous jumbled-up voices bounded from wall to ceiling to floor as they reverberated up the stair. Giving up on her gravy, Maggie trotted over to Wart's side as he clasped his hands over his ears. He hoped that this time the guard might do his duty, thus allowing him a reprieve from his determined fate. Unfortunately for the boy's hopes — as well as the guard — the next thing the residents of the castle heard was a resounding *bang* followed by the clattering of sword against stone. For the second consecutive night, Castle Ektor had been breached. Wart craned his neck towards the kitchen door, listening. Quick, soft footfalls could be heard coming up the stair. Maggie clutched Wart tight to her apron. Neither cook nor child had any doubt as to whom it was that could be climbing the stair.

In short measure their thoughts were confirmed as the dark robes and long white mane of Merlin rounded the stair leading past the kitchen and to the Hall. Wart was sure that the old man would see him, deep as he was in the kitchen. Merlin, however, shot straight past the kitchen at a surprising rate of climb and continued upon the stair without the slightest glance in Wart's direction. Leaving Wart's side a moment, Maggie trundled over to the door and shut it quietly, scurrying her way back to Wart thereafter.

"Artie, me boy," she said, "If you're scared as ye seem of that old vagrant wot's just passed along the stair, then mayhaps you should run along and hide behind the potatoes." The smile on her face was warm as ever, but had an urgency to it. Wart did exactly as she suggested, skidding a bit as he rounded his way behind a looming mound of potatoes in the farthest corner of the kitchen. Moments passed without sound. Then murmurs and mumblings could be made out from beyond the thick sealed door.

Bam! The door to the kitchen swung in with a lurch. In tramped Merlin, a jovial smirk upon his face, followed by a disheveled and fiery Sir Kaye. Maggie stood her ground aside her great mixing pot, ladle in hand, stirring slow circles in her evening stew.

"Aah! The kitchens!" exclaimed the old man, "I do so enjoy a good mess! Ha... ha ha!"

"Crackin' jokes *and* crackin' heads is it tonight, you ol' bag of rot?" countered Kaye. "I'll carve you like a goose for this, I will!" Kaye reached for his sword. He did not, however, find it.

"Oh, my dear lad!" said Merlin, his smile curling at one side, "You're looking for that pig-sticker of yours. I do believe you've left it halfway up the stair. Rather carelessly, I should say."

Kaye sneered at Merlin. "You won't be snickerin' about in a moment, *Merdus*! Mark my words!" With this parting insult he was back out the door, leaving only Maggie, Merlin, and a softly snickering pile of potatoes in the kitchen. Wart was still quite fearful of the prospect of leaving with Merlin, but he did very much enjoy hearing Sir Kaye so put out. Maggie did not turn away from her stew, but greeted Merlin with a short and curt "How d'ye do, graybeard."

"Quite fine my dear lady," smiled the old man, answering that which hadn't really been a question and eyeing the still-snickering potatoes. "I do so hope you can help me. You see, I've lost my eyes and I was hoping to borrow one or two from one of your potatoes."

"Lost yer *wot*?"

Maggie turned to the man, startled and somewhat dismayed. She'd thought her hiding spot much better than to have been found out already. The look upon Merlin's face as she met his gaze was kindly (and not at all eyeless). He snuck a wink in her direction as he continued on with his ruse. "Yes, my dear lady, it is ever so sad... you see I was to retrieve a young boy from this very castle tonight, but cannot find him for lack of eyes."

The potatoes were now deathly silent. *Could such a thing be true?* From his hiding place Wart could not be sure. So numerous were the bizarre events of the last two days that he dared not disbelieve any such happenings any longer.

Merlin was now approaching Wart's hiding place. Maggie stood motionless, a strange, far-off smirk curling along her lip as she observed the old man. His demeanor had utterly changed since his battering down of the castle gate. It was now one of such folly and care that she could not seem to rouse herself to come to Wart's defense. "It does so often happen with us older folk, you see miss," Merlin continued. "Oh, but I do apologize, young lady! I seem to have barged right on into these kitchens without introducing myself to their head chef!"

He spun on his heel then, and without the slightest regard to the potatoes, extended a hand and a bow to Maggie. The young woman flushed a bright crimson to be addressed so highly by an elder and giggled a bit as he bent deeply at the waist so as to kiss her outstretched hand.

"It is a lovely kitchen, too," said the old wolf. Maggie swatted at the old man playfully and bustled away apace, squealing, "Ah, you're quite the apple polisher, you are sir!"

"I go by the name of Merlin," he said.

"Hello then, Merlin."

"And you are?"

"Maggie."

"Lovely. Now we're acquainted!"

"Fine, but I'll be havin' none of your exaggerations bein' made concernin' my kitchens!" Maggie said. "These here rooms are well wantin' and modestly kept at best. Still... it isn't oft a cook gets called a chef or a girl bowed to by her elders. For that ye have me thanks."

"But of course, m'lady. Now that we are acquainted, I do so hope that you can help me," Merlin said, taking the lid from off a spice pot and peering inside. "You see, I have come here to fetch a young lad by the name of Wart so that he may abide with me at my home. Do you know where I might find such a child?" He placed the lid back upon the spice jar and returned his gaze to Maggie, smiling.

Maggie was perplexed. A moment before she'd been sure the old man had known the boy's hiding place as clear as a summer day. "Sure, ye can't think he'd be in there, so?" She replied, indicating the jar.

Rather than respond to this, Merlin instead moved a pace closer to her and plopped himself down upon one of the stools set at the kitchen table. "Maggie, has it been a good and happy life that the child has led, being apprenticed to the groundsman here?"

Maggie stared at the old man a moment before answering. He was quite serious in his want for an answer. "Happy as us common folk can ask for, I'd dare say mister Merlin, sir," she replied.

"Are you aware of the sad goings on that befell the groundskeeper a day ago?"

Maggie bowed her head slightly. "The page, sir..." she mumbled, a glint of a tear forming in her eye, "he was made to right the place this mornin', so. Said it was a ghastly sight, he did."

"Mmm."

Merlin lowered his own gaze then, seemingly giving the entirety of his attention to a whirl in the grain of the wooden table. His long and lean fingers traced the whirl round and round in slow concentric circles. Maggie leaned in a bit, intrigued. "Is it possible," he said, "is it indeed likely, that the boy shall have to return to that place."

Maggie's eyes flicked up from the old man's hand upon the table. His eyes were still upon the table, a sadness in them she had not detected before. "I do believe he would, sir," she stammered.

Hearing this, Wart shot up from behind the potatoes, his eyes awash with tears. "No, Maggie! Don't make me go back! Don't make me leave these kitchens ever again!" he yelled, running to Maggie's outstretched arms. She hugged the child as he swung his arms about her apron.

"I'm afraid I'll not be able to make good on such a promise if I speak it, Artie," she said. Wart, his face still buried in Maggie's apron, let loose a muffled wail and pounded at her thighs mercilessly. Prying the lad from herself, she held him by the shoulders and squatted, so as to meet him at eye level. She wiped the tears from his eyes.

"There's no helpin' it, now," she said. "Lord Ektor has it in his head you'll stay there, so that's what'll be, sure. I *am* just a cook, Artie, and not a faerie queen what can do as she pleases."

"That is why I have returned, Wart," said Merlin, his voice level and soft, "or... is it 'Artie', now?"

"The boy's name isn't truly Wart, Mr. Merlin, sir," explained Maggie. "That's just the name Sir Kaye's taken to callin' the lad since we... since the boy arrived here, that is." Maggie's cheeks flushed for a moment at this slip, but she quickly recovered: "The lad's name is Arthur by right. That's why it is I call him Artie when I see him. It does seem as though I'm the only one what remembers it, however."

"Which is it you prefer, lad?" asked Merlin, looking quizzically at the boy. Wart looked puzzled by the very idea of the choice.

"Well not many'd prefer Wart, so!" huffed Maggie.

"Well then Arthur, I should very much like your company, as my home shall be ever so quiet with just the cat and me," smiled Merlin.

"You've a cat?" Wart asked.

"A recent acquisition, in all honesty," said Merlin. "I saw him wandering about in the snow as I left this place last night. He's a rather dappled and portly fellow, but seems thankful to have a bit of thatch over his head."

"You... you've got Bartholomew with you?!" gasped the lad, smiling from ear to ear. The thought of his fallen master's cat awaiting his arrival in this new home warmed the boy to the idea.

"Ah, good! I was rather hoping you'd have a good name for him, War... er Arthur!" exclaimed Merlin. "And now I find that you're already acquainted as well. How lovely! Shall we be off then?"

Arthur's smile faded. "Can... can Maggie come too?" he asked.

It was Maggie who answered first. "I'm afraid not, Artie," she said. "Lord Ektor might let a child out o' his sights without much fuss, but he'd ne'er let one of us that serves him leave, sure." Arthur looked troubled upon hearing this, so she added: "And besides that, I have become accustomed to these kitchens, so. Mayhap ye'll come an' visit me from time to time. How's about that, so?"

Arthur looked hopefully to Merlin, asking silently if such a thing was to be allowed. "But of course he shall!" said the old man. "No use having a young boy in my company if he's not allowed some mischief.

Now be a good lad and give the girl a hug, and then it's off to my cottage we'll be."

Arthur clasped his arms around Maggie once again and smiled as she kissed his cheek. Then Merlin grasped the child's hand and they were off. Out from the insulated safety of the kitchens and down the spiral stair towards the world they slipped. As they descended the stair they could hear the shouting of Sir Kaye at his father concerning the whereabouts of his sword, and they could hear Lord Ektor's booming voice calling out orders and threatening violence in return. They walked past the guard once more, who this time made no effort to stop the old man and his ward. An air of calm began to sweep over the boy and all these goings on seemed ever so far away... ever so unimportant.

It was well into the dark of the next night by the time the pair arrived in Myrddin; later still when Merlin shook open his cloak and stood a shaky Arthur on sleepy feet in the entryway to the thatched cottage. Though the child was near asleep, the cold of the stone against his feet woke him enough to look about the yard. Though there were two new trees planted by the fence, and though the interior of the cottage looked cozy and inviting, Arthur's tired mind recognized the cottage immediately as the same place at which he had first glimpsed Merlin. It was the cottage in which that old couple had died — the one from his vision. Slowly the meaning of the pair of trees, freshly planted out by the fence, dawned upon him, and he gave an unintended shudder as he thought of what must lie buried beneath them.

Merlin was a blur of energy. Small candles were quickly lit in the corners of the cottage's main room and a cooking fire was made in the fireplace. Shadows and rays of light danced upon the sturdy wooden walls. Over the fire was hung a small stewing pot, quickly filled with melting snow and potatoes, leeks and rosemary. The old man's head popped into cupboard after nook after bin as he searched out spices and seasonings to throw into the pot. It seemed to Arthur, watching from across the room, that Merlin looked rather like a forgetful squirrel, popping in and out of the cabinetry as he was. More than once he noticed the old man check the same cupboard before reaching in and extracting his prize. All the while Merlin maintained one hand upon a ladle which slowly stirred the ever-expanding ingredients of the stew.

Clack-clack, clack-clack, clack-clack strummed the ladle against the pot. It seemed imperterbable in its rhythm, even when Merlin swapped hands to reach into some outlying bin: Clack-clack, clack-clack, clack-clack. Moving closer, Arthur took a seat at the table and stared into the cooking fire as he listened to the sound of the ladle and the pot. His sight blurred as his eyes relaxed in the still of the evening. Merlin was but a mist of grey robes and white hair now; the fire a warm and constant glow. The grey mist stopped just then and congealed. It seemed to be looking at the boy. "I dare say you'll fall asleep without your supper if I let you, child," it said. As if in agreement, Arthur's head nodded forward and down, threatening to slam down onto the hard wooden table with all of its weight.

For an instant, smoke and bracken were all that Arthur could smell or hear, ash all that he could see.

The child's heart pounded; his eyes, bloodshot, snapped open; and his spine stood straight as an elm. He was back in the cottage again. Clack-clack, clack-clack, clack-clack drummed the ladle against the pot. "Sleeping already, Arthur?" asked Merlin. Rousing himself with a mighty effort, Wart stammered something to the effect of: "Er, yessir, Mr. Merlin... that is..."

Nodding at this, Merlin turned back to his stew.

"I *can't* sleep, sir," stuttered the boy, "maybe ever again."

"Why might that be lad? You seem set for it, well as I can see," Merlin replied.

"He's there! Waiting for me when my eyes are closed too long!" blurted the boy.

Merlin turned again to the lad, his eyes wide. "Who waits for you?" he asked, peering at the child.

"I don't know his name," sniffed Arthur, his heart pounding at the thought of the creature. "He... he tried to kill me, but... but you stopped him," he stammered.

"That he is truly there, waiting for you, seems very unlikely indeed, Arthur. I dare say you and I have bested that particular evil," said the old man, though his eyes stood wide and alert as he turned once more to his stew. "I rather think you'll have forgotten all about that poor blighted husk by the time you've finished your supper."

Arthur sat at the table confused a moment, wondering how on earth the old man could be so sure of such a remark, knowing nothing of the creature's repeated resurgence. There was a soft movement against his swinging legs just then, and Arthur looked down to find Bartholomew winding around one of his calves. The paunchy feline mewed sweetly at the boy from the ground, not wanting to put forth the effort to climb upon the child's lap unaided. Dutifully Arthur obliged the cat, hefting it off the floor and plopping it down again upon his lap. Bartholomew settled in immediately, purring and kneading sleepily, happy to see a familiar face.

Turning his attention back to Merlin, Arthur was about to mention the recurrent nature of the nightmares, when the old man began to hum. It was a low and guttural sound that began as one long drawn out note and then splintered into gravelly tones and rumbling bass. Clack-clack, clack-clack, clack-clack strummed the ladle against the iron pot. Clack-clack, clack-clack, clack-clack. The stewing pot began to resonate as the ladle's strikes got sharper against its sides, adding a metallic ringing to the song — just within the realm of Arthur's hearing. Images of wheels and wagons, horses and men began to swirl about in Arthur's mind. Then, in a voice quite strange and words unfamiliar, Merlin began to speak:

Chapter Four
Johnny Reb

Clack-clack, clack-clack, clack-clack. Johnny's switch tapped lazily against the spokes of the wagon. It weren't as if the horse hadn'ta trotted the way back to the plantation from church b'fore. For years, every Sund'y, Johnny an' the missus had trundled the boys out o' the house round about dawn and piled into this here wagon on their way to services. The trip to church was a cold one in the mornin's pale light, an' the missus would usually cuddle up with the boys in the blankets linin' the wagon bed. Up in the drivin' seat, Johnny just grinned and bared it. This bein' the trip home though, the weather was a sight warmer. The squeals and giggles o' tomfoolery could be heard all 'round — even from the missus an' the boys in the back — as Johnny's wagon trundled on down the dry dirt roads o' town. Johnny paid it no mind. This here time was his own. Early mornin's were no good for thinkin', bein' too cold fer the mind t' get up to speed properly. Sund'y afternoons though — them were Johnny's ponderin' hours. Sometimes Johnny'd ponder about the sermon in service, if'n it'd been any good that is. Sometimes he'd ponder on workin' the plantation, but that only ever got his dander up. No... them weren't Johnny's thoughts most often. Most often Johnny'd think on his glory days in the confederate army, an' today weren't no different. Visions o' firin' lines an' whizzing bullets cuttin' through the tree lines blew through Johnny's mind like so much powder-smoke. Voices o' friends and officers echoed to an' fro in the clouds Johnny'd conjured up outta the past. The rhythm o' the wagon seemed akin t' that o' a long day's march, with its easy sway. Johnny started hummin' hisself an old marchin' song as the wagon rumbled on down the lane. Hmm-mm, Hmm-mm he went, right along with the pulse of the switch in his hand against the wagon wheel. Clack-clack, clack-clack, Hmm-mm, clack-clack, Hmm-mm....

It hadn'ta been that long ago, Johnny mused durin' his tune, that he'an the rest o' his regiment had come a-marchin' on down this road on their way home from the war. Sure they'da known Lee'd given up the ghost to that wretch of a man Grant. They'da known, too, that the south was in fer a bundle o' trouble after the last skirmishes were sorted out. Johnny didn't like to focus on that part though... what he remembered most from that final march was the folks linin' the streets, waitin' t' see their loved ones comin' home. One could'a almost forgot the outcome o' the war, there'da been so much joy linin' the streets that day. Ladies screamin' an' a-shoutin' for their boys an' never mindin' that their skirts were gettin' all muddied up in the road.

"Huh," Johnny muttered, stoppin' his tune a minute. A funny thought'd popped into his head that moment. He turned it over a couple o' times, but kept on thinkin' it was right. "Darlin, you reckon you r'member that day me an' the boys came home from the war?" he asked the missus.

Her head popped up from the bed then, little John Junior cradled up in her arms like an infant — even though he was goin' on four now. The sound o' little Nic's new game, whizzin' an' sendin' off sparks, followed her through the openin' in the wagon cover.

"I s'pose I do at that, Johnny," she replied. "What's buzzin' around up in that head o' yours that you're thinkin' 'bout them old times?"

"Nothin' much, Margaret," Johnny said, turnin' round so as to see her face. "Only, it seems like that was the last time I can recall it havin' rained real good is all."

"That's a silly thing to go on about, Johnny," she remarked, turnin' back to the game she was playin' with the boys.

Johnny turned back to the front of the wagon an' thought 'bout rain the rest o' the way on back to the plantation.

Late that same night, Johnny stood on the porch o' his plantation home, a big ol' metaphorical bee bumblin' about his bonnet. Johnny hadn't never had no love for the North. The plantation had been ransacked durin' the War o' Northern Aggression, had been driven into the poorhouse when the slaves had been "freed," had suffered the arrival of carpetbaggers and more. "Damn fool unionists," muttered Johnny as he stepped lightly across the porch, makin' sure to skip the boards he knew t' be squeaky. The grounds o' his lifelong home looked shabby in the dim light of the moon. Gone was the luster o' the young years Johnny remembered so fondly. It was all the North's fault, an' now they'da up and gone one step too far! That man Lincoln'd been one thing — Johnny had at least seen Lincoln as a man o' principles an' action. That those principles were in direct disagreement with his own had irked Johnny somethin' fierce, but at least in Lincoln there'da been a sort of a worthy foe. 'Anyhow,' thought Johnny, 'Lincoln'd gotten a bullet in the head for all them Southerners who'd died on his watch. Maybe Mr. Lincoln an' history were square.'

"Hmph," was all Johnny said into the dark as he snuck across the steps and along the grass. Stopping a few paces from the porch, Johnny stared at a bald and cracked patch of earth. 'That soil won't never recover none o' its fertility,' he thought to hisself. 'Just one more bit o' this country that's gone an' ain't comin' home again.'

Resuming his stroll, an' continuin' his mental diatribe, Johnny thought next on Andrew Johnson. A half smile cracked its way into Johnny's scowl. If'n there'da been a man t' find a way forward with that "reconciliation" idea it'da been Johnson. Johnny was sure of it. Even Johnny, with his self-proclaimed capacity for readin' a man had spent half of his time revering Johnson and the other half o' it spitting at the name. Sure Johnson'd made Johnny and all his fellow Southerners pledge allegiance all over again (for which they'd gotten nothin' but a pat on the back an' a look o' contempt from the North) but at least the man'd been a decent old-fashioned Democrat from Tennessee. A man o' good plantation values who'd allowed for "black codes" and the like in the South. It was the North again, with their Liberal... no — they'd called 'emselves "Radical Repubs" or some such. Either way, Johnny knew who they were. They were the Liberals from up north that'd changed the Constitution an' made it impossible t' get a Confederate into Congress. 1866 had been the year. Black folk were "citizens" all over. Johnny chuckled to himself at that.

'At least that's what the Libs tell *us*,' he thought. He'da seen them dark folk carted off an' he knew the truth of the matter. Them Northern hands were just as bloody as the wealthiest cotton plantationer's.

Johnny aimed to prove that soon... but first things had t' come first.

Johnny's pace hastened as he approached the shed, fingers tremblin' ever so slightly out of either anticipation or fear. Johnny didn't know nor care which. The minute Johnson was out o' office an' *that man* had replaced him Johnny'd known something was up. Now there wasn't nothin' right in the North and not much right in the South neither. Johnny scoffed, his mind flashing back t' that patch of bald, dead earth on the lawn. No sir. There wasn't nothin' right in the nation now that that drunk, bleary-eyed, buck-shot deer was in the...

"Grant!"

Johnny'd near puked as they'd announced it — an' now he'd gone and filled his own ears with the wretchedness of the name. Johnny bit down hard, his cheeks flushed. The god-forsaken simp-of-a-man made Johnny boil deep in his belly! A watering can caromed off the shed's door, recently havin' been introduced t' Johnny's right boot. One o' Johnny's teeth made as if to burst from grindin' so hard against its fellow ivory brethren and Johnny forced his jaw t' relax.

"Of all the... this is all Grant's..!" Johnny knew it wasn't productive to stew over the man like this, but... "The man's an idiot," he ranted t' himself, "a damn fool!"

The last word hung in the musty rafters o' the shed. Johnny'd been standing there grumbling t' hisself for God knows how long now. The air, whisperin' its way through the cracks in the shed, seemed colder now than it had durin' Johnny's stroll across the porch. Johnny'd been letting his mind run away with his thoughts again an' he knew how long such an escapade could last. He flushed. Tonight wasn't the night to be mutterin' and tinkerin' in the shed. Tonight Johnny bore more on his back than his own daily weight. He pulled from his pocket the pages o' the note, checked them over twice, an' with his rucksack over his shoulder, Johnny set out.

Dead and dormant branches scratched an' snapped against one another in the gustin' wind, sendin' twigs t' the floor o' the wood as Johnny passed through its dark heart. The smell o' dry ash hung in the wood that night, remindin' Johnny once again how long it was since he'da felt the rain fallin' down from the heavens. The lush greenery this land was once home to was now all but forgotten by the burnt out trees an' the parched, cracked earth. Twigs cracked under Johnny's feet an' he paused, thinking he'da heard somethin' followin' alongside him in the dark. The only other plantation out this a-way belonged t' the Jenks family. Johnny knew 'em well, but that family'd always been a "bed by nightfall" sort. Abner, the head of the house, was an early riser, always workin' out in the fields with the slaves — when he'da had 'em. To Johnny that was all a lot o' tomfoolery. Knowin' this, Johnny sure would'a been surprised if ol' Abner or any o' his kin were traversin' this same patch o' wood, 'specially at this time o' night.

Now the note *had* mentioned a meetin' o' "like minds," but Johnny wasn't sure that meant Abner neither. If somebody else was out in the wood, Johnny figured it was somebody who knew what he was up to. Maybe even the same somebody that'd left the damnable cryptic note sittin' on his hitchin' post durin' the mornin's homily. Now if you were t' ask Johnny 'bout that sort o' timin', he'd likely tell you that it weren't very Christian t' be out o' services on Sund'y mornin'. He'd also tell you he didn't like knowin' some stranger'da been snoopin' about.

Be that as it was, the note sure had struck a chord in Johnny somewhere, an' here he was followin' its instruction to the letter. Johnny waited another moment, his mouth ready t' hurl all manner o' chaw an' bile at whoever it was that was sneakin' 'round in the dark. The branches creaked above him an' the cold wind blew at his back, but there came no more movement upon the earth — if there'da ever been any t' begin with 'tall. Johnny's coat slapped, leathery against his calf.

Chalking up the noise to some squirrel or 'possum, he set off again through the dark wood, his stride hastened a pace. Johnny told hisself it was because he had t' make up the time he'da lost pausing like some child caught doin' wrong, not outt'a fear or nothin'.

The night carried on in its dark way, the moon hardly able t' peer through the trees. Johnny knew he had t' be makin' good time now as he slunk up an' down gulches and boulders. How he hadn'ta reached the river yet, he didn't know. Hours it must'a been had gone by, and still Johnny wasn't past the small ford beyond Byron Beane's 'stead. Normally it'd take him no more'n ninety minutes t' clear that patch o' land. Maybe it was just his own wantin' not t' be late tonight that made his progress seem so slow, he thought. He went over his preparations again. It calmed him some to think he'da been doin' right so far.

He'd been good and slipped away without any incident from the missus or little Nic or John Junior. They'd only figure out he'da left come mornin', when they saw that he'd "locked" the front door with a chair an' snuck out the window. Johnny never had fixed the lock on the front door. The damn thing still bore the splinter'd marks o' when it'd been kicked in by Northern boots durin' the war. Nowadays, Johnny never left the house unguarded without makin' sure no one was a'comin' in unwanted.

B'fore leavin' the house he'da swapped his church clothes for dark grays and blacks and slung his ol' rucksack from the war over his shoulder. In it were some small provisions and a small pouch of shot, along with a small flask o' whiskey rolled up in a handkerchief. Johnny knew it was a bad sign when you were asked to bring a hidden bit o' whiskey. You weren't hidin' it from others, you see. You were hidin' it from yerself until you needed it. Whether that was when the night got terrible cold and buildin' a fire meant death, when you needed t' pour it over a wound t' keep the maggots out, or when you needed the pain o' an amputation numbed by any means necessary, smugglin' whiskey was never a joyous man's errand. This thought was reinforced by the cool o' Johnny's hunting knife, hidden against his back. The rifle was here too, her muzzle sticking out from the top of Johnny's rucksack.

As fer the rest o' the note's instruction, Johnny felt pretty content he'd not have t' worry much about that nonsense. There'da been some sort o' over-suspicious hand that'd written that note. Coverin' your tracks when you were bein' followed was one thing, but to make sure as no one *could* follow you when you weren't even expected t' be gone? That was foolishness itself. An' that hadn'ta been the end o' the damn fool warnings, neither. Johnny wasn't worried a bit if the *moon* had seen him tonight, but the note's writer sure had been. Whoever the man was, he'da felt fit to say it more'n once: "Don't let the moon see you depart," the first time an' "go across the river where the trees hide you from the moon's eye," the second. If'n the note hadn'ta resonated in Johnny's heart and mind when it promised they'd be able to take back their land and their livelihoods, he'da never given it no credence 'tall. Johnny was a god-fearin' man and there was somethin' in the fire o' that Sunday's sermon that echoed loud and strong in the writin' o' the note, almost as if it were fate what brought it t' his home that very mornin'.

Where *was* that damned river? Johnny'd been thinkin' too hard and not mindin' hisself well enough. The strange circumstance o' the night had him on edge. The more ridiculous parts o' the note flew before his eyes: "Make no fire, save the one in your belly," and "Measure your gait, know your tread and pace." Johnny'd only thought it'd been his nameless friend's way o bein' funny. Funny in that redundant and stupid-as-dirt sort o' way. Now, frozen in mid-step, he wasn't so sure. He listened hard into the dry woods. When the second twig had snapped, he'da lent no mind to it. The spooked crow he'da heard a moment afterword worried him a bit more, but now Johnny stood transfixed, listening. He could'a *sworn* there'd been a voice, could'a sworn somebody'd whispered "*damn*."

'Who the hell would be out this time o' night?' he thought. 'What if that note had been dead serious 'bout the moon seein' me?' Johnny knew he'd seen the moon through the trees an' clouds once or twice along his way. He'da welcomed the light along the path. Had he been handed a warning in earnest and thrown it aside as lunacy?

There was a sort of a shuffling just then, like heavy branches creakin', but more metallic. Johnny turned swiftly, facin' the noise. Leaves rustled and crunched about his feet. Silence again. Seconds passed like drips o' molasses. Johnny slid his knife out from its sheath, hidden between his rucksack and his lower back. Out o' the dark came a voice: "H-Hello?"

Johnny's eyes went wide as cow pies. "Abner?! Abner Jenks?"

"Johnny?" replied the darkness, "I'zat you, Johnny Schaffer?"

Abner's footsteps were comin' through the brush. Much closer than Johnny'd thought, the man popped into view. He was holdin' a rifle, cocked and at the ready. Johnny couldn't help but notice that Abner had on the same sort o' dark clothing that he wore hisself, and looked to have a similar satchel slung 'round his shoulders. No doubt Abner was thinkin' the same.

"You get a powerful strange note this week, Johnny?" he asked.

"That I did, Abner. Showed up sometime while the family an' I was at church. It was waitin' fer me as we got back. Same thing happen to you?"

"Sure 'nough did," said Abner. "Found it hangin' from a strap o' leather on my plow first thing yesterd'y mornin'." Abner shuffled closer to Johnny through the leaves. "T' tell you the truth Johnny, I don't know whether I'm in this ol' boy's corner or not," he said, gesturing t' a corner o' familiar-looking paper sticking out o' his coat pocket.

"You carryin' that damn paper 'round in yer pocket?! Abner you know the thing's treason if yer stopped!" Johnny hissed through his teeth.

"I know it Johnny," said Abner, castin' his eyes downward in shame. "Fool thing had so many rules in it, though. I didn't want t' fergit any o' 'em an' get lost out here." Abner wouldn'ta seen it, but Johnny'd given him such a look just then as to scold the white wash off a fence.

"You been followin' it to the letter, Abner?! Any ol' fool can see half o' that nonsense is t' git ya riled up," Johnny said, tryin' t' convince more'n just Abner with them words. "Hell, I'll bet ham-hocks to horse-feathers you been hidin' from the *moon* on yer way out here tonight," he snorted.

Abner was quiet a moment after that, his eyes fixed on Johnny. Then a wry smile trickled its way across his face, startin' in his right cheek and pooling up in his left a moment later. "You sure do have a way of makin' yourself out t' be above all o' this, Johnny Reb. 'Specially considerin' that, as I see it, we both been slinkin' through the darkest part o' these here woods, carryin' the same bag o' gear on our backs, an' maybe even lookin' fer the same dried-up river?" At that, Abner's hand slapped down heavy on Johnny's shoulder and he was off again through the wood and the dark, measuring his step as he went.

Johnny didn't like how easily Abner'd seen through him. He'da planned on waitin' a good while before followin' Abner down to the river. Now, though only a couple score o' seconds had passed, Johnny found the strange feelin' o' his bein' watched through the trees comin' back. No sooner'd Abner disappeared than Johnny'd wanted t' holler at him to wait up a spell... but that'da gone against the note's rules too harsh-like, even for Johnny. Waitin' a few precious seconds longer, Johnny started feelin' icy fingers risin' up his spine. An' so he set out, his pace not quite so metered as he'da liked to admit. Johnny also didn't like thinkin' about the fact that the direction Abner'd set off in — and that he himself was now headin' — wasn't exactly the way he'da thought the river *was*. Sure enough though, the land was startin' t' slope downward an' the soil and brush was startin' t' soften underfoot. There'd be a slow bank soon, and then he'd be in the river... or the dry spot where it used t' be.

Johnny's left foot lost traction and he lurched forward, lookin' like a man fixin' t' dive into a lake. He threw his left arm in front o' his already blind eyes and reached out frantically for somethin' t' slow his fall with his right. Rushes licked his fingertips an' Johnny grasped for 'em, reachin' out far as his arm would go. Dry tendrils o' the weeds snapped an' cut along his palm. Sailin' through the air, he caught ahold o' a big ol' bulrush and held on for dear life. Anchored t' the bulrush, Johnny somersaulted as he fell, the plant twistin' in his grip. His right thigh slapped into the bank, his pack and rifle swingin' t' ground right after.

Still holdin' the bulrush, Johnny tried to sit hisself up in the slick mud an' moss. The bulrush snapped. Johnny's head an' shoulders lurched forward and he got a good look at the muck on his ankles as he tumbled past 'em. A quick flash o' light an' a thud against the back o' his skull told Johnny he'da found the ground again; the pain shootin' down his spine told him he'da landed on his rifle. Johnny let out a raspy cough that petered out into a wheeze. He made no move t' get up immediately. The way he figured it, he was down an' down was a place from which you couldn't fall. That suited Johnny just fine for the moment. His eyes were comin' back into focus now, the ringin' in his head diminishin'.

Still flat on his back, Johnny looked up at the thick windin' branches o' the old oaks that lined the riverbed. Each seemed t' be tryin' t' shove the others out o' the way for a chance at the sky. Another deep breath an' Johnny felt ready to try sittin' up. The soil was cold against his palms as he pushed and pulled hisself up out o' the muck. Tucking a leg under his backside, he hefted hisself up t' a crouch, and was just straightenin' his spine when he saw 'em.

Not but two paces from him were a pair o' boots, boots black as tar an' big as snappin' turtles. Attached t' the boots was a figure the like Johnny'd never seen. A great big bear o' a man, he was. Furs an' leather wrapped their way 'round his body, matted down with mud an' loam. Craning his neck, Johnny looked up t' the man's face. A heavy dark hood made o' skin, maybe elk, shrouded the man's features from view. As Johnny stood there cowed, the man came at him. Johnny shrieked, lost his footin' and landed square on his hind end, back in the muck.

The man stopped movin'. Johnny couldn't see the man's eyes, but the pit o' darkness behind the elk skin was fixed right at his face. He could feel the man's gaze on him, an' a heavy weight settled in his throat.

"John Schaffer," came a deep and pitted voice. It did not seem to come only from the man, but rather from all about the woods. "You are later than I expected."

Johnny stared into the darkness that hid the man's face, hopin' t' catch a glimpse o' who might be staring back at him. Was this his unknown sympathizer? Johnny figured it was more likely that this man was one o' the reasons for all o' the note's crazy precautions. His hand moved instinctively t'wards the sheathed huntin' knife against his back.

"You are right to be wary, John. It is a dangerous thing you do this night," said the giant man, stepping closer. Johnny meant t' move away from him, but something about the manner o' the big feller kept him frozen as a crawdad in winter. The man stayed just out o' Johnny's reach, crouched, his head at Johnny's eye-level. "You have neither the means nor the need to injure me, John Schaffer," he said. "The weapon you seek lies above us on the riverbank."

Johnny touched the empty sheath at his back and cursed.

"As I have said John, you have no need of your blade," repeated the man. "Excepting the fall you have just taken, you have followed my instruction well enough."

Johnny sneered at the giant as he got t' his feet. "Saw that did ya?" he said. "If'n you're the one what brought me here, I've got questions a-plenty. For starters, who are ya an' how d'you know me?"

"Time, as I have said John Schaffer, is short," the man said, his voice soundin' like the far-off rumblin' o' thunder. "These questions will find their answers soon enough. I have guided you here because you are a man of strong conviction and, I believe, of action. Are you that man, John Schaffer?"

Johnny stared at the man a moment and then blinked hard. The feller was intimidatin', there was no question o' that. Johnny normally spoke his mind no matter who it was that was listenin', but this man had him off-kilter.

"Well?" rumbled the thunderous voice. "I seek those who wish for a world not so long gone! Those who would in due time rise up of their own accord and fight to return this land to its fruitful past! I had thought you to be one of these men, John Schaffer, but you now seem fearful and clumsy, and not half the revolutionary you claim to be in the churchyard."

Johnny's gut burned with brimstone. Standin' square an' facin' the oak o' a man, Johnny erupted. "No damn mountain man is gonna stand here and question me an' my devotion t' the South!" he yelled, findin' more conviction with each word spoken. "I've fought for this land year after year! I killed all them that I could in the war, just t' save it! The people from this here river t' them far hills sang my praises when my regiment marched home! Hell, we only stopped because Lee gave us up at Gettysburg!" he declared.

"It has been three and a half long years since that day, John," said the big man, "You have grown complacent; your fire has gone out."

"Damn that talk!" Johnny came back at him, "Johnson was a Southerner an' a man of peace and Northern atonement. There was a chance at that life we lived b'fore the war with him!"

"And now?"

"Now?! Now we got the murderer o' all things Southern sittin' in the big chair! We got our very *end*!" Johnny was really burning now. "Grant will end us all if'n we let him, he proved so in the war! I thought I was comin' t' find a man who knew that! Somebody who'd help me put *down* that fox an' roll his damn carcass out o' the henhouse! I didn't put up with all o' your damn fool warnin's and superstitious talk t' be turned away as yeller!"

The man's head rolled slowly to the side. The blackness beneath his cowl struck Johnny all the way down t' his soul. The air seemed t' lighten then, the night gettin' a little less dark. "Good," said the blackness which hid the big feller's face. "You are indeed the man I thought you to be, John Schaffer, I shall excuse your clumsiness and your lateness. I ask you now to make haste due north of this riverbed. Twenty minutes quick-march from here you shall find our meeting. Those others who have been found worthy are there already. I shall follow you momentarily."

"What sort o' place is it?" asked Johnny, lookin' 'round as if t' see the meetin' place through the trees.

"Look for two lamps set beside one another. It is a symbol used by revolutionaries since the beginnings of this nation. Your brethren await you there. Now go. Our errand grows dire."

Johnny looked back t' the man, wonderin' what that last bit meant. He'd disappeared, enveloped by the dense wood. Shakin' his head, Johnny turned t' the north and set out, quick-march.

Marchin' all on one's lonesome wasn't quite the same as marchin' with company, Johnny quickly noticed. Moreover, 1869 wasn't the same as 1865. His legs weren't as marshaled as they had been in the past, an' he was in a hurry. He was half sure he was double-quick marchin' after five minutes — an' downright certain after ten. Three minutes after that, Johnny was seein' the beginnings o' a clearing up ahead. The trees grew less thick as he approached the open space, almost as if the forest had given up on growin' there out o' fear. Not twenty paces from the last brave trees stood a barn, dark and rottin' away. On the near side a door hung open, the lower hinge o' which had rusted off entire-like. In a low-set window, behind smoke-blackened glass sat a pair o' lanterns, glowin' dimly through the soot.

Johnny kicked the soil from his boots, pounded on his right thigh a few times t' stop it from crampin' an' sauntered across the dry grass t' the barn, duckin' his head as he swung through the open door. The barn smelled o' dry tinder an' rotten hay. Thick ropes hung loose from the rafters, a couple o' rusted pulleys visible on the grimy floor. T' his left, in the corner, sat the two lamps on a scarred, tooled hobbyhorse. Behind them, fillin' up the back quarter o' the barn was an enormous pile o' crates. Once they'da been stacked neatly, one on top o' the last, but sometime over the years many of 'em had rotted away. The boxes were a jumble now, fallin' into and through one 'nother. Steppin' further into the barn, Johnny saw a group o' figures sittin' hunched-over like in the center o' the open space. All the light in the barn comin' from the lanterns in the corner, Johnny could only make out the most bare o' their features. He stepped closer, tryin' t' make out a face or two. Surely Abner'd be one of 'em. There were seven men he could see; each occupyin' one o' nine high-backed chairs sat in a circle. There was somethin' small an' soft lookin' set dead-center o' the circle.

Johnny was two paces from 'em when he noticed somethin' funny. He'da been lookin' at the thing in the center so fixedly that he hadn'ta noticed it before then. Now he was so close t' the group that it was obvious as shootin' whiskey durin' church! No one'd moved. No one'd even looked up at him as he came close. A feelin' o' dread came over Johnny. It'd started even b'fore he'd taken his eyes off o' whatever the damn fool thing on the floor was. His gaze raked its way up along the inanimate forms o' those men seated closest t' him, an' directly into the face o' the man across the way.

Deep shadows danced slow-like across the man's face. They cut deep along the furrows o' his brow. His one eye not hidden in shadow stared into Johnny's. The man's terror shot into Johnny like greased lightnin'. It charged from the man and into Johnny, raw and fresh. The man was afraid *now*, afraid for his life this very second. Rope held the man tight against his chair. Leather an' oil filled the man's mouth, trickled from the corners o' his lips. The man's eye darted up from Johnny, up t' the rafters, a panicked look o' warnin' in 'em. Oil sputtered afresh through the leather as the man gagged, his drowned moan barely escaping into the barn.

Too late Johnny looked up, seein' only stars and broken rafters above. Too late he turned, havin' felt the floor shudder beside him. Too late did the smell o' hide and loam reach his nose. Already a giant hand had lifted him by the throat. Already he'da been forced backward an' down, his feet havin' stumbled over the wet, amorphous thing at the circle's center. Coils o' thick rope wrapped their way 'round Johnny's body as his spine slammed into a high-backed chair. Johnny's mind was a'firin' right an' left like a blinded sentry. "I ain't done you no wrong, Mister!" he yelled. "S'you that asked me out here tonight. I'm only doin' that what you bade me!"

"It is too late to play the sheep, John," came the now-familiar, thunderous voice. "I am well aware of your character."

Johnny let out a *"Whoopf"* as a rope thick as a crabapple hit him in the belly an' cinched him t' his chair, knockin' the breath right out o' his lungs. The rope coiled 'round him again, this time 'bout his neck. Breathin' was a bitch after that, an' movin' was her bastard son. The back o' Johnny's head was flush 'gainst his chair. He stared at his nameless captor, unable t' look away. "Why'd you go t' all the trouble o' gettin' me here if'n all you was gonna do was string me up?" he spat. "I thought you an' me were like-minded men!"

Slowly the big man pulled hisself up t' his full height. There, encircled by his captives, the man's shoulders an' head climbed too high for the dim lamplight to reach.

"John, you have been a tracker of men, a hunter of beasts... do you still not recognize a baited lure when you encounter one?" the darkness replied.

Johnny's mouth fell wide open. A moment passed, neither man movin' as the weight o' the big man's words sunk in. Then, slowly, the giant bent at the waist an' crouched directly over the small shape in the center o' the room. A large hand drove its way deep into the thing, making a soft, dull sound like an old boot flung into a swamp. Johnny could see the eyes o' the men around him darting back an'forth t' one another. They knew somethin' was comin', an' Johnny wasn't too keen on findin' out just what it was.

"Why, then?" he asked. "Why go writin' somethin' so cryptic as that damn note o' yours? Why have me dress all in black an' follow yer foolhardy rules?! What's the *moon* mean t' you anyway?!"

The large man, who'da been in the process o' drawin' his fist back out o' the thing on the floor, halted what he was doin' an' sank t' one knee. "You have done me a kindness, John Schaffer," he said, "and as such I shall return the deed."

Right then the lamplight flickered just right an' Johnny saw the barest o' the features o' his captor. Two eyes burned at him from out o' the man's hood, wild an' hungry. They were the eyes o' a predator, alert and exacting. Below them, Johnny was almost sure he'da caught a fleetin' glimpse o' a crooked smile.

"It is a rare thing for me to learn which of my trap's barbs has hooked its prey," the man said. "The moon means nothing to me John.

Its inclusion in your note was meant only to assure that you and your brethren here were careful enough not to be spotted during your pilgrimage here... my chosen end to this little sojourn."

Johnny wanted desperately t' stall, t' find some way out o' this spot, tight as it was. "You didn't answer my question," he said. "Why? Why do any o' it? If you don't see things as we do, why not just let sleepin' dogs lie?"

"Because sleeping dogs shall one day wake!" said the giant. "Because a change has come over this land, John Schaffer, one which those I represent would not see undone!"

With that, the giant yanked his hand from the bundle on the floor. Somethin' lookin' like oil-soaked leather an' straw were clenched in his fist. It only took one short stride for him t' cover the space between the two o' them, standin' then so close that Johnny could feel his breath. The other men rattled an' shook in their chairs. "Speak your last," he bade Johnny, his clenched fist inches from Johnny's mouth.

"You'll never kill the spirit o' the Sou-Aaaggh!"

Johnny's threats were drowned by oil an' hay. He gagged, his body tryin' t' force up that which was already runnin' down his gullet. Leather pressed the hay down farther an' Johnny choked.

"That, John Schaffer, is exactly what I shall do. Those who would fight for a different world will perish, and those who have run or sat complacent shall thrive. That, John, is how I will kill all that you believe to be true about your people."

The mountainous man disappeared for a moment, only t' reappear holdin' the two lanterns in one o' his whoppin' mitts. Oil crept down from his clenched fist, dripping down along the glass o' the lamps. The small flame from each leapt for its new fuel, climbin' its glass-walled prison. Johnny watched horror-struck as the man slapped the lamps t'gether, shatterin' the glass an' sendin' sparklin', flamin' shards rainin' down on the pile o' oil an' hay b'fore him. Smoke, then flame, rose from the bundle, cloudin' his vision. Slowly the barn, his captor, an' even those seated near him were enveloped by the smoke an' the fire.

The chill o' the wee hours was swiftly dispatched by flame an' smoke. Through the brush an' branches the blaze shone bright, fingers o' red-orange light thrustin' their way through what had, moments

74

b'fore, been a very good hidin' place. Abner hardly noticed the change. He was focused on the billowin' black smoke an' the barn that it was quickly eatin' up. Johnny'd walked in there not five minutes ago. Abner knew this because he'da been followin' Johnny nigh on ten minutes now, since b'fore they'd gotten t' this place.

Johnny'd come a'crashin' through the brush like an ornery hog while Abner'da been shiverin' behind a big rock. Peekin' out he'da seen Johnny an' he'da wanted t' shout over t' his friend. The look in Johnny's eyes'd been far off, though. It'd looked somethin' akin t' sleepwalkin', Abner'd thought. Somethin' 'bout that look'd kept Abner quiet, an' so he'd followed Johnny here instead. Abner'd thought it odd, an' still did fer that matter, t'find a barn out here all broke down an' with no farmin' land 'round it. Johnny'd walked right in though, so Abner'd figured he'da been expectin' t' find it. The longer he sat in the bushes watchin' the place get more an' more covered in black smoke, the more he wanted t' run in an' see if Johnny was still in there.

Just then one o' the barn's windows blew out, sendin' fresh flames out into the night. Abner stood, leavin' the questionable safety o' his hidin' spot, ready to run in fer sure. Then the creaky ol' barn door, the same one Johnny'd gone through, cracked an' shifted, liftin' entire-like off the ground. The one hinge that'd been keepin' the door fixed t' the barn screeched an' tore. Beneath the raised door stood a massive figure, holdin' it aloft one-handed like so much pressed tin. Abner knew him right off. He'da met that man briefly in the forest an' turned tail quick as he could.

Icy fingers gripped his heart on seein' the giant again, an' Abner dove back into the brush, shiverin' despite the heat o' the blaze. He watched as the man tossed the door aside. The sound o' snappin' tinder was just meetin' his ear when he saw the giant silhouetted figure snap its head in his direction. It was then that Abner realized how patchy his hidin' spot had become in the light o' the fire. The huge man stood motionless. Abner dared not even breathe. Seconds passed, the light and the cracklin' o' the fire the only things to mark their passin'. Then, quick like a bee to pollen, the great big man shot off into the woods. Abner watched him go, terrified by the speed o' such a big man.

The giant was well an' gone before Abner dared move again. The barn was near completely covered in smoke. The spot where the door'd stood was marked now by a deep orange glow that shone through the billowin' ash. Abner ran at it. 'Johnny'd been in there for sure when the barn went up,' he thought. The appearance o' that giant in the doorway'd only made Abner more sure that Johnny'd need his help.

Almost to the barn, Abner covered his mouth an' nose with his arm. Smoke folded over him, layer after layer, as he flew through the door. Nothin' was visible inside, exceptin' the glow o' the fires burnin' all 'round the barn. Abner's pace slowed t' a cautious crawl as he tried not t' run over anythin' hidden in the smoke. One o' the fires, straight ahead o' him, was glowin' in strange hard angles. Somethin', or maybe a few somethins, was in the way. They'd be too short an' too stationary t' be men, or least-wise men o' any reasonin', figured Abner. Even so, he crept closer to 'em. The nearest o' the shapes was right in front o' him now, its top a straight horizontal line in the dim light. Wrapping the cuff o' his shirt over his palm, he grabbed onto the thing. Sure 'nough, heat shot full-tilt right through the shirt an' into his hand, makin' him let go right quick. Tooled and wooden the thing was, an' much sturdier than the rest o' the barn. Some kind o' tall, bulky seat.

Abner bent low over the thing, waving the smoke away from it as best he could. Smells o' sulfur an' somethin' akin t' charred pork leapt up Abner's nose an' down his throat. Somethin' was in the chair alright, an' it weren't nothin' livin'. His face inches from the thing, Abner finally saw it through the smoke. The face o' a man, or what was left of it. He'da been bound t' his seat with ropes so thick they'd yet t' burn through, though the hair'd been scorched from off his scalp. The man's skin was shiny an' brittle lookin', an' somethin' white an' milky was leakin' from his molten eyes. Abner pulled away, tryin' not to wretch. It hadn'ta been Johnny. It couldn'ta been.

Abner took a couple steps farther into the barn, tryin' t' get some distance b'tween hisself an' the damned. Somethin' was burnin' an' smokin' awful-like next t' his foot now. He aimed a boot at it an' hoped t' God it wasn't another body. When it went sailin' away, makin' a crackly, wooden sound Abner sighed in relief. His eyes were tearin' up good now, an' he knew he'd have t' get out sooner than later. The smoke 'round him'd cleared out a touch, that bit o' tinder bein' cleared away. He could see more square-backed chairs round-about, sat in a circle. Figures were sat in each of 'em... each of 'em save one. Those near the one he'da passed looked real bad, an' Abner tried not t' look at 'em. The flesh o' some was actually catchin' alight. Workin' with all his resolve, Abner kept his eyes on the one seat without somebody in it. A spark o' hope flickered in his mind. He moved t' the chair right quick, hopin' t' see signs o' someone — Johnny hopefully — havin' worked their way t' freedom b'fore the fire 'n smoke'd started up. Lookin' down at the seat, Abner saw neither cut ropes nor marks o' violence; nothin' that could tell him someone'd broken free o' the chair. Actually, the thing was damn near pristine lookin', like no one'd ever sat in it.

'It was meant fer me.'

The thought slammed him in the skull like a bale o' hay. The impact o' that sort o' thinkin' can leave a man dizzy, an' so Abner stood there transfixed, starin' at what could'a been his end. Then somethin' moved beside him. The movement was small, but it kick-started Abner's mind again, bringin' him back into the world an' out o' his head. Still a bit fuzzy, his eyes shifted their way over t'ward whatever had moved. A man was seated in the next chair over, an' he was alive. The man was covered in smoke an' soot, an' somethin' that looked like an oily rat was stuck in his mouth, but there was no doubt in Abner's mind: he'd found Johnny.

Quick as a wink, Abner tore the leather out o' Johnny's mouth, scoopin' out a bit o' smokin' hay with it. Johnny wasn't breathin' so good. Abner figured he'd better get Johnny out t' the clean air real quick, an' he went t' work on the ropes that held his friend prisoner. The fires were growin' now, an' the smoke couldn't quite hide how much o' the barn they'd eaten away no longer. Takin' an eye off o' his hands an' the rope a second, Abner checked Johnny's breathin'. Johnny was still with him, but he didn't look good. Abner tilted his friend's head back a bit an' blew hard into Johnny's lungs. Abner's own lungs didn't like that much, an' he wheezed as he stood back from Johnny, tryin' t' catch his breath. That's when he saw some o' the flames lickin' an' eatin' away at the barn's roof above him. The fire sure was makin' quick work o' the barn. A flamin' bit o' roof landed with a spark an' a *thunk* a foot away from the men. If'n it hadn'ta been so hot n' dry in there, Abner sure would'a *started* sweatin' by then. The smoke was gettin' t' him now an' he was startin' t' have t' near cross his eyes t' see straight. Finally somethin' gave an' Johnny slumped forward in his seat, coughin' weak-like.

Abner threw Johnny's arm over his own an' hefted the man up an' onto his back. His legs quivered an' gave a bit, his sight gettin' real dark for a terrifyin' heartbeat. Breathin' in deep, smoke be damned, Abner pulled hisself back up and swung 'round. Fast as he could go, he retraced his steps from the barn door. As he got close, it seemed as if a breeze had kicked up from back in the barn. Smoke was blowin' past him and out o' the barn so fast that it damn near pushed him an' Johnny over. There was a crash like dynamite goin' off. Abner got one good look at the night sky as he pulled Johnny an' hisself free o' the smoke. Cold night air flew into his lungs. The stars flew down from the heavens an' smacked him square in the brain-pan. The last thing Abner remembered b'fore passin' out was feelin' his knee hit the ground real awkward-like an' seein' Johnny slap full-bore against the dirt with a groan, right next t' him.

Smoke was still fillin' all corners o' the sky when Abner awoke an' pulled hisself up from the dirt. Rememberin' the crashin' sound that'd gone on when the sky'd seemed t' come fallin' down upon him, Abner swung his head 'round t' get a look at the barn. The whole roof'd caved in. Nothin' in there'd be alive any longer. Tryin' not to think o' the man with the meltin' eyes, Abner chose instead t' look over toward where he'd seen Johnny fall. Johnny was still there, sure 'nough, but there was somethin' wrong with the way he was lyin'. Pullin' hisself up t' his knees, Abner crawled over t' Johnny. Johnny's back was hunched over an' his neck had a strange sort o' crick in it. Gettin' closer now, Abner saw that Johnny's hands were clenched real tight into fists but weren't holdin' on t' anythin' in particular. Abner's chest seemed t' collapse in on itself as he pulled hisself even closer. Johnny's eyes were open too, but Abner could tell he wasn't lookin' at anythin'. Johnny wasn't there no more. Not wantin' it t' be true, Abner took Johnny's shirt in his fist an' shook real hard, like a child wakin' his Pa on Sund'y mornin'. Johnny jus' slumped closer t' the earth.

Tears blurred Abner's eyes as he picked up Johnny's body, cradlin' it gently as he got t' his feet. It didn't seem right. He'da suffered tribulations a'plenty t' get Johnny out o' that damned barn while he was still alive! He'da done it, too. Abner knew that. If'n he'd kept his head an' not passed out when the barn collapsed, he could'a breathed into Johnny's lungs some more. He could'a saved Johnny for sure! Carryin' Johnny's body away from the barn, Abner cursed them old timbers for not holdin' longer. He cursed hisself for a coward an' a weakling. He cursed the smoke for stealin' his breath an' Johnny's life away. Most o' all, he cursed the giant of a man who'd brought such death t' his small corner o' the world. He reached the edge o' the forest an' set down Johnny real careful-like. He sat down hisself, too. He sat, an' sat, an' sat, the smoke an' fire burnin' away behind him as the first light o' mornin' climbed into the sky.

Clack-clack, clack-clack, clack-clack shook the cart behind its single horse. She was a short black filly an' a benign sort o' creature. She followed whoever held her reigns dutifully, relyin' on their judgment t' lead her t' wherever she was needed. Not even when the cart hit a particularly deep rut, sounding as if it might splinter t' pieces, did she startle. The man at her reigns reacted even less. On he plodded in his slow measure, oblivious t' the shudderin's o' the cart. Abner knew no harm could any longer befall his forlorn cargo. Followin' along behind the cart sobbed the Widow Schaffer an' her boys, Johnny's only bereaved. They was headin' from Johnny's plantation down t' the churchyard, where the parson waited. Along the way they passed through the town proper. It was in the market that Abner's ears first perked up an' he was given reason t' raise up his head an' look 'round. There, along the storefronts and alongside the road, stood ladies an' gents, babes and bare-boned codgers. As the cart passed, the gents doffed their caps an' ladies wept. Abner wasn't sure how it'd gone about, but 'round about halfway down the market road a gang o' folks'd jumped in behind Widow Schaffer and her young'uns. Seein' 'em, Abner ducked his head low, wishin' they'd just go on home. Every one o' 'em that joined up was one more heart he'da cut into when he'da let the smoke an' the fire take away his neighbor an' friend. None o' them knew it, a'course. Only Abner did. He knew it an' every footfall followin' that cart down the road weighed heavy on him, heart and soul. Those few o' Abner's heartstrings that hadn't snapped two nights prior, when he was holdin' Johnny's dead body in his exhausted arms, drew taught. Boom ba-doom, boom ba-doom-doom beat his heart. Abner hated it for beatin' so hard, especially when he knew it was breakin'. By the time the ol' cart reached the churchyard, Abner's chest was beatin' so hard you could see the poundin' through his shirt an' his vest. By the time he an' the parson'd laid into the earth the pine box that was to forever be Johnny's bed, Abner's eyes'd fogged over somethin' terrible. The blood pounded in his eyes, creatin' flashes o' red 'n white light that beat along irregular-like in time with the the poundin' o' his chest. As the parson began his prayers, Abner swore he'da felt one o' them last heartstrings give. A heavy, hot liquid poured down through his insides an' settled in his gut, pullin' his shoulders down apace in kind. He felt his knees shakin', tryin' t' hold aloft the extra weight that sat in his gut. His hands trembled as he braced hisself against his knees. Tears slapped down against them hands, hard and wet.

Just then somethin' like a dove alighted on his hunched shoulder. There was somethin' about its soft presence that let a bit o' air an' light into his lungs. Given that bit o' encouragement, Abner heaved in some sky an' worked at shakin' the cloud away from behind his eyes. It took a bit o' work, but after a moment his eyes cleared, an' Abner turned to see what it was that'd taken it upon itself t' show a guilty man kindness. Abner sure wasn't expectin' the thing upon his shoulder t' be the hand o' the Widow Schaffer. Her eyes were heavy as his own, but there was thanks in 'em. Thanks that seemed aimed at Abner hisself. Nothin' in the world could let Abner make sense o' that look. Nothin' that was, until his ears started hearin' the world outside hisself again an' the words o' the parson came floodin' in. The man was speakin' clear an' loud, an' in his words there was praise for Abner. He was speakin' o' bravery and o' friendship. Abner stared at the man, glassy-eyed. The parson went on, his pitch rising on words like "our sons" an' falling on ones like "Northern aggression." Abner felt the irregular *boom-ba-doom* of his heart pick up the rhythm o' the parson's words, heard it right itself t' a regular *ba-bum, ba-bum*. The parson turned t' recantin' stories o' Johnny's glories durin' the war. As he listened t' these, Abner's mind swept him back t' the sight o' that great big man standin' b'fore the burnin' barn wherein Johnny'd sat dyin'. The parson couldn'ta known the goings on o' that dark night, but as he spoke

Abner saw 'em again, this time in a new light.

The parson began leadin' the assemblage in a choral refrain. Abner let the voices flow into him. They rushed in through his ears an' flowed down the still-poundin' veins o' his neck. Down they went, carried by the current o' his blood, down an' into his cleft heart where they set fire. The fire burned, hot like molten iron, as it flowed down his shorn heartstrings. Down it poured until it found that weight in his gut. The molten flame scorched an' gnawed at the weight an' ate it all up. Then it hit somethin' so central t' Abner you'd have to call it his core. Abner's shoulders picked back up, his eyes shinin' with the flames that was burnin' from deep inside, an' he sang loud an' strong with them that was around him. He sang in words, but what was flowin' from him that day was more than just lyrics. It was more'n song or prayer even. What was flowin' out o' Abner Jenks that day was molten an' miraculous fire, an' it was a flame that would not soon be put out.

Chapter Five
Shadow and Regret

It was like waking from a dream: one replete with sounds and scents, its own time and place. A dream that had thrust its presence upon reality, had supplanted it. Merlin had drawn quiet some moments ago. Yet still before Arthur's eyes hovered vestiges of the graveyard and its inhabitants. Shadows reflected in mist, they flickered and dissipated like so much fog before the morning sun. Lazily the wood-grain of the table came into focus as Arthur became aware of his surroundings once more.

Bartholomew still sat upon his lap, purring contentedly in his sleep. An empty bowl, once ladled to the brim with stew, sat before him upon the table. Arthur's eyes shifted, still focusing poorly, toward the bowl. As he did so, a final image of Abner, crying as he sang with the choir, winked back into sight. Arthur's throat closed tight around a sob. He could not breathe. Swallowing hard, Arthur forced new air down into his lungs. Once there, however, the air condensed and built in pressure, surging upward once again, this time in the form of tears. These fell heavy from his red and bleary eyes, splashing down into the basin of the empty bowl before him. The sad reality of Arthur's recent past mingled with the dreary imagery that had forced its way into his head. For sheer lack of space they pulsed and pounded their way out through his temples. They fell as weights trussed up in tears. They swept forth from his stomach as wails and cries. The child shook, overcome by such emotional blood-letting.

To Arthur's left, his back to the embers still glowing in the fireplace, sat Merlin, his own eyes still clearing away the clouds conjured by his tale. Sadness did not dance all across his face as it did upon that of the boy, but clung, hardly visible, along the edges of his eyelids. More prevalent upon his countenance was the mask of horror and shock that hung from his sunken cheeks and strung itself across his down-turned lips. His ancient frame shivered with regret and apology. He shook visibly as he stood, his heart crying out for the child who sat at his table to forgive him. He wanted to embrace the boy, to comfort him. Yet his own guilt held him in place. It whispered in the old man's ear: "You can only bring this child more pain. You have cut deep into an already open wound." The old man knew this well. The sights of death, the smell of ash, the very world of his tale had echoed too strongly in the child's own fate.

"My lad, I fear I have done you great ill in telling you such a tale," he said, his voice returning to its gruff and aged timbre; all hint of the strange vernacular of his tale dissipating back into the æther. "I dare not wonder why such a tale would come to me at such a time." With this he whisked his traveling cloak from the hook upon the wall and draped it around the child. He did this without touching the child even in the slightest way, for guilt still hung beside his ear assuring him that his mere touch might somehow injure the child further.

"I want to go to bed," spoke the boy.

Scooping Arthur up from his chair, Merlin carried him down the short hall to a small room. Therein had been laid a small bed with a pair of soft wool-stuffed pillows and a heavy blanket made from the same. Arthur was placed on his feet at the door by the old man and walked in of his own volition, the traveling cape still wrapped tight around his shoulders. Bartholomew snuck into the room, hardly noticed by either the boy or the old man.

"I'm terribly sorry for telling you such a tale, Arthur," said Merlin, his voice so soft as to be difficult to hear if one wasn't listening properly. With that he began to shut the door after the boy. From within the darkening room came the quietest of replies.

"S'ok, Mr. Merlin," was all that the old man heard, but it gave him a bit of hope that the child was not too damaged by this last trauma.

"I shall not sleep tonight, but shall instead stand watch," he said, through the small crack that remained between the door and its frame. "I shall be close at hand, should you need me."

It cannot be said that either Arthur or Merlin truly rested that night.

Both man and boy had far too much upon their minds for quiet repose. Merlin sat, deep in thought, at the fireside all through the night. Arthur, while asleep, had only fitful dreams of fire and of death, of giants and of men in lands far away. He did not, however, dream of crackling bracken or swirling eyes.

Chapter Six

Upon a Summer's Day

It was back-breaking work, Arthur decided. In fact, he was sure he'd heard something pop somewhere near his shoulder an hour ago. The summer sun beat down upon his scrawny shoulders. The scent of rotten, smoldering thatch permeated the air. Little cuts and scratches bled and itched as he scooted himself about the roof, replacing what was rotten with fresh thatch.

"Can I come down for a while, Merlin?" he asked, trailing off into a whine as he spoke the old man's name.

Thok

"Can you still see through to the flagstones?" replied the old man from below.

Thok

"Well, not as easily as before..."

Thok

"I wouldn't yet call it a repaired roof then, Arthur."

Thok

Arthur sighed. There hadn't been much hope to begin with. He scooted himself down the slope of the thatch and peered over the edge of the roof. He could see Merlin hunched over the woodpile below. The boy craned his neck, leaning further over the edge of the roof, so as to catch a better look at the old man at work.

Thok

The axe slammed down upon its fodder. The log was split in a single blow and the next replaced it, quick as a light.

Thok

Again two blocks of tinder lay where before had stood a single core. The boy marveled at how deft and practiced the old man's motions were. One hand swung the axe down upon the logs while the other cleared the fallen tinder and placed the next piece of wood, all in what seemed to Arthur as one smooth cyclical motion. The old man's back arched upright.

"This is not the most productive way to go about thatching a roof, Arthur," he said, looking up to face the child.

Arthur startled, his hand slipping along the coarse thatch. He caught himself again, but not before a firm sliver of thatch had driven itself deep into his palm. "Yeeeaaaoooww!" yelped the lad, grimacing at his still-clenched hand upon the roof.

Merlin sighed. Arthur, it seemed, was a relatively accident prone child. Just one day prior the boy had tried bounding over a fence, hooked his ankle and scuffed his chin upon the earth.

"Ooh! Aagh! Merlin, it hurts!" cried the boy.

Smothering a chuckle, the old man laid down his axe. If the child was willing to injure himself to get out of work for a mere moment, perhaps the break was one well paid for. He strode across the patch of dirt which separated the wood pile from the cottage and stretched out a hand.

"Grab ahold, boy. I'll take a look at what you've gone and done to yourself," he said.

The boy reached out with his good hand, the hand which had been his anchor to the roof, and toppled headlong from his perch. Just as deftly as he had handled the axe, Merlin scooped the child out of the air. Arthur made a wide, spinning arc, swept up in the old man's grasp. His sight blurred for a moment, his brain addled by the falling sensation in his stomach. Then, just before his face, there was earth. It swung slowly to and fro before him. His arms were outstretched, probing about for a handhold as if he were still falling. His chest felt tight against his lungs.

Above him, the old man cleared his throat. Arthur looked up, craning his neck so far that his skull touched his shoulder blades. An upside-down Merlin swung into view, his arm outstretched and holding a piece of cloth which very closely resembled Arthur's shirt.

"Th-thanks," gurgled the boy from his contorted windpipe. The old man squinted tersely. His bespeckled old hand released its hold, and

Arthur's chin, for the second time in as many days, met with the dirt.

"It is a remarkable thing, Arthur," said Merlin moments later, "that a boy can put such energy into sloth as to make it into an occupation."

Arthur lay now upon his back, his head propped up by a spare bundle of thatch. A stern-looking Merlin dabbed at the boy's chin with a bit of wet cloth. Above the old man, Arthur could see the very hole in the roof which the old man had wanted him to patch. This, Arthur was sure, was by design. His chin stung. Merlin lacked the soft touch of Maggie, or even Bedwyn. As the old man treated his cuts and scrapes, Arthur pined for the company of his prior benefactors, wincing every so often out of pain and indignation. The old man was certain he'd tumbled off the roof on purpose, but that sort of reasoning was daft to the boy's way of thinking. Who threw himself off a roof? For what gain? Still... despite the old man's chiding, there was entirely something to be said for resting upon the thatch rather than scraping the skin from one's palms to patch the roof with the stuff. The boy sighed, staring up at the heavens through the loosely bunched roofing.

"Was the barn ever rebuilt, Merlin?" he asked.

The old man looked about, seemingly half-expecting to see a barn just out the cottage window.

"Barn? Never *been* a barn here, Arthur," he said assuringly. "What are you on about?"

"Not *here*," Arthur said, "I meant the one that the big fellow burnt up with Johnny and Abner in it."

Merlin sat back at this and heaved a slow sigh. Arthur could tell that his question had been entirely unexpected. The old man's breath was ragged now, his hands folded together. For a moment both man and boy stared fixedly, the old man's eyes delving into the wrinkles of his hands, the boy's into the sky.

"No," spoke the old man, his voice deeper, quieter than before. "No, as far as I can recollect the tale, the spot was left to be eaten up by whatever leaves of green would venture within that blighted clearing — though I doubt very greatly that any ever did," he added.

This was not the response Arthur had wanted. "Well, what happened then?" he asked, a bit put out.

"The same thing that always happens when lives and lands are torn asunder," replied Merlin quietly. "People rebuilt."

There was a twinkle creeping into the corner of the old man's eye which Arthur noted with interest. "But you just said..." he pried.

Merlin was standing then. The twinkle in his eye had grown and was spreading like an infecting confusion across the old man's face.

"Come and help bring in wood for the fire, Arthur," he said. "I suppose the thatch can keep for the night. We'll not have a drop of rain tonight, after all."

Arthur hadn't the foggiest idea how the old man knew such a thing, but of the things he'd borne witness to while in the presence of the wizard — for such had the old man become in the eyes of the boy — predicting the weather was practically benign. He followed Merlin out to the woodpile dutifully, all the while noting that the light still flashed, bright like a far-off star in the corner of the old man's eye.

Once his spindly arms were laden with all the tinder they could carry, Arthur dutifully followed Merlin back into the cottage. He took care as he trudged along. There were only so many times the boy would allow the earth to do him harm in a short period. To keep from falling he had to take large sweeping strides, designed to avoid — or at least detect — the attacks launched upon his equilibrium by errant pebbles and forgotten stumps. The spectacle of such an act was not lost upon the old man as he held the cottage door open for the child. The look of worry and confusion upon Merlin's countenance softened.

"How can people have rebuilt and yet *not* have?" Arthur asked, laying the wood by the hearthside.

"What? Oh. Haha!" chuckled Merlin. "Yes, it does seem a bit paradoxical in a way, does it not?"

"Para-what?" Arthur was entirely confused.

"Let us tend the fire and I shall endeavor to explain," said Merlin. The logs were laid and a flame struck. Little tendrils of orange light wrapped about the tinder, looking for footholds and, finding them, rooting themselves in wooden pits. Merlin watched them climb as he lit his pipe.

"Do you see this bit of light here?" he asked, pointing to a flame which had just caught alight upon a small log.

"Yes," said Arthur.

"It is just now catching hold, having left the brother from whence it was spat. Do you see that?" asked Merlin.

"I suppose so," said the boy.

"What do you suppose would happen if I were to snuff out the flame that birthed this new bit of light?" mused the old wizard.

Arthur stared into the fire, trying to work out Merlin's meaning. In silence, he opened his mouth and closed it again, not knowing what to guess.

Before the child could work out the answer to his riddle, the old man scooped up a mug of tea and doused the lower flame. At first the second flame flickered violently. Then, it weakened and shrank upon its perch. The two stared at the small flame, waiting to see what it would do. A moment passed as the flame glowed dimly. Then, as quickly as it had shrunk, so leapt the flame, its light taller and brighter than ever. Still the man and child stared on, as slowly the new flame widened upon the tinder. Eventually the thing was so large that it enveloped the wood and shot off sparks and a fiery brood all its own. These flames in turn climbed higher up the chimney than could their father have done.

"So too it is with man," said Merlin. There was a hint of wonder in his voice as he spoke, as if even he did not know by what mechanism such things were set in motion.

Arthur began to turn toward the wizard, meaning to glean from the old man's face what internal thought had stolen away his attention. Before his eyes found Merlin's face, they caught a glimpse of something shining and strange. A peculiar spark had popped and spun from the bark of a large log upon the fire. It seemed to the child that the spark moved differently than the others. Firstly, the thing had been in the air for quite a few moments and had neither landed nor gone out again. Secondly, when the fire leaned and bent in a certain direction, this little spark failed to follow along. It was as if the thing had its own agenda and couldn't be bothered to remain simply a spark any longer. Arthur was almost sure that, on one meandering which had taken the spark especially close to his face, he had even made out tiny wings and legs upon the thing.

"Now what do you suppose..." said Merlin, trailing off transfixedly.

Another spark joined the first just then, this one winking in and out as it flitted about. The two of them leapt and spun until they were joined by a third and then a fourth point of light — and then a fifth and sixth. The fireplace fell away then and all was dark, save for the little points of light dancing before the boy.

The old man spoke...

Chapter Seven

Embers Amongst The Ashes

Abner sat, smokin' his pipe upon his stoop. His eyes followed the last few wakin' bees o' the day, buzzin' about in tired little loops an' droopy curly-cues. Contrastin' the tirin' bees were the lightnin' bugs, growin' in number an' as energetic as the first cock-crow o' the mornin'. The first dark ambers an' deep pumpkin oranges were beginnin' t' follow the corn-cob yellows which danced across the sky. Night was comin' soon. Those that worked the fields were done or finishin' up the day's work.

Every now an' again, one o' the bees' lazy meanderin's was interrupted by the zippin' and winkin' trails that followed the lightnin' bugs through the darkenin' sky. For a moment, the bee would zip about as if he'da been set on fire, but soon enough he'd settle down again into his slow, whirlin' descent toward home an' sleep.

Abner sighed. It'd been weeks since Johnny'da been laid t' rest. It may've been off-color t' say it, but the story o' "The Barn Fire an' the Behemoth," as it had been called in the papers, had spread jus' as fast as had the flames on that ill-fated night. The events o' that night'd spread across four states already, an' still had plenty o' steam.

Abner'd jus' come back from the Widow Schaffer's home, where he'da visited with the lady an' handed over a rubber ball an' a woodwork pea-shooter t' the boys. 'Them boys'd seemed cheery enough t'day,' he thought, 'even though them toys ain't 'xactly as fancy an' electric as little Nic most liked.' It was bafflin' t' him how oft-times the young'uns were the quickest t' get right again after some kind o' tragedy. Them boys went whoopin' and hollerin' about jus' as soon as they got their play things; whereas the Widow Schaffer, it was easy t' see, was workin' her hardest jus' t' soldier on, as best she could. Abner felt he might really be doin' the same as she, sittin' all by his lonesome on the porch an' starin' off at nothin' too particular.

Somethin' told him he'd need a few minutes b'fore seein' the faces o' his own wife an' babies. It tore him up somethin' ferocious, thinkin' 'bout Johnny an' 'em others that lost their all for reasons he hisself couldn't place. More an' more Abner felt there was somethin' what had t' be done. Sure, there'da been a town watch set up once the people in town knew about what'd happened, and sure nothin' else terrible'd gone on since, but that did powerful little t' sate Abner's gut feelin' on the matter. Somewhere, out in the wilderness, there was a predator o' men. A great big goon o' a man who'd burned and murdered good men, an' for what reason Abner didn't know. It was hard t' feel sated in a world like that, Abner thought t' himself. Somethin' had t' be done. The world had t' be put back to right. For the life o' him, Abner didn't know how that sort o' thing could be done, but each day that he went t' see the Schaffer family, he felt more an' more that it *had* t' be done — an' soon.

'But how?' Abner thought t' hisself. There'da been no sign o' the big bastard since the night o' the fire. Abner was sure there'd *be* none neither, until some other tragedy came thunderin' out from the woods an' into town. He clenched his fists as he thought on the problem, finally slammin' one down upon the planks o' the porch.

A moment later, there was a soft pitter patterin' on the porch an' a small bundle o' cotton an' lace plopped itself down upon the steps beside Abner. "Hello, daddy," it sang. "Are you mad at them stairs?"

Despite his worries, Abner had t' chuckle at such a thing as that. "No, Mazie," he said, "I'm not mad at them stairs."

"Well, did they do somethin' they shoudn'ta then?"

"No, darlin'... it's me that's in a pickle, not these here stairs. I suppose I jus' know they can take a little bit o' frustration every now and again is all," Abner replied, turning t' face his daughter. She had a dolly in her hands an' was smoothin' out its dress an' petticoats, never mindin' that her own were gettin' ruffled by the steps.

"You done somethin' wrong, Daddy?" asked the little cherub.

Abner hadn't told her the truth o' Johnny's death, nor would he ever willin'ly do so. Little girls didn't need such ruin on their minds.

So, like any father an' husband worth his salt, Abner dodged the question. "T'aint *that* so much darlin'," he said, "more like I'm tryin' t' find a feller."

"Has he gone missin' like Mr. Schaffer done?" This is what she'da been told o' Johnny.

"No, no darlin'. It's more as if he picked up an' left town all o' a sudden. Don't you fuss yerself 'bout it though."

"But Daddy, you're always sayin' how it's damn near 'mpossible t' up an' leave this town."

"Don't say that word, darlin'."

"Well it's so, Daddy — besides, you say damn more often than your prayers."

Abner sat up at this an' squinted at his daughter inquisitive-like. She stared back into his eyes, a strange twinkle in her own. They sat there a moment, durin' which Mazie slowly raised her dolly's head up t' hide the growin' smirk upon her face. 'Yup,' thought Abner, 'the signs are all there. The missus' wily prints're all over this turn in the conversation.'

"Now, Mazie... Momma didn't go an' put you up t' this, did she?" he asked.

"Noooo..." Mazie blurted out, between bursts o' giggles.

"Mazie, are you fibbin' t' me?" Abner scolded, raisin' his hands t' his hip in mock seriousness. The little girl squealed behind her dolly, realizin' she'da been caught at her mother's game.

"No Fair!" she wailed, a mask o' false dismay upon her face. "You always know when Momma has me trick you!"

Abner's hand darted over an' tickled his daughter on the belly, sendin' her into fits an' squeals. "That," he said, "is because your momma isn't quite so sneaky as she thinks."

Forsakin' her dolly, Mazie rolled herself sideways and away down the steps, still snickerin' an' a'huffin' an' a'puffin' from bein' tickled so. Father an' daughter sat quiet a moment then, both wearin' smirks upon their faces an' soakin' in the warmth in their hearts.

Slowly, little pudgy fingers walked their way back across the steps. Abner pretended not t' notice. Closer an' closer they crept, finally pouncin' upon their prey, the little cloth dolly. Mazie swiped her toy t' her chest again, just as Abner spun 'round, wearin' the greatest look o' surprise across his face. The girl gasped, still smilin' ear t' ear. Little trails o' laughter puttered their way out from between her pursed, smilin' lips, like an auto-trolley chuggin' uphill.

B'fore she really got goin' though, Momma was at the door. "Now what's all this laughter, then?" she asked from the threshold.

"Uh-oh, Mazie, the jig's up! The ol' warden's gone an' showed up. It's solitary confinement for the both o' us, I'm bettin'," Abner gasped, shootin' a sly wink at his daughter.

"Abner Jenks! You'll have my own child turned against me if you keep up like that," said the missus, a hint o' seriousness behind her jovial tone. "Now come along, Mazie. I won't have you mussin' up your nice lace dress by rollin' all around the porch like a prairie dog!"

Mazie dutifully picked herself up off o' the steps, a pout upon her face. "Two more minutes!" she said, stampin'.

"Mazie, you can come back out after you change your dress an' do your chores. Lord knows your layabout father will still be there, growin' roots into the porch." She said this last bit with a wry smile on her face. Mrs. Jenks knew full well how hard her husband worked at runnin' their plantation, especially now that it was only him an' the couple o' freed men who'd opted t' stay on for an honest wage an' a share o' the crop. She loved her husband, but was not so pure in her adoration that she could resist a good jibe now an' again.

Abner knew what she was up to, alright. A loud and exaggerated "Harrumph!" an' a snort for good measure were his reply.

With this, the missus walked back into the house, a little smile curlin' 'round her lip. Mazie lingered a moment. "Maybe he'll write you," she said.

"What?"

"You said somebody'd left an' you wanted t' know where to, right Daddy? Maybe he'll write you," Mazie chimed. "When you went off t' fight in the war, you wrote Momma an' me." An' then she skipped off into the house.

A long moment went by, durin' which a bee landed upon Abner's shirtsleeve. So wrapped up in thought was he that it was a full five minutes b'fore he saw the bugger an' swatted it away. That little act seemed t' break Abner's trance-like thought process. He stood, still starin' out across the fields. "Or maybe he already has done," he murmured. Abner spun on his heel, ran t' the doorway an' shouted into the house: "I'll be back b'fore nightfall! I gotta get somethin' from the Schaffer place!"

"What?!" came the voice o' the shocked Mrs. Jenks from somewhere deep in the house. Abner never heard it. By the time the missus'd bustled out onto the porch again, Abner was on the plough-horse an' kickin' up a trail o' dust t'ward the Schaffer place, his saddle still restin' in the barn.

It was late that evening when Abner an' the ol' plough-horse came amblin' back up the road. Steam an' spittle poured from the poor beast's face as it plodded along. The creature's expression was one a man wears when he'sa been chased by the devil apace, an' only just out-run the bastard. Its eyes stared longin'ly t'ward the barn an' its pile o' hay. It was the thought o' this refuge alone that likely kept the ol' boy goin'.

Abner couldn'ta been less interested with the needs or wants o' his horse. It weren't that he was all that uncarin' or any o' that sort o' nonsense. More like he was too fixed on the slip o' paper he had in his mitts t' bother about some horse, or anybody else for that matter. He was havin' trouble readin' it now, as it'd gotten true an' dark out. The only light t' go by now was that o' the moon an' the late-to-risers of the lightnin' bug community.

As the horse plodded labouredly into the barn, Abner swung his right leg across the left an' slid off o' its back. The horse kept goin' straight ahead into the barn slow-like. Abner was a good twenty paces off t'ward the house when the sound o' his horse collapsin' into its bed o' hay met his ears. There followed a groanin' and a mumblin' in the vernacular o' horses from within the barn. Even if Abner could o' understood it, he wasn't about t' be side-tracked by the bellyachin' of an old an' grumbly equine. He took the stairs up onto the porch in short, quick leaps an' practically exploded through the front door. Finally havin' t' look away from his treasure, Abner shot up the stairs t' the room he an' the missus shared. The light was out already, an' the missus most likely along with it, but there were important things that needed doin'. Placin' the slip o' paper down on the bedside table, he struck a match an' re-lit the lamp. The far side o' the bed shifted an' groaned.

"Sorry, darlin'," whispered Abner.

"S'it late or early?" replied the covers.

"Only just gettin' on toward late, s'all," said Abner as he rummaged about in the closet. The blankets grumbled again as Abner found what he was lookin' for. Out from the closet came his knapsack. It was the same one he'd carried with him on the night o' Johnny's demise, an' it slapped down onto the wooden floor with a heavy *whump*. Abner winced.

Sure 'nough, the blankets were thrown back an' the missus was up in earnest. "Abner, what on earth is it you're up to?" she asked. Then, noticin' the knapsack on the floor an' the manic look in her husband's eye, her tone took on an altogether darker note. "Abner *Jenks*! I'll not have my husband runnin' off into the night again!" Her voice changed from a shout to a hoarse whisper. "Not after John Schaffer's death an' all the woe o' it!"

Abner was in a tight spot. It looked bad for sure. "Now darlin'," he began.

"Oh, no you don't Mr. Jenks. I'll not be *darlin'ed* an' *sweethearted* into widowhood, no sir!" She was up an' out o' the bed now, her nightgown rumpled an' her bonnet askew. Lazy curls o' hair had snuck out from under her bonnet an' bounced an' coiled as she stomped her way over to her husband.

Abner stood, momentarily quittin' his fevered search through the bag. His wife was difficult t' sway when she got like this, an' that was an understatement. "You've got this wrong, Tess," he said, optin' t' use the missus' proper name rather than keep on bein' rebuffed for usin' her pet names. "I'm not goin' anywhere... leastwise not tonight."

"Oh, I'm sure it'll be the wee hours again b'fore you climb your way out the window an' out o' our lives!" Tess replied, swingin' her raised fist down and into Abner's chest. It wasn't so much an act o' violence or anger, just one o' desperation.

"I'll prove it to ya, then," Abner replied. "There next t' the lamp, there on the table, what's that?"

Lookin' over, Tess gasped. "What's *this*, Abner? What's *this*? Well it sure as shinola looks like another note, sent by what devils I'm sure I don't know!" She was burnin' like a fumarole now. "Whatever it is this asks, you can't go off and do it! I won't have it, Abner!"

Abner kept his voice calm an' metered as he went about replyin' t' that. He knew there'd be no reasonin' with her 'tall if he fed that head o' steam she'd gone and built up. "Tess, that letter ain't even addressed t' me. Jus' read who it's to, Tess. You'll see it, clear as well-water, you will."

Tess looked the note over quick-like. The right side o' her nose flared. Abner was sure there'd be a heavy blast o' steam plowin' out o' there. Her brow furrowed. She looked the letter over again, readin' it further the second time.

"It's Johnny Schaffer's letter, Tess."

"Well that much I can see, Abner," replied the missus. "What's odd t' me is that *you've* got it." She was calmin' down a touch. No longer did her nose seem cocked and ready t' explode with exhaust. Her worry was bein' bled out, replaced by a sort o' charged curiosity.

"It was Mazie's idea," Abner said, "Well... she put the thought into *my* head, more like."

"*Mazie's* idea?"

"Most ways, yeah," Abner continued. "See I wasn't jus' settin' while I was out there on the stoop this afternoon. I was ruminatin'."

"Uh-huh," squinted Tess. She was still starin' down at Johnny's ol' note, her grip tightenin' around it an' crinklin' the poor thing.

Abner saw the sharp glint in her eye. He was on thin ice tellin' her the next bit that was comin', an' that was for certain. "See," he went on, "it don't sit right with me how Johnny Schaffer is lyin' in a pine box an' that big lummox what murdered him is still out there, hidin' out along the borderlands somewheres."

"Abner Jenks," said Tess, her tone steely, "you wouldn't be fixin' on tellin' me that you're lookin' t' go off on some harebrained search for revenge, would you?"

"Well..."

"Because if you are, you can hang that idea from the nearest tree!"

"Tess, it ain't like that. I ain't about t' go traipsin' off into the woods an' the wilds after some beast o' a man what stands as tall as a locomotive an' walks them borderlands like a will-o-the-wisp."

Tess' grip on the letter slackened, but her gaze remained piercin' as Abner went on.

"I was more thinkin' that I might figure out where he's holed up, or find some way t' flush him out o' his hidey-hole. T' be honest, though, I wasn' havin' no real luck at it."

"Mm-hmm."

"Then sets down our little girl-child, an' she spouts off a line 'bout how I wrote y'all letters t' let you know I was alive, an' whereabouts the fightin' was at durin' the war." Tess was sittin' on the bedside now, listenin'. "Now, after she went inside, I kept on thinkin' on that a while. I was rememberin' how I'd get goin' in them letters an' tell y'all more'n I ought o' done 'bout our troops an' the war an' the like — an' then it hit me. Here I had a piece o' correspondence from this hill-man, this borderer. I had it in my own knapsack right here!" Abner gestured excitedly at his knapsack, pointin' with both hands an' near stompin' his feet. "What's more, I knew right where another bit o' his correspondence was! It was settin' around collectin' dust an' misery with the rest o' Johnny's final effects, right 'round the bend on the Schaffer homestead!" Abner finished, havin' gotten more an' more exuberant in the tellin' o' his scheme.

"Abner," said Tess, "you ain't makin' a lick o' sense, hon."

"Well sure I am, darlin'!" Abner beamed. "Now I got two o' these here letters, penned in the very hand o' The Borderer! I'd bet land rights t' lunch meat there's a slip-up or two in 'em, maybe even enough o' one t' figure out the man's whereabouts from! If'n that's the case, then all I'd have t' do is write the local authorities an' he'll be greetin' the devil so soon as t' make all o' hell itself surprised t' see him!"

The fire was back in Abner's eyes, and Tess saw it. It was the same righteous fire that had sparked an' shone from his very bein' the day he'd come stormin' home from Johnny's funeral. There was somethin' different about Abner when that fire started goin', somethin' Tess knew not t' try an' snuff out. To the woman who loved him, the glow that shone out from Abner's eyes when he got an idea in his head was like t' the beatin' o' angels' wings from on high. It was for this reason that her heart sank. That, an' that she knew Abner's idea was a good one.

"Well there's no use in lookin' fer yer letter in there, then husband," she said. Suddenly it was hard for her t' meet Abner's gaze, an' she knew why. Tryin' t' get as close as she could t' meetin' him eye t' eye, she settled fer the corner o' his smile. "See, I took yer letter," she swallowed.

Abner startled at that. Right quick he knelt an' started rummagin' again through his knapsack. After a moment, he knew what she'd said was true; the letter weren't there. He clenched a fist around the open lip o' his bag out o' frustration. Still kneelin' beside the bag, he burned holes into his wife's cheek with his stare. "Now, Tess," he began, tryin' t' keep the tremblin' resentment out o' his voice. He weren't half as successful at it as he'd probably wanted t' be, for Tess took the question as a sort o' assault.

She shook a bit, but didn't let her fear take hold right yet. "Now, d-darlin'," she stammered, "I was only tryin' t' make sure you didn't go off an' get yourself killed."

Abner was up on his feet like a light, the knapsack still clenched in his fist an' swingin' about. "Tess!" he shouted. "Tess, that was my own property! An' what's more it was somethin' I could o' gone an' used t' git even with that borderer what did away with my friend an' neighbor!" Abner was practically boomin' now. He threw the swingin' knapsack down t' the floor with a wail o' vexation.

Tess shook a bit. There weren't many things that made her scared no more, not after the war. One o' the few that got her goin' right quick was the sight o' her husband's anger. It was a thing that'd gone and changed since he'da come back from the war, y'see. It'd been the worst jus' after he'da come marchin' home alongside Johnny Schaffer. There'd still been rancor in his veins then, as if he'da still been fightin' the Union Army. It didn't show up so much no more, but when it did Tess couldn't handle it. Somehow she took it on herself, y'see, lettin' Abner go off an' get tangled up in the war 'tall. Somethin' in her took blame for lettin' him go, for not tryin' hard enough t' keep him home. That bein' said, any hurt the man had gone through or change that'd come over him since the war... well, she figured that was her doin' as well.

"You have t' promise me!" she blurted out. "You have t' promise me you ain't gonna go an' get yerself killed, Abner!" Her eyes were fillin' up with tears as she said it, her throat closin' up around the words as she forced 'em out.

"What?!"

"You have t' *promise* me, or I won't let you have the letter back," she said, finally bringin' herself t' look her husband in the eye. As she locked her gaze t' his, the man and wife saw deep into each other's hearts. Abner's furor slackened, seein' that his wife only meant t' safeguard that which she had, an' which she loved. Tess' fear abated like a spent gust o' wind as she watched the rancor leave her husband's eyes, t' be replaced with understandin'.

"Tess, I done fought my war," Abner said. "All that I'm doin' nowadays is tryin' t' make my little corner o' this land as good an' right as I can. I know you don't want me puttin' m'self before the cannon, darlin', but like I see it there ain't no one else what's got a clue as t' how t' track down The Borderer. Now, I just might."

Tess looked at her husband a moment. Then, makin' her decision, she strode across the bedroom an' unhitched a daguerretype from off the wall. In the photograph was a young, spry-lookin' Abner. He'da sat for it b'fore he'd headed off t' war, at a fair deal o' expense. Tess flipped the photograph over an' popped off the wooden back. Pressed right up against the photograph itself was Abner's letter. She handed it t' her husband, lookin' him in the eye as she did so. He held onto her hand as she gave him the letter, scoopin' his other arm 'round her waist as he did. Pullin' her close, he kissed her, after which she rested her head on his shoulder, the two o' them standin' pressed together.

"Thank you, Tess," said Abner.

Chapter Eight
Points of Light and Dark

The fire had burned down into a dark and fragile pile of dimly glowing ash and char. Even that bit of wood which had been doused in tea had now burnt up and turned to pitch.

Merlin picked up the drowsing Arthur and carried him to bed. "I shall sit awake before the cottage door tonight as always, Arthur," he said, "but by morning's light I shall depart."

Arthur's eyes opened blearily.

"Fear not, for I shall return before evening's last light. There is merely something that needs my doing," said Merlin.

Arthur let his eyes droop again. A day to himself sounded fun. Merlin was at the door now, but just before he shut it behind himself he added one last instruction: "I will expect the thatch to have been repaired in my absence, Arthur." The latch clicked and Arthur was left alone to grumble his last waking protests of the day into his pillow.

Merlin sat himself down before the dwindling glow of the fire. No heat emanated from its small and dwindling points of dim red light. He chuckled to himself softly. As the fire had been a reflection of man's existence, offering up insight to the child, so might the ashes be to the old man. For weeks now had his once-bright hopes dwindled, the spark which had set him upon the path he now trod fading away into sloth and befuddlement. There was need of illumination: of that there was no doubt. Scratching around blindly in the dark could not be helped with merely the spark of impulse to light the way. And yet, for the life of him, he did not know what it was that he was meant to do. It was as if *something* was hiding away his knowlege and memory, the fuel which his mind craved — something itself bleak and dire.

An unseasonably cold breeze swept past the fence outside, buffeting the gate and whistling through the window shutters as it wisked about. A chill swirled, serpent-like about the old man's skull, skittering down along his aged frame before it was gone.

Dim, quiet eyes peered from beyond the fence at the dozing old man within the cottage. The night grew still as they hung silently beyond the slim wooden barrier of the gate. By morning they had gone.

The dew was beading upon blades of grass as Merlin quietly latched the gate and headed, walking stick in hand, down through the quiet town of Myrddin. Naught but the hardest-working of the townsfolk were yet waking as the old man made his way down the cobblestones. Those few that were awake and fussing over the preparation of breakfast would later tell of a shuddering in the earth and of a biting gust of wind which whined momentarily at their doors. The old man traversed the town's borders and was again trudging along dirt roads and fields in what seemed the blink of an eye, such was his haste that day. His feet stamped the earth; his staff cleft the clay, and a dark cloud could be seen hanging about his countenance. He would have his answers this day. He would have them, or dire payment in their stead.

The sun was high in the sky at Castle Ektor and would have been beating down upon Gregory's mailed shoulders save for the bank of cloud which had, late that morning, rolled in from the north. The castle guard smiled at his good fortune. This day's watch was faring quite well, indeed. Gone were the days of having to shoo Wart from about the main gate. Further gone were the days of raiding parties and war — praise be to the Sibling Lords, Ambrosius and Uther. 'Yes,' thought Gregory, 'the life of a guardsman is quite the delight in these affable times.' And here, to top it all, was a cool summer's day.

Gregory's sated sigh was cut short by oaken timber — his blissful smile sent clattering to the stone walk, along with the rest of him, an unconscious heap of man, mail and splintered wood. Over Gregory's placid form stepped Merlin, his eyes like two dark, brooding pits. Up the stairwell, echoing in deep resonant tones, rang the failure of the tower house's fallen protector.

As the echoes subsided, Merlin listened to the sounds of the castle proper. High above, he could hear the muted boomings of Lord Ektor as he railed against one serf or another. Upon the main stair there could be heard the mutterings and scufflings of sleeping hounds, their dreams inexplicably uninterrupted by the cacophonous shattering of the gate. Then came to the old man's ear the sound he had been searching for — a faint and rhythmic humming which emanated from somewhere halfway up the stair. It was a warm and happy intonation, but Merlin's eyes did not soften at hearing it. Instead, he took the stairs two at a time until he was before the small wooden door leading to the castle kitchens. The humming was louder here and a wisp of warmed air rose from beneath the base of the door.

Maggie had not heard the thunderous closing of the main gate. Neither, to her great content, could she hear Lord Ektor's yammering while nestled in her kitchens. The popping of her cooking fire, the bubbling away of her cauldron's contents, and the cheery meter of the tune which she hummed to herself were all the noise of which she was aware.

Thus, it came as quite the surprise to her ears when the little kitchen door flew inward and banged violently against the wall of her little world. The sound of it made her heart stop-start and then catch in her throat. Her breath and song cut off, she spun about, not knowing what to expect at the door. She yelped when she saw within her kitchens not Lord Ektor or Sir Kaye, but the tall, lank frame of Merlin, his shoulders bowing slightly beneath the low ceiling. Dark and glowering, he strode toward her, already well within the warm and close border of her realm. In the space between breaths he was before her, bringing with him an ætherial chill which choked away the warm, spiced air of the kitchens. His spine curled further as he lowered his face close to hers. The last time Maggie had met with the old man he had been cordial, downright charming even, but now the look about him — this piercing stare — it was foreign and frightening to her.

Merlin squinted, breathing rattling breaths down upon her face in silence. Her heart raced. What did this fell creature of a man want?

"I have need of answers, Maid," rasped the old man, "answers which you shall give me without protest. Do you understand this?" The girl had flinched as he said it. She cringed now, shivering in spite of her proximity to the cook-fire. "Well?!" he demanded. "Tell me that which you know, that which you kept from me before!"

"I... I d-don't," stammered the girl.

The wrinkles upon the old man's face spread like cracks upon glass and his glare widened into a grimace. He gripped the collar of the girl's dress and dragged her, slant-ways away from the cooking fire. Her hip banged heavily against a stout prep table, sending vegetables toppling to the floor.

"Oww!" she cried out, startled and scared. "Please sir, Merlin sir, I dunno what it is ye're expectin' me t' know sir," she pleaded. "I'm just the cook here, as you know, sir!" She could see the old man's teeth through his sneer now, could tell he believed none of these words. What was it he wanted? She could hardly think from the fear in her belly. She'd *liked* this man the last time they'd met. Now all she could think of was trying to get away — far, far away from this strange and fearsome man.

"You'll not evade my questions, Maid," he said, "not while I know you've hidden what it is that I seek!"

She gasped, gulping down air through the throbbing of her hip, despite the horror filling her belly. He was still gripping her collar, pulling her chest sideways across the tabletop. She had now to look out of the corner of her eye to see his glowering face above her. Her bodice felt tight against her lungs. A bit of lace tore along her neck. She panicked and struck out at the old man's chest. He was thinner than his robes led on. The impact of her hand against his bony chest was like to that of striking a flagstone. Merlin did not even seem to notice her having struck him. His eyes bore into her, bore like bottomless funnels trying to fill themselves up with what lay secret within her.

"Let me go, sir!" she screamed, "I dread what it is you want!"

"What I want, girl," he yelled, matching her by volume, "are answers!"

She grabbed ahold of his wrist, just as the force of his arm pulled her freshly-bruised hip up and onto the table, sending the carrots and radishes thereupon tumbling to the floor. Wincing from the pain, she cried out in desperation: "Then you'll have t'start askin' me questions, so!"

The pull against her collar ceased. The air grew warm again in the kitchens and the smell of soup over the fire once more permeated the air. The old man held her still in the iron vice of his grip, but the malice had gone from about him.

"I have forgotten myself," he muttered. His eyes, shifted away from her, refocusing, seeming to see the room about him for the first time. When his eyes landed upon her again the desperation in them remained, but it was no longer ensconced in the swirling dark as before.

"Maggie, I must know," he said, his voice now grave but steady, "all that you know of Arthur."

Maggie was taken aback. She did not know how to respond. Her eyes tore themselves away from the old man, scanning the dust mice and radishes upon the floor for inspiration. "Have... have ye not thought t' go to Lord Ektor for what ye're lookin' for, Mister Merlin, sir?" she stammered, in a half-hearted attempt at feigning helpfulness.

Again, wrinkles widened across the temples and down the old man's cheeks. "That pompous old lummox knows only half as much as he presumes," he admonished, "beside which, why should I inquire with the stable master whilst I have the horse by the teeth right here, eh?"

"But how can you possibly..." Maggie started.

"Child, it was you that told me," Merlin said, cutting her off, "so please do not any longer pretend to be ignorant of the information of which I speak!"

Maggie could see that he was straining to contain himself. The rancor which had so recently passed from him was building behind his eyes again. A shiver whipped up her spine.

"You're right!" she cried, "I can't tell how you know it, but I admit it. It was I that carried the child here, wee bairn as he was. What I can't see is how it matters any t' yerself, sir," she said.

"We shall see what it is that you know," muttered Merlin, finally pacing away from the girl. She remained perfectly still, sitting upon the prep table as he found a large spare kettle and upturned it so as to create a seat for himself. Her perch was quite higher than his new seat, yet the old man made no attempt to crane his neck and look at her eye-to-eye as he spoke. Instead, Maggie's view was of knotted and mussed curls of grey hair.

"What *is* he?" asked the old man.

This first question caught her entirely off-guard. She had no idea how to answer it. "H-how do you mean, sir?" she stammered, adding quickly so as not to appear evasive, "d'ye mean is he Pict or Breton, Irish or Roman, like?"

"I have no knowlege nor care for such strange names," came his response. "I do not seek a list of begattings, if that is what you offer. These are merely leaves and branches. I seek the root!"

Maggie had thought she had been in the right line of inquiry. Thinking now that she was not, she could think of naught to do but sit dumbfounded.

"I do not wish to be made to guess this day, kitchen-maid. Is he god, is he monster, is he something left unnamed? Answer me!"

The wizard stamped the foot of his staff against the leg of the table. Startled and compelled into answering quickly, Maggie shouted out something which she had sworn to keep sacred until her dying breath. "He is son and heir to Uther, the Lord Pendragon!"

Slowly the staff was lowered to the ground. The old man breathed in and out softly. "This comes as a great admission from you, Lass, so much I can tell. Yet I know that name only from my dealings with Ektor. It is little, indeed, which I gleaned of Uther, for it is next to nothing for a man to be called brighter than the proclaimed 'lord' of this house."

Maggie shook her head in disbelief. "I'll be thrown in the Iron Maiden for this," she lamented. "I was never to speak such a thing. I'm finished for sure, so I am."

"This Lord Pendragon is so severe as to have you slain for speaking the name of his child?" asked Merlin. "Such cruelty seems unwarranted."

"Warrant's got nothin' to do with it," Maggie said simply, "not where Lord Pendragon's concerned. Artie's not what you'd call... legitimate, so."

"What sort of being is this Pendragon? Is he winged serpent? Demon? Beast?" asked Merlin.

"Beast of a man is more like," said Maggie. "It's him an' his brother Ambrosius what drove the wretched Roman Legions from our shores. Hahaha," Maggie laughed nervously. "Slaughtered and dumped 'em into the sea, sure. Are you sure ye've never heard any o' this? A grey-beard like y'self never wondered where Vortigern and all his Brass-Heads shuffled off to?"

"Brass-Heads?"

"Blimey. Never you mind, then," Maggie said, shocked. "Must'a lived under a tree to've missed all that, so," she muttered to herself.

"There is much I do not recall," admitted the old man, "How do you come by this knowledge?"

"I've just told you: everyone under the skies knows of Lord Uther, him and his elder brother Lord Ambrosius, long may his soul rest."

"I rather meant the child, Maggie."

"Oh. Artie. I suppose dead is dead, eh? No sense in keepin' secrets, now I'm doomed, sure?" she sighed. "I was aide to the midwife at Artie's birth, and meant to be his wet-nurse." Her voice faltered at this. "My own child didn't survive the birthin'." Her shoulders shuddered visibly then, as tears fell upon her apron. She heaved a terrible sob and tried to force a smile, saying, "What's the use o' all that milk goin' to waste, right sir?" She could speak no longer, so constant were her tears.

At this the old man stood. His eyes never meeting hers, he stepped to the girl's side and reached out a thin hand which he rested softly upon her shoulder. He held it there a moment, a gesture of comfort, after which he strode toward her cooking pot, saying "Please continue."

Hours later, Maggie would determine that this had also been how the lace of her dress had been mended. For the moment, however, she merely hiccupped and soldiered on in the telling of her tale.

"We wasn't at Lord Pendragon's castle when the boy was birthed," she sighed, "Y'see the whole problem o' the matter was that little Artie's mum was wife to Marquess Gorlois, who was lord of Castle Tintagel at the time. Bit of a bloody mess it was, when Gorlois found out. I'm afraid sendin' me an' little Artie out the front gate was the last thing his mum ever done. Burnt at the stake, she was.

"Thing of it was," she went on, "Lord Pendragon refused us at the gate when we arrived. Didn't want a reminder o' his crimes starin' at 'im every day, I imagine. What he did do was run off to war with Gorlois. Sacked Tintagel itself, he did."

Merlin raised an eyebrow. Maggie wasn't sure, but it seemed as if the old man had heard something worth hearing at last.

"How then did you come to be cook here, with the boy apprenticed to the house's groundsman?" he asked.

"That was a bit o' luck!" said the girl. "Me an' the lad was eking out a livin' along the roadside, somewhere near Athetney, so. One mornin' while Artie was busy cryin' me to wakefulness, a page-boy I'd known at Tintagel came runnin' up to us askin' after the child's name. Imagine my disbelief, so, when after hearin' his name was Arthur, the boy said we was both expected here, an' would be workin' for Lord Ektor! I suppose you could say that Lord Pendragon did look after the boy, so. After a fashion, like."

"And this is all you know of the child's young life?" asked Merlin.

"Well, that's all there is of it, sir. He's naught but a lad, sure," said Maggie, laughing as she added, "He hasn't had the years yet for a storied past, has he? Hahaha!" She would have gone on chuckling to herself, had it not been for the grave look upon the wizard's face. She couldn't tell for certain, but the old man looked almost worried, or perhaps frightened. Whatever it was, the look had disappeared before Maggie could work out what it had meant. As she looked on, the old man's face became calm once again, placid even, like that of a man resigned to his fate.

It was just then that the kitchen door swung violently inward once more, striking the wall with a resonant crack. Lit by the dull red of the cooking fire and filling the small doorway to the corners, there stood Sir Kaye, armored head to toe and already brandishing his longsword.

Spying Merlin by the stewpot, he shouted, "You again, eh Greybeard?! You were fortunate enough to find me at table with my father when last we met. You'll not be afforded such graces this time, Spindle-shanks!"

It was as Sir Kaye was taking his first step, bold and clattering, into the low and cluttered kitchens, that the wizard had moved. It had appeared as a blur and a flick of gnarled hair, Maggie would later recall. As if underwater, she could remember single tendrils of grey locks whip across Merlin's face, seeming to pull wide the old man's calm expression until it was a scowling mask of bared teeth and fiery resolution, fit to startle a wild beast. Then, quick as the flicker of a shadow against the wall, the old man had swept up his staff from upon the floor and hurled it javelin-like at Sir Kaye. Steel warped and wood shivered to splinters as the staff struck Kaye in the breast. The knight shuffled backward to the doorframe, the air bludgeoned from his chest. A hollow rasping could be heard from within his armor as he fought to re-open his lungs. Before Kaye knew it, the old wizard had leapt upon a table and raced beast-like, hand over foot, to his side. In vain defense, Kaye heaved his sword toward the low ceiling, readying himself to cut down this preternatural villain. A long, bony hand gripped like iron about his clenched hands, bending the gauntlets thereupon. Shrieking in pain, Kaye was forced to drop his blade. The old man's eyes appeared, gleaming in the slit of his visor.

"You know not with what forces you deal, boy," said the wizard. Kaye was flying backward then. As he flew, he caught a glimpse of one of the old man's hands, outstretched in the place his suddenly tight breastplate had been a second before. In the man's other hand there hung what looked like a pair of crushed gauntlets. Then Kaye hit the wall of the stairwell and all was black.

Maggie shivered in the corner. Throwing aside the pair of gauntlets, Merlin turned to face her. "Where is Lord Uther?" he asked.

"Castle T-Tintagel, on the coast to the w-west," she replied, still shaking. The wizard's eyes burned still with an intensity which Maggie could not help but fear. "W-will you go to him straightaway?" she asked, knowing that when the old man met with Lord Pendragon her life would be forfeit.

The old man thought a moment.

"No," he said, "I have given my word to the child. I shall return to him this night. Uther and his secrets shall have to wait a while longer." He turned to exit the kitchens, stooping to retrieve Sir Kaye's fallen sword as he went.

"Take me with you!"

She'd blurted it out before she knew what she was saying. Sword in hand, Merlin turned to face the girl.

"Why," was all he said.

"I'm dead useful, sir," she began, adding "and Artie does like cookin' with me, so."

The old man thought for a moment. "Did you not say that Lord Ektor would not let you leave this place when last we spoke?" he asked.

"Well, beggin' yer pardon sir, but that was before I'd told you that for which Uther will have me put to death," she said. Pointing at the unconscious Sir Kaye behind Merlin, she added "likely by the hand of that devil there, sir. Now's me best hope at leavin' with me head intact Mr. Merlin, sir. Please let me come with you, sir. I promise to be no bother at all."

Merlin turned to look at the fallen Kaye. "Power is a strange thing," he said. "To think that one with so little of it could wreak such havoc upon those with none." He was silent again a moment. Maggie dared not stir for fear of breaking whatever spell held the wizard rooted to the spot.

"Come," he said suddenly. "My pace is quick and I cannot let up. To do so would be to break my word to the boy. I must return to Myrddin by nightfall."

Stepping over the vanquished and groaning Kaye, the two of them went hastily down the stair. There was no guard at the Main Gate as they passed through, Gregory having slunk away in resignation of his post.

It was late, and Arthur was beginning to become nervous. Merlin had said he would return before darkness fell, yet already darkness *had* fallen. The boy sat at the window, peering by candlelight out along the road to town for any sign of the old man. Now and again the child thought he saw movement along the path and instantly perked up, hoping to see Merlin's tall and lank form cresting the hill that separated their cottage from the town of Myrrdin. Once Arthur had seen a rabbit along the road, and twice a squirrel. There had even been a raven which alighted upon the fence for a while, but Merlin had not yet shown. The boy's stomach gurgled. He had not yet eaten any supper.

Arthur's eyes flicked to the road again. Nothing. There had been increasing instances of this, realized Arthur. More oft than not, now that it was dark, he had looked to the road, sure that he had seen something move, yet nothing was there. An icy finger ran itself up the child's spine. He swung about, sure that some creature or another was standing just behind him in the cottage. For an instant little glowing images of eyes hung just before him, disembodied in the air. As he watched, they faded away, remaining just in front of his face no matter where it was he looked. Trying to calm himself, Arthur forced himself to realize that they were just the images of his own eyes, hanging before him because of the haste with which he had spun upon his imagined stalker.

The gate outside creaked slowly open. Arthur screamed. His heart was pounding like that of a hare. Turning about again, Arthur looked out the window only to see, from the corner of his eye, the door to the cottage swing open as well. Hidden at the window behind the mass of the door, Arthur held his breath, not knowing who or what had come into the cottage this night. Then the child saw the blade of a sword reflected in the candlelight. He scooted off of his stool and into the corner, wishing to shrink away into nothingness so as to go unseen.

"Arthur?"

The boy sighed with relief, nearly wanting to laugh. Merlin was home. Arthur ran from the corner in which he had foolishly hidden himself, stopping just before the man at the door. Indeed it was the wizard, looking somewhat tired and traveled and brandishing what looked suspiciously like the sword of Sir Kaye.

"Where have you been today, Merlin?" asked the fascinated child, adding "You're late you know!" for good measure.

"It could not have been helped, I am afraid, Arthur," smiled the wizard. "The road felt longer on the way from town than it has before. Maybe the ol' plow-horse is gettin' too on in years... or maybe it's that I'm a bit impatient these days... bein' that I had such a dire errand t' get done with."

Arthur was perplexed. "Why're you speaking so, Merlin?" he asked, the cheer shifting to worry as he looked at the old man. 'What was that smell?' he wondered to himself. It had caught upon the air of the cottage as the old man had spoken. Had it been wheat? Wheat — and dry manure?

"It was with single purpose I headed out, this I recall," muttered the old man. "No... not me," he said, perplexedly.

Chapter Nine
An Errand

"I'zat Abner Jenks comin' up my walk?" asked Tommy Horner as he leaned against the doorjamb o' the Telegraph & Post Office.

"Sho' 'nough is," replied Abner, still swattin' the dust from the road off o' his trousers.

"Don't see 'nough o' you these days, Abner!" said Tommy, "More oft it's one o' yer freed-men that's come a-callin' on me... lookin' fer news o' their kin, I do know — them what's gone off t' the North." Tommy finished this hushed whisperin' with a conspiratorial wink an' a nod. It was clear he didn't approve o' such customers.

Abner squinted a smidgen hisself, restin' his right hand on his hip. His neck craned forward an' he looked Tommy square in the eye. "You tamperin' with those boys' correspondence, Tommy?!" he asked. I know you got no love for dark-skinned folk, but a man's got the right to know if his wife's livin', he does."

Tommy held Abner's gaze a moment. "This what you come here t' ask me Abner?" he said. "My office don't see hide nor tail o' you fer weeks an' this is how you finally show up? Spittin' accusatory-like at me?"

Abner leaned back on his hip, his neck poppin' straight up again. "T' be fair, Tommy, no it ain't," he said. "You answer me straight an' I'll drop any more questionin' in the matter, sure as bullfrogs in the summertime."

Tommy snorted, a cocky smile peelin' its way across his face. "Well, I'll say this Abner Jenks. You got a good way o' seein' a man's kind o' humor. I reckon ten times out o' a dozen you'd have me dead to rights, too. Thing o' the matter is: I ain't had no opportunity t' go trippin' your boys' correspondence up," he said. Then, with a cruel twinkle in his eye, he added: "They hain't never gotten no responses. Not a one of 'em. Not even them what swears on the Bible they's got correct addresses an' names fer their families." Tommy's eyes widened, glistenin'. "Not. A. One..." he said dramatically, lettin' the last word hang in the air a bit for emphasis. "It's as if every one o' them dark folks what high-tailed it after the war up an' vanished," he finished, his smile wide as a pregnant sow.

"Huh," said Abner, scratchin' his head. "That's a damn strange sort o' thing, Tommy. Damn strange."

Tommy only nodded.

"What do you think...?" Abner began, but Tommy held him quiet with an outstretched hand.

"You said you'd leave it be if'n I answered you square, Abner. Anyway, that's all I know on the matter."

Abner chuckled. "Well, I suppose I did, Tommy, an' that's a fact," he said. "If them boys do get some kinda response, I'll drop an extra coin in yer till t' get it to 'em, how's that?"

Tommy nodded, still smilin'. "You always did know how t' get them wheels a'turnin' fer you n' yours, Abner," he said. "Now what sort o' business *did* bring yerself into my office?"

"I got a matter what needs a good scrutinizin', Tommy. Mind if we step inside a moment?" said Abner.

"Ain't no skin off o' my knee, Abner, long as you don't mind the heat o' the place," said Tommy as the two o' them stepped into the telegraph office.

A dry heat radiated off o' the wooden slats o' the telegraph office. Somewhere in the back o' the buildin' Abner could hear the rumblin' o' the furnace an' the ticking o' what sounded like one hell o' a big metronome. Across the desk sat Tommy, scourin' the letters from the man Abner'd taken t' callin' The Borderer. Tommy picked nervously at his teeth as he read. He was sweatin' more'n Abner was too, more even than Abner thought could possibly be blamed on the furnace. Another moment passed, after which Tommy straightened his back and stretched in his chair. He wiped the sweat off o' his face, dryin' his palm on his shirt.

"Y'say this man what wrote these was the same as that behemoth what set the barn fire that night? The one what killed Johnny Schaffer?" he asked.

"Near got killed m'self draggin' Johnny outt'a there, Tommy," Abner replied. "There ain't no doubtin' it."

Tommy sighed. "I gott'a tell ya, Abner: I don't rightly know what it is you're expectin' me t' pluck out o' these here letters. They're half gibberish an' at least as close t' madness, so far as I can make out. Just readin' the infernal things sets me afright, an' no lie."

Abner wasn't about t' take that sort o' answer from a man the like o' Tommy. "Tommy," he said, scowlin' a bit, "you're one o' the better read folks 'round these parts, an' moreover you're a man what reads other folks correspondence each an' every day. Now, are you tellin' me that you haven't picked up on how folks talk different if'n they're born outt'a town an' the like? Is *that* the bundle o' beads you're tryin' t' pawn for my land, Tommy?"

Tommy swore, leanin' across the table t'ward Abner, sayin' "Now you hold it there, Jenks. I wasn't goin' so far as sayin' any such thing!" He wiped his brow a second time, slappin' his palm 'gainst the table this time 'round an' settin' the ol' thing off creakin' and moanin' t' itself. "What I *am* sayin', Abner," he said, "is that this here boy don't talk like no one I ever heard... least-wise no *single* person."

Abner wondered 'bout that, but held off askin' after what Tommy might mean by it. Tommy wasn't in no mood for discussion an' Abner could tell that for sure.

"Moreover," Tommy went on, "I ain't so sure I wanna mix m'self up in huntin' down a feller what killed eleven men single-handed an' what stands tall as a locomotive. No sir, that ain't no errand I'd put on m'self or my kin."

"Can you give me a point on the compass at least Tommy? A direction from this here town he'd likely hail from?" Abner asked, breakin' into a cold sweat hisself. If Tommy didn't know how t' help him, Abner was up against a wall for sure. "Tommy, the man killed Johnny Schaffer, a friend o' yours an' mine. Killed him in cold blood, an' now he's roamin' the woods out there somewheres, free as a song!"

Tommy's eyes flicked away from Abner's gaze. "I know it, Abner," he said. "That there's the reason I close up shop here by midafternoon. It's why I'm home t' the missus by evenin' an' why I bolt the door at nightfall an' never ever lift the damn latch b'fore the sun is full in the sky the next mornin'." Tommy was wringin' his hands as he spoke. Even thinkin' o' The Borderer seemed t' set him off.

Abner shook his head at the sight. "Tommy, I rise every day b'fore the sun t' work my plantation," he said. "I stay out t' watch the sun go down every night I got the moment t' spare, an' you know what, Tommy?" Abner said, "You know what? I done *seen* the man you're in such a fright over!" Abner was standin' now. "I done looked him an' his horrible self in the eye!" Abner snatched up the letters from off o' Tommy's desk, shakin' 'em b'fore the man's face. "I even got me a personalized invite t' his little dinner party from out the depths o' hell! I was there when those men kicked off!"

Abner leaned close t' Tommy. "So why is it, Tommy Horner? Why is it I got it in me t' go after this bastard, an' all you got in your gullet is a yeller streak? Huh?!" At that Abner turned on his heel an' stamped his way outt'a the Telegraph & Post Office, mutterin' somethin' 'bout goin' on along on his lonesome anyhow. Fumin', he gripped the doorframe b'fore he was outside entire-like an' turned on Tommy, figurin' he had at least one good jab left. Tommy Horner sat, hangin' his head behind the desk. "You know somethin', Tommy?" Abner fumed, "You can sit there in yer damn fool office long as you please. Sure, you might have air in your lungs longer'n others, but you'll be dead long b'fore they put you into the earth. I thought a man from these long-sufferin' lands would'a learned that years ago!" With that, Abner figured he'd said his piece. He turned his back on the man at the desk an' stepped back out into the relative cool o' the day, slammin' the office door behind hisself.

Now, sure it'd felt good tellin' off Tommy Horner an' sure he'da stamped out the door with purpose, but truth be told Abner didn't quite know what that purpose was. Tommy'd been his best hope at gettin' a leg up on The Borderer from them confounded letters. Abner's pace slowed as he made his way back t'ward his plough-horse. 'Did the missus need anythin'?' he wondered. There weren't no use in a trip t' town bein' a total waste, after all.

It was just at that point, when Abner's thoughts had begrudgin'ly swapped over t' bakin' flour an' fence mendin', that a clammy hand slapped its damp self down onto his shoulder. Abner spun 'round, clenchin' his fists reflexively an' hopin' t' god almighty that it wasn't The Borderer, come for him at last. The face that met his wasn't the one he'da expected 'tall, but a sweatin', shakin' Tommy Horner, lookin' white as a sheet an' just 'bout as likely t' fall t' earth in a heap.

Tommy's sweaty hands clasped 'emselves tight 'round Abner's fist. Abner felt some small thing bein' forced into his hand. Tommy's eyes shifted to an' fro. His lips quavered. "Listen close," he hissed, "I ain't said nothin', y'hear? On yer grave." His eyes were still now, pleadin'.

Abner opened his mouth t' reply, but Tommy cut him off. "It's a madman's errand you're set to Abner," he said, "more so'n you know, I figure. A man'd have t' be plum suicidal t' help you, an' there's only one, I reckon, s'crazy 'nough t' do it."

Tommy held Abner's gaze a moment longer. It was just long 'nough for Abner t' see the man's eye water a touch. Then he was gone, the door t' the Telegraph & Post slammin' shut behind him. Abner got onto the ol' plough-horse right away and turned the ornery ol' equine t'ward home. He was a good quarter mile outt'a town b'fore he unclenched his fist an' had a look at the thing clenched inside. It was a small scrap o' telegraph paper. On it were two short lines, written in a hasty scrawl:

Cassius Marcellus Clay
— Lexington, Kentucky

Arthur coughed. It felt as if he was coated in dust from the road. His eyes refocused. The dark shadows and warm glow of the candlelight danced about the cottage once more. Merlin stood before him again, looking even more weathered than before. The wizard leaned heavily upon the sword in his hand, its tip wedged between two flagstones set in the floor. Arthur offered Merlin his hand and led him to the chair before the fireplace. The old man let the sword drag along the floor as he went. As he sat the sword fell, clattering to the stonework from his limp hand. In the old man's eyes there remained a far-off look, as if he had not yet returned from whatever land he had transported himself and the child off to. Seeing this, Arthur went about getting together the things he would need to make a pot of tea. 'That will rouse the old man's spirits,' he thought. There was a fire to be set, the kettle to be hung above it, water to be poured from the bucket, and the tea itself to be fetched from the top shelf. 'First things first,' thought the boy.

The night was chill and covered Arthur with gooseflesh as he left the cottage. Out at the woodpile, the boy again felt as if there were hidden eyes watching him, again felt the tickle of a spindly finger dragging its faint weight roughly against the bones of his spine. He hastened his step as he strode laboriously back into the cottage, not daring to chance a look over his shoulder. Inside once again, Arthur noticed how quiet the cottage had become.

"Sort of a strange day to have had, eh?" he joked, hoping to get a response from the silent old man in the armchair before the fire.

Faint and shallow breaths were his only response. Reaching the fireplace, Arthur sat with his back to the old man and began to set the logs and tinder in place. Every few seconds he looked over his shoulder to Merlin. The wizard sat very still, staring at some indefinable spot upon the wall, his pupils wide and unfocused.

"I mean, it's not as if a person often leaves home in the morning and ends up in some far-off land riding a mangy horse by noon, is it?" Arthur smirked. It felt good to joke about the goings on of the night. It made the boy less worried for either the sake of the old man or for himself. He struck a flame from the flint and nurtured it, watching as it caught alight. "Fancy getting mixed up like that, eh Merlin?" he said. "Thinking I wanted a story when all I'd asked for was the goings on of your day, haha! I do appreciate..."

The old man lurched forward in his chair and stared directly into the boy's eyes, his pupils focusing sharply.

"Still... mixed up, Merlin?" asked the child quietly.

The old man held Arthur's gaze a moment longer, his eyes boring their way into the boy. The fire snapped. The old man's head jerked to the side, following the noise. Seeing the fire, Merlin's expression softened. He looked about himself as if for the first time seeing his surroundings since returning to the cottage.

"Well," he said, "have you patched the roof?"

Arthur smiled. Whatever it was that had gripped the old man, it was gone now. The two of them spent the rest of the evening talking of the activities of Arthur's day in solitude — which thankfully included the successful restoration of the thatch. Merlin even got up from the chair and fetched the tea from the top shelf for the lad when the water was ready.

Arthur was careful not to ask Merlin of his day again for fear that such a question might again upset the wizard. It came as a complete shock then that, when it was time for bedding down, Merlin announced that they would have company the next day. He would not tell the boy who their guest would be, but assured the sleepy child that it was company most welcome indeed.

Chapter Ten
Wicked Sir Bart

The noon-day sun fell in sticky, radiating waves as Maggie made her way along the road. 'That old codger weren't tellin' no lies,' she thought. 'He sets a terrible pace, he does.' She had only managed to keep in step with the grey and spindly old man for a single hour before her considerably younger limbs had wearied and she had fallen behind. Her guide had said something about continuing straight on and the "hills just beyond Myrddin" before he had escaped beyond the horizon. 'For all the good that does me,' thought Maggie. She had never heard of such a place, nor had she explored these rolling hills to the north of Lord Ektor's holdings. Thinking Myrddin to be constantly over the next rise, and then the following one when proven incorrect, she had trudged onward well into the bleak of the night before finding a shifting and ungainly sleep aside a gnarled oak. The morning had brought her new determination in the form of the hope that she must have relented just before the signs of life were to meet her eyes. Thus, blindingly early, she had traipsed onward, her heart full of the expectation of an early arrival.

She had hoped, at the very least, to have been able to procure a warming cup of morning tea in Myrddin for her endeavors. Yet, since her early departure, the sun had crested the horizon and ascended steadily the slope of the sky until it hung at the apex of its journey above her, seemingly mocking her slow and laborious progress. She scowled at the thought. Maggie did not do well without her morning tea, and the utter lack of the stuff, whether from the town tavern or some passing peddler, vexed her terribly.

"What sort of peat bog of a village does the old miser inhabit that traders cannot be found upon the road at morning-time?" she asked herself aloud. "This'll be the only bloody one, I'll wager — if it even exists! Been an entire day since I left Castle Ektor, it has, and still nothin' in sight, sure!"

Yet on she trod, the hope of a new home pulling her boots along at every step and the fear of being alone turning her eyes ever toward the horizon in search of the chimney that would be her own.

Arthur had been particularly boundy all day. The expectation of a guest after a pair of months with only Merlin and a plumper-than-ever Bartholomew as company were to blame for this. His energy level had reached such a fever pitch, in point of fact, that Merlin had, just after lunch, banished the child from the walls of the cottage until supper was prepared.

Arthur, finding himself excommunicated, did what any pariah with his wits about him would: he fashioned himself a weapon and went looking for trouble. Arthur's weapon of choice was a sword (which he was quickly able to fashion out of a fallen tree branch). In actuality, it was little more than a switch, but to the eyes of the boy it was as fine a blade as that which hung across the mantle above the fire, a sword which Arthur was fairly positive had quite recently belonged to Sir Kaye. But he could prove none of that, as the old man had been decidedly silent when questioned on the matter. Merlin had also, despite much pleading, refused to allow the boy to play with it, grumbling something which the child had been quite sure had sounded very like "limbless by tea time" as he did so.

Arthur snorted at the very idea of such condescension. 'After all,' he thought, 'as a law unto myself, I am naturally adept in the ways of the blade, along with all manner of sneakery.' At any rate, this new sword worked just fine for his purposes.

A shrub behind the boy shook menacingly. Whirling about, he slashed and stabbed at the thing mercilessly, more than once whapping his own fingers in the process. The shrub let out a hiss and a yowl, startling Arthur and pausing his assault. A few seconds

passed, laden with the expectation of what vile thing might be lurking in the shrubbery. 'Might it be a viper? Or mayhaps a cockatrice, with its scaly snake's tail and the head of a rooster?' He would have to be careful if he heard clucking, Arthur decided. The cockatrice was rumored to turn a man to stone by breathing upon him and to possess the death-darting eye. Arthur squinted, so as to more quickly be able to close his eyes at the sight of the first snowy feather.

Arthur's musings on the powers of the cockatrice and their foils was cut short just then by a bedraggled Bartholomew slinking out from beneath the shrub. The tufty tabby dragged with him a smattering of leaves and twigs bound up in his hair, souvenirs of the walloping he'd undergone in escaping his napping place.

"Aha!" crowed Arthur, "Wicked Sir Bart, have at you!"

With this declaration the boy set upon the cat once more, whapping the ground about the beset feline's paws. For a moment it seemed as if the cat was prepared to endure such trials and taunts. He hunkered low and sat very still amidst Arthur's attacks, merely glowering at the child. Then, just as the wooden switch came down beside him, the cat sprang at the boy, yowling death threats as he soared. Finding Arthur's shins good sport, Bartholomew slashed and bit at them, a flurry of claw and fluff, twig and fang. Startled by this counter-attack, Arthur leapt about in small circles, seemingly trying to fly away from the cat as if he were a bird. Bartholomew, sensing he had the advantage, pressed his attack. All Arthur could do was attempt a few half-hearted defensive swipes with the switch as he frantically looked about for a point of refuge.

'The fence!' thought the boy, 'I'll climb the fence and from there I'll be able to keep the beast at bay!'

Some of the cuts upon his shins were beginning to sting and to bead with blood as the boy ran in a dead sprint to the fence, the cat in quick pursuit. A lucky backward swipe from the boy's switch caught Bartholomew upon the nose just as the pair reached the fence. The cat stopped short and yowled his indignity at the strike. This gave Arthur the precious moment he needed to climb atop the fence and gingerly spin about to face his foe. Bartholomew paced back and forth before the fence, careful to remain out of the boy's reach. Crouching upon the fence-top, Arthur swayed like a punch-drunk squirrel. The fence was thin and his ankles unsure.

Bartholomew lowered and wiggled his haunches, preparing for his next assault. Seeing this, Arthur chanced another defensive sweep with the switch. It proved his undoing. Forward rolled the boy's ankles, and

backward fell his crouched body. At the same instant, the cat pounced upward. This created an exceptional and ill-boding reality for the child. Bartholomew, his furry limbs outstretched and barbed, hovered before the boy's face, neither of them moving in relation to one another. It was, instead, all the world that spun away from them. A leaf which had been lodged in Bartholomew's fur tugged its way free, arcing away from the flying feline. The fence was below Bartholomew then, the open sky before Arthur's falling eyes. As the plush, be-clawed form of the cat slowly eclipsed the clear blue sky two events took place. The first was the appearance of a densely-knit cloud, seemingly out of the very æther, which swept quickly in and then out of Arthur's view. After this Bartholomew was curiously absent from sight, but Arthur hardly had the time to recognize this fact as the second event involved his back striking the earth with a resounding *whump*.

Arthur emitted a noise something akin to "Pfghrrrrrr…" as every last iota of breath was forced from his lungs. Points of light flashed and danced before his eyes. He felt as if he would never breathe again. Concentrating, he forced his lungs open, emitting a creaking sort of a sound as he did so. Precious oxygen expanded his chest and he re-opened his eyes, not having realized he had closed them to begin with. What greeted his eyes was a sight which had sadly become something of a norm in his young life. Above him stood an adult, the look upon whose face was something between bewilderment and the utter lack of surprise. It was not, however, the adult Arthur would have expected. Instead of the aged form of Merlin bent over the boy there stood Maggie. In her arms she held her apron, from the bulging form of which could be heard the sharp and guttural protests of one plump and rancorous feline. With one hand, Maggie gripped Arthur by the elbow and unceremoniously heaved him to his feet. Her other hand remained resolutely about the folds of her apron, a fact Arthur was all too thankful for, as constant fits of hissing and fiery escape attempts were constantly being made from within its woven walls.

"Guessin' this is the place, I am," huffed Maggie, quite out of breath. "That old codger sure can shift himself when he's got a mind!"

"Maggie!" Arthur cried out, having just forced the air back into his lungs. "Maggie, I'd hoped it was you! Merlin said we were to have company, and I'd worried it was to be Lord Ektor or Sir Kaye or, or…

maybe some other ancient task-master like himself! Oh, Maggie, how I hoped it was you!" he shouted.

And not a breath too soon, I dare say, Artie," smiled Maggie. "This beastie here would 'ave near cut you to death had he gotten his way," she said, raising her still-very-animated apron a bit, adding "might'a crushed ye' too, heavy as he is." Arthur giggled at this, still beaming up at the girl. "Head along inside now, Artie. I'll shoo the blaggard along his way," she said. With a gentle but firm hand upon his shoulder, she herded the boy toward the door.

"But, Maggie!" said Arthur, "He lives here, he does! That's Bedwyn's old cat, Bartholomew, that is!"

"What is?" Maggie asked. "Not this ginger mountain of a thing, sure! What's it ye've been feedin' him? Foxes?!"

Arthur giggled again. It truly was lovely, he thought, seeing Maggie again. "Mostly table scraps," he admitted, "Seeing as he's a bit slow for the field mice."

Maggie gave the boy a reproving look, beginning to stroke the lump under her apron. "Now that's no way to mind a cat, Artie," she said. "I can see there're a fair few things needin' my attention hereabouts."

With that, she shooed Arthur toward the cottage. "Let's go let your 'ol taskmaster know I've arrived, shall we?"

The evening which then passed was an uncomfortable one. Arthur and Maggie's entrance into the cottage had seemed to interrupt Merlin, though from what they could not tell. The old man had been sitting in the darkly upholstered chair which stood before the fireplace and staring vexedly into the empty firebox as if willing flames to burst forth from the cold ash. The instant the cottage door had swung closed behind Maggie and the lad, Merlin had shot bolt upright in his seat and swung his face about to look at the two of them. The look in his eyes had been of a searching and angered sort.

A flash of terror shot across Arthur's heart and he recoiled from Merlin's presence. Something of the ashen creature which had nearly slain the boy was reminiscent in the old man as he sat hunched in the darkened interior of the room.

Whatever it was that caused Arthur's fear, Maggie was entirely unaware of it, or was at least undaunted, for she immediately began buzzing about the cupboards of the small dwelling. She spoke to herself from time to time as she did this, filling the following hours with such mutterings as "didn't expect these to be stocked" or "well, these will have to be moved... bloody rat's nest." By evening, however, she seemed to have decided that she was familiar enough with the cottage's stores and promptly began whipping up a startlingly tasty batch of potato and rabbit stew.

Merlin had remained aloof and brooding throughout this process. The stew alone seemed to soften him, luring out a smile or two as he ate.

This was to set a pattern for the following few days. The old man would brood, Maggie would whip about brightening and altering the cottage as she saw fit, and Arthur would largely be left to his own designs. When he asked Maggie about it, she would merely wink and say, "Just give him some time, is all. Even wine takes its time to open up once it's aged."

It occurred to the boy that Merlin had invited the girl to stay with the two of them to begin with, yet the old man seemed to sallow in her presence. 'Mayhaps,' he thought, 'Merlin doesn't do well in mixed company?' But that couldn't be it. The old man was just as poor at dealing with the boy himself (and worse with Ektor and Kaye) as he was in the company of the girl.

After a week had passed, each day of which Merlin had seemed even more brooding than the last, a strange change came over the wizard. Though he was still very short with the others when they spoke with him, the look upon his face had changed. There was an air of self-assuredness about him as well as a level of activity which he had not shown in the days prior. Numerous times he would pop out of the cottage on some errand or other, always returning with his business trussed up in a small woven sack which he secreted away upon his return. One night, however, the sack sat in full view for all to see, leaning against the doorframe to the outside world. It was no great and unexpected shock, then that he announced his departure of the following morning over dinner that night. He did not give particulars of his journey, nor did he respond when questioned about his return.

Maggie and Arthur had exchanged curious looks when the announcement had been made, but were both inwardly relieved when they awoke the following morning to find both the wizard and his bag of belongings gone. Gone, too were Sir Kaye's sword from the mantle and, most noticeable of all, the sense of worry and tension which had permeated the cottage for too long.

Chapter Eleven
Parting Ways

The clay and stone of the roadway gave but a little beneath the old man's feet. The road was firm and the last of the spring rains had come and gone weeks before. There was a pregnant fullness to the breeze as it carried wisps of pollen and spore to their final fruitful resting places. 'Would that my own journey be so fruitful,' thought Merlin as he strode along at his usual quick pace.

It was good to be abroad again, dislodged from his lair as if after one long waking doldrum of a hibernatorial dream. He could nigh on feel the cobwebs and gathered dust shaking loose from his every sinew as each lank stride thrust him forward. He was nearly bounding; he felt so good to be loosed from the smothering influences of the child and his nurse.

The food, he admitted to himself, had improved during the girl's tenure in the cottage, but the incessant banter, the insufferable games of make-believe and of great deeds wore so upon the old man's mind that improved nourishment was scant consolation. The playing at house was, he was sure, not what had led him back to Castle Ektor a month prior. 'Yet,' he questioned himself, 'what indeed had it been that had done so?' It was this question alone that the old man had been pondering this last week, and still no answer had presented itself. Something had pulled him along his way that night, something which had felt like... what had it been? Familiarity? Destiny? Whatever it had been, it had brought him to the child's aid by the slimmest of margins, the act of which, too had felt foretold. That had been the lot of it, however. That had concluded all which had felt fore-written.

There had been a hope, even a surety in him early on, that his actions thereafter would bear similar marks of pre-destiny. They had not. This left him the pained question of why. Why this child? Why that night? Why could he recollect nothing at all from before that night? Another early theory, now forsaken, was that he had been traumatized by the cold and ice into a temporary loss of faculty. As the days had worn into weeks without change, however, this belief had faltered. He now felt as if he were a soul adrift on a foreign tide. He had wracked his brain upon the matter; had sat in silence and waited for insight, but all effort had come to naught.

'No more,' he had decided, 'no more will I wither on the vine whilst awaiting providence to rain down upon me.'

The child would be taken care of now, likely by more adept hands than his own. The girl cared for him as if he were her own. It had been this revelation that had encouraged him to bring the two together again to begin with. He had even hoped, in doing so, to regain the feeling of pre-destiny he had these long weeks sought. His being stymied against this effect had, in point of fact, been that which had finally settled his mind against such a docile course of action. Whatever clarity had visited him upon the night of the storm would not return of its own accord. He would have to search it out. The maid had been some help, it was true. The story of the child's young life had held some small revelations, but nothing in it had hearkened to the sense of a greater destiny. Politics and lineage could be diverting to be sure, but they were not governed by the unseen threads of fate.

Yet, here was this child, unremarkable to a fault — save for the strange events which he had been involved in during the night of the snowstorm. 'The child must be the key', he thought to himself, 'for no other has ever drawn me to their side as did he.'

It had been with this in mind that he had set out that morning toward the lands of the girl's tale. Castle Tintagel lay south, along the west coast. The people of Myrddin had given him this much, along with a few landmarks, here and there, for which to keep an eye open along the way. He wagered it would take three days, travelling at his pace, to reach the castle. Once there he would have his answers, even if he had to kick in the Main Gate. He chuckled to himself at this thought, fondly remembering his experiences at Castle Ektor. His pace quickened as a dreamy smile spread across his wrinkled cheeks.

'There is nothing quite like a bit of a journey to fill a man with the sense of purpose,' he mused. The scent of the road, the changing of scenery, and even the promise of the unknown whispered of discovery. One merely needed to place one foot in front of the other and the familiar world slipped into the past, into memory.

Somewhere in the distance a whistle blew, faintly followed by the scent of smoke and steam.

Chapter Twelve
The True American

Tess hadn't put up too big a fuss. Least-wise, it hadn'ta been anywhere near what Abner'd expected when he'da gone an' told her he needed t' go t' Kentucky on account o' some bit o' sweaty telegraph paper writ on in shaky letterin' — not t' mention he was a'goin t' find a man he'da never heard o' b'fore on the word o' the town postman an' gossip, Tommy Horner.

Abner rubbed his eye absent-mindedly. It still stung a bit an' would likely move from scarlet t' mulberry by mornin'. 'Yeah,' he thought, 'she'da taken the news right cheerful-like, considerin'.'

A whistle blew, long an' loud, signalin' they were about t' get underway. Abner felt 'round in his vest pocket, double checkin' on the whereabouts o' his ticket. Findin' it, he pulled it out an' looked it over. Under destination it read:

Lexington, Kentucky;
by way of Little Rock, Memphis, *and* Nashville

"Good thing this newfangled bullet train was passin' through t'day," thought Abner, lookin' out the window t' glimpse the massive double-decker steam engine. "Otherwise I'da had t' go the roundabout route." Steam billowed an' pumped past the window an' the car gave a hefty lurch. They were underway. Abner thought o' the missus an' lil' Mazie, imaginin' he could see their forms in the steam as the train left the station.

The dark ambers an' violets o' evenin' were spreadin' fast across the sky as the train pulled into the station. A warm breeze swirled 'bout the coaches an' up the stairs as Abner disembarked, blowin' across his face. 'What a night,' he thought as he shook the sleepy shiftlessness outt'a his legs. Sittin' all day didn't agree with him, but this here Kentucky climate would get him goin' again in no time. Were you t' add t' that the fact that by takin' the bullet train, Abner hadn'ta even lost a day t' travel an' he was downright ahead o' schedule... such as it were. From here on in there weren't much o' a plan 'tall. Tommy's note was still crumpled up in his pocket, but every time he'da asked somebody on the train 'bout Cassius Marcellus Clay he'da either been told t' go suck eggs, had newspapers rustled at him, or else been told that they'da "never heard of him, an' would rather not talk 'bout such unpleasantnesses anyhow." Abner'd thought that last reply'da been suspect to a high degree, but had also thought it better not t' pry any further. He was beginnin' t' get the picture that not only was this Clay character the only man "crazy 'nough" t' help him in his plight, but he may-as-not be deranged entire-like. First things were first, however, an' Abner needed a stiff drink an' a cot.

A short walk from the train station, Abner found what he was lookin' for: a local gamblin' hall with rooms for rent an' a brand o' hooch that passed the flame test in a lovely shade o' cobalt blue. Bein' more tired than parched, Abner just had the one drink, received a bit o' a glare from the barkeep for testin' whiskey that was "only a nip's worth anyhow," an' asked for a bed. Headin' up t'ward the rooms, he spun back 'round an' shot a question regardin' Cassius Marcellus Clay across the bar. He'da had t' yell it a bit t' get the barkeep's attention back away from the more pliant drunks at the bar, so it weren't really no surprise when the response he got was o' the "he don't live 'round here no more," variety. A couple o' the drunks leered at Abner as he went up t' the beds, whether outt'a dislike for the question or jus' general pickledness he didn't know. Slippin' off his boots, Abner reflected on the day comin' an' how it might jus' be a long, rough repetition o' swears an' doors bein' thrown in his face.

As it turned out, though, he needn'ta bothered. Hours after Abner'd said his prayers and begun sawin' away for the night there erupted such a fracas down in the gamblin' hall that you can still hear told the tale o' the dead poundin' on the rafters o' their caskets that night, askin' fer quiet from out in the churchyard at the end o' the road.

Hisself a heavy sleeper, an' especially so when havin' had a nip o' the whiskey, Abner didn't quite wake in time t' know what had started the disagreement. It sounded, as he shook the sleep from his brain-case, as if a whole heap o' somebodies were clamorin' at the barkeep from somewhere on the gamblin' floor. 'Hell of a way t' order a drink,' thought Abner, tryin' to coax the sandman back t' his bedside.

A moment later Abner's eyes popped open again, like the mouth o' a rooster at four in the mornin'. Someone'd answered the hollerin' from the gamblin' hall, but by the sound o' him he sure hadn'ta been the barkeep. The barkeep was a bald little rail o' a man with a bottle-brush moustache three sizes too large for his weak lookin' jaw. Sure he was a stern sort o' man, but his voice was soft and near tremulous when he spoke. Now, t' contrast, the man who was now hollerin' across the bar at the gambling' floor had a voice like that o' some sort o' book-learned bison. His voice was so low an' barrelous that Abner could feel the nails o' his bed frame wrigglin' loose as he bellowed from the floor below.

Somethin' so rude as t' make fresh whitewash blush was yelled from the gamblin' floor. The sound o' a bottle shatterin' against the wall left little doubt 'bout its reception. Then came the words that, more'n anythin' else, rousted Abner Jenks from the bedsheets.

"Goddamit, Clay! You was told you weren't wanted back 'round these parts! Shown it too, s'far as I recall!"

Clay. Abner was willin' t' bet that there weren't two men in the city o' Lexington goin' by the name o' Clay an' bein' so despised as the man downstairs was. Abner threw on his breeches, grabbed his coat an' boots, an' was out the door like a pastor late for church. He was halfway down the hall when the first shot rang out. A woman screamed an' a hustlin' an' a bustlin' followed that was so frantic as t' put t' shame even the most skittish o' herds o' cattle. More gunfire followed an', by the time Abner could see the goin's on in the gambling hall, there weren't much visible through the gunsmoke but a couple o' overturned poker tables an' a blur o' motion at the door as the last bystanders hotfooted it into the street. Takin' advantage o' what was a momentary lull in the gunfire, Abner tore down the stairs an' ducked behind a couple o' fallen chairs. There was a bang an' the oil lamp above his head popped sendin' slivers o' glass an' burnin' oil down atop Abner's head. Whoever the feller was at the end o' the bar, he was a decent shot.

Now, Abner wasn't no enemy t' any o' these men an' neither was he armed, savin' for the boot-knife he had stowed. Rememberin' the ol' adage concernin' knives an' gunfights, Abner kept the blade stowed. He was target enough already he thought, jus' by virtue o' bein' a movin' object in a room full o' smoke an' burnin' tempers. A punctuation t' this line o' thinkin' rang out just then in the form o' another gunshot. One o' the chairs Abner was hid behind burst to splinters.

"Shit!" yelled Abner. It was a sort o' curse he didn't generally like t' use, but a chunk o' chair'da wholloped him 'cross the thigh, makin' him think he'da been shot. Abner had just 'nough time t' wonder what kind o' hand-cannon did that sort o' damage b'fore a gap the size o' a gopher hole was blown in the wall just above his head.

"Hellfire!" he hollered, controllin' hisself a bit better this time. "Whoever it is doin' the shootin', I ain't armed! I'd appreciate a bit o' gentlemen's courtesy, for Pete's sake!"

"Best t' *get* armed, son!" shouted a voice from closer'n Abner'd expected. Sneakin' a glance across the gamblin' floor t' his left, Abner saw that a couple o' men were huddled behind one o' the upturned poker tables. One of 'em wasn't movin'. The other man spoke again.

"Once ol' Cassius gets goin', he's like t' a cannon-startled nag! Ain't no stoppin' him without lead!"

"Stuff and nonsense!" rang the barrelous voice from the bartop. "You lax-minded retrogressors fired the first shot!"

With that, another pair o' blasts sounded across the bar. Abner pulled his head back behind his would-be barricade. So this was the man he'da been sent t' find. Tommy's warnin' 'bout Clay bein' the only man crazy 'nough t' aid him jumped back into Abner's head. He wondered if'n maybe he hadn'ta heeded that warnin' so well as he could'a done.

"That always was your trouble, Cassius!" shouted the man behind the poker table, "you never got no point across but that ya' hated yer neighbors, the whole lot of 'em!" Without lookin', he wrapped his gun hand 'round the edge o' the poker table an' blind fired a couple o' shots in the general direction o' Clay.

Abner took the opportunity t' dive behind better cover. The upright piano standin' at the near end o' the bar top looked sturdy, an' was at least less cramped a barricade than a knocked-down chair. As he was scuttlin' his way across t' the piano, he caught hisself his first glimpse o' Clay.

The man stood, clearly visible between a couple o' stools before the far end o' the bar top. He was a shorter man than Abner'd thought, an' had the look o' the well-fed gentry who Abner usually thought o' as runnin' towns like this'n. His double-breasted suit coat strained about his middle like an overstuffed sack o' grain. On the top o' his head stood a tall hat resemblin' an over-eager prarie dog who'd tried t' swallow a stove-pipe in a single go. He was utterly covered in weaponry. Holstered at his hip was somethin' akin t' a revolver, but owin' t' its size, Abner figured it was the gun that'd blown the hole in the wall a moment ago. Slung over the man's shoulder was an even more intimidatin' weapon. Abner had no idea what it was, but the barrel o' the thing could'a been used fer smugglin' turnips. In Clay's hand, an' bein' raised t' the ready at that very moment, was a gun which defied Abner's understandin'. The closest his mind could get t' describin' it was that it looked somethin' like a cross b'tween an old wheel-lock pistol an' a mantle clock. The man was quite a sight, Abner decided, an' not entirely the kind which inspired thoughts o' sanity.

"I have never spoken ill o' my neighbors, Flannigan!" roared Clay. "I have only sought to educate! If that means usin' language strong enough t' clear the cobwebs out o' your willfully ignorant ears, then I am well within my rights t' use it!"

Flannigan fired again, this time shatterin' a mirror behind the bar which had been advertisin' somethin' called "Dorian's Decrepitizing Daguerrotypes."

"And," continued Clay, stridin' forward, "if maintainin' the voice o' reason in these taxin' times means silencin' yours, Flannigan, then so be it!"

With that, Clay pulled the trigger o' his clockwork pistol. There was a snap an' a whir, an' for an instant Abner thought the thing'd misfired.

"What happened, Cassius?" asked Flannigan, "your stupid toy

cain't..."

Blam! Blam! Blam! Blam! Blam! Blam!

Abner's ears popped. The shots'd rang out so fast that his ears hadn't but barely been able t' tell 'em apart. Clearin' his ears with his finger, Abner heard the windin' down o' what had been a very tightly bound spring. He didn't dare shift from his spot behind the piano.

"Stranger, if you truly are unarmed I implore you — stay where you are," said Clay. "Do not pursue me and you shall yet see the dawn." Then, reachin' for somethin' which hung from a chain upon his neck, he walked hastily out o' the bar.

For a moment Abner ruminated over what t' do. He needed Clay's aid, but the man seemed well out o' his tree an' likely t' shoot if followed. Still — Johnny deserved more'n this. What kind o' friend hid behind a rickety ol' pile o' ivory an' tinder while his best bet at redemption disappeared into the summer heat?

Makin' certain the coast was clear, Abner slowly got up an' out from behind the piano. Smoke still hung in the air an' the entire gamblin' hall reeked o' sulphur. Flannigan, or what was left o' him, slouched with the other corpses behind the poker table, a startle frozen on his face. Not wantin' t' linger, Abner stepped into his boots, bolted up the stairs, an' grabbed the rest o' his belongin's.

A moment later he was skiddin' t' a stop jus' outside the gamblin' hall with no idea where t' go next. A quick look 'round showed him where it was he *shouldn't* be headed. A block down the road t' his left, lanterns in one hand and rifles in the other, there stood a brace o' men.

"Who'zat?" one o' 'em shouted.

"That's the man what came 'round askin' 'bout Cassius Clay not five hours ago!" shouted another, "They're in cahoots for sure!"

"Shoot him!" said the first man.

Abner's eyes went wide as saucepans. It was his very first night in Kentucky an' here he was in his second gunfight already. He turned a quick tail t' the mob, makin' a mental note t' load his own rifle as soon as it was practical. Lexington was turnin' out t' be a lot less nice a place than he'da thought gettin' off the train.

It weren't far that he'd got before Abner realized his grand mistake. He was clompin' along at 'round half o' his normal clip. Jus' as the first shot rang out from behind him, Abner looked down t' see what was the matter. Like ants from a kicked hill, self-dismay spread across his face. Like some kind o' child ripe for a whippin', he'da forgot t' lace his boots. A second rifle cracked off a shot. Still steamin' at hisself, Abner scanned about for a hidin' spot. Not so much as an empty crate or barrel could he see along the side o' the road. The mob was bound t' squeeze off a decent shot eventually. Abner redoubled his efforts with his boots an' picked up jus' enough steam t' make it 'round the nearest street corner before the third rifle sounded. Abner panicked a bit. The only thing truly savin' him so far was that the mob was movin' slow an' as a group. Soon as they figured that they had the upper hand here, they were bound t' break up an' start movin' faster. He needed a hidey-hole an' he needed it right quick. Half a block up, Abner spied the perfect thing: a carriage what had been unhitched from its horses an' left t' stand empty for the night. Leper-like, he plodded across t' it, swingin' the door open hard, quick as he could.

There, in the carriage, paused in the midst o' lightin' his pipe, was Cassius Marcellus Clay. The stout man's sharp eyes darted first t' Abner an' then t' the other seat across the carriage. There, with a strange cube-like key on a chain stickin' out the side of it, was Clay's clockwork pistol.

Again Abner's eyes turned moon-shaped. "Now, wait a minute!" was all he had time t' blurt out before Clay, who was faster than his girth let on, had let drop his pipe an' lurched across the coach for the weapon. Abner slammed the carriage door shut an' made t' scamper, but his untied boots got the better o' him, an' instead o' sprintin' down the street, he fell in a heap right where he stood.

Blam, Blam, Blam, rang out the shots from Clay's pistol. Three holes, made in ascending order, blew through the wood o' the carriage door. The lowest o' them, Abner couldn't help but notice, was right above his head as he lay in the road. Thoughts regardin' whether his boots'd jus' saved or endangered his life were shoved out o' his head jus' as they were fixin' on becomin' a real good hard look at life itself in all o' its complexities. The carriage door slammed open once more, barely holdin' onto its hinges. Out from the dim interior leaned Clay, clockwork pistol in hand.

"You heard me fire this weapon earlier, sir," he said. "You'll recall that it has six chambers and that I have just now exhausted only three of them. Be assured that you shall not survive this next volley."

"Please!" shouted Abner in desperation. "Please hold off a minute, Mister Clay!"

Clay held, his frame rigid as iron an' his eyes deadly. "There's no one that's so respectful t' me as that anymore," he said, "no one 'round this town, leastwise." He surveyed Abner a moment. "You're not from the city. That and your decorum have graced you with the chance I now allow you, this *one* chance, t' explain yourself, sir. Use it judiciously."

Sweatin', Abner looked over his shoulder. The mob was closin' in on the corner; he could hear it. Soon it wouldn't matter none whether he'da convinced Clay t' read his an' Johnny's letters or not. They'd both be lynched. With that in mind, Abner spoke quick as his lips would allow.

"Mister Clay, all I know o' you i'zat you're a man well schooled an' braver than most," he said. "I came here on the train tonight, direct from Malvern, Arkansas t' ask your favor, sir. I wouldn'ta done so if'n it weren't a matter that desperately needed doin'."

Abner took a deep breath. Clay was lookin' at him different now, like a man mullin' over whether he was bein' hornswaggled or not.

"Now, beggin' yer pardon, sir," Abner continued, "but there's about a hundred armed men 'round the corner, an' they're fixin' t' do us both insufferable harm. We'd best be off t' another hidin' spot b'fore they catch us in this here shot-up wagon."

Clay's eyes flicked t' the street corner an' back. There wasn't no mistakin' the truth in Abner's words. Torchlight was flickerin' from 'round the corner an' angry voices could be heard on the wind.

"First you interrupted me in the midst of a perfectly survivable gunfight," Clay said, his tone thick with malice. "Now you've exposed a refuge as comfortable as I could've hoped t' find."

Abner was sure he'da sealed his own doom, comin' t' Lexington an' lookin' up a man so volatile as Clay. He wrung up his face an' waited for the scent o' black powder which'd be his last remembrance o' life. It didn't come, an' as Abner opened his eyes again, he saw Clay stuffin' his pipe into his pocket. Nimble as a cat, the portly man leapt out o' the carriage an' darted down the dirt road. For a brief confused moment, Abner sat, his hindquarters gatherin' dust.

"Shake a leg, stranger!" shouted Clay as he disappeared into the night. Abner was on his feet, quick as a spooked prairie dog. It was a good thing too, for just that minute, as he bumbled loose-booted after Clay, the first faces o' the mob came 'round the corner. Their eyes caught his jerky gait right immediately an' their tenacious cries sent talons o' woe diggin' t'ward Abner's heart.

"Clay! They've seen me!" he shouted.

"Dammit!" bellowed the dark road ahead, "and now they know they've got my tail as well!"

Abner cursed hisself as he ran on. The mob was doin' a much better job o' keepin' up with him this time. They'd seen their prey again an' reckoned they had the upper hand. After all, they were many an' their prey was constantly runnin' like a flushed quail. The faster members o' the mob, Abner noticed, were even gainin' on his hindquarters. Panicking, Abner shouted ahead t' Clay once more.

"They'll catch us up this time, Clay! Ain't no hidey-hole good enough t' hide us from them that see us gettin' *to* it!"

"This way!" came Clay's reply, echoin' down a small street t' Abner's left. "Try t' keep up, mind! I've got just the spot for our needs!"

Abner swung a hard left an' pelted down the thin throughway, loose boots be damned. At the end o' the narrow road, two blocks ahead, Abner spotted Clay through the dark. A spark o' light glowed in the man's hand. Abner scoffed. The man was re-lightin' his pipe in the middle o' a run for his life!

Clay finished with his pipe an' set off again jus' b'fore Abner reached the corner, the footfalls o' the first o' the mob only a pair o' seconds sprint behind him.

"They'll follow that smoke an' ember easy as a bloodhound on the scent o' a lung-shot doe, they will!" shouted Abner.

"Lovely image!" replied Clay, his teeth clamped firmly 'round his pipe as he ran. "Hardly matters now, though! We're here!"

The men turned one final corner an' Abner found hisself standin' in a small square crowded in on by buildin's on every side. The one directly across the square, though — now that was the strangest thing made o' four walls Abner'da ever done seen. Likely, back when Lexington, Kentucky had been a young an' blossomin' township, this here'da been the town smithy. Over the years that followed, however, the place must'a been built up an' out with whatever lumber goods were readily available at the time. One corner o' the place, Abner could see, was made o' aged an' fire-licked stone. That must'a been the entire smithy itself, for the other side o' the structure was a mass o' oaken timber. B'tween these two discordant halves o' the buildin', which stood a good three floors high an' cast quite the imposin' shape in the small square, was fixed a door which wouldn'ta been so out o' place had it been fixed t' a great big barn. Bein' that it was stuck dead center o' such an odd buildin', though, it gave a strong impression o' bein' the door t' a doll's house. The image o' little girls o' tremendous height pawin' the entire structure open an' meddlin' with the people an' furniture inside shot into Abner's head all o' a sudden. Unfortunately, he didn't really have the time t' mention such a thing t' Clay, who had already reached the front o' the place.

Above Clay's head an' beside the great big door hung a sign bearin' a strange ol' anchorless ship an' the writin' o' a careful hand which read:

'The True American'
Cassius Marcellus Clay, Editor and Proprietor

Beneath the sign, however, there was a number o' hasty scrawlin's which the local population had, no doubt, added at a later date. Abner read such unpleasantnesses as "Turncoat" an' "Snollygoster" an' "Jesse Scout" cut into the wood.

While Abner'da been starin' at the sign, Clay'd run over t' the giant door, slipped his fingers b'tween two planks o' wood an' slid open an odd little triangle o' a door. Noticin' that Abner was starin' 'round like a idlin' layabout, he clapped his meaty hands together an' bellowed "in!" so simply an' so loudly that even the simplest-minded o' cattle would'a got his message.

Snappin' to, Abner made fer the squat door lickety-split. He had one foot in the door, with Clay on his heels when a voice rang out behind 'em.

"Halt! Don't go no further!"

Clay turned first, his gun drawn, and scoffed. Pullin' his head back through the door, Abner quickly understood why. Standin' there b'fore 'em, holdin' a squirrel rifle, there stood a boy no older'n thirteen. The rifle, too long for the boy t' heft properly, shook in his grasp.

"Don't make me kill you, child," said Clay. "It'd be a right shame to kill one young as you."

"Th-the rest of 'em are right behind me, so they is!" stammered the boy. "Now I've caught you fair as square! Jus' give yourself up an' no harm'll come t' you."

Clay sighed. "I'm afraid none o' that holds true, lad," he said. "Firstly, that mob that's comin' behind you is out for blood 'n vengeance an' neither I nor this gentleman will survive their clutches. Secondly, you haven't caught me."

The boy looked indignant at that an' gripped his gun all the tighter, but Clay went on.

"That there squirrel gun might sting somethin' painful, but trust me son when I say that it won't fell me nor any man worth his salt. Now this gun here," Clay said, gesturin' t' his own weapon, "This gun here's a blunderbuss. Even if your pappy and General Stonewall Jackson himself were with you none of you would have the time t' recant your sins before meetin' god and all his angels, not if I pulled this here trigger."

The boy was shakin' a good sight more then, an' his eyes'd lowered from Clay's gaze, restin' instead on the wide-horned barrel o' the blunderbuss.

"You, being a bright lad, must have by now realized my third argument with your statement o' a moment ago," smiled Clay, taking the opportunity t' shove Abner backward through the little doorway. "Life is hardly ever fair." With that and a nod, Clay stepped back through the door quick as a cat, his eyes never leaving the boy until he was safely within the buildin' an' Abner'd slid the paneling back in place.

It was only after the door'da been latched that Abner had a chance t' look 'round the interior o' the strange buildin'. The first thing that struck him was how empty the place was. Behind him, Clay let out a shriek o' dismay as he noticed the very same thing.

"Dammit, they've taken her! I don't know how they did it, but they've gone and ripped my heart out while I was away!" he stormed.

'Now, if Clay'da been the buildin' itself,' Abner thought, 'then that's exactly what looks t' have happened'. It was as if someone'd come along an' stolen away with the guts o' the place. T' the left there were a couple o' piles o' papers an' crates an' what looked t' be a great big heap o' furniture all stacked up under a hodgepodge o' bedsheets. 'Gainst the far wall was a skeletal sort o' scaffoldin' which gave the distinct impression o' havin' been affixed t' somethin' in a number o' places. Abner could see spots where the platforms lead t' empty space an' others where hooks an' ties had'a been torn an' rent asunder, as if some great beast'd come through the giant door an' ripped apart whatever it was that had needed all this riggin' t' begin with.

T' Abner's right, Clay was a'grumblin' and a'bustlin' over t' what appeared t' be a small two-story apartment built into the larger structure. He threw on a light once he got there, sendin' rays o' orange-ish light across the empty floor. Suddenly a number o' long an' rusty chains, hangin' from the rafters, were visible. Some o' them dangled near all the way t' the floor. Abner's heart started a'beatin' somethin' ferocious as images o' another buildin', tall an' ominous as this 'un, danced b'fore his eyes. He was back in the barn, back amidst the flames an' smoke an' death. The weight o' Johnny's corpse hung down once more over him, the burden so great that Abner couldn't hardly breathe on account o' the load. He wasn't gonna make it. The flames were gonna swallow him up like they had ol' Johnny.

Somethin' glass shattered nearby an Abner snapped back t' the present. A brick lay on the dirt-streaked floor along with a few shards o' glass. The mob had grown outside an' evidently weren't too shy t' start breakin' windows.

"Otva'li, mu'dak!" yelled Clay, emergin' again from the lit room, which Abner could now see was a sort o' discombobulated office.

"What?!" said Abner, not havin' the foggiest notion o' what the man had said, but pickin' up the tone right quick.

"Nevermind!" said Clay, "just a saying I picked up in Cossack Alaska!" He was carryin' a shotgun now in addition t' the weaponry he'da already had with him. He traipsed right on up t' Abner an' chucked the weapon into his hands.

"There's a real gun for ya," he barked. "If I don't miss my guess, you'll need it before the night is out." Clay then strode back across to the great big door an' peered through the crack between the two large wooden frames. A group o' men, lookin' winded an' angry, had joined the boy. More still were arrivin' every second. As each new man showed, he first strode right up t' the great door itself an' chucked down his torch. A small bonfire was growin' there, sendin' flames into the night air in great leaps an' bounds. Still, unlike their fire, the men o' the mob looked tense, on edge. None that had yet arrived looked as if he were willin' t' do much more'n throw stones.

"What're they waitin' on?" asked Abner, edgin' his way close 'nough t' see through the crack between the doors.

Clay grunted somethin' akin to a chuckle. "Mobs are funny creatures, friend. A man alone can often be braver, and is always smarter, than he is when he's part o' a group. I'd wager that this lot here will need t' double their number before they've the potency t' start shootin'."

Abner pulled his eyes from the growin' crowd an' turned t' look at Clay. "I'm not one t' drown my neighbor's cat, Mr. Clay," he said, "but even if what you say is true, I reckon we've only got a minute or so b'fore them that's out there wind up the vigor t' blow holes in the both o' us an' this here warehouse o' yours right along with us."

"Warehouse?!" spat Clay. "*The True American* deserves a sight more respect than that slander, stranger! Now, sure we're no *Daily Gazette* or *Tribune*, but this here's the most righteous periodical south o' the Delaware Bay!"

"Periodical?" asked Abner. "But where's the printing press? Where're next mornin's papers?"

"I've many a suspicion as t' what the answer t' those questions might be," replied Clay, "and, truth be told, I'm betting it's a tale worth tellin', but it was you that mentioned how little time we have before the boys outside gain enough numbers t' surrogate for nerve. For now let's just say that I've been out of town long enough for the rats to have their day!" He practically spat this last bit toward the door behind which the mob was gatherin'. He was about t' storm back t' the little office when a calm, clear voice rang out, seemingly in response t' his hurled insult.

"Your days of spinnin' your propagandist, Northerner prevarications through the heartstrings o' Kentucky are drawin' t' a quick an' bloody close, Cassius!" The voice rang out clean and clear, echoin' off o' the back wall o' the gutted *True American*.

"Looks as if they've achieved fermentation, doesn't it?" Clay sighed, "and in the pickled old form o' Brian A. Scates, t' boot." With this he raised his sonorous voice t' the very roar o' a wild beast. "You may have run off my boys in my absence, Scates! You may have absconded with my Rotary Press! None o' that changes me from the voice o' reason and none o' it elevates you from being a simp and a fop! And believe you me, Scates, the day that I let the mewling, puking refuse o' humanity that you have stirred up tie their strings 'round my neck and hoist me from their gallows, well that's the day all hope for humanity in the South dies as well! I'll not let that winter begin this night!" With that, he shoved the barrel o' his blunderbuss through the broken window and fired it blind into the crowd.

Abner'd taken a step toward Clay as the man raised the weapon, hopin' t'stop him. Screams an' cries from outside proclaimed his failure. All he could do was stare, dazed, at Clay. Slingin' the wide-barreled gun 'round his shoulder, Clay noticed the look o' dismay painted all over Abner's face.

"Rock salt," he said, gesturin' to the weapon. "Hurts like a blighted whore's craw, an' their wives'll know they were in a fight, but it's not lethal save for point-blank." Then, gesturin' t' the shotgun he'da given Abner, he added, "that's loaded with the same stuff. If anyone starts forcing his way in, give 'im a barrel full. If it's Scates, blow both barrels down his throat!" With that, he set off toward the office again.

"Me?" asked Abner. "Where're you goin?"

"The roof!" bellowed Clay, disappearin' into the office again. Abner wasn't sure he liked the sound o' that too much. Here he was, alone again, holdin' off a mob o' men he had no real quarrel with, an' armed only with a couple o' rounds o' rock salt an' his own unloaded rifle. 'To top it all,' he thought, 'this Clay feller seems more crazy than he does helpful.' He'da have t' thank Tommy Horner somethin' painful the next time he saw the man — if he survived t' do so.

The screams an' shock o' Clay's assault was windin' down outside an' bein' replaced by the grumblin's an' rumblin's o' indignation. 'There's happenin's aplenty that a man'll forgive," thought Abner, 'but getting' shot ain't capital among 'em.'

"That was foolish, Cassius," rang out Scates' voice again. "The simple and violent act o' a cornered animal. Us civilized folk won't tolerate feral beasts in our midst!"

This time there were shouts o' agreement. 'Where'd Clay got off to?' wondered Abner, 'an' what in hellfire did he need from the roof?' Then the pounding started. First with their fists an' then with their boots an' shoulders, the mob were hammerin' at the door.

"Shit," hissed Abner, entirely sure the word was warranted this time — this wasn't gonna end without blood, not now. Steelin' hisself for the worst, he pulled back the hammer o' his first barrel an' squared his shoulders. He stood there a moment, silent an' still as a sentry. The thunderin' against the door rose an' was joined by the creakin' an' strainin' o' wood. The door, big as it was, wasn't gonna hold fer long. It had been built t' stand 'gainst the forces o' nature but not those of men.

Wham!

A plank o' wood broke an' fell t' the floor o' the building. Somethin' fell loose somewhere else at that same moment an' everything changed inside Abner. Gone was the hope o' getting' out o' this predicament. Gone, too, was the man who'd married Tess an' raised little Mazie. Back an' mad fer his time away was the soldier, the grey-clad warrior who'da killed an' maimed, shot an' stabbed t' pay fer his supper. The butt o' Abner's shotgun slammed down on the hand that was gropin' 'round the hole it'd made in the door. The man's thumb snapped an' he yelped in pain as he pulled it back out o' sight. Another hole burst open t' Abner's right. Quick as a dog on a hare, Abner's boot met with the flank o' another man's knee. Abner smiled at the yelp an' the thud that sounded from beyond the crumblin' door. If'n they were comin' through, they'd have t' wade through the hellfire that had been silently festerin' in Abner's gut since Johnny's demise. Now the sulfuric stuff was loose, an' them that got too close were burnin' from exposure. Somethin' soundin' like an auto-trolley slammed inta the locked doors just above Abner's head. Reflexively, he jumped back. They'd be through any moment now, an' welcomed justly by the demons they'd awakened in him. The shotgun spun 'round in his hands carvin' a smooth arc 'till its barrel pointed square at the door. A second an' third heavy blow thundered 'gainst the door. On the fourth, the heavy iron lock buckled an' the doors swung arduously open. Two bulky men, pickaxes in hand, leered down quizzical-like at

Abner. They'd wanted t'find Clay standin' there for certain an' couldn't quite figure on what t'do with what they'd got instead.

The contents o' the first barrel hit them both flat in the chest an' they buckled an' fell. The crowd that surged forward over 'em got the second. Abner's chest pounded as the shotgun spun again in his hands. The barrels were hot against his grip, but he couldn't feel it for the fire radiatin' out o' his fingertips. He advanced on the mob, a single man covered in dust an' powder an' awash in fury. He had his first target all picked out, a big lanky feller who'd be visible when he went down. 'Clay was right', Abner thought, 'at the very least they'll know they was in a scrap t'night.'

B'fore he got t' his mark, though, Abner was stopped; not by the crowd an' not by their weapons, but by a voice. It boomed over the entire square as if amplified by a fistful o' bullhorns.

"Mr. Scates, gentlemen of the shiftless and ignorant population!" it sounded. "I wish t' thank you properly for your treatment o' my colleague and myself tonight!"

It was Cassius Marcellus Clay, an' sure 'nough he was on the roof, his already sonorous voice echoin' off a the buildings o' the square.

"Please, now!" he bellowed. "Stay exactly where you are, you bigoted massing of slack-witted murderers!"

Abner couldn't see what was transpirin' upon the roof, but every pair o' eyes which had been fixed on hisself was now turnin' skyward. Each pair o' peepers that found Clay froze the instant they did so, knockin' every jaw open t' boot.

"I'm speaking especially to the venerable Mr. Scates and those men standing nearby his all-too-convenient perch at the center o' the square!" Clay boomed. "Those of you in the alleyways may live t' feel the burns you receive when this shell detonates, but I wish those o' you near the soon-to-be defunct Brian Scates a charitable reception at the gates o' Hell, for it is your next and final harbor!"

A smile traced in hellfire smoldered its way across Abner's face. Clay had a loaded cannon livin' on his roof. 'The man might be a bedlamite,' thought Abner, 'but he sure is primed for a fracas.'

Self-preservation plunged into the minds o' the mob, burstin' the bubble o' bloodlust that had been there b'fore it like a toad under its heel. Panic washed over the mob, sweepin' 'em in all kinds o' directions. Abner was sure by their flailings that the fuse on the roof was lit — lit an' short for that matter. Heels flew an' elbows swung, often findin' friends an' neighbors so as t' get by. One man, havin' had Abner's death in his eyes a moment b'fore, an' now facin' his own, ran t'ward the open door o' *The True American*. He was face first on the floor b'fore he realized the folly o' his actions.

Abner raised the shotgun again, waitin' fer his next victim. He needn't o' bothered. Just as the members o' the mob were reachin' the corners o' the square, the cannon let fire. The whole o' the square shook with the force o' the ball bein' loosed; shook again when the ordnance exploded dead in its center, right where Scates'd been standin' a moment b'fore.

Abner's ears buzzed like a shook hive o' honeybees. When he raised his eyes t'ward the square again it looked as desolate as a saloon on Sund'y mornin'. B'fore he could register much more'n that a firm hand was grippin' his shoulder an' steerin' him back into *The True American*. Clay was sayin' somethin' t' him. Shakin' the buzzin' bees out from between his ears, Abner squinted hard at the man. Slowly the words took clearer form in his ears. Clay was over near the ol' pile o' furniture that was sittin' in the corner an' askin' Abner t' help him with the sheets hangin' over it. Abner stumbled over, wonderin' as he got ahold o' the sheets which one o' the two o' them was more shell-shocked.

"Took my press, the wretches! Good thing they're dumb as they are ignorant or theyd've thought t' look around for other treasures!" smirked Clay.

It weren't until the covers'd been all but removed entire-like that Abner could make out what it were that stood b'fore hisself. Clay wasn't shell-shocked. Hell, he hadn't even lost a step when that ol' cannon'd let fire. Four wrought-iron wheels, spoked in walnut, sat upon the earth b'fore Abner. Cables an' sheets o' metal-work wove 'round one another until they peaked in the form o' four spires bedecked with rectangular brass railway lanterns. Curlin' its way up t'ward the lanterns there was spun a kind o' nautoloid canopy. Rear t' that lot was a sealed brass vat, the like t' boil soup for an entire regiment. Smack-dab in the center o' it all sat a claw-footed chesterfield, decorated with all manner o' levers. Juttin' straight up b'fore the regal-lookin' piece o' furniture was a brakeman's wheel.

Abner'd seen auto-trolleys an' heard o' other sorts o' horseless transport, but he'da always thought o' them as lumberin' shambles o' things, meant only t' grab a whole peck o' bankers n' clerks from one plundered estate t' the next. That sort o' thing was too big an' cumbersome, not t' mention costly, for a private individual t' own outright, he'd thought. Yet here was Clay, mountin' the thing an' tossin' his knapsack behind the chesterfield like it were an ol' worn-out horse-cart. Abner's mouth hung agape. He didn't know whether t' revere the thing or t' fear it.

"Oh, for god's sake, man!" boomed Clay. "Don't stand there on ceremony! Get in the vehicle!"

Still marvelin' at the wood, brass, an' iron contraption, Abner leapt up the fender an' landed heavily on the seat. Noticin' how wide Abner's eyes'd gone, Clay plopped his arm down on the armrest and casually leaned t' look at him, a smile on his face.

"Know how I came about to have this darlin'?" he asked.

Abner shook his head hastily. He had just begun ponderin' the series o' levers curlin' up from under the seat o' the couch. He wondered for a moment 'bout what sort o' ominous use each might come t' have, but was stopped short by Clay's response.

"I knew a trader, a quite respectable man, who often ferried odds an' ends about the country by rail. He and I formed a sort o' standing agreement that, were he t' find any unique sort o' item bearin' a trigger or which could be loaded with black powder, I would certainly take it off his hands." With that, Clay flipped forward the grip of the armrest he'da been leanin' on an' exposed what looked t' be the stock, trigger and part o' the barrel o' a very ornate rifle. "Imagine my surprise, then, when one fine day he rolled up in this apparatus!" he said, his hand gripping the trigger. "Nowadays, I just call her Petunia!"

Abner caught the glimmer o' excitement which danced about b'hind Clay's eyes an' braced hisself, for what he didn't quite know. The former editor o' *The True American* whooped an' squeezed the trigger, an' with a thunderous bang an' a rumble, Petunia roared t' life. Her four brass lanterns flared a bright yellow, flames burstin' up from tubes in their bases. A brassy rumblin' an' bubblin' began t' beat out its watery tune from the great big cistern to her rear. The chesterfield gave

a lurch an' the whole o' the contraption, occupants an' all, bounded away from the wall.

"Cost me quite a few circulations worth," whooped Clay, in his element down t' the soles o' his shoes, "but she's the damn finest thrill you'll ever get from pulling a trigger just once!"

Clay whirled the brakeman's wheel b'fore him an' the carriage spun in a close arc an' tore out through the great door an' into the night. The first mutterins an' swearin's o' the fallen rioters could be heard now, along with a few stirrin's here an' there.

"Throw the first lever!" bellowed Clay, indicatin' the largest o' the set beside Abner. Abner did as he was told an' was near thrown out o' his perch for it as the carriage bolted into the distant dark, leavin' those that remained t' lick their wounds an' ruminate on what it was t' stand b'tween a man an' his freedom.

About a mile down the road Abner an' Clay were carousin' an' partakin' o' the drink as they remembered the events o' the night. Clay was tellin' o' how plum gargoyle-faced Scates had looked, starin' up at the mouth o' a cannon, lit and glarin' at hisself. Abner sucked at the bottle o' drink, smilin' away the fear an' adrenaline as he listened. It was hardly a wonder at all that the auto-carriage was a-waverin' back an' forth about the dirt road in the dark o' the night. Neither man noticed until it was too late that they weren't alone on the road. The form o' a woman, draped all in golden dress, flashed in the flickerin' light o' the gaslamps. What she was doin' walkin' along the outskirts o' town in such finery an' at such a late hour, the men did not know. Nor did they have the time t' ponder any o' that, for she was near two feet from the wheels o' the carriage by the time they saw her. Her eyes flashed in the gaslamps an' she was gone again b'fore they could swerve the auto-carriage away from her shinin' self. The men winced as they saw her disappear.

There was no impact an' no yelp o' pain. The men were sure they'da gone an' hit the woman, but the carriage bore no sign o' havin' hit her, even when they chanced a momentary stop t' see if she'da been caught in Petunia's undercarriage. It was only then that they saw somethin' movin' slow-like along the road behind 'em — somethin' which looked a whole heap like the woman, still walkin' along the road as if nothin'd ever altered her pace. Abner took one last look at the liquor an' hurled it into the bushes b'fore gettin' back in the auto-carriage. The atmosphere was a whole lot more somber upon the chesterfield after that, both men sure they'd rather not labor too much over the strange woman or her miraculous state o' well bein'.

Chapter Thirteen
The Dreamer Espied

The boy awoke with a start. He was sweating; his heart was beating like a hare's, and questions tumbled about like leverets in his mind. The dream had been just like one of Merlin's stories. He half expected the wizard to be sitting by his bedside at his waking, yet the room stood empty. Why had he dreamt of those same strange men of whom Merlin had told him before?

'It felt so real,' he thought.

Could it have *been* so? Was this even truly part of the same tale the old man had told him? Was it just some silly extrapolation invented in his own imagination? All these questions bombarded the boy at once as he pulled his mind from the realm of the dream. Above all the rest floated one question, the importance of the answer to which seemed so dire and yet so impossibly elusive that it sent the boy into fits of panic as he dwelled upon it: who had she been — that shining woman who had walked, nearly floating, by the roadside? Arthur had never heard nor conceived of someone of such grace. She had looked directly at him as well, as if she alone amongst the inhabitants of the dream could see him. Those golden eyes had bored into him until he had awakened, drenched in this cold sweat. Even if the rest of the dream was something of his own imagining, Arthur had no idea whom she had been.

Maggie, he could hear, was already awake and bustling about the cooking fire. Deciding that he would rather not be alone with his thoughts at this very moment, he hurried to dress and ran out to the main room. He smiled awkwardly at Maggie and pulled a seat away from the table for himself, sniffing at the air for hints of breakfast.

"Sure'n you're up early Artie!" she exclaimed as he scooted his chair noisily back toward the table. "What brings you t'be waking so early?"

She was right to ask, the boy noticed, for looking out the open window he could see that the sun was only now just peeking over the horizon. Staring at the morning sun he absent-mindedly asked her the same thing.

"What're you doing up so early as this Maggie?"

The girl smiled warmly, chuckling to herself and patting the boy on the head.

"Life of a kitchen maid, I suspect" she said. "Early to rise and late to bed. I'm afraid I'm just plain groomed to it now, I suppose. You haven't answered, though Artie. What is it that's rousted your young bones from sleepin' so early, like?"

Arthur shrugged. "Had a dream," he replied.

"Not another nightmare, I hope," she replied, looking at the boy a bit closer as she said this.

"No, not really," muttered Arthur, peering around Maggie at the cookpot. He'd just decided that whatever it was that was in there smelled delicious. "Well," he went on, "there was an odd bit at the end, but…" He was smacking his lips now, not really paying attention to the conversation.

"All right, all right," said Maggie, "I'd wanted to let it simmer a bit longer, but let's tuck in, shall we?"

She ladled out two small bowlfuls of the stew and set them upon the table. Aromas of pheasant and thistle arose with the steam from each bowl. Arthur smiled warmly and tucked in, a feeling of safety and care trickling down his throat with each spoonful.

"Now then, let's hear about this dream," said Maggie.

Arthur decided to start at the beginning, telling her of Merlin's stories and of how each seemed so real, as if he were actually there watching them happen. He spared no detail, trying to recall as much as he could at every turn of the tale.

The old man's eyes popped open and he shot up from where he lay like a flushed fox. 'What was it', he wondered, 'that had just happened?' Who was the gold-clad woman who had so abruptly entered into and interrupted his dreaming? As he sat there pondering, his face and cloak beading with the morning dew, a speck of something drifted before his eye. 'Some piece of flotsam or spore, wending its way toward disintegration,' he thought, sweeping it from before his eye.

His thoughts had no sooner lent themselves to the mustering of muscle and bone than he noticed the return of the speck. Puffing it away with a bit of breath, he began the process of standing, taking stock of which muscles protested the greatest upon *this* morning as he did so. Upon reaching his full height he was again greeted by the selfsame wisp of naught which had hung before him twice before. The thing hung so close to his eye that, come there the slightest gust of wind, it might inadvertently scrape the surface of his pupil. Now, too, there was a faint scent upon the breeze. It was a musty smell he recalled for reasons long forgotten. Bringing his focus close as he could to his own face so as to examine the bit of stuff, he let in a sharp gasp. "Death," he said, "that is how I know you. You smell of death."

What it was that hung before him so closely was the tiniest barbule of a feather. Now focused upon it, his keen eye could discern the beginnings of decomposition upon the thing. It had been borne to him upon the wind from a creature whose passing had been days prior and which was long out of its misery. As if the thing were somehow familiar or precious to him, Merlin had the impulse to reach out ever so gently and pluck it from the air.

'What a strange sensation', he mused with himself, 'the thought that I knew this bird.'

The edge of the featherlet seemed to twinkle as he thought this.

"Oh," he said, "so we do know each other, though I cannot recall how. All right then, little forlorn friend, let us see what it is you wish to tell me."

He stepped forward, directly toward the little thing. As if upon some unseen string, it pulled away from his eye as he did so, only to hang once more before him. It hung at a slightly greater distance this time, but not so far as the tip of his nose.

"I half expected as much," said Merlin, smiling. He took another step forward, larger this time. Before him, the bit of fluff danced and swirled, bounding along on its minute currents of air. Again the old man stepped forward, following his tiny, shining guide. Presently, another wisp of stuff joined the game, floating in little winding spirals about the first. There was a golden sheen to the new arrival which shone due to some inherent quality or to the dawn's fair light. Merlin knew not which. He decided to forego discovering the source of this second speck's shining, however; for a new and far more intriguing prospect had just come into his mind. Shifting his focus from they that were before him, he instead scanned the greater sky. At first, he was sure he had misguessed in his theory, for nothing presented itself readily to his eye. Then, as if to make itself known, a tiny procession of glistening downy specks shifted themselves about. In such wondrously perfect alignment behind their nearest brethren had they been hidden that, had they not moved, they would surely have remained invisible to him still. Now, though, they sparkled and shone like a dusty and fragmented bit of spider's silk.

Their whirling dance beckoned to him. Their entire procession now in sight, he was able to hasten his step, and hasten he did, passing along the tiny glittering highway as he went. Each bit of fluff danced along with him for a while as he strode onward, in due time relenting its privileged position to its kin. The ousted featherlets did not abandon him entirely once removed, but instead chose a new circuit to make about his person. Some elected to swirl about his crown in tight, winding coils, while others blustered wildly about his shoulders. Still others billowed about in the currents which the old man's feet kicked up as he trod onward. All of these had a shared and steadily growing effect upon him. His strides grew more spry, his gait more loping. He could hardly feel the regular creakings and aches that came with age. It was second nature to him to be following along with the specks now, as if he had been doing so all his life.

Gently the bits of fluff arced their way northward, coercing him in their little way to continue along with them. The land grew softer and the grasses tall. Reeds brushed against his knees. The sensation of water seeping into his shoes and about his ankles made known to him the presence of a pond or river. Undaunted, he waded onward along this, the proper path. The water was up to his waist, then to his chest. It pressed against him, trying to push him downstream.

'It certainly slows a person down,' he mused. It wasn't anything to worry about, though. After all, the water's drag merely gave him more time to watch his pixie-like friends dance about. There were willows upon the bank as he rose from the water, their branches hanging deep into the current. 'Everyone's in for a dip,' he thought, chuckling to himself. Winding himself through the curtains of willow branches, he found himself looking upon the first strange object that he could recall ever encountering.

'Is that right?' he wondered 'haven't I just recently seen something peculiar... or some*one* perhaps?' It was no matter, for he could not at that moment ever recall feeling such a way before.

Standing before him was a tall and be-columned structure, the face of which stared down upon him through all-too-familiar eyes. 'It must be some happenstance,' thought Merlin, 'which gives this structure such a face.' There, supported by a dozen columns of stone, was a great triangular façade. Therein, surrounded by the images of a spear, a pair of helmets, a globe, and an owl, there was carved a great stone shield, emblazoned with a man's head. His own head. There was no escaping the exactitude of the likeness in features. There, encircled by strands of stone hair and beard, was set his own brow, his own nose, his own eyes. These giant facsimiles stared motionlessly back at him, as if to ask how he came to bear their same carving.

Chapter Fourteen
Time and Tide

Something popped inside Merlin's ear and he was immediately aware that he was drenched from rib to toe. The cold morning air gripped his skin and he shivered, pulling his gaze from that of the stone figure. Gazing down, he wondered how he had come to be so soaking wet. Looking about he located a quick-flowing river and deduced that he must have waded in for some reason, though what it was he could not fathom. Indeed, he did not recognize his surroundings at all, nor how he had come to be in such a place. The temple before him he knew he had seen before, and so turned his focus back upon it. This gave him a bit of a shock, for he stood not before the building he recalled. It was the same in general construction, to be sure, but the stone pillars were deeply cracked in places and vines grew about their flanks. The stone face upon the façade had changed as well. While it still bore great likeness to his own, the focus had gone out of its eyes and it no longer seemed to be staring directly at him. Strange changes seemed to have been made in the detail of the carved face. Firstly, the great stone shield was held aloft by three creatures. Half man and half sea-beast, Merlin recognized these as Tritons. He did not recall how he had come by this memory of their existence, but was certain of it none the less. Secondly, not all of the stonework strands that surrounded his likeness were hair. Some bore the scales and winding muscular bodies of serpents, their faces peeking out from the curls of the beard. Lastly, there sprouted feathered wings from amidst the hair upon his head.

Merlin wondered how he had overlooked such details at first glance, for they made him more uneasy than he would have liked to admit. The serpents amidst the beard gave him such pause alone, that he passively dug his fingers through his own bristles, not entirely sure that he would not find a serpent coiled therein. The Tritons, too, discomfited him, for he could not remember how he knew of them, but only that it was not a happy recollection.

Scouring the entire façade for further missed detail, he found none, but his eye lingered upon the smaller and lighter of the two helms. He rather fancied the image but, like the Tritons, could not figure why and, after a moment more, decided to leave such feelings be so that they might be mulled over by his subconscious. His eyes fell next upon the image of the owl. This, above all the other symbols, he knew he should find as a portent or clue to the riddle of it all.

'An owl,' he thought, 'have I not recently been visited by such a creature?'

A small wisp of naught drifted before him, shining in the morning light. He brushed it aside as a nuisance, his mind still working upon the image of the owl. When the little thing flew before him again, an impulse gripped his mind and in one swift, delicate motion he acted upon it. The small bit of fluff lay still now, pinched between his forefinger and thumb. Turning his focus to the little thing, recollection swept over him like a fell breeze. The tiny featherlet lay still, though he had half expected it to struggle against his grasp. It was one of the bits of glittering decay that had entranced him as he had awakened upon the roadside that morning. His memory of the dream-like journey he had taken in getting to this place had returned to him.

"How strange that you were able to beguile me so easily," he said.

He parted his finger from his thumb, releasing the bit of feather to the air once more. It promptly took flight, but did not resume its place just before his eye. Rather it swept about in a lazy curling circuit before him apace. The wizard's eyes flicked back to the image of the owl upon the temple gate.

"Now we shall see to your owner," he said, "but I would much rather do so in my right mind, thank you."

As if it had been waiting for this cue, the little bit of feather whipped away into the sky and did not return. This seemed good to Merlin, for his thoughts would have to be his own if he were to meet whomever or whatever it was that had drawn him to this place. The answer lay within the temple, he knew. But whatever was to be found inside was truly something of great power. The way in which he had been made to come to this place was evidence of that. Evidence, too, was it of the wild nature of the power within the temple; for force, passive as it had been, was not something to which men responded well. Had he been another man, Merlin might have taken offense himself, thinking the temple to be some oubliette or pitfall set for his ensnaring.

As luck, or whatever else was at work in this place would have it though, he was a soul seeking something, and as such was not beset by all the doubts of a regular man. The strange familiarity of this place, that it had sought him out, these things meant recognition. Recognition in turn meant knowledge, and this was what he sought for himself.

'Still,' he thought as he ascended the steps to the temple, 'this day has marked the first loss of my memory since I have met the child. Herein, it would seem, lies a power great enough to overwhelm my waking mind. I shall have to be cautious in this place, lest I give myself over to it again. My remaining years are fleeting enough without the loss of more of them to forgetfulness.'

Standing at the doorway, the temple held an impenetrable darkness, and so as he entered he did so in utter blindness. The first thing he detected was the scent of rot and decay. There was also a humidity to the air, which made the rot seem to hang in curtains of hot damp about him. As he worked his lungs against the damp, he breathed in spores and mold. Something sloshed against his feet.

As his eyes adjusted, Merlin could see spots of glistening liquid pooled in the depressions of the floor, from which thin tendrils of steam rose. Mold and moss grew along the banks of these Lilliputian lakes, giving the room at large the feel of a miniature wetland, no doubt peopled by spore and salamander alike. There was a spring somewhere in this place, Merlin decided, which gave it its heat and water.

Cracks in the outer wall sent thin rays of light down toward the floor where they reflected in the pools, scattering their golden rays about. A thick haze of dust and spore hung, sparkling in the light like heavy curtains. In amongst the dust there were mixed more feathers, though these were not the mere fragments that had led him to this place but whole, patterned plumes. Their glittering in the reflected light gave the effect of a starry nightscape which swirled about the old man as he crossed the stone floor. For all its mold and age the temple felt inviting to him, its warmth comforting.

A door presented itself along one wall as he moved through the room. Not really knowing why he did so, Merlin meandered through it to the adjoining room. Warm water enveloped his already-soaked ankles as he stepped across the threshold. The floor of this room was submerged, and the water trickled back into the room behind him as he stepped inside. The effect of the water about his ankles was a soothing one, as if muscle and tendon were returning to their desired state. There was a mineral scent to the air as well in this place which chased away the spores and rot. Stepping further into the room, Merlin was suddenly gripped by the sensation that he was standing at the very edge of a precipice, the bottom of which was made invisible by its depth. The water grew progressively darker the deeper into the room he looked, turning entirely black before it reached the center itself. Hardly visible and only inches from his feet, Merlin could see a ledge in the pool, after which the floor fell away entirely. Peering over this edge, he felt an imperturbable uneasiness descend upon him, as if the pool were peering back into him from the depths.

The heavy closeness of the air suddenly felt as if it were pressing in around him, the black water as if it were pulling him down. The dark of the room blanketed him, weighed upon him, beckoned him to delve deeper and deeper into the hot dark murk. He was bent over before he realized it, hinged at the waist. His beard drooped close to the surface of the pool, his feet curling over the lip of the chasm. His heart pounded in protest. Some small, frail voice from within the old man was shouting desperately at him to leave, to run from this deep, hot tomb of a place. Yet he could not bestir the will to do so.

The tip of his beard dipped below the surface of the water. There was a tug and his beard went taught. Someone, unseen in the black, was yanking him downward, hard. Despite the old man's every attempt to pull free, his unseen assailant drew him steadily deeper. There was nothing in the bare room to grab ahold of. Every inch of the floor was submerged beneath the water and the walls were too far away to grasp. Surely any further part of his body that sank beneath the placid surface of the pool would only provide his assailant further aid in tugging him downward.

Merlin groped for the sword that hung from his hip, hoping to slice his beard away and free himself. He was halted in this just as his hands touched the sword's hilt, for in doing so he had inadvertently shifted his center of gravity. Off-balance, he was being pulled even faster into the pool. His face drew close to the water's surface. Then, just as his nose was about to be drawn beneath the water, from whence he knew there could be no escape, something glinted in his periphery. One of the feathers from the antechamber had glided into the room. It curled its way toward him, flitted before his eyes, and settled itself down between the tip of his nose and the water's surface. Its quill puncturing the water like that of a pincushion, the little feather bowed under the weight of the man but, supported only by its own spine, held. Its vanes tickled the tip of his nose, but he dared not sneeze for fear of plunging himself into the dark. In a different light, the old man thought he might have found the sight of himself quite humorous. The image of Arthur popped into his head, this being a predicament Merlin could easily see the child getting himself into. He made a mental note never to mention this particular adventure to the boy, and took stock of his options. The tugging upon his beard had ceased, but he remained set in place, neither sinking nor rising. The portion of his beard which was submerged seemed to have grown heavy with the weight of the water, but whatever had been tugging him downward seemed to have been scared off for the time being. Slowly at first, and then in a metered, steady pace, Merlin straightened himself to his full height.

Once he had righted himself, the feather plucked itself from the water. It went its way up toward his face, hung there but an instant, and set off through a second door, one set caddy-corner from that through which he had entered. Perhaps more zestfully than was prudent, Merlin followed. So great was his uneasiness in the room which held the dark pool that, no matter what lay before him, he was sure he would do well to put that place behind him.

Beyond the door of that room, he was washed in brilliant light. The sun hung before him, having risen while he had been in the dark. So bright was it, so contrasting from the dark in which he had been, that he was forced to turn his gaze away. He blinked hard, forcing his eyes to refocus in the light. Slowly he turned again to look about his new surroundings. He stood in a great hall of some sort, the roof of which had caved in at some point, letting the sun shine down into its once elegant trappings. Like the previous room, much of the floor was covered in water, this time a glistening viridian in color. Arches and pillars which had once held the domed roof of the hall protruded from the water like giant stone bathers. Strings of bubbles rose about these, releasing steam as they burst against the surface. Turning his gaze upward toward the sun again, Merlin could detect a mezzanine to the hall, along which ran a stonework walkway. At one spot, just where the rays of the sun shone upon the walkway, there stood a figure. Merlin tensed. He had thought himself to be alone in this place and admonished himself for the oversight.

'This place,' he thought to himself, 'it has affected me in ways both subtle and grave. It is rare to the point of invalidity, the number of times that I have been ambushed. Yet here I find myself, again at the mercy of the denizens of this place.'

The figure along the mezzanine stood still, frozen in place. This was odd, but stranger still was the realization he had just made. His thoughts about being ambushed had not been merely concerning the recent days, but rather a feeling he seemed to have about his entire lifetime. Despite his perilous situation, the old man smiled at his insight. Perhaps his past was not so lost after all.

He raised his hand in hail to the figure upon the walkway and waited for a response. When none came, he raised his voice in a haloo, thinking that the figure had somehow not noticed him. When there came still no response, he stepped further into the great watery hall to get a better look at his silent companion. The rays of the sun fell no longer directly into his eyes and at this change a second smile, bordering upon a smirk graced the face of the old man.

"Hmm," he said, walking further into the hall.

Sure enough, he picked out a number of similar figures standing upon the edge of the mezzanine in even intervals. Each stood still as the first, but in differing poses. Some held weapons, some ceremonial objects. None gave the slightest hint that they had noticed him.

"And why should they?" he asked himself. "Statues rarely *do* take notice of men as we pass them by."

He chuckled to himself openly as he found his way along the side of the great bubbling pool and deeper into the hall. At a spot along the far wall there was a space where there should have stood one of these stonework men, but it appeared that the ceiling had claimed it as victim during the collapse. Other than this damage, however, the hall was remarkably pristine. No mold or decay could be detected upon the air here, only the heavily mineralled scent of the steam rising from the pool. Gone too, were the mosses and vines which crept about the entrance to the temple.

Leading himself to the far wall of the place, Merlin discovered the remains of the statue that had fallen from the mezzanine above. Broken now into numerous large pieces, the figure looked as if it had once born the attitude of a bather, though the state of the thing made it hard to tell for sure. The head and torso lay apart from the rest, resting near the corner of the room. A hand was missing as well, having once been placed above the statue's marble curls. A close look at the face of the statue lent a feeling of justification to the wizard. The thing was expertly carved and did, indeed, seem to be staring back at him as he looked upon it. A soft slopping sound met his ear then, and he tore his eyes from the broken thing in search of its origin.

Around a bend, in an alcove which adjoined the hall, he discovered an ancient conduit. Constructed of cairn stones and tarnished by mineral deposits left upon it over hundreds of years, the stone channel now bore a tawny coating. Water poured in a steady, quiet stream from its stony maw, pooling in a small basin. From there, the water was guided along a finely-cut stone gutter toward the viridian pool. Here, lying in the gutter, was the bather's missing hand. Held in its grasp was a small stone tankard, the source of the slopping Merlin had heard from the hall. Tiny waves of the hot water surged and ebbed within the tankard before returning to their journey to the great pool.

Stooping to pick up the tankard, he noticed something peculiar. One of the fingers of the stone hand lay outstretched, making its grip upon the tankard look entirely unnatural. In point of fact, it looked more as if the hand were pointing to something. The old man followed the line of the outstretched finger across the floor. It did not quite point at the ancient drain, but rather at something just beside it. There, cut into the stone wall, there was a gash which looked more like the wearing of time upon the temple than a purposeful door. Behind it, however, could be seen the rocky walls of a cavern. Merlin's heart drummed a quickened beat against his chest. His recent memory of the dark places within this temple was not a favorable one. What hidden dangers might lurk in this new-found chamber?

Something glittered, deep in the cavern. Thinking it to be another one of his enchanted featherlet guides, Merlin bent low, shifting his lithe frame easily through the entranceway's crumbled bulwark. The feathers had after all, he thought, not tried to kill him thus far, and had once even come to his aid.

Stalactites dripped from the invisible ceiling of the cavern. The floor of the place was warm and soft to the touch. The air within embraced him, seeming to welcome him, to draw him inward. Again the now-familiar feeling of his being watched bristled the hair upon the old man's knuckles. The only light in the place was that which flooded in behind the old man himself. As he moved away from the crack in the rock, the rays of light lent meek luminescence to the cavern, revealing in the rock a dusty, coppery glow. To his left, a small emerald pool bubbled up from the rock, its edges frothing with minerals and salts dredged from deep within the earth. This was the mouth of the spring, the very womb of the temple. Turning in place, as if hung from invisible cords, were a handful of the glistening feathers. A pair of objects stood along the far bank of the pool. Upon approaching, Merlin discovered that the larger of the two was yet another statue, this time of a woman and forged in bronze, rather than the carved stone of the bathers outside. She was nude, save for a thin sash of woven metal cord which draped about her waist and down her leg. She stood upon a bronze pedestal, upon which was also laid a helm which bore striking similarity to the larger of the helms upon the facade of the temple.

'Truly,' thought Merlin, 'I have found the god of this place.'

Nothing he had thus far seen in the temple had been wrought with such care. Instinctively, he reached out to touch her. The woman was so finely cast that, at the caress of his hand, her very pores could be detected. There was a warmth to her metal flesh as well, likely owing to the heat which rose from the spring. A single ringlet of her hair draped down her breast, seemingly asking to be replaced amongst her braids. He wove the curls together again before he knew he was doing it. The wizard had half expected her to startle as he had touched her, but she remained fused in position, her sash swaying lightly in the air.

Beside the shining woman and her helm there lay a second object, small and forlorn in comparison. This was the final source of the numerous feathers which Merlin had observed throughout the temple. Its life long extinguished, the owl was now no more than a pile of bone and feathery ruin. And yet, still the feathers and bone of the creature glistened with a near preternatural beauty.

Merlin bent low over the relic, wondering how such a creature could draw him to this place. Surely something so long deceased could not have any spirit left within it. No. Bending closer, he found there was nothing left of it in spirit either. The owl was merely a fallen shell of a beast. Yet, there hung still a sense of presence in the cavern. If anything, the feeling of his being watched had intensified the deeper he had delved within. Somewhere, perhaps deep within the shadows, someone was watching him in silence. He turned his gaze upward so as to better scan the hidden places about him. He needn't have looked so far.

Bent at the waist and peering over him, the statue bore a quizzical look upon her face. The old man's heart stopped. His breath shivered from his lungs. He had not heard the slightest movement, had not recognized the presence in the cave as emanating from the statue at all. One of her hands had drawn so close to his head that she might have run her fingers through his grizzled mane, had she wanted to. Her eyes, now open and lustrous, stared into his. Finding his lungs empty, Merlin tried to force the air back into them. Before he could make a sound, she spoke to him.

"Brother-That-Was, that would, should, have been!" she exclaimed, a tinny bubbling laugh bursting forth upon every word. She gasped then, returning her outstretched hand to cover her mouth. "You that, with she, were lost and gone these many years! Yet — now! Returned to the day and the land! Does *she* come along presently?" With this, she stood straight and whipped her head about briskly toward the cavern entrance, a look of expectation upon her smiling face.

Merlin took a step away from the shining woman, unsure of what meaning to take from her words. She seemed to recognize him, yet no pang of familiarity resided in his breast concerning her.

The hopeful guise the statue wore upon her face shifted to despair.

"No," she said, "no, she remained after and... changed, like all the brethren." She returned her gaze to the old man. "Your change is most peculiar, young Brother-That-Was, would-have-been.

"Oh!" she exclaimed. "Believe, know that we were furious with him, all of us who knew! You must know this, or tax your false-aged heart we must all!"

Again, Merlin stood confounded. Whatever it was that this bronze nude wished to convey to him, he could not discern. "Was it you then, who drew me here like fish to bait?" he asked. "I had thought it to be this fallen creature."

The statue's breast heaved as she looked down upon the carcass of the owl. The strands of hair which Merlin had righted fell again before her face, but she did not move to replace them. She stooped over the creature, releasing a sob that echoed, low and metallic. She was quiet then a moment, seeming to will herself to composure. When she stood again, the sadness had not entirely drained from her beautiful face. She held in her hand a single feather, plucked from the wing of the creature. "My friend and aide," she cooed at the feather, "my companion and spy, servant and messenger." Her fingers traced the edge of the feather. For a moment she looked as if she were going to lose her composure once again. The moment passed, however, and she smiled warmly at Merlin once more, righting her curls and placing the feather amidst them to hold them in place.

"Yet, though unmade, splintered, and cast to the wind, look what he has found for me," she asked, reaching out her arms as if to embrace the old man, who did not move to do the same. "You... you perchance do not see me?" she said, her lips once more curling in a pained frown. "Have I, too, passed too far along that final highway to visit with the day?" She looked utterly distraught by this prospect, and so Merlin hastened to reassure her.

"I can see you quite well," he said, "but I do not know you, nor do I know what it is you mean by summoning me to this place."

"Is it too much to visit with your own kin?" she asked, drawing nearer to him. Her skin was stippled with goose flesh and gave off strange tinkling noises as she moved. "You may have wizened and carbuncled in form, but I see you for who you are." She was so close now that her metallic breath broke across his face. "Tell me you do me the same courtesy?"

"I believe that I would recall being acquainted with bronze-hewn maidens," said Merlin, smiling.

"I," she said, pushing him away, "A mere statue? A carving made by mortal hand?" Her voice rang in his ears. "I am no mere craftwork, Brother-Cousin," she exclaimed, "I am god in this place!" her arm swept about the cavern. "Here and all the lands of the empire!"

Her voice died down then, as if she had recalled herself. "Though it may be true if you say it that those far-off lands are dark to me, I would protest in belief that I yet hear their whispered prayers on the days of my polishings — do you... truly not recognize me, Brother-Cousin?" she asked.

"In truth," Merlin replied, "I have had great troubles of the mind of late. My recollection fails me more often than not. Give me your name and perhaps that shall aid me, goddess of the spring."

"This news pains me," she said. "I am your... but, no: I was never that to you. I wished it to be, Cousin-Kin; you must hear me in that. *She* did so as well, but that you must know... or perhaps not?" She stopped for a moment, a tender look upon her face as she stared at him. "But maybe, in this alone, you have been spared some grief, if you are not in your right recollection."

She spoke in riddles to the ear of the wizard, riddles which he grew tired of deciphering. He was quite sure he was not the one of the two of them who was out of his mind.

"Your name, maiden," he said, "What is it?"

"But, I am Sulis!" she smiled. "Surely that much you can recall?" Then, as if remembering something she had long forgotten, she proclaimed: "No! No, it was not. You did not know me by this name! It does not fit well upon my tongue when I gaze upon you. Was I to you Sulis-Minerva?"

"I can recall no such name," Merlin sighed. He made to leave, thinking the entire day a waste. This Sulis goddess could no more tell him of his past than she could remember her own, had she even known him at all. "I am sorry," he said, "but your pet has found the wrong confused old man."

"NO!" she cried. "No, I know you! I have seen, through the very eyes of that beast whose last deed you do now doubt! My sister! You who loved my sister will not leave me so readily after it has taken me these long years to find a familiar face!"

Her pleas succeeded. The old man ceased his retreat. Here named at least was the *she* of whom the statue had been speaking. He turned to face the goddess.

She was hunched over, her fists clutching whole tufts of her shining hair. Her eyes were squeezed shut and her mouth hung agape in a masque of excruciating pain. Her knees screeched, pressed against one another so that she might endure whatever trauma she was undergoing. "Minerva, then!" she shrieked between gasps for air. "Just Minerva! It pains me to recall myself to that form, for Sulis does not go quietly from me. It is not all of me that *is*, you understand, that was she that I once was! Please! Please, do not leave me, Brother-That-So-Nearly-Was!"

"You call me by many a wandering sort of name, Minerva," said Merlin. "Do you not know by what name you knew me? If you knew me at all you would know by what name I was called, would you not?"

"Much is in a name, Cousin," she replied.

Indeed it seemed that she was right, for upon his calling her Minerva, she had straightened, her knees no longer grinding bronze shavings from one another.

"But ours was never the tale," she went on. "Had you been born to woo the spear and the shield, mayhap my memory would still ring with the songs of our love. But then, knowing *her* own tale... perhaps you would be dead, for I am the more savage by right."

Her jaw was stiff now, as if she had remembered something unpleasant. She looked down and plucked up the helm from her pedestal, wiping the moisture from off its surface. Instead of flicking the wetness from her hand, she moved toward the emerald pool and plunged her hand beneath the surface. When she raised it again, the base of something long and thin sat cradled between her outstretched fingertips. She drew the thing, which shone with the same bronze gleam that she herself did, from the pool until it was as tall as her shoulder. Then her hand twisted quickly, gripping the bronze pole in her clenched fist. The tip of the thing came up from the water then: a flat, pointed, deadly thing; the tip of a spear, which she held aloft as if examining it in its entirety. She spoke then, but not to Merlin. She spoke in quiet tones as if to herself, or perhaps to the weapon.

"Bairn of the Far-Springer, chooser of the bow and horn, Brother's-Bane, sky-seen seeker damned never to score his prey... why this loss, so early departed, still thought held aloft eternal... why this one returned?" she muttered.

"Do you speak, goddess Minerva of the spring?" asked Merlin, seeking to interrupt what he perceived as the mad rantings of the statue. She looked up from her thoughts, found his eyes again as if doing so for the first time. "Of the spring?" she said. "I suppose it is so. But it was not always mine. It was hers who now perches behind my eye and breathes within my breast." She paced forward, her spear still held aloft. "I loathe her. She is more oft the sustainer now and I the parasite. She!" She paused her striding toward him and squinted at him, hard.

"It is you, Brother's-Bane. You, like some heirloom tarnished but once shining, hearken me back to my beatific truth! Praised be the triumvirate fathers eh? Yours, and mine, and the dark one too! Look! Look as I glisten in my skin!"

As she said this, she had begun to glisten and shine in a way entirely new. She was no longer forged of metal, but of flesh and bone. Her hair fell in curls of natural shining black. Her eyes twinkled, a strong dark brown in color. The moisture of the cavern beaded upon her shoulders, dripped down her naked olive skin. The change was miraculous. No longer did a statue stand before Merlin, but a goddess, living. She laughed a light and chiming giggle which sounded as if it were a thousand tiny bells ringing in the echoing reaches of the cavern.

"I am split from her!" she proclaimed. "I am Minerva and she, Sulis! Our unnatural binding is now undone! Let her remain as patron of this place as I," she sang "I am free!"

Giggling, she dashed toward the old man, wrapping him in a heavy embrace. She was strong. He could feel her muscles against him, and the woman could have lifted him and tossed him across the room if she had wanted.

"I am a goddess, unbound once more!" she proclaimed, still holding him tight. "Seek me oh ye mongers of war, ye delvers of wisdom, ye crafters, ye just and ye plotters! I am yours to call, your light and salvation once again!"

She released the old man from her embrace at this, but not before she had planted a molten kiss upon his lips. She spun and whirled about the cavern upon her tip-toes, only returning to him after, still chuckling to herself.

"She will be furious at me for that, Brother's-Bane!" she said. "Do not take my embrace as an attempt at thieving you from her. I merely meant to reward you for my freedom! Tell her this straightaway or shall doubt spring where it ought not. Go!"

She waved her hand at him as if to dismiss the old man from her sight. Merlin did not stir.

"That is all well and good, Minerva. I am glad to see you as you are, as you want to be, but," he said, "go to whom? I still do not recall you nor this sister you speak of."

"But this cannot be!" she exclaimed. "Surely you recall my sister! If even this, my true form does not recall me to you, you must remember her!"

He shook his head. "I recall nothing, save for in dreams and tales that happened to me or any other before my appearance upon a lonely hill to the north of this place two months now since. I knew then nothing, even of myself. I have taken, in my way, the name of that place as my own. I am Merlin to those that know me and, save for the life of a small child, it is all that is beholden to me in this world." He sighed after saying this. It seemed such a hard admission for him after watching the goddess before him regain all that she once had lost.

"Then you have forgotten much," she said, a knowing smile upon her lips. "Here, let the goddess of wisdom grant you a boon."

Gripping the shaft of her spear tight, she lunged at the old man. Her strike was swift. The old man lurched backward and off his feet, the spear embedded in his abdomen. His back sank into the soft floor of the cavern. A golden light began to emanate from every bit of stone in the cave. All faded to white... and then he awoke...

Chapter Fifteen
In the Beginning

My father taught me to hunt. He taught me what it is to master another creature so completely that it has no chance of escape, of survival. He did this so that I might myself survive. I learned very quickly that to live, one must be both capable and willing to kill. In these mean times life is a race: a race for food, a race for breath, a race from those that would give chase. Those that would feast upon me and those I protect. Beasts. Gods. Demons. We men race against them all... and sometimes alongside them. All these things my father taught me. His name is Hyrius. He is a warrior, a hero, a hunter. My name is Orion and I am proud to call myself his son.

People will tell you that I am a liar. They will tell you that my father is none of these grand things. That he is a beekeeper, and nothing more. These people have no idea what sort of man my father is. They hear tales of him, perhaps, from the soldiers who oft demand tribute from my father as their battalions pass our homestead on their way to war. Or perhaps their tales come from the traders who tout the wax and honey from my father's hives as the best quality and the most reliable in the whole of Greece. I assure you, my father is, indeed, a beekeeper. He is a wonderfully talented one, in truth. It is not the trait that defines him. I was taller than him by the age of eleven, and yet my father towers over me to this day. The spirit of the man burns brighter than any god's. There is a light in him that I strive to contain every day. I have yet to stand up to the test.

When I was very young a woman brought me to my father in a bundle. She looked upon him with what he has told me was a mix of sorrow, regret, and the slightest glimmer of hope. My father tells me of the woman's eyes: a steely grey color, haloed in the green of a forest at midnight. She begged him silently with those eyes, pleaded with him to take me from her. He has told me that he felt himself fall deep into those forested eyes, that he did not know when it was that he reached out for me, did not know when it was that her arms no longer supported my tiny frame. He only knew that the instant I was in his arms and safe, she was gone. No footprints did she leave upon her departure. I was all that marked her presence at my father's house.

In those years my father was not yet a beekeeper. He was a man without a profession and without marketable skill. All that my father knew of hunting, of fighting, of character, he had learned through the wisdom of earth herself and from his failures to best her. To say this may sound as if Father was not intelligent. Were I not the benefactor of his teachings, would I be able, through force of my own sheer will, and armed with naught but that of my own creation find the skill to fell a boar? Would I know how to master a sling and stone with which to silently fell a deer? Would I have found in myself the perseverance to carve into the unfettered wilderness a life for those I might one day call my own? When called, would I have stood my ground when faced by a very god? I know that I would not have been so bold as to laugh at the prospect of battle with the lord of all the seas of this world. Without his hand at my back, constantly helping me forward, I would not have known how to stand my ground. This is the man whom I call Father. This is Hyrius.

It is night and I am thirteen. I stand a full head above my father's height and chide him over this before setting the table for dinner. There sounds a rapping on the door of our home. Its heavy timbers shudder with the force of the blows. Father waves me toward the door and I answer it as is my duty. I feel trepidation at opening the door, for Father built it himself and it has never let in the slightest draft or shuddered against the pounding wind or rain that came during winter. With the warmth of my father's gaze upon my back, however, I hesitate but a moment before opening the door.

There, upon the clay that is our stoop, flops a fish. I turn to Father, begin to ask the very obvious question of how such a creature has come to be at our door, and at such a strange hour of night. No sooner has *my head turned from the fish than its eyes fix themselves upon me and the thing swims through the air, directly at my foot. I cry out in pain as the fish's teeth clamp themselves around the hook of my heel. Something barbarous pulls me, out and down, through the doorway. I am dragged by my foot out across the plain in front of our small shack, all by a fish no larger than the span of my palm. Father is on his feet the instant I fall and follows me through the door faster than I had known a man could move, his hunting knife in hand. The fish, with its preternatural strength, is immediately outmatched by the sinew of my father's muscle as he catches us up. As I have done before, I watch for the signs and am rewarded as the animal's wit is stripped from it. He stays ahead of the creature, predicts its dodge to the left. Its very sight is taken from it next, as Father slices its eyes from their sockets before it can dodge away again. I feel my foot fall to the dirt, the tugging at my heel ceased. The teeth detach themselves from the bone of my heel and I am free.*

A shrill, gurgling sound fills the plain. Father is at my side, helping me to my feet. The fish flaps and bounces blindly against the dirt, its cry growing — not in volume, but in strength. The sound fills my ears and presses against my chest. It crushes in on me from all directions. The fish is now bounding, higher into the air with each attempt. My ears pop and I lose sight of our strange and dangerous visitor. When my eyes find it again, the fish hangs in mid-air, swimming in place ten feet ahead of me at a height twice that of my own. The pressure still crowds all around me, my chest struggling to expand enough to gain my next breath. The blind sockets of the fish's eyes locate me. Father steps before me. He is so close to me that it is an easy thing to see the effort it takes him to breathe. He shudders with each breath. His steps are metered, however, his resolve unshaken. A voice deep and powerful presses itself down my ear canal.

"You are mine, child," it booms. "The scent of the sea is in you. Your flesh is that which came from mine. I claim you now, child, and return you to the seas." My temples pound in hearing these words. It is as if the speaker is within my very skull!

"Your claim on my son means nothing to me," I hear Father say then. His voice sounds far off. It is muffled, as if he is speaking from within a sealed room. "My son's life is mine to mold, not that of some

fish-sprite sent by the demons of the blue," he says.

The voice in my skull erupts with rage. "You dare speak so to me, human? You are naught to me. You are a man, a member of the frailest of races that dwell upon the earth. I am that which sustains you and all those that reside here upon the land. I am Lord and Master to all those that call the sea home. I am a GOD!"

With this, the fish goes rigid. Its head spreads outward, split like a fruit, and peels itself apart. From the opening steps the god Poseidon. His form is that of a man, yet he stands fully twice the height of my father, his hair flowing in some unseen current. He points his hand toward me. As if we are beneath the sea, I feel the wake of this movement push past Father through the air.

"That child is no longer yours, fragile man-ling. He was absconded with whilst I rode the tides; but now I reclaim him to the sea, for his strength is mine."

"My son is indeed strong, oh god of the waters," Father says, "but I do not see any water here, and it is into a man he will grow, not a god. It is I who shall make sure of that, not some fish who appears on doorsteps and drags children into the night."

"You speak boldly for a creature so thoroughly outmatched," says Poseidon then. "You dare insult the god of all the waters of the earth. The thread of your life began to be stretched over the shears of the Moirai when you defied my wishes. Now it most surely is fraying along their blade, soon to be cut."

Poseidon raises his hands, grasping the very moisture from the air. The earth trembles beneath my feet. The air moistens around me and I feel a warm vapor rise from the earth. The moist topsoil around my feet cracks and dries. The field in which we stand withers, its own moisture joining into droplets with the steam rising from the land. Poseidon clenches his fists and the droplets — thousands of them — hover in the air all about us.

"Do you see now, mortal? Do you see what power it is I control? The oceans drive themselves into all the lands of this world. There is not a scratch of earth that I cannot claim as my domain," he booms.

I see Father's back tense. I have never seen him afraid, but faced with such a being how can he but be so? Fear seeps into my bones. The effort it takes to breathe now makes my chest burn. Lights dance before my eyes and I fall to my knees. Father hears me fall and speaks.

"My son, stand with your father. The danger is not so great."

He is not afraid. I struggle with my footing but cannot find it. My lungs will not fill. I feel myself slipping into darkness... my eyes closing of their own accord — and then there is Father's hand pressing against my own, dragging me upward and to my feet. I stand again. Somehow, breath finds its way into my lungs. I open my eyes and look into the face of my father. His face is stern, yet kind.

"Stand with me, my son," he says again.

There is a rush of wind and water and I feel many tiny impacts sear across my arms and shoulders. Water speeds past me along currents of air, scratching my flesh as it passes. Father's eyes widen and he heaves a deep sigh, taking great labor to do so. Only now do I notice why only my arms had felt the burn of the droplets as they passed. Father stands between me and the god.

"You dare insult me so as to turn your back upon me mortal? Did you think that atop your many defiances thus far, I would suffer such disgrace? You shall suffer before your death this day, farmer," speaks Poseidon.

"Your boasts and your bravado will win you neither the day nor my son, monster!" says Father, turning to face the god. It takes him a great deal of effort to do so.

"You are barely able to stand, human — and you shall not be able to do even that for very long. I shall tear your soul from this plane and send you to meet my brother in the land of the dead. It is then that I shall take what is..."

"You are wrong, Poseidon! I can do ever so much more than stand! You shall not have my son this day!" roars my father, his eyes blazing. He is as a wild beast before my eyes. I am too swept up by Father's zeal to know to cringe before such ferocity.

Father holds aloft his hunting knife, and before the laughter can escape the lips of the god of all the seas, hurls it as hard as he can. His aim is not at the face of the god. The knife instead flies back toward our home, back toward the small squat structures that sit in the front of our meager dwelling. The hilt of the knife thuds soundly against the wall of the closest hive.

Poseidon's laughter is that of pure mirth. "You cast off your blade as to face me unarmed, whelp? It is indeed a pleasant day on which I find someone so deserving of the torments which I shall now rain upon you," he chuckles. He raises his hand to send thousands of droplets down upon Father once more. The droplets congeal, they form a wave which hangs in the air, a wave meant to come crashing down upon Father's head, meant to drown him where he stands.

As he begins to lower his hand I become aware of a new sound. The pressure against my ears must have masked it until now. Now as clear as the first sounds of morning, I hear it — a low hum that seems to come from all directions, at once near and far away. The stars twinkle above as tiny specks of black whiz past me. On they fly past Father, some alighting upon him for a moment before continuing on to their enemy.

The swarm is immense. The hives have emptied themselves in response to the attack that has come unwarranted upon the small walls of their home. They move in no one direction at any time as they descend upon Poseidon, but in all directions at once. There is no one target for the god to aim his wave at any longer but thousands, hundreds of thousands. I begin to notice welts upon the skin of the god... they are small, but marks they are — and their numbers are growing. Poseidon tries to fend the bees off with his wave of congealed droplets, but the bees dodge it as if it were so much muslin flapping in the wind. The god bellows his pain:

"This cannot be! Such lowly creatures cannot harm a god!"

"You are the one who was arrogant, Poseidon," Father replies, a grin spreading upon his face. "You traveled far from your realm to come here tonight. Did you not think that I knew of how your power diminishes the farther you go from your true home? Did you not think that I would notice that your form this night is that of a man? With your form the same as mine, with you so great a distance from your realm, you are naught but a shadow of a god. Your flesh is as weak as my own, oh 'great' lord of the seas!"

Poseidon's eyes go wide. I am sure he can feel the venom of the bees building within his flesh, even as their spent bodies fall at his feet. On and on they hurl themselves upon him, on and on until the god can no longer keep hold of his grip upon the water that he has pulled from the earth. His wave comes crashing down upon the land at his feet, and *the great god of the seas begins to thrash his arms about in vain like a common peasant.*

"Beekeeper! I shall not forget this day!" he cries.

The body of Poseidon explodes into foam, leaving only his eyes to hover where he had been, the two connected to one another by the body of a small, black crab. The creature falls to earth and begins to scuttle away through the fields, a small cloud of bees still stinging it between the joints of its armor as it goes.

Father turns to me. Only now do I see the blood running down his back and his arms, only now do I see his knees trembling. I throw his arm over my shoulder, crouching to keep my shoulders below his. Father accepts my help.

"Let us go inside, Son," he says. "I would like a warm cup of soup."

It is not until after I have carried Father to the hearth and built a fire, after I have dressed and attended his wounds, after I have mixed his soup and set the kettle to the flame, that I can allow my mind to return to the events that took place outside our door. Questions swim in schools through my brain. I — the son of mighty Poseidon? How could such a thing come to pass? Why would the god-brother of High Zeus come to steal me away in the dead of night? And — most wondrous of all — how in the name of all the gods had my father, a mortal man and mere beekeeper, been able to fend off one of the greatest of all the gods?

Father raises a hand to me as I begin to stutter what would assuredly have been a malformed question in his direction.

"Hush now, Son. It has been a troubled-enough night, already. Let us not add to our burden this day with that which can be told in its own due time."

I dare not question him again this night. I finish preparing our soup, help Father to swallow his and to keep it down, and then, against many a protest, carry the great man off to his bed. I make sure the door is latched solidly before shuffling off to my own cot.

Sleep comes slowly, amidst images of gods, weapons, bees, and the greatest man I might ever know... commanding them all as if they were mere toys.

Chapter Sixteen

Godfall

The old man awoke coughing water from his lungs. Once more he lay upon his back on the floor of the cave of Minerva. Recalling his having been gored by the goddess' spear, he searched his abdomen for the weapon. His body was unharmed. Even his robes bore no mark of having been run through.

The cavern was oddly dark as he rose to his feet. The images of the giant boy and Poseidon, of Hyrius and the bees still swam in his head. He wondered if such a vision could be truth, if he could trust what the spear of Minerva had shown him. As he stood there pondering, a voice solemn and quiet carried across the cavern to him.

"It was Athena," the voice said. "That was the name you knew me by in our fleeting time together, so long ago."

His eyes found her then, a dark figure across the grotto. She spoke again as he approached her.

"Had I known, had I remembered how deep into the past we had to dive... I may not have ruled you worthy of such a boon, Orion," she said. Once more she knelt beside the desiccated pile of feather and bone which had once been her owl. Now and again she raised a handful of the downy corpse, watching as the feathers sifted between her fingers only to float back down to the floor.

"What does this mean?" he asked. "What can I make of such a vision of the past, so long gone?"

"I had thought," she said, "that in seeing it, you would be freed of this, your carbuncled form." She waved a hand at him haplessly, quickly returning it to the body of the bird. "Memory had broken me from Sulis, and I believed you to have undergone a similar binding to some native deity. I thought to show you your own true self again, Orion." There was a note of sorrow in her voice now. "But that was fallacy from the start, Cousin-Half-God."

This new manner of speech did not suit the beautiful and vibrant goddess he had seen emerge from her mental and physical shell, thought Merlin. Had the loss of her pet truly been so great as to eclipse her own joyous release? He stepped closer to her still, trying to discern her shape from those of the shadows. There was something wrong. Even in this dim light, her body should have luminesced.

"Come no closer," she said. "I do not wish you to look upon my ruin."

Merlin stopped. What had transpired during his time gazing upon the past? Was Minerva indeed injured? What could have injured such a being as this?

"Knowledge of myself has proven my unwitting destruction, Brother-Never-To-Be," she said. "It was Sulis, for all her mangling of my memory, that sustained me." She stood then, her eyes visible and dimly twinkling in the shadows. "I fed upon her, taking the prayers of her worshippers as my own." There was a definite air of despair in her voice now. "She was the goddess of this spring before I came here with my Legions. We came to conquer this land, to make it part of the empire. We succeeded in body, but the savages of this land still clung to Sulis and her ilk for prayer and healing. Thus did I come here and bind us together. I had meant for her to be enveloped and woven into the thread of my being. I did not understand the risk."

She laughed, a resonant and brassy laugh devoid of mirth. "I, the goddess of wisdom, the oracle of Athens, did not understand." She stepped toward him, showing herself in the reflected light of the pool. She was now neither statue nor woman, but some tarnished version of both. Her flesh bore spots of rust and oxidization. Bruises and open sores leeched droplets of what looked like molten blood. A deep crack ran across her belly. "For what is a goddess," she continued, "when her followers are slaughtered? Does she even persist, or does she sink with the jetsam of the forgotten to be buried in the silt of history?"

Her gaze wavered a moment, the light in her eyes dimming further. When she looked back upon him, her eyes were not focused. It was as if she no longer saw him, but merely saw that place where she knew him to be.

"You have a strange buoyancy," she said. "The tides tell me they have washed over your frame nigh on twice as long as they have my own, yet I can recall the very moment of your conception. Tell me how this has come to pass, Orion, so that I may yet stretch these waning hours of my own into centuries."

Merlin could make no sense of her meaning. "That I was conceived as long ago as you say, Minerva, is quite revelation enough. I cannot know how my years have weathered me like the cliffs when yours have not aged you in the slightest. Let us say that it is likely that I have had a harder go in this world. Let us say, until proven otherwise, that how it is that I have survived these many long years has not been so graceful as to be encased in a metal hide."

The goddess snorted at this, coughing rust upon her wrist. "Call me by Athena, Orion, for it is as she that I may see you clearly. And I do so wish to see clearly before my untimely end." She smiled weakly. "I am young for the years of our kind yet, as should you be. Your mother in perpetuity is evidence of that. I have merely lost my flock, and so myself."

She was quiet a moment then. Still she could not focus her eyes upon him. Her gaze lazed, unfocused about the cavern. Now and again, her eyes broadened and she seemed to smile, as if recognizing a particular column of rock or shadow.

"Was ours so short-lived a house, Orion?" she asked. "All but one of my family are gone. Did we burn ourselves out, shining so brightly? Would that we had foreseen this day, for we may not so readily have spilt the blood of your forefathers. My sister... you and she might have been a salve to our self-inflicted wounds." Her head lolled back toward him. "You were so happy, you and she. But alas..."

Her sobs shook her frame now, metal grinding upon flesh. He caught her in an embrace, more for want to cease the strain upon her body than anything else. She felt lighter to his touch than before. The rust had taken much of her frame already. Comforted, her shuddering lessened.

She pulled her head from him suddenly then, so violently that he feared for her form. Her eyes were focused but she did not look upon him directly, rather at a spot just above and to the left of his left eye.

There was a look of incredulity upon her face.

"You mention it so lightly!" she said, nearly disgusted now. "Yet you hide away that which is most precious to our ilk."

He did not know of what she spoke, but instead looked questioningly upon her.

"The life of a small child, you call it!" She shook with rage, wanting to strike at him. He held her tight, not allowing her to do him, or her ever-weakening frame, further harm. "Where is *my* Savior? Where is that which comes from the very æther to rescue me? Do I not warrant it? I — who was once worshipped by fully half the world of man?"

"The child?" he said. "What do you know of the child I now claim as my protectorate?"

She raged at him once more, this time freeing her fist from his grip. He felt a rib crack under her blow, but held her still. Wheezing himself now, he knew he must gain what knowledge she had of the boy.

"I saved the child," he said, "because of a tug from deep within my heart. It was as if I was guided by a hand incorporeal and beyond my own understanding. I would do the same for you if I knew how!"

He was shouting now, trying to force his meaning into her struggling mind.

"Fool!" she proclaimed. "It was not you who did the rescuing! You, nameless and forgotten and half-blooded! It is a rare stone indeed that skips along the surface of the tide, heeding not the æons as they spin beneath it. And you have caught hold of it?! Caught one of the stones that skips across our realm, sending out its ripples as far as can be tracked!"

"I do not understand of what you speak, Athena!" said Merlin. "But you shall shake yourself apart if you persist in this assault!"

Her eyes shifted, looking upon his at last. She relaxed her arms and allowed herself to be quieted. Her breast, now cracked itself, heaved a great sigh.

"What folly it is to be an oracle," she said, "to see others live and know it is not for you. I go, very soon now, to meet my father and kin."

Her face turned serious, her tone dire. "I shall call you Orion until I sink beneath the tide which now rises to capsize me, dear Cousin," she said, "but do not use that name beyond the border of this place. Do not even think it as your true name to yourself. As I was bound to Sulis, so are you tied to this child's word for you. If his belief in Merlin falters, if he does not believe you his hearth and home and guide, so shall you fall as I do now. For better or worse, you are no longer the child as whom you were born. Leave this place as Merlin and persist."

"What if something should happen to the child?" asked Merlin.

"The child shall one day die, Orion. Then shall you sink into the silt as readily as I do. Keep safe and strong your flock of one, long as you can, and learn. For in that one you have caught the power which sustains your own."

She was now weaker in his grasp, her weight too much for her to hold aloft. He lowered her to the ground to ease her pain.

"Can you not regain your place upon your pedestal, Athena? Can you not return to a metal form?" he said.

"That is the pedestal of Sulis now," she replied. "My followers were forced from these shores by the very blood that sired your salvation. Such has always been the story of our two houses, eh Demi-Cousin? Both houses, tied to the ever-present tides which buffet us in perfect meter upon our opposing shores. Both, shining or rough, erode at their whims.

"Learn to float, Orion!" she pleaded, "Watch the spin of the skipping stone and learn, for the depths of the sea are dark and would soon swallow you up. We are not so quick as to skip, our ilk. Learn to float."

At this she seemed to slip away, her eyes glazing over and her once-more metal frame going stiff. In his mind, however, her voice persisted a moment more. "Do not visit the darkened pool again, Orion. I can no longer save you from the clutches of that which resides therein." Her body then gave a final shudder and crumbled before him. Only her shining head remained, staring lifelessly up at him from his hands.

For hours he sat there, holding her in silence.

No longer did the shining feathers hang in the air as he exited the temple. The little glittering things had all sunk beneath the water that pooled upon the floor. Unseen eyes watched him from beneath the surface as he turned to gaze upon the temple once more before his departure. They hovered a moment upon the charm which now adorned his wrist: a simple bronze coil. Then they too sank into the utter blackness beneath the surface of the water.

Chapter Seventeen
Revelation

The whole of the morning had passed by as Maggie and Arthur sat at the table over their now stone-cold bowls of stew. Arthur had been so wrapped up in the telling of the dream, and Maggie so interested in the thing, that the sun was already past its zenith before either of them noticed. Maggie let out a bit of a gasp when she saw this, realizing that she had let the bulk of the day slip away from her. By then, Arthur had just been getting to the appearance of the strange woman at the end of his dream, though, and she figured it best to let the child finish.

"I was sure she looked right at me, too," he said, "as if she knew I was there — which nobody else did! It was like she was telling me I shouldn't be there!" he finished, his chest heaving a bit from the exertion.

"Shouldn't be in your own dream?" asked Maggie. "Seems a bit presumptuous, doesn't she?"

She laughed at this, but Arthur looked less sure.

"Well, what if it wasn't my dream, Maggie?" he said. "What if it was another of Merlin's stories... but he's just telling it to me from farther away?"

Even Arthur himself seemed to be pondering the possibility of this as he said it. Maggie gave him a playfully questioning look.

"Sounds to me lad, that it's you what's seen everythin' so clearly, so. Who's to say that that lovely, strange place you see durin' the stories isn't the work o' your own imagination an' not the old man's witchery, hey?"

Arthur hadn't thought of this. He screwed his eyes up, in deep thought.

"Seems to explain how it is you'd know what's next, mmm?" she said, almost to herself as she got up and tossed the remainder of their morning stew out the window. Bartholomew, who had been lurking underneath the table for some time now, made a streak of himself bounding after the plunder.

"Sort of," said Arthur, "but I didn't know who this Abner was at all until Merlin told me, and I still haven't the foggiest idea what the story has to do with anything whatever."

"Hah!" chuckled Maggie, "Sure'n a child never needed reasonin' for his mind t' go a-wanderin'?" She patted Arthur's head, waving him away from the table. "Run along and scrape up your knee, now Artie. That's a good lad."

Arthur did as he was told, even going so far as to actually scrape his knee as he bounded about that afternoon. All the while, and this was the likely culprit of the scraped knee, he mulled over the conversation of the day. Eventually, he came to the conclusion that, as Maggie assumed, the stories and their vivid nature were due to some working of his own mind. How, then, had this dream depicted the very next bit of Abner's tale? How had his dream told so much of this new Clay fellow?

Surely, it must be Merlin's doing. If that was the case then likely there was a reason to all of it. What that could be the boy did not know, but as the shadows of evening stretched across the fields a theory began to form in his mind. The longer he dwelt upon it, the more certain he was that it must be right. He did not share it with Maggie, however, upon returning to the cottage for supper. Nor did he do so the next night, nor the night after that. In part, this was because he thought that she might disbelieve him; but more than that, he didn't want her to somehow disprove him. So dear and so important had his theory become to him that he now handled it as if it were so delicate a thing that the mere utterance of it might cause it to come undone.

And so it went, Maggie blithely unaware of Arthur's secret; he silently keeping watch over it, always waiting for the next dream.

Chapter Eighteen

Castle Tintagel

The evening wended its way toward night, the first stars beginning to wink their tiny lights down upon Tintagel. The night watchmen, now finishing their supper, would soon relieve the day's honor guard. In waiting for their replacements, the honor guard had begun to fidget and pace, their overall feeling being that, at such hours, a proper changing of the guard was unwarranted and flamboyant. This in part was due to Tintagel's being set upon a great stony karst of an island, unto which only a thin sliver of a causeway allowed entry.

The road snaked down the cliffs of the mainland to this causeway then wound its way up the karst to the castle gates. At any hour passage proved a laborious journey, but after nightfall the causeway was nigh on impassible. Over the years, the lack of light upon the cliffs had sent many a brave soul crashing to the rocks and waves below. The rising of the tide, too, had claimed its fair share of would-be travelers to this far-flung islet. Even as the sun still clung to the further reaches of the sky, the waves began to wash over the thin tongue of land by which the mainland clung so perilously to Tintagel. By the time the night watch had settled into their posts, the causeway would be fully submerged, undetectable below the swirling currents and foam until late the next morning. It was only due to these natural protections that the honor guard of Tintagel were able to gaze deeply into the orange and pink clouds and to wager upon which stars would shine first each evening.

It could have been noted upon this particular evening that the Burin, the arrowhead affixed to Orion's drawn bow, shone like the eye of the devil himself. Unfortunately, this portent was overlooked as a much more obvious and equally unwarranted apparition appeared at roughly the same time.

A boom echoed against the gatehouse walls, seemingly coming from all corners of the earth at once. It took those closest to the gate a moment to locate the source of the noise and when they did they could hardly believe what they beheld. There, standing near flush with the Main Gate stood a curled and bedraggled figure of an old man. A dirty travelling cape was mortared about him, from which only a bony hand protruded. The man looked as death himself come to call upon Castle Tintagel. The bony fist raised and then fell once more, rapping again at the gate, sending sound and shudders throughout the gatehouse.

A summoning haloo was called across the walls then, and a brave voice called down to the man. "Sirrah!" shouted the voice, "I am called Pelias and am Captain of the Guard here at Tintagel. What means this assault at my gate in these perilous hours of night?"

Below, the old man took a stride away from the gate so as to see who had addressed him. In tandem with this motion, the hood of the man's cloak fell about his shoulders, revealing a tangle of grey hair and beard. The old man smiled up toward the battlements.

It was a smile that Pelias did not return. The Captain of the Guard had a hawk-like look about him, from the hook of his nose to the severe glint which at all times inhabited his gaze. The old man felt this gaze upon himself for but a moment before Pelias spoke again.

"You wear the robes of a pauper, a traveling vagabond Sirrah, but they belie your true nature," he said. "Upon your wrist there is a bangle so fine that I have never beheld its peer."

Again the old man smiled up to Pelias. "A recent acquisition," the aged man replied, his voice clear and strong, "though I admit the full cost of the thing I have yet to bear out."

"And that sword, Sirrah, is it too..."

"I am charmed that you find my possessions so fine as to warrant such inspection Mr. Pelias," said the old man, "but what I carry with me tonight is no matter of import. I have business this night with your Lord Pendragon. Let me in." At this the old man moved toward the door again, but Pelias shouted down to him again, this time allowing a fair amount of warning to be carried in his tone.

"Your sword, Sirrah!" he shouted, "I can see, even in this dwindling light that the blade which you so carelessly hang at your hip was wrought by the skill of the western tribes. The hilt is bronze and the guard carved in the pattern of lizard-scale."

"I am glad you take note of it!" said the old man, "but my business is with your lord..."

"Your business is with me, Sirrah!" commanded Pelias, "not only because I am commander of this gate which bars the way irrevocably to my lord, but because I would have you tell me what ill you have done to Sir Kaye, my brother-in-arms!"

With this he held aloft his own sword so that the old man below might see it. It was unmistakably the twin of that which the old man wore. The old man smirked a third time. Pelias prickled with indignity. His wrist twisted, turning the blade of his sword above the head of the old man. Six arrows nocked quietly into six bows.

"You are friend to Kaye, are you?" The old man asked. "I half expected you to know him. It would seem that the brash and the wicked have wriggled their way behind every wall and edifice of import to be found here-about."

Pelias ground his teeth. He indicated his sword with a nod. "This sword and its brother, which you now bear, were awarded Sir Kaye and I for services martial, rendered to Lord Pendragon and to his brother Ambrosius before him, gods rest his soul. We were but squires in the war with Rome, but were honored as knights bold by the Sibling Lords. And now you dare to assault the very door of Uther bearing that which was forged to protect it."

The old man seemed to ponder this revelation for a moment, fingering the hilt of the sword at his waist. When he looked up to Pelias again, much to the guard's torment, his smile had broadened. Indeed, the old man practically chuckled in his reply.

"I had wondered," he said, "why this blade was so reluctant to do its work upon this place. You see, before I took to your gate with my fist I drew this sword, meaning of course to knock the gate from its hinges and be done with the matter. The sword merely hung before the gate as passive as a lamb, and so I was forced to knock and to be graced with your pleasant discourse. Open your gate, Pelias. I shall not ask again."

Pelias exchanged an incredulous look with the assembled guard. It was clear that they thought the man below mad. Whether it had been the old man's belief that he could force open the gate of Tintagel or that he somehow thought that a sword had a will and could impose itself upon its wielder that drove them to this conclusion it was hard to say, but mad he surely must be. Mad and dangerous. Sir Kaye's sword was evidence enough of that.

"You have not answered me concerning Sir Kaye, Stranger," said Pelias. "Tell me of him and my guards may yet spare you."

"Then we stand at a mutual impasse, Pelias," said the old man. "For you have no more granted me audience than I have granted you tidings of Sir Kaye."

Pelias made to reply to this, but the old man held his hand aloft and continued on.

"I propose a trade. I shall tell you of Kaye and you shall let me pass peacefully to the hall of Lord Pendragon. In thanks for this kindness, I shall spare your lives."

It was Pelias' turn to guffaw, and he did so with as much mirth as he could muster.

"No one merely strolls into Castle Tintagel and demands the ear of her lord, Stranger," he said. Your greatest hope is to set yourself at the mercy of my men. If your message is worthy of it, it may find the ear of the lord in due time. If not..."

"Do not think that I have not noticed that you call me 'stranger' now, instead of the more kindly 'sirrah' which you offered up so eagerly a moment ago, Pelias. I would also have you know that I have not failed to notice the signal you gave to your men a moment ago."

The old man's hand rested now upon the hilt of Sir Kaye's sword, a movement that would have signaled danger had his predicament not seemed so hopelessly disadvantageous.

"Further," he continued, "I need neither your permission nor your aid in meeting Lord Pendragon, oh Captain of the Wall. "I shall meet your lord. The only change, in the entirety of this outcome, is whether your castle maintains its gate and how many guards remain to stand atop it."

Not seeming to wish to fell a man both ancient and mad, Pelias opted for a new tactic in dealing with the situation.

"The hour is late and growing later, *Sirrah*," he said, visibly restraining himself from using the harsher terms he so dearly wished to call the old man. "In these late years of our lord, his health does not permit him to sit at court so well into the night. Give me your name. I shall see to it that Lord Pendragon is made aware of your visit at the earliest possible moment tomorrow."

The old man considered this a moment.

"The name Merlin shall suffice as well as any, though it shall mean nothing to your Lord Pendragon, I assure you." A wry wrinkle wound its way about the corner of the old man's mouth then. "I shall tell you, as a sort of down payment upon our agreement Pelias, that it was your friend Kaye who gave me that moniker."

Pelias' face made a sort of flattening motion, as if bracing for whatever was to come next.

"Kaye would tell you now if properly goaded, oh Knight of the Gate, that my disdain for obstruction is made ever the more evident when that which stands in my way is the stubbornness of foolish men. Pray do not keep me waiting long in the morning or you shall learn this for yourself," he said, turning. "Or I shall have a *pair* of these lovely swords to wear at my hip."

"You shall not have any more such princely gifts, Merlin. Of that I assure you," said Pelias.

The old man laughed.

"This blade is nothing as compared with the treasure I come to speak of with your lord, Pelias, nothing at all."

"Oh? Well pray tell me, *Sirrah*: What is this treasure of which you speak so that I might tell Lord Pendragon of it? Mayhap this shall be what secures your audience, eh?"

One of the guard stifled a laugh. Pelias shot the man a chastising glare, but it was clear that the captain regarded Merlin in the same light as did his men: a perilous old beggar and a ruffian.

Merlin merely smiled back up to the lot of them. "At my humble table, in my far-flung hovel there sups a boy who is heir to this and all of his father's lands. He is the little Lord Pendragon and I would see him reunited with his line. Tell me, Pelias, what do you think he is worth to your lord?"

For a moment the top of the wall was as silent and as rigid as the great hall of the temple of Sulis. Not a man uttered a word nor stirred in his mail. It was Pelias who broke the silence.

"There is no such child!" he said. "Long lost is the Lady Pendragon, and herself barren at that. It is a cruel thing you say to us this eve, Merlin. An heir would indeed mean many a thing to this land, some of them which I daren't imagine."

"Tell your lord, Pelias. Tell him I bring tidings of his son," smiled Merlin. With that the old man strode away from the wall of Castle Tintagel, his step light and gay. Pelias and the guard merely stood, stunned and confused as they watched him depart. He was nearly down to the causeway when they saw him turn. A voice strong and clear rang in their ears then.

"I shall return at first light, Pelias! Make sure that the gate stands ready to welcome me!" said Merlin's voice, and with that, he was gone from their view.

Chapter Ninteen
Dawn

A gossamer pink veil, the first harbinger of the dawn that was to come, was still caressing away the dark and the stars. It was that very moment when all was still, as if the earth herself held her breath in anticipation of the day. Seabirds soon would begin to rouse in their nests and send their calls echoing about the cliffs below, rising to beckon the residents of Castle Tintagel from their beds.

Of the many pleasures Tintagel offered its residents, this method of waking was one of the more cherished. Yet today, the calls of the gulls and swifts would not be given their due. Their calls would fall upon deaf ears, for the castle was mustering. The clattering of mail and the creaking of doors bounded through the stillness of the pre-dawn. Against the keep and curtain wall bounced the voices of men, shifting themselves to the ready. A glimmering plate helm bounced in and out of sight between the crenellations of the gatehouse. Pelias had arrived at the watch.

The old man, seated upon a sizable stone which lay a few paces out from the gate, could not help but chuckle to himself as he saw the younger man's haughty face appear, red with indignation, above the battlements. Pelias' face was gone as soon as it had appeared, but his indignation remained naked upon the air as his bellowed remarks bounded down through the stillness to the old man's ears.

"What is the meaning of this?!" Pelias barked.

A second voice, stammering as it replied, followed the captain's down from the wall.

"Beggin' the Captain's pardon, Sir! We thought you should know he'd returned, Sir."

"And WHY, might I ask, has he not been dealt with as I ordered?" Pelias said.

"Well you see, Sir..."

"Did I not give you precise instructions to fire upon the old man the moment he was seen at the gate again?"

"You did, Sir!"

Merlin's eyebrows rose in a nonplussed sort of way as he listened from below. He smacked his lips, noting their dryness. He had a skin of fresh water somewhere in his robes, he thought, but where had it got off to? He was still rummaging about, his right arm a foot up his left sleeve, when Pelias' shining helmet bobbed over the side of the wall again. The Captain of the Guard thrust his arm out in the old man's direction, his face visibly reddening.

"Then WHY does he still breathe?!" Pelias spat, again disappearing from view.

"We — we did fire upon him, Sir. To be sure we did, but..."

"Spit it out man!"

"None of us was able to strike him, Sir."

The man sounded ashamed. The only shame Merlin could see was that he had yet to locate his water-skin. His hand finally closed about something soft, and with a triumphant smile Merlin pulled forth from his sleeve — an apple. He squinted at the thing. It was decidedly not a skin of water. Furthermore, it looked to be well past its prime. 'But', thought the old man, 'so is its owner, and who am I to turn it away for that?' The apple was soft but not without refreshment, and the old man smiled as he turned his attention back to the wall, a dribble of juice running down into his beard.

"You missed EVERY time?!" Pelias shouted.

"Well I wouldn't so much as call it a miss, Sir..."

"Did you hit him?"

"No, Sir."

"Then you missed!"

"Beggin' your pardon, Sir, but..."

"How many of you did I post at this gate through the night, Watchman?"

"There's four of us, Sir."

"And how were you armed?"

"Sir?"

"How many arrows, Watchman? How many arrows were you given?"

"Oh, the full twenty, Sir! Just as ordered!"

The Watchman seemed pleased with this answer, Merlin mused. It was likely the man's first correct response of the whole exchange. It was a pity really, what the man was bound to have to reveal next.

"That's *eighty* arrows!" said Pelias. "Are you telling your captain that in eighty attempts, none of you managed to strike the feeble old bastard down?"

"Oh, no Sir! We had the word sent down for more arrows twice, Sir."

The man still sounded chipper. An astounding fellow, Merlin thought. He did not envy the captain the command of such a charge.

"Twelve quivers emptied and not a hit!" Pelias roared. "What, pray tell did you attempt after such an authoritative display of ineptitude?!"

"Well, we stopped calling for arrows, for one. Didn't seem much use, did it? Anyway, we reckon he isn't so feeble as he lets on."

Pelias' grimace could be felt through the stone of the wall.

"You mean to say you did nothing?"

"We thought we'd wait the situation out, as it were, Sir. It was only when we saw the dawn approaching that we thought the idea a bad one and sent word to wake you and the garrison, Sir."

There was a moment of silence from the wall then. During this time Merlin had the time to notice that he had eaten his apple to the stem and, pitching it over his shoulder, proceeded to wipe the juice from his fingers with the corner of his sleeve.

"How long has this farce of guardsmanship been going on, Watchman?" Pelias' voice was quieter now but no less dangerous, Merlin thought.

"Well, that's the fantastical thing of it all, Sir. He showed up at the gate some three hours ago, he did," the watchman said, his tone perplexed. "I don't see how he done it, m'self."

"I begin to doubt whether there is an occurrence upon this earth that does not send you into fits of stupefaction, Watchman."

"But sir," said the watchman weakly, "Three hours ago it was blackest night. The tide would've been up above the causeway, wouldn't it — and the waves all crashin' about, as you like?"

"And?"

This was odd, mused Merlin. It was Pelias' turn not to understand the other man's meaning.

"Well the blighter arrived dry as a pauper in a pub, if you will Sir."

"I see," said Pelias. "And how do you suppose that he managed such an impossible feat?"

The man must have given no answer, for the next sound was Pelias' voice again, louder and once again full of rancor.

"Well perhaps instead of standing there gathering dew, you would do well to examine the facts of the case! The man clearly never left as we had thought him to, but rather stuck out the night behind some boulder or other down along the cliff-side, waiting for you half-sleeping, half-addled bastards to grow so feeble as to not be able to strike at him given ten thousand arrows!"

The old man stood, taking a moment to straighten his aged spine with care. The time was approaching now. He hiked a knee close to his chest, pulled it close, released it, and held his ground before the stone. One hand rested upon the hilt of Kaye's sword in a relaxed sort of manner, the other wheedling the last droplets of juice from his beard.

"There will be lashes, Watchman, make no mistake of that. There will be lashes for this incompetence!"

There were then the sounds of a scuffle atop the wall and the sound of someone being knocked onto his back. Pelias then appeared, his face a violent shade of maroon. In his hand was the watchman's bow, an arrow nocked at the ready. The arrow was loosed faster than a man takes to draw breath, Pelias letting out a shout as he let it fly.

For an instant, the look on the Captain of the Guard's face was that of manic triumph. He was on the verge of letting out a fit of victorious laughter until the arrow began to waver. By the time it fell, short of its mark, he had broken into what appeared to be a cold sweat. As the shaft splintered and rotted, his arm began to shudder. As the arrowhead, now a dull pebble, bounced along the ground, the bow dropped from his hand. Merlin let the bow finish its clattering before he spoke.

"Yesterday we spoke as civil men," he said, "but today you have taken to savagery, Pelias. I fear I shall have to return it to you in kind."

Three strides and he stood before the gate. With the fourth he brought it crashing down. Through the dust and timber he strode into the walled city of Tintagel. A pair of guards crawled about in the debris of the gate. He was past them before they were on their feet, already winding his way along the wide and lazy stair that serviced as the main road within the castle. Only small alleys split from the road as it wound its nautoloid way toward the High Bridge and the heart of Tintagel, the Keep of the Precipice.

An alarm had been raised as the gate had gone down and here and there a guard would dart out of a shop or alley before him, but none offered Merlin any true resistance. Shouts and the clatter of armored footsteps could be heard from atop the wall. No doubt Pelias and his men were keeping pace with him as best they could. It was of little concern to the old man. Already his business had been waylaid by them longer than he had been prepared to wait. Rounding a final corner and mounting the narrow stair that gave access to the High Bridge, Merlin nonetheless was made to stop. The High Bridge stood aloft, high as the curtain wall; and on either side of the Keep of the Precipice the wall wound about to meet the bridge. The bridge itself, a thin fifty-foot-long blade of ivory stone was manned to the very edges with a dense bramble of guardsmen, their shields a solid wall over which only their spears and pikes could be seen. The wall on either side was manned with archers, their arrows nocked. At the far side of the bridge stood Pelias, his red face defiant. As Merlin surveyed the scene, he thought he detected a wary smile upon the man's face.

"Out of room, old man?" Pelias shouted, the uncertainty in his voice almost masked by his bravado.

"Young man," said Merlin, his tone stern, "I have offered you only glad tidings and have received only threats and attack in return. Lord Uther is due the tidings I bring him, tidings of his son and heir!"

As he said this, the old man noted the shifting of a number of the guard. Along the wall, an archer lowered his bow slightly. He went on.

"I come to deliver these tidings, by means peaceable or otherwise, and no mere nettle of guards nor their over-eager captain shall keep me from this task."

More bows were lowering now; the spear wall splayed itself akimbo; and whispers were to be heard from behind shields. Pelias' eyes darted about, and he was just about to chastise his men back into formation when a deep and rumbling sound stole the breath from his lungs.

The door to the Keep was opening. Merlin inclined his head. Pelias spun violently on the spot. The door rumbled slowly forward until there appeared a slim and dark aperture. From this seemingly impassable crack slipped an old and matronly wisp of a man. He wore the fine silks and bangles of courtly life and had a low paunch that spoke of a cloistered and sedentary life. He raised a milky arm in a sort of hail and addressed Merlin.

"I am Conrad," he said, "and I am council to Lord Pendragon. Do forgive Pelias his impetuousness, for he is merely doing what he interprets to be his duty."

Pelias looked shocked at this. He looked about to his men for affirmation, but none met his gaze.

"Pelias," said Conrad, "do show our guest some manners will you? Make a way across the bridge; there's a good man."

Conrad rested his bangled hand limply upon Pelias' shoulder for a brief moment, removing it in a sort of condescending caress. Pelias slumped at this and gave only a nod to his men. The shield wall parted down its center and Conrad beckoned at Merlin to come across. Wary glances and a nervous silence floated along the bridge as Merlin made his way. Once he was across, Conrad, whose eyes had never left the old man, addressed him again.

"Tell me Stranger," he said, "what is your name and from whence do you hail?"

"I am called Merlin," the old man replied. "I have travelled here from the protectorate of Lord Ektor, and I would speak to your master, Conrad."

"Has Ektor taken to calling himself a lord now?" said Conrad. "Last I was aware, he was merely a knight with a small holding. Well, no bother. Do come in."

Merlin could not help but note as he followed Conrad within the Keep of the Precipice that Pelias had returned to a deep shade of maroon.

Chapter Twenty

Conrad

"I am afraid," said Conrad, once the two of them had entered the Keep, "that I cannot allow you to see Lord Pendragon just yet."

Merlin whirled about to face the man, and for a moment could not find him. The Keep was utterly dark inside and his eyes had not yet adjusted to the shift in the amount of light.

"Do not worry," came Conrad's voice, a whisper voiced from Merlin's shoulder, "It shall not be long that you will have to wait. I merely wish to confirm your claim so that we might present a coherent tale to the lord. His time is so very scarce, you see."

Merlin's eyes, now more adjusted, picked out the shape of Conrad sweeping silently along the entryway before him. He followed closely behind as the councilor wended his way down a hall and up a stair and around a corner into a small room with a low door.

Inside, there were lit a pair of fat candles that sent low shadows dancing about the room. The walls were lined with shelves upon which sat stacks of scrolls, loose parchments, and a smattering of bound tomes. Stacks of papers were piled about on the floor where they did not fit on the shelves, giving the already small room a feeling of choking closeness. Here and there an empty bottle of wine could be seen amidst the mess as well, and a large goblet sat at a small desk at the far end of the room.

"The spoils of war, I'm afraid," said Conrad. "These documents once belonged to the Romans. The brothers Pendragon discovered them after the sack of Londinium and appropriated them."

He moved across the small room with practiced care. Not a scrap of parchment stirred as he settled himself upon a dainty seat behind the desk.

"It was a tremendous find, though the Pendragons hardly took the time to discover its value. Here in this room," he said, with a grandiose wave of his hand, "lie the family histories of every king, chieftain or self-styled lord in Brittania." He raised his head and stared fixedly at Merlin. "You see," he went on, "the Romans were quite meticulous. Were it not for the sheer tenacity of the brothers Pendragon, I dare say they would rule us to this day. All claims to land or fealty are accounted herein," he said, adding with a smile, "that is all *true* claims."

His eyes having adjusted to the buffeting dark, Merlin strode across the small room, accidentally brushing a stack of papers with his robe. Conrad sighed dramatically.

"You do understand the importance of maintaining the order of these documents, my good fellow?" said Conrad, a heavy note of exasperation in his tone.

Merlin made a small sort of a noise akin to a 'tut', but could not be made to care any further. He thought he knew where this line of talk was going and he would have none of it.

"You say that the Romans kept these documents?" he said, glancing down upon the pages which he had disturbed. They seemed to be responses to some sort of census of lords and holdings. Merlin's eye paused upon a good number of names and holdings before resting languidly once more upon Conrad.

"Indeed," said Conrad, pursing his lips so tightly that they appeared as a thin penned line in the gloom.

"The Romans were driven from these shores many years ago, by your own lord I might add. So I must profess my ignorance upon how or why such a... remarkable horde?" shrugged Merlin, "is at all relevant to our business here."

Conrad was haughty now and was going to great lengths, thought Merlin, to show it. He rolled his eyes and harumphed, standing with his hands on his hips.

"I have *of course* maintained the research the Romans began!" he said. "Why, not a month goes by that I do not receive tidings from some lord or other, demanding that his heir be recognized in these pages!" He pointed a billowing sleeve at the parchment upon the desk.

"Here is all you need to concern yourself with, however: the line of Pendragon, from Uther and Ambrosius all the way back to the very first muck-dweller to bear their name! Now you will scarcely be able to read it, no doubt..."

"I can read it plainly as any," said Merlin, then pointing at the name Pendragon atop the page as evidence to his claim. There, it does indeed say Pendragon."

Conrad tutted dismissively.

"This is written in the old Roman, fool. Only those schooled by the Romans themselves can read it," he said. "You shall have to take my word for much of what is written here, but look there, at the bottom. I am sure that you can discern the strong 'U' in Uther's name?"

He lifted the scroll so close to Merlin's face then that the 'U' nearly eclipsed his field of vision. The parchment stank of mold.

"As you can see," said Conrad from behind the parchment, "Lord Uther never took a wife. He never fathered an heir. Of all of my labors here, you can be sure *that* one I have documented most correctly." He removed the parchment from Merlin's face, revealing his own smug grin.

"I could not help," said Merlin, kindly as he could muster, "but notice that someone — presumably yourself — has drawn a line beside Uther's name? Perhaps he was indeed to be wed at some time?"

"Bah!" said Conrad, "the hopes of a young and over-eager councilor. Nothing more, I assure you."

But there was a tremble in the man's wrist as he lay the parchment down upon the table again, a tremble which belied his words and emboldened his opponent.

"Am I to understand," said Merlin, "that you offer up this rotting scrap of ink upon stretched goat's flesh as proof irrefutable of a lifetime? A lifetime I might add, that by all accounts has been filled to brimming with conquest? Is this your incontrovertible proof that I have come here bearing false tidings?"

"Incontrovertible," smiled Conrad, showing his stained, yellow grin once more.

"Well," said Merlin, "as one wizened old beggar speaking to another, I presume you to know that marriage is hardly a prerequisite for the germination of a seed."

Conrad's smile broadened sickeningly.

"Ah, but what good is such fallow seed? Clearly any resulting sapling would be unworthy of such breeding?" he said, gesturing again toward the parchment upon his desk. Any self-respecting greenskeeper would raze the blight from his fields. I shall recommend that Lord Pendragon do the same. You may see yourself out."

Conrad then turned, in a pantomime of sudden interest in his shelves. Merlin did not move save to reply, his voice steely.

"I am afraid that you have mistaken the terms under which I entered this keep, Conrad," he said. "You see, I did not come to find the sort of teachings which goats-flesh and ink can impart. I did not come for pleasant horticultural conversation, nor did I come to discuss your inane system of land and title claims. Most certainly of all, I did not come to this little spit of land to be turned away by some frail and pompous advisor."

Conrad's smile wilted notably at this, the man shuddering visibly at the use of the term "advisor." It took him a moment to regain his composure, and when he spoke it was with a desperate air of dominion.

"Well, Mr. Merlin," he said, "I am afraid that you shall be leaving us much less successfully than you might have hoped."

He placed his hand upon Merlin's elbow in an attempt to escort him from the room and indeed, the Keep. Merlin cocked an eyebrow and stared at the man. A good deal of toil must have been going into the effort, for the frail old councilor was sweating and his arm shaking more than ever. He had, Merlin thought, the look of a tutor trying to unseat an unruly student, only to find that his pupil was carved from granite.

"You know," mused Merlin, "I do believe that this cramped little room has yielded me all the revelations I can stand for the time being."

With that he strode to the door, paying no mind whatsoever to the little man affixed to his elbow.

"Well, I suppose you know the way out," said Conrad, "Though I cannot guarantee your safety from Pelias and the guard."

"Then it is fortunate that I both remember the way out and shall not be heading in that direction," said Merlin. And with that remark he unhinged the surprised Conrad from his elbow and placed him within his little record room, shutting the door between them. Lord Uther was himself within the Keep somewhere and Merlin would search him out. He returned to the main stair and began to climb. The Keep of the Precipice was of a similar sort to Castle Ektor, but built on a grander scale. Every few steps there were rooms of varying size that broke off from the stair. As he climbed, Merlin caught glimpses of living quarters, food stores, an armory, and even a pair of dining halls that each put the Great Hall of Castle Ektor to shame. Merlin glanced into each of these, startling a page or two here and there, but saw no sign of anyone who might be Lord Pendragon. If the Keep had indeed been built similarly to Castle Ektor, then the Lord's apartments would be atop the Great Hall. A beautiful and ornate double door sat at a landing some four flights up the spiral stair.

'And here is the Hall itself,' thought Merlin, but as it was quiet and dark and not a time fit for supping, he sped on along the stair. Twice more around the stair and the old man found what he was looking for. Another ornate door stood before him, smaller this time, but bearing a deep relief of a winged serpent coiled upon its face. At each side of the door was a stonework guard post. These, however, stood empty. Merlin found it odd that even the Lord's own honor guard would have been called to the gate, but as this worked to his advantage he did not dwell upon it long. The latch of the door sat in the coiled serpent's open mouth. 'A man would have to be daring indeed to brave such a vile ward to assail Lord Pendragon in his apartment... if he believed in such superstitions,' thought Merlin as he tried the lock, ready to break the door down if need be.

The door slid quietly open, giving only the slightest resistance to his touch. A cold whip of a breeze burst forth from the chamber as the door cleared its frame. The room within was black as the grave. From the darkness came a sharp gasp and the sound of someone clattering about. As he peered into the chamber, Merlin could first make out a delicate pair of female hands hastily fumbling with a bit of flint. A spark was struck then and he saw it fall into a small pool of oil, and instantly there was light. The glow of the lamp revealed a young and frightened-looking chamber maid.

"Who's there?" she asked, raising the lamp from its sconce. She gasped a second time as he stepped into the tiny room. "Wh-why, you're not Lord Conrad!" she exclaimed. "Y-you aughtn't to be here."

It was clearly taking all of her courage to speak to him, Merlin noted. Yet, the girl was standing her ground. She was an admirable young maid, he decided as he surveyed the room before him. It appeared to be a heavily curtained ante-chamber. The lord's apartment would be just beyond the curtains, then. He made to pass through the curtains, but again the little maid stepped before him. Still shivering with fright, she held the lamp before her like a ward against evil.

"Sir," she said, "please, it's only Lord Conrad that's permitted any further... if you please," she said, trying to look brave.

Merlin placed a strong hand upon her shoulder and moved the girl aside. His grip was firm but did not hurt her and she stayed where he had moved her. He thrust open the curtains, a hint of trepidation in his throat.

The room beyond the curtains was little like what he had expected. The bedchamber of Lord Pendragon stood empty. Against the far wall stood a large oaken bed, its covers immaculate and untouched. The air about was crisp and cold and bore no hint of habitation. No tapestries were hung upon the walls to insulate the room. The only decoration of any sort was an ornate sword which hung, gathering dust in its sheath, above the bed. A sliver of pale light blinked in and out of existence where a curtain billowed against the outside wall, letting in a faint scent of salt and sea.

"What dark machination is this?" he whispered into the darkness. To his surprise, an answer was whispered back to him.

"Lord Pendragon is no more," came the voice of Conrad, soft and deadly beside him. "He has been dead these past three months, in truth."

Merlin spun on the spot. Conrad stood not a pace from his side, clutching in his hand the bit of parchment containing the Pendragon lineage. The smile had returned to his face.

"Of course there are precious few who are privy to that knowledge," he said.

Merlin reeled with the revelation. Here at long last he had hoped to discover something about the child. If he had only looked into the eyes of the boy's father, had only wheedled some secret clue out of the man. He sighed as he looked across the long-vacant room, wondering where to turn. Had it been folly to come here? And what if it had been? Where would he turn next?

"It has been a bit of a conundrum, to be honest," said Conrad. "You see, at some point the people will have to be made aware of the death of their lord, but to tell them immediately would have left the high seat vacant in their minds, and things left vacant want to be filled. Naturally, they would each have had some idea of who should carry on their stewardship, but how likely do you think it would have been that they would all have come to the same conclusion?"

Merlin stared at the man, saying nothing.

"More to the point," said Conrad, "what do you think the chances would have been that they all chose *me*?"

He ducked through the curtains and strode into the late Lord Pendragon's bedchamber. His eyes passed over the large bed and across the room, a self-satisfied look upon his face.

"No, better to invent this lingering illness. Better to show the people that Lord Pendragon himself wanted me to take the reigns and look after his people whilst he recuperated. Otherwise my rise to power might have been viewed in rather an ill light, might it not?"

Conrad swept close to Merlin then, his smile broadening so that Merlin hardly knew why the man's cheeks did not tear themselves into ribbons.

"Imagine my good fortune then Mr. Merlin, when you appeared. As violent and heathen a thing as ever I could have hoped to discover, delivered unto my very doorstep."

Merlin turned away from the frail man. The surprise of the moment had passed through him now, but he did not wish Conrad to see it. He wondered — was there yet opportunity here? If there were he would bleed it out, even at his own peril.

"How did Lord Pendragon die?" he asked. "Was there ever an illness?"

"Oh!" chuckled Conrad. "No no, there never was such a thing — not along the lines which you must be thinking at least. I merely contrived it as a handy excuse as to why Lord Pendragon could not be seen at court."

"Poison, then?" asked Merlin.

"You judge me too harshly, my dear man," gasped Conrad, gliding away and turning to look at Merlin over his shoulder. He would have looked coy, Merlin thought, had he been a young lady. "I am no killer, skulking about in the shadows! The lord was very old and, as you may know, certain eccentric habits are wont to crop up in those who outlive their adventures."

This struck something within Merlin. It cut into the soft tissue of his own doubt like a carver's knife into a fatted calf. "You have evaded my question," he said, grimacing. He did not wish to look at the man's face, did not wish to smell his fetid breath.

Merlin strode toward the curtained window where he could feel the saltwater breeze. Conrad followed close behind.

"I suppose there is little harm in telling you," said Conrad. "After all, I should think you would like to hear what it is you shall stand accused of?"

Merlin's eyes narrowed.

Conrad took Merlin's continued silence for acquiescence and went on. "Very well," he said, "I shall tell you of the last hours of the so-called Lord amongst Lords, Uther Pendragon."

This was the first that Merlin had heard ill spoken of Uther. For the man's advisor to speak with anything but reverence of him was surprising.

"You did not like your lord?" he asked.

"Come now, my good fellow," replied Conrad, "don't tell me that you believe one man could have been such a successful warrior and have also orchestrated this time of 'peace' which now graces us? Such a dichotomy never graced a single man.

"No, Uther was a warrior's warrior. He was a conqueror! Every breath he drew, every step he took, he advanced against the enemy. He and Ambrosius drove Rome from our shores; the last of them were made to swim for lack of boats. It was a resounding victory. But what happens to a conqueror when the enemy is vanquished? Do not bother to answer me that; the answer is to find a new foe.

"Ambrosius was closest to his brother and so he was the first to meet with Uther's disdain. The brothers had meant to unify this land under one king, and Ambrosius was the elder. Uther would not yield, however, and so the Twin Fiefdoms of the Sibling Lords were formed. Ambrosius ruled from Londinium in the East, while Uther ruled here in the West.

"That was not the end for Uther, however. He did not know what it was to stop. I tried to make him see reason. We appointed him vassals to watch over parts of his land, to keep him protected and wealthy. Each he picked himself, from the ranks of his very own army. Each did well for him, too. But our conquering lord was not satisfied. Ever did he scrutinize the actions of his vassals, eventually finding fault with each. Some were reprimanded; some were punished; but those who resisted, who saw the mania that had swallowed their lord and sought to be free of it... they were ground into sand beneath His Lordship's foot."

Conrad waved an arm about the room. "Did you know, Mr. Merlin, that this was once the fortress of Marquess and Lady Gorlois? They lived here for a good many years, charged with keeping watch over the western sea for Lord Uther. That is, until upon one of his many visits here, Uther perceived that Marquess Gorlois was conspiring against him."

Here was something that truly piqued Merlin's attention: the Lady Gorlois. Had not Maggie named her as the child's mother? He wondered how much he could glean of her from Conrad without forfeiting the secret of the child's parentage.

"Was it so?" he asked. "Did Gorlois plot against Uther?"

"Who is to say?" sighed Conrad, "Uther was mad! Mad with loss, the fool was. The man had everything. He had freed and conquered more of this isle than any save the Romans themselves, yet his little personal defeats vexed him.

"I think it began with Ambrosius. Uther never saw himself as Ambrosius' equal, not truly. Of course he fought with the man and railed against him publicly, but privately he loved him. Uther's world diminished when Ambrosius died. There was no longer a star in the sky to reach toward. And so Uther tightened his grip upon that which he already had. Gorlois was ordered to amass troops to protect the land, and did so — and was deemed a conspirator and a traitor for it."

"What happened to him?" asked Merlin.

"Sand beneath Uther's heel," said Conrad. "Uther came to Tintagel with all his host, saying that Gorlois was to mingle his troops with those of the realm. The Marquess mistrusted this request and a battle ensued. It was not long fought. That very night the town burned. The troops that Gorlois had trained here were slaughtered to the last man, and Gorlois was himself made to walk naked through the streets and out the gate. Uther called that 'laying the sin bare' and Gorlois was not the last to suffer it."

"And what of the lady?" Merlin asked, almost nonchalantly.

Conrad cocked his head to the side.

"Igraine? She was Marquess Gorlois' final revenge. Her charred remains greeted Lord Pendragon upon his entering the gate. But surely you know that part. It is her child whose claim upon this land you have come to assert, is it not?"

Noting Merlin's silence as an affirmation, Conrad pressed the point. "I have long been aware of that particular indiscretion of our late lord's. Thankfully the whole messy business was sewn up when Igraine was burnt at the stake. Naturally neither Gorlois nor Pendragon ever acknowledged the child, though I do recall signing a writ of payment to Sir Ektor, or 'Lord Ektor' as he seems to fashion himself these days? By your presence here I deduce that he has earned his payment and that the child still lives. A pity."

Merlin smiled. "Yes he lives," he said, "though through no work of Ektor or Kaye is it so."

"You mean to tell me that you have been his warder?" said Conrad. "It is all the more fitting then that you shall be my scapegoat. You, the sole barrier between me and my rightful seat."

Conrad had been dancing about this point for quite some time, thought Merlin. He had gleaned much from the man's tale thus far, and to let him spring his trap before he could glean what more he could seemed a wasted opportunity.

"I suppose Uther threw himself on the pyre?" he asked, brushing aside Conrad's threat, "mayhaps to join his fallen love in the afterlife? Is that the fate you wish for me as well, Conrad? A stake and a spark to remember me by?"

"Your fate may very well resemble that of the poor Lady Igraine, Mr. Merlin," smirked Conrad. He absentmindedly fumbled about with the tassels that hung from his robe's neckline as he said this. He was in a state of childish glee. "Though perhaps I shall give you the rack. The people shall call out for vengeance at your slaying of our infirmed lord in his very bed."

His eyes flicked to the bed and back to Merlin, giving the distinct impression that he was stifling a laugh. "You are wrong concerning Uther's fall, however." He winked and flitted to a small door that stood in the corner of the room, resting his withered hand upon the handle. "Through this little portal lies the final fate of the mighty Lord Pendragon."

'Was this where Conrad hid the body?' thought Merlin, thinking himself about to find the desiccated remains of Uther.

Conrad's flesh twisted like a bit of tissue as he unlatched the door and pushed it open. To Merlin's surprise a brilliant shaft of light burst forth into the room. He stepped toward it, unable to resist its brilliance or the secret that it held. As he drew close, the scents of the sea washed over him. Salt and stone and seaweed pulled at him as he stooped through the doorway and onto a small parapet. Low, decorative battlements adorned the masonry. As his eyes adjusted and the sky and sea bloomed into view, Merlin marveled at the beauty of the place. To stand in this spot was to seem to fly above the sea and below the sky. It was exhilarating.

He realized that his hand was resting upon something. Looking down he found it to be the back of a stone seat. There were two of them, both molded into the floor and facing out to sea.

"A curious little hideaway, isn't it?" said Conrad from the doorway. "I admit to not understanding Uther's purpose in ordering this place constructed. The few times I saw him here, he was seated just there," he said, indicating the seat upon which Merlin's hand rested. "He never sat in the other seat. His hand would lay upturned and open, as if he expected Lady Igraine to seat herself beside him at any moment."

Conrad strode out onto the parapet. He was just beside Merlin now, gazing over his shoulder. "It was from here that he flung himself into the sea," he said. "It is an odd notion to try and join someone consumed by flame by enveloping yourself in the sea, is it not? But as I have said, there was madness in him, increasingly so toward the end."

Merlin stepped toward the edge of the low, crenellated wall. The drop from the parapet was sheer. Hundreds of feet below, the sea lapped against the stone cliffs which comprised the outer wall of the Keep of the Precipice. Conrad was behind him now, the man's rancid breath warm against his neck.

"I wonder," mused Conrad, "was he drowned or did the impact crush him first?"

"You will not push me from this ledge, Conrad," said Merlin. "You do not wish to sacrifice your pawn just yet."

Conrad retreated a pace. "You are right, of course," he said. "It was but the thought of a moment." He cocked his head to the side, realizing something for the first time.

"You have waylaid me in my duties quite long enough I dare say, Mr. Merlin," he said, "but there shall be no more. You know now as much as I do of the final fate of Lord Pendragon. It is time for you to make compensation for such rare knowledge. I am afraid the price shall be quite dear. Do follow me now," he said, beckoning Merlin back into the Keep.

Merlin followed close as Conrad stepped through the squat doorway. It took the aged councilor's eyes a moment to adjust to the darkness. It was a moment that Merlin had been counting on. It was the mere work of an instant and he was done. When Conrad, having no doubt heard the scuffing of Merlin's feet upon the floor, turned to look at him, Merlin was placidly fumbling with the locking mechanism of the little door. There was a soft sort of smile upon his face as he latched the door and straightened himself.

Conrad turned his nose up in a sneer. "Smile stupidly if you like," he said. "It shall not be long before you cannot do so at all. Come, come."

He raised the curtain, revealing again the little ante-chamber in which the chambermaid sat. She looked up at Conrad, a fearful look upon her face. He gave her a curt nod and again waved for Merlin to follow him. The maid curtsied in thanks for the acknowledgement.

Merlin, following Conrad now, had just stepped before the maid when she let out a blood-curdling scream.

"His sword!" she yelped. "He's taken Lord Pendragon's sword!"

Conrad's eyes darted, hawk-like to the blade that hung at Merlin's hip. There, where Kaye's blade had hung not a moment before, rested the Blade Pendragon. Conrad was aghast. Admonition and threat pulled his face taut, and he would have hurled insults at Merlin, but for the palm covering his mouth.

Merlin flung the man — none too lightly — against the stone wall and bolted out of the lord's apartment. The maid shrieked again as Conrad crumpled to the floor in a daze. Merlin took the stairs three at a time, building speed as he went. Below him was the gate out of the Keep, and beyond it Pelias and the guard.

Merlin shook his head in a moment of self-reflection. What star was it, he wondered, that had fated him to hurl so many doors at so many dim-witted guardsmen?

His shoulder slammed into door, the door into Pelias, and he was away. The commotion behind him was still reaching its fever pitch as he bounded the broken gate and stepped lightly across the causeway to the mainland. Water was already over-lapping the stones there as he passed, and it would be hours before Castle Tintagel recovered well enough to start a proper search. Glancing down toward the sea, he saw a high-roofed tidal cave which looked still somewhat accessible. It was as good a place as any, he thought, to weather the night. What, after all, was the difference between a foot and a mile if one could not bridge it?

"Keep safe and strong your flock of one," Athena had said. Merlin knew that she had meant the boy. She had commanded and pleaded with him to safeguard the child, but had he done so?

It was well into the night now, and Merlin had lit a small fire from driftwood in the cave below Tintagel. The tide had risen now and both the causeway and the approach to the cave were flooded. In his hand he held the Blade Pendragon. He had stolen it in hopes of handing it to the boy, a symbol of the child's stolen birthright.

But now, the echoes of Athena's words swirling in his head, Merlin wondered if he had done rightly. The sword was nothing but a symbol of power, and one that Conrad and the Castle Guard of Tintagel would fight to reclaim. He had no doubt that by morning Conrad would have spread his lies through all Tintagel. He would be thought a killer and Conrad a hero. Had he not then put the child in greater jeopardy? What fate might he expect for himself if the child should come into peril? Had Athena not warned him that his fate was entwined with that of the child?

He turned the sword about in the air. It was a finely wrought thing, to be sure. Numerous chips of amber and garnet decorated the guard and inlaid in the pommel there sat a formidable ruby. The flames of the fire danced upon the sword's blade and from the gems sent sanguine points of light about the cave. It gave the sword a wondrous effect. The blade shone and glowed and seemed alight with fire.

Merlin half expected it to turn molten in his grasp. He turned the sword about in the air again. A bit of the ichorus light from the ruby caught in his eye and all went orange and molten before him. Thoughts of the child and of Athena and of his own survival poured forth from him, glowing and hot. They split and wound about him, a fiery mail of interwoven destinies. In them he caught white-hot glimpses of innumerable faces and events.

He blinked hard, suddenly feeling as if hours had passed. All was as it had been. He sat in the cave as before, holding the Blade Pendragon in his grasp. And there before him, a smoldering ember of the moment before, hung his answer. He contemplated it a moment and then stood. From within his robe he drew Kaye's sword, hidden when he had fetched the Blade Pendragon. He held them together in his hand, smiled, and pitched them both upon the fire. Upon the swords he piled wood and then stone, and soon the heat of the fire was so great, its light so bright, that nary a soul in high Castle Tintagel could not feel its brilliance.

The wee hours of night began to slough their weary way toward dawn as Merlin sat back from his work. Smoke and char blackened the walls of the cave. Here and there embers were scattered, giving off a waning red glow. He could not help but smile at his handiwork.

Before him lay the Blade Pendragon, by all appearances the same sword that he had held aloft some hours before. Kaye's sword was nowhere to be seen, save for a bit of slag here and there about the makeshift kiln.

Merlin rubbed his bare, aching wrist absentmindedly as he began to allow sleep, at long last, to embrace him. If he met Athena in his dreams, he thought, he must remember to thank her once more.

Chapter Twenty-One

The Great Hunter

I awoke to rays of the morning sun creeping across the floor toward my bed. A light breeze wisped through the open front door. The door! I had latched it firmly the night before! I knew so! I ran out the door, grasping the broom handle as I went. The light of the day caught my eyes and stars danced before me for a moment. "It's nice to see you so full of initiative, Orion, but the sweeping to be done is only where you let bits of food strike the floor as you made my soup last night." Father's voice caught me even more off-guard than had the sun. It was early and he was injured. Surely he could not have risen from bed yet. Yet there he stood. As my eyes adjusted to the light, I found that he was tending the hives for the morning. The bandages still gripped themselves around his flesh, the blood of the night before dry upon them now. His knife was back in its sheath now, attached to his hip. As he stood from tending the last of the hives, I could have sworn that all of Father's strength had been restored overnight. I began to ask how THIS miracle had occurred and was silenced just as quickly as I had been the night before.

"I have been thinking since I rose this morning of how to answer some of the things you would ask me, Son" he said. "I have decided that today we shall go for a hunt together. This shall do much to appease the demons I see dancing upon your skull, but not before we get a bit of breakfast into you." With this he walked past me and into the cottage, ruffling my hair as he went. "And put some clothing on you naked fool," he shouted from inside.

As I clothed myself and then ate, Father re-dressed his wounds. He then set a sling in my hand, and tucked another into the leather cord around his waist. He packed a satchel of food for the day and tied it across his shoulder and under one arm so that the weight of the bundle rested snugly against his back. A less-attendant son might have offered to carry the satchel for his father. A less-attendant son might also have had to cook all the household meals for a month, as payment for such insult.

The sun was a quarter of its way across the sky as we set out from home and into the wood. As we approached the first trees, I could contain myself no longer. "Father how will a day's hunt answer that which I wish to know of gods and men? Of my birth and parentage?" Father simply knelt by a patch of mud and began to smear it over his skin. He beckoned me to do the same.

"Without forethought, Orion, we are no better than any of the other beasts of this world," he said. "The eyes and nose of many a beast are as keen as those of any man. Those of a deer, son, are much keener. It is in our knowing this that we are his master." With that, we delved into the woods. As father walked his feet made no sound. They seemed to evade every small twig, every dry leaf that would give them away to the eyes of the forest. I think to this day that, had a falcon alighted on the same spot as my father trod, the bird would have made more noise. My feet were another story. Snappings and shufflings seemed to echo around us as I blundered through the brush. After a few moments of this, Father again stopped and crouched to the ground. I followed his example and crouched beside him. "Orion, what do you hear?" Father asked. In the stillness of the forest I could hear only the song of distant birds, and answered him thus. "Listen closer Son, listen to the forest itself, not to its inhabitants. What do you hear?" I listened. I sat and listened and could not hear what it was that my father asked of me.

"There is nothing, Father. Nothing but the chirruping of the birds." I told him.

At this, I was sure my father would become upset. Again, he did not do as I thought he would. Father sat flat upon the ground and crossed his legs. Again I followed his example. Resting thus, Father clasped his hands together and closed his eyes. "Follow my lead in this, Son. Let the questions you still hold to leave your mind. Like a trained dog they will return when bidden. Listen now, not to the forest, but to your own breath." I thought this folly, but did as Father asked. Closing my eyes, I could feel my breath flowing in and out of my chest, flowing down into my body and being pushed out again. I sat there for what might have been a moment and might have been hours, doing just as father had bidden me. As from a dream, Father's voice found its way to my ears. "Now, Son, listen to my breath and not your own." My own breath fell away from the focus of my ears, and I found the breath of my father. I listened only to his breath, though farther away and fainter it was than my own. "Now, Orion, my Son. Listen to the breath of the forest." Father's breath faded from my ears, and a hushed whisper made itself known. It was that of the wind through the branches and the tapping of leaves falling to land upon the loam of the forest floor that I heard, the swaying and creaking of each trunk as the breath of the forest danced around its trees. Far off, a brook was bubbling down a hillside.

I opened my eyes. Father was standing again before me. I took the hand he offered me and stood beside him. "Every bit of land on this earth breathes thus, Orion. Breathe with the forest, become as one with her, and she shall shelter your every move. Come now."

Father set off at a quicker clip now. The wind ran with him, making the brush and branches bow in his presence. My ears perked as I heard the breath of forest dancing through the loam and leaves behind me. As the gust of wind met my back, so met my foot against stone. I was following Father through the trees and brush. Quietly now I followed, now quieter still as I found my rhythm with the wind and breathed as the forest did. Deeper we delved, now, deep into those places where light itself found it difficult to trespass. It was dark and cool as evening when father stopped next. Crouching by the roots of an ancient tree, he beckoned me to his side. I stooped low beside him.

"What is it we have done thus far, my Son?" he asked.

I knew not what he meant, and so answered as well as I could. "We have covered ourselves in mud and run through the wood looking for deer."

"True, those were our actions," Father said, "but it was not a recanting of the actions that I wanted you to tell me. I would rather you tell me what we have done with respect to capturing our prize."

"Is that not what I have said, Father?" I said, now confused.

"It is, Orion, but think of it thus: each animal of this earth can detect the world and those in it with five organs. If we are to find our prey this day we must rob him of each of these organs. Then he will have no way of escaping our stomachs this night. First, he sees his world through his eyes. We have covered ourselves with the mud of the forest to rob him of those most telling of his organs, for it is when a creature sees you that he knows you. Second, among his organs is his nose. The creatures of this wood can, any of them, smell a man from as far off as he can hurl a stone, and more. Thus does the mud serve us again, for it smells of home to the deer and not of the hunt. In our first act today we have stolen from our prey his most trusted allies. Can you guess what he will rely on next, since his two best defenders have deserted him?" Father asked.

"I do not know, Father." I said, for I had not thought of any of this before that day.

"Think of what we did next, Orion. It is how we next stripped our prey of his would-be defenders."

"It is his ears." said I, trying to keep the excitement from my lips as the thought came to my brain. "We stole his ears away as we trod upon the breath of the forest to this place."

"Very well thought, Orion," said Father. "We have now taken all that we can from our prey before we face him. His feet and his tongue yet remain to defend him. We shall take them both from him at the last moment of his life, for they are such dear qualities that none but the gods can take them away from afar."

"What sort of a defense is a voice, Father?" I asked. I knew, of course how a beast could strike at a man, but was puzzled as to how a voice alone would defend a creature.

"Did you not call out when you were in the teeth of the god Poseidon?" he replied. "A simple cry can muster aid or can provide warning to those who would take flight. We must also take care to keep him quiet in a place such as this, for the cries of a wounded deer may provoke other hunters, man or beast, to descend upon us and demand what is ours. If we are fools enough to tell them of this opportunity, then the price is ours to pay when they come to collect it."

With these words and a wink, Father disappeared over the knot of root beside which we had been huddled. Upon following him, stealthily *as I could, I was shocked to discover myself mere paces from a small gathering of deer. The beasts had not heard our conversation, nor had they noticed us as we crept up upon them. To my right and near the trunk of the tree, Father was already setting his sling with a small, smooth stone. The words of a question had already formed in my mind and were on their way to my lips when Father's eyes found mine. There was blood and death in them. I was startled at the change that had come over the man in the instant that he had been out of my sight. Here before me was a predatory beast. Gone was the teacher, the mystic I had delved into the wood alongside. With a darting glance to my hip Father ordered me to arm myself in kind. I did so out of abject fear of the man who stood before me. Father's eyes shifted to the nearest beast. I followed his gaze with my own and took stock of the animal.*

It was a sturdy creature. The muscles in its legs and neck pulsed strong with the life carried from its heart. Its eyes gleamed with a sight clearer than that of a man's. Its nostrils flared as it took in the scents of the glade in which we all stood. Its ears perked at the slightest rustling of the wind through the trees. And yet there stood Father, a mere fifteen paces from the animal, already spinning his stone in its sling, invisible to this pinnacle of nature's senses.

There had been naught but the slightest gust in the breeze. The stone had loosed, the deer fallen. The others had heard no warning, no call for aid. They paced warily. Their hooves were raised in flight and then lowered in doubt. Father was beside and behind me now. His breath was as the breeze. I less heard him tell me to take my aim than felt the command in my sinews. A doe fell. The muscle of my arm tingled from the swiftness of the shot, the blood catching up to the place it was needed. The rest of the herd flew from the invisible death that had rained down upon their fellows, their hooves sounding like so many Titans thrashing through the bracken.

Father stepped forward to the fallen deer. As his gaze shifted to the victim of my sling, I saw what I must describe as pain in his eyes. He motioned to me to come to his side. I did so in silence. As I followed father's gaze to the face of the deer, I became shocked with what I saw. The eyes of the deer were not clouded and pale, as I had thought they would be, but darting left and right. The creature was silent and still, but not dead! A gasp of panic left my lips as I tried to think of what to do next. I had done just as Father had, had I not? How was it that I had not slain the beast? Was this some sort of magical beast hiding in the form of a deer?

Before I could answer any of these questions, Father had materialized a small knife from a fold of leather along his waist. He stooped beside the deer and cut along the back of its neck until the head of the beast lurched forward unnaturally. The life faded from its panicked eyes. It was dead. "Well done, Son" said Father. "Catch her upon the temple next time, and not the jugular, and you'll put her down without pain or fear." These were the last words said before we left the forest.

Chapter Twenty-Two
Prophecy and Peril

The sun hung high in the sky as Merlin emerged from the cave. At his hip hung the Blade Pendragon. From his pocket he drew a pile of small, tightly bound bits of parchment. From each of these, affixed with a bit of twine hung a strangely reflective bit of feather. One by one, Merlin raised the bits of parchment to his lips. His eyes fixed upon the little featherlet for a moment and then he exhaled, placing the next feather in the place vacated by the last. They took to the air with transcendent ease, and soon the old man had produced a small procession of notes, gaining altitude along the sea cliffs. And then, with a final twinkle and a whirl, they were over the cliffs and away.

The old man smiled warmly to himself. He had nearly expected the little things to fall right into the sea. He had placed his faith in the relics of Athena however, and she had not disappointed. Nor had the dolorous boon which she had granted him, for that matter. Though full of lament and sorrow, these now-recurring visions of his young life as Orion clung to him, even after his waking. Like lost children wending their way home, he welcomed them back warmly, even the sorrowful ones. For their sorrow was his own; with each new returned memory, he knew himself all the better. There was strength and solace in such knowledge.

He took his time ascending the path that connected his cave to the causeway and in turn to Tintagel. 'The more time the guard has to raise the alarm, the better,' he thought. He was across the causeway and beginning his ascent to Tintagel when he heard the now familiar sounding of the horns. There was shouting across the battlements then, and a genuine roar of voices was building from behind the wall.

Despite his having purposefully taken his time, Merlin found that no guards were yet outside the propped-up shamble which had once been the Main Gate. In waiting for the guard, he perched himself once more upon the stone that sat before the gate.

To pass the time he drew the Blade Pendragon from its sheath. 'How long did it take to raise the guard of a castle?' he wondered. He began to absent-mindedly draw lazy, curling shapes in the dirt before the stone. He hadn't balanced it quite so well as the original smith had done, he realized. It was no great matter.

After a moment Merlin became aware of a change in the level of noise from beyond the gate. The castle had gone quiet, save for a muffled voice or two. 'Finally,' he thought, 'the guard must be readying themselves to confront me.' He stood, holding the Blade Pendragon before himself, its point still touching the earth.

The gate shuddered aside. There before him stood the populace of Castle Tintagel, down to the very last man, woman, and child. At their head stood Conrad, his simpering grin already affixed from cheek to cheek.

Merlin could not help but feel for these people. The devotion they showed to their fallen lord was truly touching. It was a pity how readily they had fallen into Conrad's clutches. He hoped that their eyes would be opened to the man's treachery in due time. 'Hope,' he thought, 'that shall have to suffice for the moment.'

The mob closed rank about him, grumbling insults and brandishing what weapons they had. Pikes and swords fanned out about him, accompanied by ploughman's forks and shepherd's hooks, cook's knives and rough sticks. The mob stayed close together and out of his sword's reach. When this was done, Conrad strode towards him from their ranks.

"You see!" he said. "Here has returned the murderer, bringing with him the evidence of his crime!" He pointed a withered finger at the Blade Pendragon. "We who so loved our lord, who honor his memory, we shall retrieve that which was stolen from him! With the Blade Pendragon we shall slay this demon hidden in the visage of a man! We shall reclaim Lord Uther Pendragon's legacy and honor, and we shall take them with us into a bright tomorrow! For Uther!"

Conrad raised his fist into the air. All about the mob, fists were raised aloft in unison, and from the walls and the cliffs of Tintagel echoed the cry — "For Uther!"

Here was the moment Merlin had waited for. He held the Blade Pendragon aloft, making sure that all could see. He let it hang there in the air for half a heartbeat and then spun it in his grip and thrust it, dagger-like into a deep cleft in the stone on which he stood. A heavy metal clang resounded from the walls, startling the children and a fair few of the adults gathered about. Even Conrad looked perplexed.

"People of Tintagel!" said Merlin, his voice as loud as the ringing of the stone. "You are indeed bereft of your lord! Let he who would lead you now, he who would honor Uther's legacy, free the Blade Pendragon from this stone!"

The stunned look on Conrad's face shifted to wary zeal. He approached Merlin and the sword.

"At least you know when you are out-matched, Murderer," he said, loud as he could muster. "Do not think that I or my people shall show you lenience, however. Blood must be paid in kind!"

Fists and cheers rose from the crowd once more, and Conrad reached for the sword. Merlin gave way, allowing all to view the silken-clad councilor. Conrad's wrinkled hands clasped the grip of the Blade Pendragon. Every eye of the mob was fixed upon him, every mind ready and waiting to see the blade held aloft.

The seconds ticked by. Necks craned. Shoulders jostled and feet shifted. Yet the sword did not budge. Whispers passed from child to mother, from man to wife to sister and brother. "He is old," said some, "Poor man," said others, and "... needs help?"

Conrad could hear them and redoubled his effort, grabbing the guard now with his free hand. His form strained and shuddered visibly in his silks and his eyes burned with indignity. Someone stepped forward from the ranks of the crowd. Conrad did not notice until the man stood beside him, fixed upon the blade as he was.

"Allow me to assist you, Lord Councilor," said Pelias. "You are aged, after all, and perhaps Merlin would make light of your frailty. Let me help you in this."

"No!" spat Conrad. "The Blade Pendragon is mine! I alone shall free it!" His footing slipped just then, his frame buckling with exertion.

"The Blade Pendragon," said Merlin, "was and is Uther's. Only he who is rightly heir to the high seat of Tintagel can release it."

The murmuring of the crowd grew at this. Weapons began to lower and questions abounded. Conrad fell to a knee, shuddering.

Pelias scanned the crowd. He could readily see the doubt amongst the citizenry and even amongst his men.

"Stand aside, Lord Councilor," he said. "I shall retrieve the blade for you."

Conrad gave no reply save to redouble his weakening efforts against the blade. Pelias tightened his hand around the remaining free guard of the sword and pulled. A cry of support came from the crowd. Surely now the sword would be freed.

All too soon, the cries of support gave way to gasps and to dismay. Pelias forced a hand onto the grip despite Conrad's protests. The larger man gave a tremendous yank.

For an instant the crowd, wanting to see the sword freed, thought that he had done it, that Pelias had retrieved the Blade Pendragon for them. But the thought was merely hope and illusion. Pelias had not raised the sword from the stone, but had jerked his frame so violently that he had fallen to his knees.

Eyes began to flit to Merlin and then back to the stone. No one seemed to remember that they were carrying weapons. When enough eyes were upon him, Merlin spoke again, this time in a calm and somber tone.

"I did not slay your lord," he said. "This charlatan who is now affixed to sword and to stone like a tick on a dog has been leeching your lord and lands for much longer than you know. I have merely arrived here to burn him from your wounds and to see this place healed of his contaminant."

"Liar!" shrieked Conrad. He was ashen and his silks were damp with sweat. He pressed upon the Blade Pendragon, using it as a crutch to raise himself up. He thrust a bony finger toward Merlin, leaving the sword to Pelias for the moment. "You would twist these people's minds! You would have them place you upon Uther's throne, the very throne which you yourself so recently made vacant! You have placed a witchery upon this sword so that only you can retrieve it again! We are not so easily fooled, Wizard!"

"On the contrary!" said Merlin, raising his voice enough to carry over the crowd. "I shall never lay a hand upon that sword again, nor claim to the seat which it symbolizes."

Merlin then turned to address the crowd about him. "Good people!" he said, "In the coming days many will come to this place. They shall be drawn from near and far to lay claim to this sword, but all shall fail. All save one, for whosoever pulleth this sword from this stone shall be king! Not only of the lands of Uther Pendragon, but of all Brittania!"

As the crowd gaped and stared, murmured and wondered about Merlin's words, Conrad let out a guttural howl and hurled himself bodily forward. He grasped at Merlin, his fingers like claws.

Merlin moved so quickly that few in the crowd saw his fist strike Conrad's belly, saw the elbow that spun into Conrad's spine. A few would later recall the sound of cracking bone as Conrad's ribs broke, but most would remember only the startled look upon their would-be ruler's face as he hurtled side-long over the cliffs of Tintagel and out of sight.

Such was the end of Conrad, his only inheritance from Lord Pendragon a watery grave, his only headstone the rocky shore.

No one recalled Merlin's departure that day. Some stared in shocked silence at the sea, some watched Pelias as he struggled against the sword in the stone. Slowly the crowd returned to the castle. The last two upon the cliffside were an exhausted captain of the guard and a quietly weeping chambermaid. By nightfall they too had gone within the castle's walls.

Chapter Twenty-Three

Eyes in the Dark

It began as a nearly imperceptible tapping. Arthur woke to it slowly, unsure if he was still asleep. He had been dreaming of Bartholomew and innumerable little minced-meat pies which had sprouted tails like mice. The portly cat had just missed cornering a pie but lost it under the dresser, and Arthur could not tell if he was still hearing the terse tapping of Bartholomew's tail or if the sound was emanating from the waking world. Tap, tap, tap it would go and then remain silent just so long as to cast doubt in the child's groggy mind as to its ever having happened; then tap, tap, tap it would go again in the same soft far-off way.

Tap, tap, tap it came again and this time Arthur shot up with a start. How long had it been going on like this, he wondered. How many times had he drifted back to sleep only to wake to the same sound? How long had he written it off as some figment of his dreams? It was cold in the cottage and through the gaps in the shutters, he could see a handful of stars. 'Why', thought Arthur, 'must all manner of strange goings-on begin in the dead of night?'

Tap, tap, tap it came again, as if some nocturnal creature had come calling at the door for a pawful of butter, but was not so bold as to want to wake the sleeping inhabitants of the cottage. Now that he was aware of the tapping, Arthur was sure he wouldn't be able to sleep without knowing what it was. He threw aside the heavy sheepskin that was his blanket and set out to investigate.

The chill of the night caught him immediately, sending chills up his spine and causing his knees to quiver. Gripping the sheepskin in his small hands, he hefted its bulk tightly about himself, his knuckles white with the effort. The sheepskin kept him from shivering, but as he crept along the narrow hallway, the flagstone floor sent sharp pangs of cold up through his feet.

He heard the tap, tap, tapping again. There was no doubt now that it emanated from beyond the heavy front door. Perhaps it was because he was closer now, or perhaps it was that he was cold and it was dark, but Arthur thought that he could detect a faint scraping sound that followed the tapping noise. Again the thought of little claws came to Arthur's mind, though now they did not belong to something so innocent. The dark and the cold of the night were beginning to play on his nerves.

'What if it is a man, tapping and scraping at the door with his thumbnail? Surely nothing but terrors could be in the mind of a man such as that,' he thought to himself.

Somewhere behind him there came a rustling from up in the thatch. He startled, spinning upon the spot. There in the black of the hall, where he had been only a moment before, Arthur swore that he had seen something move. Something black as the night itself.

'I mustn't scare myself,' he thought, 'It must be my imagination getting the best of me.'

He tried his best to mean this too, but staring into the black of the hall it was hard to shake the unease from his bones.

Tap, tap, tap came the sound again, so close to the boy this time that the scraping sound was like someone scraping their nails along his scalp. He had backed himself into the door without knowing it. Spooked, he stood still as a stone, marshalling his thoughts.

"I'm just scaring myself," he whispered aloud.

After forcing down a pair of deep breaths, he turned his back to the dark hall and fixed his eyes upon the door. Tap, tap, tap came the sound again, faster this time, as if whomever or whatever it was that lay beyond had heard him whispering words of encouragement to himself.

Arthur took one last deep breath and wrenched the door open. There, in the dark of the doorway, hung a small scroll of parchment. It hung in mid-air, affixed with a bit of twine to a small and gleaming bit of white feather. The thing drifted gently forward, twinkling in the starlight. It stopped just before Arthur's chest and hung there, suspended it seemed by some unseen bit of spider's silk. Abandoning the sheepskin to the flagstones, the boy reached across the threshold into the crisp night air and took hold of the little bauble. It was a strange little thing, he thought. How on earth it had come to hang about on his stoop he could not say.

As he stared at the little thing in his still-outstretched hand, something stirred. Arthur refocused his eyes. There, just behind his outstretched hand, somewhere in the black of the night, he was sure he had seen something move. He tucked the bit of parchment to his chest and stared out into the gloom. It had been somewhere near the gate, he thought.

As he stared, his eyes transfixed upon the gate, a strange thought occurred to him. There was something odd about the gate, wasn't there? It looked sunken somehow, as if it had warped or aged in the few hours since the sun had last touched it.

Leaving the gate be for a moment, he scanned the rest of the area as best he could from the relative safety of the threshold. There was a space under one of the bushes where Bartholomew was wont to lie in wait for the passing ankle or bug. In that space he thought he spied something, a shapeless thing, hidden in shadow. Yes, he was sure of it. Something bulky had been stuffed beneath the bush and lay there in a most unnatural way.

Just then, whatever deep and dark cloud had been obscuring the moon parted, sending a ghostly haze of white light down into the yard. There, visible beneath the bush lay the wooden gate, a splintered wreck of tinder and iron.

Arthur gasped. His eyes flicked back to the thing that now hung low across the walk. Shuddering and crackling, the dark planks of wood shifted and split. A withered, briery hand swung heavily to the earth. Fingers cut into the soil, shivering dark little splinters from their tips as they scraped about for purchase. A beam broke and a hollow shoulder raised itself from the gap. The scents of ash, of bracken and loam, of rot and spore filled the air.

Arthur shuddered violently. He had feared the thing in silence since the moment he knew it to exist. He had tried to push the memory if it, of Bedwyn's death, of that horrible falling, dying feeling that came when it was close, to the back of his mind. But now, as the thing's knotted, bottomless eyes tore their way open, his secret fears were made true.

Merlin had not slain the awful thing after all. He had only startled it, driven it off and lied to the boy to pacify him. He scolded himself for fearing that this day might come and for saying nothing when the old man had been there to ask. Now it was too late and the thing had returned, had come for his blood and for that of Maggie. He had doomed her, his friend and protector, simply by keeping close to her. She would take the place of Bedwyn, he realized, crumpled and broken upon the floor.

The creature opened its shattered mouth, an earsplitting, keening wail erupting from deep within its gullet. The sound buffeted about within his eardrums, rising in pitch as it went on. Now nearly free of the wall, the creature crouched low against the walk. There was something predatory in its stance, thought Arthur, something he had seen while watching Bartholomew in the yard.

Just then the creature's wail broke off, replaced by a deep and resonant baying. It was something between the howling of a great hound and the war cry of a man. The creature skittered and bounded forward, heading straight at the boy.

Arthur was one step ahead of it. He had known the creature was about to charge by its stance and whirled his little body through the doorway, once inside slamming his back into the door as hard as it would go. The creature's baying was all about him as he felt the door close tight to its frame. The sound entered his skull and shook him inside and out, filling his mind with muck and horror. Forcing the latch down and into place was all he could bring himself to do.

And then Maggie was beside him, hurling the sheepskin about his shoulders and wrapping him in her big warm arms.

"Artie, what're you doin' up and about at an hour such as this?" she said. "You'll catch your right death o' the cold, you will."

Arthur came to his senses slowly. He was aware of being cold and that he was shivering. He touched his fingers to his face, but both his hand and the skin of his cheek felt far away, as if he were deep beneath the sea and groping about above the surface for land. Long moments passed this way, Maggie swaying gently side to side as she held him tight.

After a while, he could not say how long, Arthur realized that he was once again able to see clearly, able to feel the warmth of the blanket about him. He tugged gently at Maggie's shirt, just wanting to feel something tangible. The sensation of fabric against his fingers calmed him and he let out a shuddering sigh, letting go of the last vestiges of the fear that had burrowed into him.

Maggie took his face in her hands then and plopped a heavy kiss upon his forehead before turning his face up to look him in the eye.

"Now tell me, Artie," she said, "what's the meanin' of your bein' up and terrible affrighted at such an hour as this, so?"

Arthur hardly knew where to begin. The details of his encounter fell out of his mouth, a mixed-up verbal stew. Maggie stared at him as the tale tumbled out on top of itself and out of order, concern growing upon her features. When he was done, she shook him at the shoulders and hugged him once more.

"Whether what you've told me just now was a dream or a trick o' the light Artie, I'm glad you're alright," she said. "But let's get off to bed. You can curl up at the foot o' mine with the cat if you like."

She began to pull the child back toward the bedrooms, but he would not stir. His eyes were fixed upon a dirty bit of bracken that lay upon the floor. The little thing terrified him. In his mind, he could see it stirring, growing. Maggie looked from the boy to the twig and back again. Then, with the distinct air of an Irish matriarch, fed up with tales of the child, she swept up the piece of wood and swung the door open to hurl it from her sight.

A bit of grime stuck to the doorjamb squished and stretched as the door pulled from the frame. Arthur gasped. Maggie froze.

"Sure'n there used t' be a gate hangin' from the stonework o' that wall," she said, a knot of perplexed trepidation in her voice.

"Come away from the door Maggie! Come away!" shouted Arthur, shuddering again in his sheepskin. There was such pleading desperation in the child's voice that Maggie could do nothing but obey. With a fleeting, worried look to the stick in her hand, she hurled the thing out into the dark and wrenched the door closed once again.

The heavy wooden thud of the door echoed violently through the cottage, as if the structure itself were waiting for the sound of some intrusion. Arthur's heart pounded in his ears. He could have sworn that the creature would have been standing before the door, waiting to strike when Maggie had loosed the latch. Where the thing was now he did not know, but he feared the moment that he learned of its hiding place. Like a thunderclap the sight of stars beneath the thatch struck his brain.

"My room!" he cried. "It'll try burrowing through the thatch, there where it's thinnest!"

He wasn't sure how he knew it, but once he had spoken the thought aloud, it filled his mind so entirely that he could see no other course of action that the creature would take. Maggie stared at him, his terror now visibly eclipsing her wonder. A shiver washed over her as she turned and strode toward his room. He followed her, gripping the sheepskin tight as he could about his small frame. His heart felt as if it were about to beat through his ribs and out of his skin.

Then, just as Maggie leaned into his room, her hand upon the latch, there began the scraping and keening wail of the creature once again. Maggie stared, frozen where she stood. Fingers dark as pitch wormed their way through the thatch just above the wall, just where Arthur knew they would be.

The room darkened as the burnt fingers dug their way into the room. The keening wail sounded closer now. The smell of burnt flesh and bracken intensified, and any moment now Arthur knew he would see those whirling, endless eyes push their way up and into the room. Pressing past Maggie, he grasped the latch himself and threw all of his weight against her side, forcing the girl from the doorway and shutting the door behind them.

The sound of the door slamming inches from her face broke whatever spell that had held Maggie transfixed.

"Keep an eye on the door, Artie," she said, not daring to take her eyes from it herself. "Make sure nothin' comes through!"

Quick as a spark she shot to the fireplace, returning with the poker and shovel. She handed the shovel to Arthur and then went about securing his bedroom by passing the poker through the latch and embedding it in the doorframe. This done, she took the shovel back from the boy and hurried down the hall to her own room. She firmly shut and secured the door in similar fashion, the shovel taking the place of the poker.

"Looks like we're sittin' up through the night, Artie," she said, leading him back out of the hall and plopping him into the chair facing the fireplace.

She then whisked away again and Arthur, the ardor draining dizzyingly from his frame, was vaguely aware of the sight of the table being raised to its side against the kitchen door. Maggie grunted and strained under the effort, but she did not return to his side until the door was heavily barricaded, the benches placed behind the heavy table as bulwarks. This done, Maggie knelt beside the fireplace, her knees shuddering as she did so. Her hands shook as she set about rekindling the fire, and she winced at irregular intervals.

She was terrified, Arthur realized. He had never seen Maggie like this. She had always been a safe haven for him against the likes of Kaye and Ektor. As he stared at her, coaxing the few remaining embers of the fire back to life, he wondered what had changed in her, or perhaps in him, in the last few minutes.

'She might have died,' he realized, 'had I not shoved her out of my room and shut the door.'

Something batted about against his hand, startling him. He wrenched his hand up and away from whatever it was. Maggie jumped and yelped at his sudden movement, her eyes darting to his hand to see what was the matter. There, held aloft in his clenched fist was the small bit of parchment, still affixed with a bit of thread to a single golden feather. The feather batted gently against his hand from its tether.

"Now where did you get that?" Maggie asked.

"It was knocking on the door," said Arthur. "It's why I opened it to begin with. I'd nearly forgotten."

"Well let's have it opened then, Artie," said Maggie. "There's no sense in receiving such strange correspondence as that if you don't read it."

"Are you sure it's for me?" asked Arthur.

"And who else could it be for?" she replied. "Sure'n my life's been too drab an' ordinary for it t' be mine, so; savin' that is for the times you or the old codger've come barreling through it like a pair o' kicked polecats."

Arthur could hardly contain his imagination as he tugged at the string about the scroll. There was no need to try and untie the knot. No sooner had he tugged at the string than it lay loose in his palm. The feather too lay flat and did not stir. His little fingers worked against the tightly scrolled bit of parchment until he revealed a short note saying simply:

The note included a series of quick symbols, the meaning of which neither Maggie nor Arthur could decipher. They could almost have taken them for Merlin's mark, but that too had been included.

Maggie lent a fervent glance to the barred bedroom doors. "Shall we say first thing in the morning, so?" she asked, with a wry smile.

Neither of them got much sleep that night, Arthur only nodding off for a spare couple of hours just before dawn. Even as he slept, the boy's thoughts were not his own. Something creaked and clanked about in his brain; a thicket of knives carved their way toward his heart. Black brambles grown the size of trees eclipsed his every thought, shading him below their sharp and twisting vines. A billowing breeze blew through the thicket and with every gust the brambles constricted about him, their every leaf a blade yearning to plunge into his flesh. Once or twice he thought he had heard a voice upon the breeze, thought someone close and quiet had whispered the word *kill* to the bramble and blade.

Then, in a wash of gold and blue, something else alighted upon his mind; something smelling of dust and sweat and which announced itself with the rhythmic chirping of cicadas.

Chapter Twenty-Four

Hunter, Hunted

It'd been three days since Abner n' Clay'd fled Lexington. Three very long days, in Abner's estimation. Most o' the time'd been passed watchin' the countryside bump an' jostle by from their seats on the plush chesterfield. There weren't much t' talk about, an' maybe that was a blessin', bein' that between the gurglin' o' Petunia's boiler an' the whirrin' o' her engine a man could hardly get a word in edgewise. The only real time there was for conversatin' was over supper.

The first night Abner'd practically blurted out the whole business concernin' Johnny's death without so much as a pause t' take a breath. When he'da finished, somewhere just after Tommy'd handed him the note containin' Clay's name an' whereabouts, he looked up an' saw a mask o' utter bewilderment on ol' Clay's face.

"Many a part o' your tale sits poorly with me," Clay said. "Not the least o' which is why this Tommy fellow thought that I would be some special kind of use to you, my boy."

With that, the barrelous man had thrown back the remainder o' his whiskey, makin' his drunkenness unassailable the rest o' the night.

The second night there weren't no time whatsoever for banter. It seemed Mr. Brian Scates had put a bounty on the both o' their heads back in Lexington an' had the word sent out on the wire. Not but thirty minutes'd passed in — come t' think of it they hadn'ta even gotten the town's name — than a posse'd been formed an' gettin' outt'a town 'tall made the boys feel 'bout lucky as a pair o' wild turkeys the day after Thanksgivin'. They'da finally bedded down round about sun-up in a cornfield, havin' by some grace or luck only a handful o' bruises apiece t' show for the adventure.

That afternoon, due to sleepin' through the heat o' the day, they awoke feelin' as sticky an' worn as rundown taffy-pullin' machines. The cicadas were already chirpin' away the daylight when they'd hauled themselves into the auto-carriage. They stuck t' the back roads once they got on their way, generally keepin' out o' sight. Fer the last couple'a days, Abner'd been gettin' the feelin' that the way they were havin' t' rough it weren't sittin' well with Clay. The man's scowl was well fixed t' his face an' hadn't been removed for nothin' nor nobody. It was just when Abner was fixin' on hollerin' over the commotion o' the engine 'bout findin' somewheres t' wash up an' grab an apple, that Petunia herself forced the issue. Her boiler let out a gurgle and a whine, followed by a lurch an' a shudder an' then finally silence.

Clay swore an' slapped his hat down upon the wheel. Before Abner'd had a chance t' ask what'd happened, Clay was down from the chesterfield an' headed 'round back toward the boiler.

"We're gonna need more whiskey!" he said.

"Ain't it best we keep the drinkin' 'til after our drivin's done for the day?" asked Abner, hoppin' down hisself. "It's only that I still ain't sure what happened t' that young woman we done seen the night we left Lexington, Cassius."

Roundin' the back o' the auto-carriage, Abner found Clay fiddlin' with a latch right up near the top o' the boiler, holdin' somethin' that looked midways b'tween a ridin' crop an' a ladle. The latch shot open with a burst o' steam an' a whiff o' somethin' like burnt caramel an' barley. Clay dipped the skinny little ladle in through the hole an scraped about a bit. Drawin' it out again, he looked at the thing an' cursed. In the ladle's scoop, there sat a small molasses-black pool o' liquid.

"The whiskey's not for me, dammit," he said. "It's Petunia that needs a drink, and a damn tall one by the look of it! Now put that phantasmical woman outta' your head, boy'o. She was some sort o' apparition an' I'm well and certain that no good can come from the like o' her. Go an' grab my bags from behind the seat. We're goin' whiskey huntin'."

Abner chuckled t' hisself as he climbed behind the chesterfield. 'One thing goes wrong with this here contraption,' he thought, 'an' the ol' boy needs a stiff drink.' He'd seen Clay hurl the bags back there durin' their escape from Lexington, an' he figured they'da been full o' extra provisions. This bein' the first time he'd had t' inspect 'em, what he found inside he deemed mighty peculiar. One bag was full o' bank notes, both Union an' Confederate, along with a jumble o' what looked t' be all manner o' valuable brick-a-brack. This sort o' thing seemed sensible, bein' that a man never did know what currency a feller was like t' ask fer what with the unsettled nature o' the states. The problem was that the rest o' the bags didn't have nothin' Abner could make hide nor tail outt'a. They were crammed chock full o' books, periodicals, documents an' every other sort o' printed material imaginable. Abner could'a swore there were even a couple o' bits o' animal skin all scrawled on an' rolled up. He was just reachin' fer the bag the strange bits o' skin were jammed into when Clay popped his head 'round the far side o' the seat.

"What in the inferno could be takin' you this eternity?" he asked. Then, seein' Abner's hand stretchin' toward the bag, he quickly sprung right up an' smacked the man's paw aside. "Now, either you're dumber than I ever thought you t'be son, or you're far more sly than I gave you credit for. Now, mind before you answer: if it's the latter I'll burn you down where you stand, Sonny."

Abner was flabbergasted, an' that was somethin' that you could always see on Abner's face if it were true. It was a good thing too, on account o' his bein' too surprised t' make any sort o' sense concernin' why he was fetchin' that bag instead o' whichever other one it was that Clay'd wanted. Clay's eyes softened, though his scowl didn't. He reached past the satchel Abner'd been gropin' fer, right over t' the side o' the vehicle where a pair o' leather haversacks hung. He tossed one at Abner who caught it an' slunk outta' the automobile with his tail between his legs. Clay followed him a moment later, stuffin' inta his pocket a wad each o' Confederate an' Union notes. He turned a sideways glance Abner's way, mutterin' a quiet "sorry 'bout that" under his breath. When Abner didn't reply, Clay decided t' clear the air entire-like an' turned t' face his companion.

"Y'see," he said, "to some men there's things more precious than bank notes an' contraptions."

Abner nodded, still sayin' nothin'.

"That bag there," Clay said, "well, it's full o' some o' the most precious things t' me in this here world. To the right man, they're nigh on priceless, an' as irreplaceable as a thing can be." He looked close at Abner. "Do you get my meanin', Son?" he asked.

The look Abner returned him was cold as a witch's teat in winter.

"D'you recall my reason for huntin' you down t' begin with?" he asked. "It was on account o' the death o' my friend Johnny: a man I done fought beside in the War Between the States, a man I tilled the soil beside in the days that followed. He died in my arms, Cassius. I'll have you remember that the next time you go presumin' me t' be a sneak-thief."

Clay found he was at a loss for words, an' he couldn' remember bein' that for quite some time. Mayhap he'd seen the man what resided in Abner's heart for the very first time.

"You told me that some men hold certain things above the value o' coin," Abner said. "Well I presume that's true for all good men, but what that thing is likely changes from one man t' the next."

Clay opened his dumbfounded mouth t' respond, but Abner beat him t' the punch before he could find a single word.

"For me that thing's them folks I call my own," he said. "My own little girl, Mazie; my own wife, Tess; my own friends! It's one o' them that's been taken from me, an' when I catch up with the man who took him, I'll be demandin' dire recompense indeed.

"So you can keep yer bits o' old writin', Brother Clay. They ain't the tender I'm in need of."

"Point well taken," said Clay, findin' his voice once more. "Now we'll do well to get moving. Those hills are our best bet."

He cleared his throat an' set off at a decent pace, though a slower one than he could'a done. Abner noticed that, an' took it fer a good sign: a sort o' invitation t' come along an' walk together-like. For a while there was silence between 'em, both men wavin' away the bees an' the heat with their hats. Presently, somethin' occurred t' Abner, an' seein' how it didn't have nothin' t' do with honor or pride or nothin', he figured it was safe t' say it.

"Say," he chirped up, jus' a tad too casual-like t' be anythin' but awkward, "What makes you think these here hills are a good bet fer findin' whiskey?"

He gave the hills themselves a nod o' his head as he asked an' found that they'da been a fair piece closer than he'da thought. 'That, or by some trick o' the light them hills hain't got no closer 'tall,' he thought. There was somethin' odd 'bout 'em for sure, like a case o' reverse vertigo.

By the time Clay got 'round t' answerin' him, Abner'd got a bit winded an' figured he didn't much care one way or the other.

"Well," said Clay, "we're keepin' off o' the roads now, an' that patch o' dirt we ran dry in didn't resemble a town any more than the mile o' dirt before it."

Abner nodded, only ever half-listenin'. He was starin' at them hills again. The longer he looked their way, the more certain he was: somethin' weren't right about 'em.

"That, along with us passin' through what are undoubtedly corn an' rye fields at this very moment has me convinced," said Clay. "We've run smack dab into the heart of a moonshiner's Eden." He smiled an' pointed ahead. "Where better for the boys t' set up operation than a handful o' low, shady hills, I ask you?"

Clay smiled at Abner like a magician at the end o' his trick, but Abner wasn't lookin'. He was still starin' out at them hills like a man bewitched. There was a far-off bee buzzin' about somewhere in his field o' vision an' without knowin' he was doin' so, Abner raised a hand t' try an' wave the bugger away.

Now this looked mighty odd t' Clay, on account o' from his angle Abner was wavin' at somethin' that weren't there 'tall. He almost asked what Abner was up to, but Abner cut him off, whoopin' an' a hollerin' like a hound on a hare.

"That was him!" he hollered. "Did ya see him go? Damn! He's a quick one for such a big feller."

Abner shot off like musket-fire then, an' even Clay was hard pressed t' keep up with him, so hard was he runnin'. They were through the fields an' into the shade after a minute an' there Abner slowed, lookin' perplexed. He darted this way an' the other, doublin' back on hisself as he tried t' catch the trail. After a fair few moments o' this, Clay decided that Abner might be ready t' listen t' reason.

"Now here I thought we were tryin' t' quash the bees in our bonnets an' act civil t' one another," he said.

Abner's hand shot inta the air quick-like an' Clay understood. The man wanted quiet. Clay looked at Abner. The man was starin' up inta the treetops, a look somewhere b'tween hunger an' fear in his eye. Clay craned his own neck an' scanned the canopy. There weren't nothin' outta' the ordinary in them trees, s'far as he could see.

Moments passed, the only noise the wind passin' through the leaves. Both men waited, waited on a sign that Clay weren't sure he'd know even if it came. Then, like rain in the desert, the moment was past. Abner sighed an' lowered his eyes. Clay stared at him, hand on his hip an' a furrow o' exasperation on his brow. There weren't really no point in askin', but Abner asked anyhow:

"You really didn't see him?" he asked.

Clay sighed, fannin' hisself with his top hat.

"I didn't see so much as a Northern Democrat," he said, "much less a man who might actually exist."

An' with that, Clay plopped his plump self right down in the dust an' leaves. A moment later Abner came an' crouched down beside him.

"You *really* didn't see him?" he asked again, more to hisself this time than Clay. "He was right there in the treetops, big as life an' more. Now, it's true I only spied him when he moved. Damn near felled the tree he was perched in, he did."

"Is that what you were grabbin' at, far away as you were?" asked Clay.

"Huh?" said Abner. "Oh! Naw, there was a bee what got in the way o' me seein' straight was all. I might'a caught a better look at him, come t' think on it, if the damn bugger hadn'ta been pesterin' about."

"To be clear," said Clay, "You *are* talkin' about this ten-foot behemoth o' a man, the same one that killed your Johnny Schaffer? That's the man you're sayin' was perched up in the treetops an' obscured by a little ol' bee. That great big lummox of a man?"

There was a look in Clay's eye that Abner didn't quite like. His lip curled an' he asked the question Clay hadn'ta asked.

"He don't move like an ordinary man," he said, "an' he sure ain't no lummox, that much I'll swear by!"

"I'll take your word on it," said Clay, throwin' his hands up in defeat. "I've read stories strange as yours oft enough t' know truth from a yarn, an' you've the light o' truth in your eye for certain. I just wish the true tales wouldn't stack up so like they've done lately."

"What sort o' stories?" asked Abner, sittin' down proper-like.

"What say we break for lunch?" asked Clay. "I'll regale you as we gorge ourselves."

Out from the haversacks came a pair o' apples, a tart ol' wedge o' cheese an' a collection o' rolls, most o' which it turned out were hard as stones. Abner portioned out the apples an' cheese right quick an' Clay set his knife t' work on the rolls. After a moment o' no progress against an oat bun, Clay set the knife down.

"It's funny," he said, "on the train back t' Lexington from the Alaska territory, which incidentally I recently procured for the United States of America from Cossack Russia, I made a point to catch up with the recent events put to print. One of 'em contained an article relatin' the business you an' Johnny Schaffer got wrapped up in. Called it 'The Incident o' the Behemoth an' the Barnfire' I believe.

"That's what they called it," said Abner.

"It was quite a thrilling tale," said Clay, hastily addin' "from a reader's perspective," after a look toward Abner's consternated face.

"That night I know enough about," said Abner, focusin' his eyes down upon the apple an' cheese he was settin' up t' eat. "Tell me one o' your other stories, somethin' that rivals mine an' might take it from my shoulders a moment."

"Well, that's a tall order," said Clay, shruggin', "but I do think there's somethin' more t' your tale... somethin' you might not yourself be aware of."

Abner looked up so quick he was lucky not t' bite off his thumb an' two o' his fingers t' boot. "Well spit it out!" he said, hisself spittin' out the bite o' apple he'da been chewin'.

"As I said, I was readin' up on the events o' the last few weeks when there appeared to me, upon reading so many papers in rapid succession, a strange undercurrent in the many reported violences ocurrin' in our beloved South. Had I been readin' the news as it had come, I likely wouldn'ta noticed. But a long train ride and a volume o' print such as I had affords a man a special allowance for rumination.

"I found myself settin' aside incidents from all over the Southern states, orderin' 'em by date, an' perusing 'em for similar odd details. I enjoy creatin' timelines, you see. A coherent catalogue is imperative to proper research, in my opinion. It is, incidentally, why I am in posession o' them ancient vellum manuscripts we had our squabble over earlier. Which, o' course is water under the bridge."

"I agree an' that's fine," said Abner, "but I ain't heard no details yet, an' your story's wearin' old."

"Indeed?" said Clay. "Let me supply a few for you, then. Have you ever heard o' the 'Autotrolley Abberation' that ocurred in Georgia? Or the 'Paddlewheel Horror' from Mississippi? There was also the singular incident o' the 'Wilderness-Day Assassination' reported by the Virginia Voice. That last report, perhaps due to its exceptional writing, was instrumental in the creation and support o' a hypothesis in my head."

"What sort o' hypo-thesis, exactly?" asked Abner, the word foreign on his tongue.

"It is a strange thing to put into words," said Clay. "Let me continue the story as I was telling it, and I may find the proper words.

"Through deduction and research, I compiled the articles and broke them down mentally into raw data. Their shared characteristics became unmistakable, them being so odd an' seemingly disconnected from common practices. I could not help but continue along the trail they set before me. You see: in each incident, numerous people — often local officials an' public figures — died. In each, their having gathered together in the place and time o' their deaths is unaccounted for. No events were scheduled, nothin' o' note at the least, an' yet a disproportionate number o' people o' influence were gathered together an' died. Also peculiar was that, saving for your reported giant, there were never any suspects. Wrongdoings were committed, but not a soul could say a lick about who might'a perpetrated 'em. Again, this is excepting your giant, but everyone just wrote him off as the... ramblin's of a yokel," he said, an air o' shame in his voice as he said it.

"So, by your way o' thinkin'," said Abner, "The Borderer done all them things as well as killin' Johnny n' 'em in the barn, an' no one even supposes he exists?"

"That seems the likely sum o' it," said Clay.

"But, Clay... there weren't no persons o' import in that barn with Johnny, were there? Maybe we don't fit the rest o' that hypo-thesis o' yours after all?"

"Ah, but there were such men in that barn, Abner. Had you read the news o' your own frightful experience, you'd know it," said Clay. "Why, among Johnny's compatriots that night were businessmen, land-owners, an' even Mr. Joseph Brooks, a gentleman with an eye on the governorship. In short, they were some o' the most influential men in your neck o' the woods."

"The most ornery about, t' boot!" said Abner. "I've heard o' that Brooks feller an' he was every bit the rabble-rouser Johnny was," he smiled. "Why more'n once Johnny got us outta' a tight spot durin' the war just' by mentionin' the ways the north wanted us t' live. He had a way o' gettin' men t' give the enemy what for, I tell you what."

"An intriguing point," said Clay, slappin' together a bit o' cheese an' a bite o' one o' his hard biscuits an' tryin' his luck at it with his teeth.

"Clay," said Abner, after a moment o' chawin' on his apple, "if them men was all rabble-rousers an' men o' influence, well wouldn't that make 'em men like yerself?"

"In a way, I suppose," said Clay. "More than one, if truth be told." Clay looked at Abner, a bit o' suspicion stuck in his eye. "Are you suggestin' that that man might be out here on account o' me?" he asked.

"It sure looks that way, don't it?" said Abner. "I mean we wasn't exactly lookin' fer him today, though I had meant t' get onto his trail somehow. An' there he goes, showin' hisself hidden up in a tree in the middle o'... where is it we've got to anyway?"

"You ain't in the middle o' anywhere, boys," said a voice just behind Abner n' Clay. "You're teeterin' right on the border o' Indian Territory."

Abner an' Clay spun 'round quick as cats caught by their tails. Standin' there, not ten paces from 'em was a wire-thin feller in overalls an a dirt-browned shirt. In his hands he held a musket, the barrel o' which was leveled at Clay's chest.

"The way I figure it," said the skinny feller, "that gives me leave t' be as savage as I like with ya. Now grab some scalp!"

Both men obliged, puttin' their hands behind their heads. What seemed odd, both t' the new feller and t' Abner was that Clay was smilin'.

"You ain't right, are you?" said the skinny feller. "No one but sick folk like the sight o' a gun pointed at their chests."

"On the contrary," said Clay, "It is merely that I am quite happy to see you, an' for more'n one reason. Firstly an' foremost: my friend had me convinced that there was a giant of a man whom he calls 'The Borderer' somewhere about these hills. Moreover, he'd told me that this great big monster of a man was out for my head. You are clearly not he, and so I am glad of you."

The skinny feller looked 'round, spooked.

"That tale's pretty tall," he said, "but this here land ain't been tamed yet, an' I done heard plenty that was tall as that an' turned out true. What's yer other reason?" he said, turnin' back toward Clay.

"Hmm?"

"I said: what's yer other reason fer bein' happy t' see me?"

"Ah," said Clay, "well I believe you are the man I have been looking for. You are, I presume, the proprietor of the still which resides somewhere nearby?"

The skinny feller scowled at Clay, none too sure how t' respond.

"I'm lookin' t' purchase a good deal o' whiskey," said Clay, "and I have a good deal o' money with which t' do so. How would you like t' sell your entire stock in a day?"

Well that was all the skinny feller needed t' hear. He put up his gun right quick an' swapped his scowl fer a smile.

"Name's Hardy," he said, "Jeremiah Hardy!"

It turned out that Jeremiah's still weren't far off, an' it weren't just the one, neither.

"What we ain't exactly got is yer proper whiskey," he said, as the stills came inta view. "We got yer Tennessee Bourbon; we got a real nice Old Tom Gin, an' what we got most o' is somethin' we're callin' White Lightnin'. We mostly got that on account o' we haven't quite got the whiskey figured out yet."

Comin' 'round the bend, Clay smiled wide. Tucked inta the small shady gully were some dozen or so copper an' bronze stills o' varyin' size. Fixed up t' each of 'em were copper tubes an' big ol' glass jugs.

"Not since the icy cliffs o' the Alaska territory have I seen such splendiforus spectacle," said Clay. "What do you say to a bit of a tasting before we buy?"

"Well," said Jeremiah, "I do have t' see that you're payin' in real money first."

Clay raised an eyebrow, but went ahead an' reached inta his vest pocket where both the Confederate an' Union notes were stashed. Before he took his hand out again, he went ahead an' asked Jeremiah right out: "That'll be the Northern money?" he asked, smilin' real wide.

Jeremiah 'bout lost his mind. "N-Northern!?" he sputtered, half-raisin' his musket again.

Clay just kept on smilin', wide as the sunrise. He let out a guffaw an' pulled the wad o' Confederate notes outta his vest, leavin' the Northern money right where it was.

"Boy, did I get you goin'!" he said, still smilin' at Jeremiah, but sneakin' a wink over in Abner's direction as well.

Abner couldn't but be impressed with how sly Clay'd handled Jeremiah. He wagered Clay'd got all o' Alaska from the Cossacks for a cart o' potatoes. Jeremiah'd laughed right along with Clay, never suspectin' a thing, an' when they'd quit hemmin' an' hawin' he went an' grabbed three tin cups full o' bourbon, handed 'em out, an' the three boys fell in like a band o' thieves. After 'tasting' a few rounds, Jeremiah asked 'bout The Borderer again. Bein' that he was well an' warm behind the ears, Abner told him the whole gory business.

"An' this happened t' you, yerself?" asked Jeremiah when the tale was done. "Not some cousin who cain't be trusted?"

"Saw it with my own eyes," said Abner, shufflin' off t' draw hisself another dram o' gin, which by then he'da decided he liked the best.

"Shee-it! Now that's soberin' stuff!" said Jeremiah. "'Course, I count that a blessin', so thank you, sir, from the bottom o' my next cup."

The boys all laughed at that, an' Jeremiah the hardest of all. He'da thought o' that phrase a few years back an' loved sayin' it as oft as he could.

"Heheh..." he chuckled, tryin' t' compose hisself. "The only tale I can conjure up t' rival that 'un is 'bout a man out west they say is entirely unkillable. He rides out with his posse 'gainst the Indians, the Mexicans, cowboys; whoever'll stand an' fight really! An' no matter how outgunned he is, no matter how many o' his posse are laid low, he comes lopin' on home with nary a scratch on 'imself!"

Clay an' Abner swapped looks o' doubt between 'em.

"Well... I got a cousin says so, anyway," said Jeremiah, sendin' everybody inta hysterics again.

"Clay, you gotta know one!" said Abner. "Tell us a doozy!"

Clay swirled his bourbon an' raised an eyebrow.

"Fact is," he said, "you're lookin' at the baddest man I ever have met. I ain't found my equal yet, an' I don't ever plan to." With that he swallowed his drink an' slammed the cup down with authority. Then he belched, an' everyone was rollin' 'round in the dirt laughin' again.

After a minute, when it'd gone quiet an' Clay'd got hisself another drink, he leaned forward an' stared serious-like at the other two men.

"Now: I do know a tale," he said, "but it's a real loo-loo an' I'm not entirely sure you boys're up for it."

"Oh, come on Clay!"

"Do tell it!"

"Well," said Clay, "alright, but this ain't a regular story, you see. This is what some folks call a riddle an' others call prophecy. That'll depend on who you ask. Now, Abner: you recall those bits o' old goat's flesh which I have rolled up in the auto-carriage, I'll wager."

Abner nodded.

"Well, you're about t' hear how I came to have 'em an' what it is the first o' them I ever read says."

Drunk as he was, Abner perked right up at the mention o' them old bits o' vellum. After the grousin' Clay'd done when he'da nearly touched them rolled-up skins, it startled him 'bout as much as a flushed hare that Clay wanted t' talk 'bout 'em.

"Now, you know I have a friend who travels all over these states," Clay said. "I purchased the auto from him an' a good few o' my firearms, an' that's what I asked o' him. The thing is, every now an' again he'll show up at my door with somethin' altogether different under his arm. Well, on one particular dark an' stormy night..."

"Horse shit. Ain't been a storm 'round these parts in years."

"I live in Lexington, Kentucky."

"Ain't been a storm 'round there neither, I'll wager."

"Jeremiah, I will have you kindly shut the hell up an' let me tell my story!" said Clay. "Now it just so happens that this stormy night was a few years back, so you're right anyway. I was a fair sight skinnier than I am today, an' the war hadn't yet broke out. So here comes into my office my friend, soaked an' tired from ridin' the rails, an' he says he's got somethin' I'd like. Abner, do you recall that there was a symbol above the door o' my press-works?"

Abner thought a minute.

"Why, yes," he said after a moment's thought. "It was an odd sort o' masted ship with a broken anchor chain."

"Precisely right!" said Clay. "Now, outta his coat my friend pulls these scrolled up bits o' skin..."

"Hain't your friend got a name?"

"Jeremiah! What did I tell you about shuttin' the hell up?"

"S'awful peculiar that you ain't got a name for him is all I'm sayin'."

Clay sighed.

"His name's Jones, dammit... but that ain't important in this tale so would you just shut up an' stop interruptin'?" he said.

"Hmph," said Jeremiah.

"He pulls the scrolls out o' his coat," said Clay, ignoring him, "an' guess what's on 'em?"

No one guessed, fearin' that Clay might consider it interruptin' t' do so.

"A big ol' seal, made o' dry an' ancient wax. An' wouldn't you guess it: that very same ship an' broken chain was pressed onto each of 'em. I opened one of 'em that very same night after buyin' 'em off Jones outt'a some sort o' sense o' destiny or duty or somethin'. The writin' was English, but some kind that was older than anythin' I've seen. It took me a minute t' see the letters properly, but here's what it said:

The dead yet living,
The skin-wrapped son of the beast,
The old-named-young-named-old again,
The dreamer, the seer, the believer,
Shall skip, spin, rise upon the new tide,
Shall reign when he who lurks in the cold and dark is felled.

"Now what do you say t' that?" asked Clay.

"Wow," said Abner, "I ain't never heard nothin' like it."

"S'easy," said Jeremiah.

"What?" said Clay.

"Well, s'easy is all," slurred Jeremiah. "The riddle, I mean. There ain't *hic* much to it if you know the feller well enough."

"What are you blathering on about?" asked Clay, fair incensed at the moonshiner's cockiness.

"Well it means Davy Crockett, don't it?" said Jeremiah, smilin'.

"Davy Crockett died at the Alamo!" said Clay.

"No, he made it outt'a there, but he drowned crossin' the Mississippi a year later," said Abner.

"He lives 'bout thirty miles up the road!" laughed Jeremiah. "An' what's more, he's the answer t' your riddle. You two already got that whole 'dead yet livin' part figured, I'll wager. What you might not know is that he went an' got 'imself a missus, an' they went an' got themselves a boy-child, t'boot! An' wouldn't ya know they went an' named the boy Davy, after his daddy? So now Davy calls 'imself David t' keep things simple, y'see?"

"What?!"

"Davy was old when he went by Davy, though that's a youngin's name, right?" said Jeremiah. "Well, now that he's got a boy o' his own, he goes by David, which is an older feller's name. See?"

"No, but go on anyway," said Abner.

"Well, Davy — David that is — wraps 'imself in animal pelts when he hunts; an' I heard him called worse than a son-of-a-beast, I tell you what! The man's the best night hunter you ever did see, so I'd call him a see-er o' sorts as well. See? S'easy!" said Jeremiah.

"Son of a bitch," said Clay.

"What about that part about the feller that lurks an' reignin' after he's dead?" asked Abner.

"Well, that's the easiest part," said Jeremiah. "That's your 'Borderer' feller, that is, an' Davy Crockett's gonna shoot him dead!"

"Son of a bitch," said Abner, "I'll drink t' that!"

"Cheers!" said Jeremiah.

"Budem zdorovy," said Clay.

Jeremiah gave Clay a queer sort o' look. Abner said somethin' 'bout Cossack Russia, an all three o' them slung their drinks back.

"Whoo! What in... Whoo!"

Clay'd slammed his cup down an' was shiverin' like a sheep shorn in winter.

"*Hic*, wh-what in Sham Hill...?" he slurred.

"Tried the White Lightnin', did ya?" said Jeremiah. "You shouldn'a done that!"

"God's holy hole!" said Clay, fallin' on'ta his side in the dirt.

He lay there a minute b'fore the other boys knew he was asleep. Jeremiah followed suit right quick, an' Abner wasn't too far behind, neither.

A moment later, somewhere in the trees, somethin' big an' quiet slipped away into the night.

Chapter Twenty-Five
A Home no More

Dawn came long before it seemed due. Bright golden ribbons of light pulled themselves through every nook and cranny of Maggie's barricades. They wrapped the boy in warmth and security as he awoke, the voice in his ears still whispering of death.

Maggie had not slept but a wink. She darted here and there, a frenzy of nerves and worry. Arthur could hear her muttering to herself as she loaded two travelers' bags for them. After a moment, she noticed the boy staring bleary-eyed at her from the cushiony depths of the chair by the fire.

"Oh good, you're awake," she said. "Come and have a try at lifting your bag, Artie. I've made it the lighter of the two, but there's just so much we might want, isn't there?"

The bags did look rather large, Arthur thought as he slid down from the seat. He stole a wary glance toward the bedrooms as he crossed to the kitchen. Both doors remained barred and still, yet he could not keep from shuddering at the sight of them. The dining table had been pushed aside, presumably by Maggie herself as she seemed not to mind its having been moved.

"Come on then, Artie. There's no time to waste now the sun's up," she said. "I'd like to put a fair distance between ourselves and this place today. Don't you agree?"

Arthur nodded, trying his strength against the weight of his bag. It was surely not the lightest thing he had hefted in his life, but the hopeful look on Maggie's face quelled any protest he might have made.

"Yeah, I'll manage alright," he said.

No sooner had these words escaped his lips than Maggie clapped her hands excitedly and bolted back to the cupboard, fished out a pair of apples and a loaf of bread and stuffed them roughly into his bag atop the rest.

"Oh, don't fuss Artie," she said in reply to his groans of protest. "We'll have eaten those by lunchtime, sure."

She was off again, throwing various sundry items into her own bag. Arthur stared at her, pondering exactly how many kitchen knives or spices they might truly need, until a realization dawned upon him. Maggie did not mean to return to this place. Turning about on the spot, he sighed. Much as the horrors of the night before still hung upon his thoughts he could not help but remember the sanctuary the place had offered him for the last few months. Here he had been free of the cruelties of Kaye and the demands of Ektor. Here he had been able to wander and spend whole hours as he liked. Wherever they were headed to next, Arthur doubted he could be so lucky again.

"Ready, Artie?" Maggie asked, her hand upon the door.

He nodded solemnly, and with one last glance to the barred bedroom door, he followed her out into the morning light. About a quarter mile down the road, Bartholomew popped his head out of a bush and, guessing their intent by their demeanor, took up a trot beside Arthur's feet.

Chapter Twenty-Six
The Young Lord Pendragon

The preceding week had been an entertaining one; Merlin could say that at the least. For the first couple of days he had waited with baited breath, hoping and wishing to hear the sound of approaching footsteps. It had seemed like an eternity.

Soon, however, it was proven to him just how useless his worry had been, for early upon the morning of the third day a horn sounded. It had echoed down the cliffs, reverberated about the cave, and wakened him from his fitful slumber. The old man burst from his makeshift bed and sloshed straight out into the high morning tide. There, as the waves rolled gently past his waist, he saw a young man cross the causeway toward Tintagel carrying a pair of banners. The first — and largest — was the flag of his lord, Ban. The second, smaller banner was the white flag of truce. At the sight of the lad, Merlin let loose a raucous cheer. Then, fearing that he might unwittingly undo his own machinations, he darted back into the cave. Soon thereafter he heard the customary "haloo" from Pelias atop the wall and knew that that for which he had hoped had begun to come to pass. This prompted much splashing about in the shallows, followed by the lighting of a fire for practical reasons.

It was as he was drying himself by the fire that a second horn had echoed down the cliffs, sounding very different from the first. A second lord had arrived on the very heels of the first. Merlin restrained himself from dashing into the waves a third time, but let out another loud whoop despite himself. This did nothing to better his reputation, for each time they were asked about the howling cave by the sea, the denizens of Tintagel responded quite vociferously that a madman and wizard lived there and warned travelers not to go near it.

The following days had contained a veritable procession of lords, marquesses, earls, and at least one self-styled king. Each had come, proclaimed that one god or another had sent him, and demanded to see the sword — which of course stood in full view before the walls of Tintagel, stuck as it was in the stone. Most, when pointed toward it by an ever-tiring Pelias, dismounted then and there and, with varying levels of pomp, vigorously grabbed and groped at the sword. None were successful.

Their numbers were so great that, from his vantage point, Merlin had witnessed at least one altercation; which arose between a lord still tugging away at the sword and another, freshly arrived. Words and then blows were exchanged; and upon the following morning, with the entirety of the many assemblages attending, a duel was waged. It had been meant as a duel to the death, the winner to take the crown and damn the sword and its stone, but that concept had faltered when neither man could injure the other. This was likely due to their both having worn their most ornate and heavy armor and neither man being any longer in his prime. It was only a short while before both men were sprawled upon the grass, heaving in their suits. It was then decided that they would both make second attempts at the sword, giving each other fair time to prove his worth. This would have settled the matter, but for their discovery upon climbing again the path to Tintagel of yet a third lord, his hand already upon the blade.

Recently, there had been so many of these disagreements that a sizeable camp had appeared atop the cliffs. No lord, nor any of his travelling vassals had dared depart. None wished to miss the great event of the pulling of the sword, and beside that there seemed no end of entertainment in the camp. Sir Kaye, having arrived upon the fourth day, had supplied much of it. He had already made four attempts at the sword and fought in three duels, all of which had been avoidable.

Merlin was, of late, the only one about that seemed in anything less than high spirits. It was true, though no one knew it, that he had been the one to set all of this frenetic circumstance in motion. It was true too that he had much enjoyed watching his plans come to fruition and discovering that he had correctly directed the feathers he had taken from Athena to the destinations he had gleaned from Conrad's books. This realization, however, came with its own doubts. Arthur and

Maggie had not yet arrived and, though all the earls and lords and whatever-they-weres had arrived upon horseback, he felt that the boy and maid were well past due. Even the young Brothers Saracen, named for their darker skin, who ruled the lands of Londinium in three equal parts, had each now tried his hand at the sword. None but Merlin knew it but, save for Arthur and Maggie, they had been the last of the invited guests to arrive. If the boy did not arrive soon, many would tire of their frivolity and begin to depart. They would not see the boy pull the sword and likely not believe the news when it found them.

It was with great relief then that, upon the sunset of the eighth day, Merlin discovered the source of a scratching, scrabbling sound outside his cave. There, looking disheveled and much the worse for wear, were Arthur and Maggie, the girl carrying a much bedraggled knot of fur in the shape of a feline, barely recognizable as Bartholomew.

"Oh, thank the fair folk ye're here," said Maggie as Merlin poked his head out from the cave. "Artie'd half convinced me we were climbin' down to the home of a beast." She smiled an exhausted smile and allowed Merlin to take her bag as she hopped down into the already-rising tide.

"It's not just me that thought it," said Arthur. "Half the people camped on the cliffs think a demon lives here! They say it's him, er... you," he said looking at Merlin, chagrined, "that they're here to stop stealing away the sword. Some swear they've heard wails and shrieks coming from down here."

"Some unfortunate amalgam of rumor from Tintagel and my getting a bit excited a few days ago," said Merlin. "I assure you Arthur: there is no one but me in this cave, and I am no sort of demon at all."

His smile was returned timidly.

"I've figured as much!" said Maggie, "There weren't no sign of you in the camp an' only wild accusations when we asked after you at the castle. I think we're just a bit nervous to be out so close to dark is all, as we haven't had the best o' luck come nightfall these days."

Arthur shuddered and reached for Bartholomew. Maggie handed over the tousled feline and watched as the boy took the cat into the cave.

"Is the boy alright?" asked Merlin, also watching Arthur and

Bartholomew as they traveled deeper into the cave. "He's clinging to the cat as if for his very life."

"Artie's less a boy than he used to be, Merlin," said Maggie, "and he's holdin' on to that cat for good reason. It's more'n once that cat's saved our skins these last few days."

Merlin gave the girl a worried look. He had not considered their having trouble on the road. Now, having heard the mention of it he felt that he must, somehow, be to blame.

"What has happened?" he asked her, absentmindedly dropping her bag upon the cave floor and inspecting her more closely. She did not seem physically injured, but the marks he had first taken to be merely the accumulation of travel now took on a worrisome bent. She did not meet his searching gaze, but instead gave a quick nod in the direction of the boy, now nearly eclipsed by the darkness of the cave."

"Well, whatever it is, he doesn't seem to be afraid of the dark any longer," said Merlin.

"'Course he is," said Maggie. "All of us are, now we know what's in it."

Again this caught the old man visibly off guard, which was something that would have sent Maggie into fits of laughter had she not been so tired and afraid. She merely tramped over to where he had dropped her bag and collapsed beside it.

"The thing of it is," she said, gesturing to the place where Arthur and Bartholomew had disappeared, "it's far better to know you're in trouble than supposin' you're safe, and that cat'll tell us whether we're bein' watched or hunted straight off."

"Hunted?" said Merlin, worry washing over him. He suddenly felt uneasy with the boy out of his sight. "Wait here," he told Maggie. "It is perfectly safe."

"For a little while yet," she said, keeping an eye on the setting sun.

Merlin did not hear her. He was already striding into the dark recesses of the cave after the boy. He had not yet lit a fire for the night, making the far reaches of the cave well and truly dark. It took him an anxious moment to find the boy, and when he did, the sight of him did nothing to subdue his worry.

Arthur was standing silently in one of the deepest corners of the cave, staring up into the dark. Over the boy's shoulder a pair of yellow eyes shone and blinked at the old man. Arthur stroked the cat absent-mindedly. Then, noticing that Bartholomew had seen something, slowly turned to look at what it might be. The look on the boy's face was white with fear, yet steely and brave.

"Who are you?" he asked.

"Why, it is Merlin of course," said the old man.

Then, all at once, the boy dropped the cat and thrust himself at the old man, gripping him tight about the waist. Tears streamed down the boy's face and he sobbed into the old man's robes. Merlin heaved a sigh of relief and lifted the boy into his arms. The child had been traumatized, it was clear, but a weeping Arthur was a familiar one and as such an improvement on the silent and wary one of a moment past. Merlin carried the boy back toward the fading light at the mouth of the cave. Bartholomew plodded along before them dutifully; but when the cat spied Maggie sitting by the opening of the cave, staring at the last rays of the sun dipping beneath the waves, he began to bristle and yowl. Arthur shuddered in Merlin's arms. Without turning to face them, Maggie stood.

"We'll need a fire," she said, "the biggest and brightest you can keep fed 'til mornin'."

She began searching about the cave for wood and, finding some piles of driftwood set against the cave wall, began arranging them in a sizeable heap. Merlin watched her a moment.

"I assure you, Maggie," he said, "that once the tide is up, as it shall soon be, this cave is quite inaccessible."

The girl stopped what she was doing, flung the last piece of wood down on the pile and turned on him.

"And I assure you, you old bastard, that it's nothin' o' the like!" she yelled.

"I have seen enough!" bellowed the wizard, his voice caroming off the walls of the cave. "I will know what it is that has happened! Who is it that has been after you?"

Maggie stood her ground.

"We need a fire," was all she would say.

Merlin assessed the girl for a moment and then shifted Arthur's weight to one side. The boy started at this, but did not cry out.

"We will make a fire, then," said Merlin, "but then I shall demand that you tell me what it is that has happened!"

Maggie nodded and the two of them set about adding kindling and preparing the fire. When it was ready, Merlin, still holding Arthur, pulled a flint and striking stone from his robe with his free hand and sparked the fire to life. Maggie tended the burgeoning flames, and soon the fire shone like a beacon in the dark.

Arthur had finally released Merlin and sat beside the fire, looking tired but less afraid. Maggie sat beside him, looking much the same. It was not until Merlin cleared his throat that either of them looked away from the flames.

"You have promised me explanation," he said. "I can see that you have both been beset along your way, and I must know the reason for it."

He had directed the question to Maggie, but to his surprise it was Arthur who spoke.

"The reason!? You want to know the reason?" he said.

The child was shuddering again, though from anger this time, and his eyes did not waver as he stared incredulously at the old man. Merlin began to open his mouth to speak, but the child cut him off.

"It was because of you! Because you lied!" shouted Arthur. "You said it was dead! You said it wouldn't be coming back, but you lied!"

The echoes of the child's words died in the stunned silence that filled the cave.

"What d'ye mean he lied?" asked Maggie into the void. "Do you mean to tell me that this old sod knows what the vile thing is, so? Am I the only one at all who's runnin' from somethin' she knows nothin' about and has done nothin' to provoke?"

Arthur stared at Merlin, daring the wizard to refute what he had said. A chill ran up the old man's spine.

"You cannot mean the creature that I destroyed," he said at last. "The one whom I unmade the very night upon which we met, Arthur?"

Arthur nodded his head sternly.

"That's what you said that night, but it's a lie!" he said.

"It is not," said Merlin, shaking his head earnestly. "Arthur you must believe me. There is no way that that creature should have returned. It was torn and sundered and scattered to the wind."

"Sure'n somethin' tried to kill us the night we got your note,

Merlin," Maggie said. "Sure'n that same somethin's been stalkin' us every night since, and sure'n we haven't but barely kept our necks in runnin' from it. Whether it's the same as what Artie thinks it is or not, I'll swear to my dying breath that the thing is real — and likely somewhere about these very cliffs at this very moment."

At her saying this, all eyes were cast about the cave. Even Bartholomew seemed to understand the ill portent of Maggie's words.

After a moment of listening and hearing only the fire and the surf, and seeing nothing dancing in the shadows but those cast by the flames, they returned their attention to one another. Eventually, it was decided that they would sleep in shifts and that whoever was awake would keep close watch over the moods of Bartholomew for signs of danger.

Though he had been appointed a shift of his own, Merlin stayed awake all night talking to either Maggie or Arthur in turn. It was thus that he learned the full details of their harrowing journey, and that they in turn learned the details of the fate of Lord Pendragon and of Conrad and of the sword in the stone. The only detail Merlin omitted was of his encounter with Athena, for he neither knew how to relate it nor what might happen if he did so.

They woke later than Merlin had intended the next day. Arthur, it seemed had been so reassured by Merlin's presence that he slept long and deeply, such that neither Maggie nor Merlin had the heart to wake him. This set the entire rhythm of the day off in Merlin's perception and resulted in his constantly forgetting things and rushing about. When the child finally did wake, Maggie mentioned that he might want to wash up in the lapping waves, as he had not had the opportunity since getting on the road. The old man blustered, eventually acquiesced, and then promptly forgot to offer Arthur breakfast. Instruction was hastily given to both Arthur and Maggie as to how they were to behave during the day, and was then repeated as a precaution.

It was early afternoon when Arthur departed the cave alone, as was Merlin's wish. Maggie followed after a while, but under strict orders not to be seen near the boy. This, Merlin had said, was of utmost importance. "The child must draw the sword from the stone without aid or supervision," he had said, "or the endeavor will be ruined." It was for this same reason that Merlin meant not to leave the cave for the duration of the day.

Arthur was nearly at the top of the cliff when he realized that, in the bustle of the morning, he had neglected to ask Merlin about the strange symbols that had been written on his note. He reminded himself to ask the old man about them later and pressed on. He was too excited to worry about it at the moment, anyway. The very idea that he was the son of a lord, and to be proclaimed one himself that very day, was nearly enough to push even his instructions on how to accomplish the task out of his head. Nothing else seemed to matter much.

The plan was that he would go to the center of the camp atop the cliffs and proclaim that he meant to pull the sword from the stone. Then, with a throng of interested onlookers at his heels, he would ascend to the gate of Tintagel and draw the sword from the stone, a thing which Merlin had assured him would be very simple.

'There's another thing I meant to ask the old man about,' he thought, 'but I suppose if it's that simple a thing, then it doesn't really need explanation, does it?'

Reaching the top of the cliff, Arthur immediately strode to the camp and, finding its center, shouted at the top of his lungs:

"My name is Arthur!" he said. "My father was Uther Pendragon, and I have come to pull his sword from the stone!"

He then looked about for the throngs of elated followers that he was sure he had lured to his side. The camp stood still and quiet. Save for a single knight breathing heavily in his plate, no one seemed to have noticed the boy at all. This was for a pair of reasons, though the boy knew neither of them.

The early afternoon had, by this time in the life of the camp, developed into a sort of unofficial lull in the daily goings on. The morning's duel had already been fought, and the victor's subsequent attempt at the sword witnessed. Some knights and lords had already begun to take advantage of this structured way of life, challenging newcomers the very instant they arrived so as to usurp their chance at the sword through victorious combat. The seated, solitary, knight who watched Arthur make his proclamation was one such predatory individual, and had indeed just returned exhausted from the sword a few moments before.

The second reason for the quiet of the afternoon was that a particularly vicious fight had broken out amongst the spectators during this recent attempt at the sword, and one of the men involved had demanded immediate satisfaction. So it was that, as Arthur proclaimed his intent, most members of the camp were either too busy watching two men assault one another or too engulfed in finishing their mid-day meal to be bothered by his shouting. Shouting, incidentally, which every boy and girl in the camp had uttered in one form or another already, usually more than once. Not knowing what else to do, Arthur strode as purposefully as he knew how toward Tintagel. Only the solitary knight watched him go.

Maggie saw Arthur crossing the causeway just as she was reaching the cliff top. She noticed how utterly alone he was and her heart sank. Something was wrong, she thought, but as there was no throng of followers and bystanders for her to blend into she could find no way of getting closer to the boy without disobeying Merlin's instruction. She would have to satisfy herself with keeping a watchful eye on him from across the causeway.

So it was that Arthur approached the sword in the stone entirely by himself. Looking ahead, he saw that not even a solitary guard stood atop the battlements. Tintagel was still without its main gate, but Pelias had declared it "defended beyond all reasonable measure" due to the presence of the lords and knights camped across the causeway. As such the guards had taken to crossing over to the camp so that they could witness the daily duels.

There, before the walls of the mightiest castle he had yet seen, stood Arthur. Before him was the sword of his father, plunged deep into the stone. He approached the ornate weapon warily, not sure of what might happen next. He had the impression, as he inched closer to the blade, that some bit of Merlin's magic might take hold of him as he neared the sword, telling him what to do.

He was atop the stone before he knew it. He waited there a moment for something to rise up from the earth and direct him, but nothing came. Slowly, he extended a wary hand toward the sword, allowing the tips of his fingers to brush delicately across the hilt. Nothing happened. There was no rush of insight, no shiver of understanding shooting up his spine, nothing. Arthur stood perplexed.

He tried gripping the sword in his hand, quickly releasing it again as if it were aflame. Nothing. He began to feel foolish. Perhaps he had been wrong, he thought. Perhaps there was no magical trick to the sword and all he had to do was to give it a good tug. Perhaps it was enough that he was Arthur, son of Uther, and the sword would yield itself to him in deference. He gripped the sword again and tugged. Again, nothing happened. Arthur became frustrated. He yanked and pulled and pushed at the sword. Futile minutes passed, his efforts beginning to falter. He let go of the sword and took a step back to ponder the thing.

Merlin had said that retrieving the sword would be simple for him, and yet there he stood before it, exhausted and bereft of his promised birthright. It made no sense to him. Staring at the sword, catching his breath, his mind began to wander. He thought of Merlin and of the safety of the cave. At least, he thought, he would be able to return there before nightfall, swordless but safe. 'Maybe then,' he thought, 'I can ask Merlin how to draw the sword from the stone. I could ask him about his strange letter, too, and those markings he put on it.' And there it was: his answer, staring him right in the face.

'It's a puzzle-box,' he realized, 'and Merlin's given me the key!'

He approached the sword once more, standing so close to it that he could not see the blade, but only the pommel and guard from above, the large ruby staring back at him. He squatted and inspected the hilt a moment and, when he was sure of himself, placed his hands in very precise positions, one atop the pommel and the other low about the grip.

Now, what was the first symbol?' he thought to himself. "A sort of a 'J'," he replied aloud.

With his right hand he pressed upon the ruby pommel while turning and pressing against the grip with his left. The hilt clicked and moved in his grip. Arthur's heart skipped a beat, nearly making him release his grip, but he dared not move for fear of losing what progress he had made.

"An 'I' was next!" he whispered excitedly. He breathed in and let go, but only from the grip of the sword. With his right hand he pulled straight up on the pommel. A satisfying *clack* emanated from the sword. The next letter had been a sort of a bent 'M'. 'How am I to make an 'M' with my hands?' he wondered. He gripped the handle of the sword once again with his left hand and, as if he were peeling an onion, twisted his hands in opposite directions. This time the sword loosed a resounding *thunk* from somewhere deep within the stone. Arthur was ecstatic. There had only been one further symbol upon Merlin's note, which meant he was one simple motion away from pulling the sword from the stone and claiming it and all the lands of his new-found father for himself. His heart beat thunderously against his ribs. His hands quivered, so excited was the boy.

'Now, what had the symbol been?' he thought.

He couldn't recall. In the nervous excitement of the moment, he had forgotten it. He felt as if the symbol was upon the very tip of his mind, yet would not reveal itself to him.

'How dim-witted am I?' he thought to himself. 'I read and re-read that note to myself every night this week! How can I have forgotten it?'

He stood there crestfallen, willing the forgotten symbol to present itself to him. As he did so, he became aware of a sound coming up the hill. It was a heavy, hollow sort of sound; one which he could almost place. Suddenly, an image of the ashen creature burst forth in his mind and he whirled about on the spot.

Before him stood the knight from the camp. As he had spun around, the knight had startled and halted his approach. The large man stood, still as a statue, his hands raised in a posture of surprise.

"How did you do that?" asked the knight, his voice ringing from within his heavy helmet.

Arthur squinted at the man, perplexed.

"How did you do it?!" the knight asked once more, gesturing angrily at the boy.

Arthur looked down at himself, trying to see what the knight might be gesturing at. There, clasped in his hands was the Blade Pendragon. His eyes went wide, his jaw dropped, and he began to stammer incoherently, a stunned smile stop-starting its way across his cheeks. The knight took a step towards him, his gauntleted hand still raised. Arthur shrank away from the knight, not knowing what the large man would do to him.

"P," he said, suddenly realizing what the last letter on Merlin's note had been, "for pull?"

"Pull?!" spat the knight, not amused in the slightest. "Is that all you'll tell me?"

Arthur stared at the man, a quizzical look upon his face. Just then, when the knight had shouted, he could have sworn that he'd recognized the man's voice.

"Damn it all, Wart!" said the knight, tugging off his helmet. "I'll have that sword and I'll have you tell me how you pulled it before I take it back to the camp!"

It was Sir Kaye, and his blood was up. Images of the torments that Kaye had inflicted upon him over the years flashed into Arthur's mind. He inched further away, yet he found that he was not so afraid of Kaye as he had been when last they had met. There were greater demons in the world than angry knights, after all. He kept the point of the Blade Pendragon pointed at Kaye's chest.

"I'll have that sword!" shouted Kaye.

"No, you won't!" someone shouted from behind the knight. Kaye spun about, his helmet raised in his hands, as if he was going to smash it down upon whomever it was that had caught him. There stood Maggie, huffing and puffing from the run across the causeway and up to the castle. Kaye lowered his helmet and chuckled at the maid.

"I suppose it's you that'll stop me?" he asked, incredulous.

It was at this precise moment, deep in his cave, that Merlin realized his error in forgetting to tell Arthur how to pull the sword from the stone. He shot to his feet and bolted out of the cave and into the surf, hoping he was not too late to help the boy.

High atop the rocks, Maggie spied the wizard splashing about in the waves.

"No it won't be me at all what puts a stop to you, Kaye!" she shouted, gesturing down toward Merlin in the sea. "I do believe he'll want to have the first go at ye, so!"

Kaye looked down at the cave, just as Merlin's searching gaze found the three of them standing before the castle. Their eyes met. So ferocious did Merlin look, standing there amongst the waves; so unexpected was his appearance, that sir Kaye dropped his helmet in the dirt and bolted down the roadway, his armor clanking about cacophonously as he went.

At the sight of Kaye's exit, and seeing Arthur, the sword already in his hands, Merlin let out a whoop and sat himself down right there in the sea, laughing all the while.

Maggie swept the boy up in her arms. Tears of joy filled her eyes as she hugged the child. Arthur hugged her back with one arm, the other holding the sword aloft in triumph. Never in either of their wildest dreams had they dared to hope for so wonderous a thing to befall the boy who had once been called 'Wart'.

There was no need for Maggie and Arthur to announce what had happened before the walls of Tintagel. Kaye saw to that. By the time they had descended to the narrow causeway, Kaye, in some self-preserving act of heraldsmanship, had already run clanking into the camp atop the cliffs, shouting at the top of his lungs about the boy who pulled the sword from the stone.

Climbing toward the camp, they were greeted with cheers and gasps. Many recalled Merlin's words from the week before and marveled at how precisely he had predicted the pulling of the sword. Rumors abounded into the night. Eventually it was decided that the boy, unlikely as he seemed, must truly be the rightful heir of Tintagel and all its lands.

It was late in the evening when Arthur, escorted by a chagrined Pelias, entered Castle Tintagel. Maggie followed close at hand. They were first led to the Great Hall, where they supped on a feast that took even Maggie's practiced palate by surprise. Four fires, two along each of the north and south walls of the Hall, warmed the room. Their effect was dazzling, thought Arthur. Ektor's castle, he mused, was dark and drab in comparison with this place. Midway through their meal, Merlin popped his head in at the door. The wizard, it turned out, was now free to roam the castle grounds as he wished, so great had been the impact of the fulfilling of his prophecy. The three of them chatted and laughed together over the events of the day for a good long while, until the hour was quite late.

Yawning, Maggie excused herself first. She had gotten very little sleep, she said, in what felt like as long as she could remember; and so a serf was called and a bed made up for her in one of the lower chambers of the castle, near the kitchens as was her wont. Not long after she departed, Arthur's head began to droop. Merlin hefted the young lord from his seat and carried him up the winding stair, taking care to hand him the sword as well. That the blade was too big for the child to carry easily was of no concern to the wizard. The mere sight of the boy and the sword together would ensure that his tale would grow.

Upon arriving at the door to the lord's apartment, Merlin set the half-sleeping boy upon his feet and ushered him into the chamber. Arthur plodded along dutifully into the dark. A sudden gasp and a yelp caught them both unawares. Arthur leapt into the air, landing hard on his hind-quarters against the stone floor. A spark was struck and lamplight filled the small antechamber. There, her eyes as wide as saucers, stood the chambermaid, her nightshirt askew and her hair tousled in the shape of a bird's nest. She blinked the sleep out of her eyes, looking back and forth between the old man and the boy upon the floor.

"Who's he?" she asked after a moment, pointing at Arthur.

"That," smiled Merlin, "is your young Lord Pendragon."

"The wot?"

"He is son to Lord Uther and has pulled the sword from the stone," said Merlin, smiling broader still.

The maid did not smile back. "He can't have done!" she said. "That is — he can't be!"

Merlin lifted the sword from the floor in response, simultaneously pulling Arthur up to his feet. The boy offered a sleepy smile to the maid. She was older than he, but not so old as Maggie, and so he treated her as a peer rather than someone already grown. The girl must have seen this in his smile, for she returned it timidly.

Thinking her smile meant acceptance of the boy, Merlin guided Arthur through the antechamber and into the apartment proper. The maid followed, looking on, but as the boy approached the bed she grabbed the old man by the sleeve.

"But," she stammered, "but you mustn't!"

Ignoring her, Merlin lay the boy on bed and wrapped him in the covers. Then, with a short glance at the chambermaid, he hung the Blade Pendragon above the bed, just where it had been when he had first taken it away. He then turned his attention back to the girl.

"The young lord is rightful heir to this place," he said. "He has been tried and tried again, and in all things he has triumphed. Chief amongst the things that he deserves now is sleep."

He gestured to the boy as he said this. To both his and the chambermaid's surprise, the boy was already fast asleep and dreaming. The girl looked pained, but the sight of Arthur so comfortable there and asleep already seemed to win her over. Merlin took her hand from his sleeve and she allowed herself to be led back to her antechamber, though her eyes never left the boy asleep in the bed. When the curtains were drawn closed to the apartment, Merlin let go of the girl's hand and smiled down at her.

"I do not believe that we have had the opportunity to be properly acquainted," he said quietly.

"I know who you are," she said, not lowering her voice as he had done. "You're the vagabond, Merlin. The man who killed Lord Conrad an' threw this castle into despair."

Merlin's smile changed to a look of concern.

"Conrad," he said, "was not lord of this place. He would have usurped that name, it is true, had he been able; but I do not think you would have liked that event so very much in the end."

The maid sniffed and heaved a sigh. Tears began to trickle down her cheeks.

"He wasn't bad to me," she said, her voice catching in her throat. "He was the only one I can remember what was kind to me before."

Merlin heaved a sigh of his own, staring down at the girl. His hand rose to her cheek almost without his realizing it, and he dabbed her tears away with his sleeve. He then patted her hair, trying to make it lie a bit more flat. She did not shrink away from him, but neither did she warm to his touch.

"What is your name, girl?" he asked, giving up on the endeavor of improving her hair.

"Morgan," she said.

"Morgan, you needn't worry," he said. "You shall be allowed to stay here as Arthur's chambermaid. You shall be given every freedom that Conrad allotted you, and maybe more if you are good."

He looked for a response, but when he did not get one he continued.

"You are a loyal maid, Morgan," he said, "and it is no fault to care for those who treat you well. I am sorry for the events that transpired between Conrad and myself in your presence, but I hope that in time you will come to understand them. Can you try to do that for me?"

The girl nodded, smiling a sad little smile that sent fresh tears down her cheeks.

"That's a good lass," said Merlin, patting her on the head once more and turning to depart.

"But..." she said, "but the boy..."

"Hush now," said Merlin, passing through the doorway and into the hall. "I shall let you tell me all about it in the morning, Morgan. I shall be below in the councilor's chambers if need of me arises."

The girl shook her head, about to say something as he closed the door. 'The girl will need time,' he told himself, 'but she will understand in the end.'

The apartment was cold as Morgan blew out the lamp. In the dark, she caught a shiver and darted back to her small mat, wrapping herself tight in her sheepskin blanket. She did not lie flat, but sat up straight, her back pressed tight against the stone wall. Her eyes darted to and fro in the blackness. Her chest heaved, shuddering as it worked against the lump in her throat.

Chapter Twenty-Seven
Blood and Ice

My name is Orion and my father lies cradled in my arms. His wounds have not healed. His battle with Posideon, god of the seas, was more taxing upon his mortal body than I had thought. Our hunting trips into the wood that borders Father's land cannot have aided in what recovery may have been made. I grit my teeth, trying not to blame him for this. What could be so important about these hunting trips that he would sacrifice his health to them. I have seen his decline given life as a cough and a shudder. I have seen it mature as bloodied bandage laid upon bloodied bandage. I have seen it strip the strength from the flesh of a man who defeated a god. I have seen it climb his frame, to summit his heights and bleed the thoughts from his very mind. They are coughed up now, blots upon a bit of muslin.

There is little for me to do for Father now. His small frame shudders in my arms. I cradle the man who raised me, holding him as if I were the father and he my child. It is not his words, mostly garbled these recent days, that convey his care, but his eyes. He stares at me, his eyes clouded yet gazing deep into me. There is more bravery and more strength in those steely orbs than I have ever been able to draw forth. Here, as his body convulses, he gives me the strength to cope. I raise my hand to brush back his blood-caked hair. Swiftly, fluidly, deftly, his hand rises and meets mine in mid-motion. His fingers curl around my palm, strong and sure. My eyes flick to our hands in surprise. There is focused effort in this motion. I look into my father's eyes. The clouds that so tightly eclipsed his sight have been drawn away. He does not blink, his gaze filled with purpose. One-handed, he pulls himself up from the cradle of my elbow, holding my eyes to his with a fixed stare. I can feel his weakened breath upon my face. His other hand shoots its way to the back of my neck, turning my head so that his lips are near to touching my ear. "Remember the lessons of the forest," he whispers. "Learn the teachings of the bees." His voice is hoarse. The hand upon my neck shudders. "Never," he says, pulling my head around so that he is staring into my eyes again, "Never underestimate the treachery of man or his gods."

With this he releases the hand from my neck. It caresses my cheek as he falls back into my waiting arms. He is gone before his head returns to the cradle of my elbow; gone before I can tell him I love him one last time; gone before I can convey what it is to be a son thankful for the life his father has given him.

My eyes water. My chest heaves. I take my hand from his and close Father's eyes. As I do so, I see a thin trickle of bloody water exiting the canal of his ear. I move to brush it away. It is frigid to the touch. Instinctively I pull my hand away, carrying with it a couple droplets of the sanguine liquid. My fingertips sting and throb as the droplets upon them turn to razor-thin blades of ice, cutting into my flesh. With a flick of my wrist they are thrown from my wounds, landing upon the floor. Swiftly the water that has exited Father's ear rushes to them, enveloping them, a small pool upon the stones of the floor. Sobbing, still holding my one-time protector's lifeless body to my own, I watch the water congeal there. The pool's edge draws inward, its center lifts. My shock and my fear choke as a suffocating, pulsing rage boils its way to the surface of my heart. As I sit, watching the water lift itself into a pillar of ice upon the floor, my heart boils over sending scalding rivulets of rage streaming through my veins. My ears grow hot and my fingers crackle, electric with wrath.

Upon the floor, the pillar of ice sprouts two thin arms. They arc their way towards the sky as they form. Where their hands should be, grow sharpened barbs. I know the symbol before it takes its final shape. It is the trident, weapon of Posideon.

I gingerly lay down the husk that for many years carried the spirit of my father and I rise to my feet, shaking with blood-lust. My temples pound with it. My sight hues red. The rage in my blood erupts and I lash out, fists clenched, at the icy implement upon the floor. It slices into my flesh, even as I shatter its form. Hot drops of blood drip from my fists, joining the mangled ice upon the floor. Where my blood touches it, the ice melts and writhes, shying away. My feet come crashing down upon the small puddles as I try to crush them out of existence. They merge as I do so. Manic, I scream my loss and my bitterness at them. The blood leaves my skull and I collapse upon my knee. I am undone, cut deeper than any wound of the flesh can delve. The puddle upon the floor boils, filling the air with the scent of brine and rot. The vapor rises, hovering before my downcast eyes. It emits a faint hiss of laughter. My eyes sting from salt. The blood pounds its way back into my face and again my sight blurs crimson. I swing my bleeding fists through the vapor with all my might. It curls around them and wafts lazily, mockingly out through the open window. I shatter the door as I run screaming into the night. I can see nothing. Nothing remains for me now, nothing but the loss in my heart and the fury in my veins, and the cruel laughter upon the breeze.

Chapter Twenty-Eight

Kilkaenen Unseen

Scrape, scrape, scrape it went. *Scrape, scrape, scrape* and then quiet. Sometimes the sound was so quiet as to be thought imagined; other times it was a deep and boring noise, like that of a rat gnawing at a barrel. *Scrape, scrape, scrape* it went.

Then came the voice: a dry whispering, crackling voice, muffled and somber in tone. "All of a piece, all in a place," it choked. "All of a piece, all in a place."

Scrape, scrape, scrape it went.

Arthur's eyes popped open. Over him stood Morgan, still as a board and staring.

Scrape, scrape, scrape it went. The girl shuddered, her breath an icy mist upon the air.

"What is it?" asked Arthur, himself shuddering now, all too sure that he knew the answer.

Morgan took a step away from the bed, raising a finger past Arthur, toward the little door in the corner of the room.

"When it comes..." she said, "when it comes, it comes from the sea-door."

"All of a piece, all in a place," choked the voice once more, louder than before. *Scrape, scrape, scrape* it went, *scrape, rip, snap.*

Arthur darted out of bed, landing beside Morgan just as something small and rough skidded toward them along the floor. Morgan stood transfixed, staring at the little door. Arthur bent down and picked up the thing from the floor. It was a bit of tinder, shorn from the base of the door. Morgan screamed.

"All of a piece..."

Tall and lank, a figure popped and snapped as it rose from the gap under the door; rose until it towered over the small doorframe.

"All in a place," it said, "Kil..."

From behind the children came a boom and a gust of air. Morgan startled, spinning on the spot to see what this new threat might be. There, pulling back the black curtains of the antechamber, stood Merlin. Though he had clearly been only recently jarred from a fitful sleep, his eyes were alight with scorn and sadness, a light which only burned the brighter as his gaze found the creature.

"Kil," it said again, "Kilkaenen, I am still."

"It has found a voice!" the old man gasped.

"To kill, it is my need, my will," it said.

Merlin strode into the room, beckoning the children to his side. The creature's eyes followed Arthur as he went.

"I had thought never to see you again, Kilkaenen," said Merlin.

The creature raised a splintered finger toward the boy. "To kill it is my need, my will," it repeated.

Arthur shrunk back, hiding himself behind Morgan.

"If it is within your ability to remember, creature," said Merlin, "you will recall me as the one who slew you once before."

The whirling, gaping chasms that were the creature's eyes glided their way to the old man's face.

"Slayer, slain, bearer, brother, captive, conjoiner," it said. "Bound to me before all this were you, Mer-lin."

The creature lurched forward. Merlin reeled, memories of blood and screams, of hate and deathless wait, fell upon him like a cloudburst.

His back struck the cold stone of the floor. Arthur was shouting. Smoke whirled all about him, hiding the boy from view.

"Fight him, Merlin!" shouted the boy, as if from far away. "You can beat him, I'm sure of it!"

The boy, standing over him, whirled briefly into view, was gone again. The smoke encircled the old man all the closer.

"Fight him!" shouted Arthur.

Then something heavy and swift lurched into the smoke. Crackling fingers which had been wrapped tight about the old man's ears and neck snapped and eased. Again Merlin felt a blow strike into the smoke. The sound of snapping and a rancorous groan echoed about him; and suddenly the room was visible again, the creature rising away from him in the dissipating gloom. He was dizzy and shaken as a stricken animal, but he was free.

His vision still spinning, Merlin caught sight of the boy. Arthur was standing, no longer behind Morgan but before her, the Blade Pendragon in his hands. The creature strode toward the boy, but Arthur did not flinch or shy away.

"Get up, Merlin," he said, "get up and we'll beat him together." The boy's voice was shaking, yet he stood his ground.

The creature stepped toward the boy. Arthur raised the sword above his head, waiting to strike. The creature halted, struggling in its advance. Its whirling eyes looked back toward the old man. Merlin smiled, still on the ground, his hand clasped about the creature's leg.

"I remember the sting of your strike now, Kilkaenen," he said, "and better than most do I understand what it is that you are."

And with that, the old man crushed the creature's leg in his grasp. Keening, the creature fell to its knee. The smell of rot and bracken thickened upon the air. Wheeling about, it hurled itself at Arthur. The boy's sword swung down hard, catching the creature's hand and hacking it to splinters. Merlin was on his feet then, raising his heel and bringing it down upon the thing. Bracken and loam shivered from the creature's flank where he had struck. The creature wailed again, struggling and scraping against the stone floor.

"Sup on their perilous ink," it said, "one final red drink."

Then Morgan was beside Arthur, holding in her hands the oil lamp from her chamber. The creature's eyes whirled toward her, as if seeing her for the very first time.

"All of a piece," it said to her.

She upturned the lamps contents upon its head.

"To kill it is my need," it said, its eyes widening at the girl.

Morgan struck a spark and the room filled with light.

Chapter Twenty-Nine

Reduced to Ashes

"Another sleepless night," huffed Maggie as she bustled about the table, setting bowls of steaming porridge before each of them in turn. Bartholomew followed her about dutifully, taking only a moment to sniff each bowl. His every effort yielding only a hot, meatless mass, the cat eventually called his scavenging attempts a loss, settling instead for the warmth of Arthur's lap.

"I'm afraid it's porridge or nothin', late as it is, so," said Maggie. "There's been much early-to-beddin' and late-to-risin' goin' on in this castle, it seems." She shook her head disparagingly. "Such habits won't stand much longer, now I'm here, sure!"

Morgan smiled up at Maggie from her porridge.

"I think it's lovely," she said.

Maggie smiled at the girl and tousled the rat's nest of Morgan's hair before plopping herself down into an empty chair and tucking into the stuff herself. Merlin shot Maggie a sidelong glance, dribbling a bit of porridge into his beard as he did so. Both Arthur and Morgan were sent into hysterics as the old man spent the next few minutes trying to sop the stuff back out again.

"I'm Morgan," said the chambermaid, introducing herself to Maggie after the laughter had died down.

"And what a lovely name it is, too," said Maggie, smiling. "What does it mean?"

"Lord Conrad says it means water faerie," said Morgan, before she could catch herself. She looked down at the table then, a sullen look in her eye.

Maggie was about to ask the girl about Conrad, but she saw the look of warning in Merlin's eye and dropped the subject.

"So, ye've dealt with the creature once more," she said, changing the subject.

"Once and for all, I believe," replied Merlin, still discovering small bits of porridge in his mane.

"But you've said that before," said Arthur, "and every time you left the cottage, I knew it was out there, just out of sight."

Merlin stopped what he was doing and stared long and hard at the boy.

"It came here before, too," said Morgan, looking up from the table.

Both Arthur and Maggie looked at the girl, stunned. Even Merlin turned a quizzical look toward the girl. Dauntless the maid went on:

"It's true," she said. "On stormy or freezing cold nights, I'd wake to the smell of it, that dusty, foresty smell?" she said, looking around for acknowledgement.

Arthur swallowed his porridge in one sizeable gulp.

"I wouldn't hear it so much as just know it was there," Morgan said, heartened by Arthur's look of understanding. "It was always standing there, just inside the sea-door. I could feel it peerin' about. Sometimes it was there for whole minutes, sometimes not long at all. It was like a dog sniffin' about for food it knew was there, but couldn't figure where exactly."

"And it never saw you?" asked Arthur, disbelieving.

"I never saw it neither," Morgan replied. "Not until tonight when I was out from my curtain."

Merlin peered at the girl from over his porridge.

"Well," he said, "I believe that Morgan has done us all a great service by setting the creature alight. He is burned and gone and we would all do well to pass him entirely out of our memory. It is for that reason, Morgan, that I ask you to give me that which you have hidden in your sleeve."

Morgan looked at the wizard, stunned.

"How did you...?" she asked.

"My eyes do not miss much, my dear," said Merlin. "Now do please hand it to me."

Morgan dutifully produced from her sleeve a tarnished and delicate coil of metal, curled about a burled bit of wood, and held it out to

Merlin.

"Put it on the table," he said, "and do so carefully. I would hate to see you cut yourself on it."

When she had done so, he nodded at the thing.

"This is the last relic of Kilkaenen the Unseen," he said. "I will not yet tell you of how we met, but let it suffice, tonight, to say that it was long before long ago. He was as wicked then as you have seen him to be tonight: a glutton, and blood his supper.

"I say this to you not to frighten, but to educate. His death is not to be honored, lamented, or marked in any way hereafter. He is gone; may we never again marvel at what he was."

He stared at Arthur as he said this, hoping the boy would, in particular, absorb his meaning. He then picked up the coil of metal and wood and hurled it into the fire, where it caught flame and began to glow, flaking away bit by bit.

Morgan watched as the thing burned, her eyes aglow with reflected firelight.

"I knew we would beat him," said Arthur, staring into the flames while absentmindedly caressing the cat upon his lap.

Maggie nearly snorted her porridge.

"Ye weren't so sure when we were barrin' the doors at the cottage!" she said.

"Well, not *us*," said Arthur, indicating himself and Maggie. "More like me and Merlin, with the proper bit of help!"

He nodded at Merlin, smiling and giving the old man a very obvious knowing wink.

Merlin looked baffled.

"What?" was all he could think to say.

Arthur rolled his eyes.

"You know," he said, goofily. "You told me we would already. Your stories?"

Merlin looked as befuddled as ever. Arthur sighed.

"Alright, I'll say it since I'm the one that's figured it out," he said. "I'm supposed to be Abner, aren't I? And you're Clay! And once we finished getting ourselves here to Tintagel, we found someone who helped us kill The Borderer, or Kilkaenen as he turned out to be named!"

Arthur looked about proudly, searching for the adulation he knew he was due. Merlin was silent a moment, a searching look upon his face.

"That you were so sure of our victory, I can only call a blessing," he said, "but Arthur: I am afraid that you are quite incorrect. The story of Abner Jenks and Cassius Marcellus Clay is neither about you and I, nor one that ends in the fashion you seem to think it does."

The old man stood. The room darkened. Ash and smoke billowed about the room. It was as if some trance had come over the winds which swept about Castle Tintagel, enticing them away from the cliffs and shepherding them down through the chimneys. The billowing clouds of ash lent an obscurity to the corners of the hall. Rather than in a castle's keep, the room's inhabitants might have occupied a winding bog or a shady glen. Maggie and Morgan looked about in astonishment as the whirling ash took more corporeal form. Grey trees and shrubs were visible now, their branches eclipsing even the table at which they still sat. All was grey and quiet. A stillness settled upon the glen. Only a glimpse of the sky could be found between the ashen trees. And then, like the dying embers of a fire, came the first glimmering light of dawn.

Chapter Thirty
King of the Wild Frontier

The mornin' went slow, mostly on account o' Abner n' Clay both havin' splittin' headaches. Jeremiah, on the other hand, was entirely unaffected by the previous night's libations.

When he saw Jeremiah waltzin' 'round like a preacher on a Sunday, Clay decided two things right quick: First, he figured on never gettin' inta a drinkin' match with a moonshiner; second, an' quite related to his first decision, he figured that White Lightnin', while nigh on poison t' any well-meanin' drunkard, sure might make powerful good fuel for Petunia. So, while Abner stumbled off t' find a creek an' wash the drunk off o' hisself, Clay set up the purchase an' payment for a pair o' stills worth o' the stuff. He even got Jeremiah t' throw in a helpin' hand in cartin' the hooch t' the auto-carriage by offerin' the feller a ride in the contraption.

They was on their way back from Petunia, havin' delivered their first load o' liquor into her belly, when they spied Abner returnin' t' camp lookin' none the better for his efforts at washin' up. He fell in step cartin' the hooch easy enough though, an' with the three o' them workin' together it weren't long b'fore the boiler was full an' ready t' go.

"You ready for that ride?" Clay asked Jeremiah.

Jeremiah didn't look too ready 'tall. He'da been fine loadin' the auto-carriage up with the White Lightnin', but now that it was time t' hop onto the contraption he was figetin' like a milkmaid without a bucket.

"Oh, come now!" said Clay. "When d'ya think you'll next have a chance to ride aboard one o' these things?"

"Well, that's the whole o' the matter, ain't it?" said Jeremiah, scratchin' his head. "I'd like t' live long 'nough t' see that chance!"

"Ha ha ha!" bellowed Clay, makin' Abner wince in the seat next t' him. "My good man, we rode all the way out from Lexington on nothin' but Tennessee whiskey. I assure you, Petunia is quite the lady."

"But that there White Lightnin'..." said Jeremiah.

"Poppycock! I'll hear no more of your waffling!" said Clay, shuttin' Jeremiah right up.

Abner squinted his puffy eyes at Clay, not at all in the mood for shoutin' so close t' hisself.

"Last chance, Jeremiah," said Clay, loadin' a shotgun shell into the auto-carriage's starter chamber. "You can either point us in the direction o' Davy Crockett's place or you can give us direction along the way. What'll it be?"

Jeremiah eyed the freshly loaded starter chamber an' its trigger mechanism somethin' stern an' sighed, but he climbed aboard just the same.

"There's a good man," said Clay, once Jeremiah was situated. "Now, let's see what your White Lightnin' can really do!"

He flung a wild look at Jeremiah an' pulled the trigger. Petunia let out a whine like an over-boilin' tea kettle an' roared t' life. Jets o' red flame shot a foot high out'ta each o' her four lamps with a hiss.

"What in..." said Abner.

Clay reached across Jeremiah an' Abner an' threw down the accelerator lever. They were off, faster than even the devil could'a followed 'em. Clay whooped like a madman, his hat flyin' off o' his head an' settlin' somewhere amongst the bags behind the chesterfield. Jeremiah weren't no quieter, screamin' bloody murder as he was. Abner was the only one not hollerin', but that was on account o' his havin' gone white as a sheet.

"Where," shouted Clay over the engine noise, "where do I turn off for the Crockett homestead?"

"We're all gonna die!" shouted Jeremiah.

"The turn, dammit!" shouted Clay. "I'll need t' know well ahead o' time at this speed!"

"You even try an' turn that wheel an' we're all jam on toast, Clay!" shouted Abner, turnin' green.

"Let me off!" shouted Jeremiah. "Let me off, let me off!" He was squirmin' so bad that he didn't give Clay much choice; not unless he really did want t' end up smeared thin as jam, like Abner'd said.

It took 'bout a mile t' slow down t' a stop, an' even then the auto-carriage was a'rumblin' somethin' ferocious. The second them wheels stopped, Jeremiah threw hisself into the dirt. Abner was right behind him, clamborin' down slow-like an' lookin' green as a sick toad.

"You — you boys are crazy!" shouted Jeremiah, his knees shakin' so hard that he had t' sit in the dirt t' stop the tremblin'. "I hain't never gone near that fast in all my life an' I don't plan to ever again!"

Abner puked.

"Ha ha!" roared Clay. "Come now, boys! We'll make fantastic time!"

"My god!" said Jeremiah, starin' in disbelief at Clay. "He really is crazy."

Abner nodded a slow, sick nod, puked again an' rolled over onto his side.

"Alright, Jeremiah," said Clay, "you don't have t' keep goin' if you don't want. Just tell me the way t' the Crockett homestead an' you can be off."

"Take this road ten more miles an' swing left at the fork," said Jeremiah, all too glad t' be done with the auto-carriage. "You'll start headin' uphill, an' a few miles further you'll find the forest. Once you're there, start lookin' 'round for a raccoon tail nailed t' a tree. That there'll be Crockett's marker, so swing a right when you see it. Don't miss that turn, now. There's a couple o' Northern boys who done set up a mine over the hill a piece. The carpetbaggin' claim jumpers'll shoot you on sight, they will."

"Watch for the raccoon tail. Got it," said Clay. "Then what?"

"Oh, don't worry 'bout that," said Jeremiah. "Jus' keep headin' up that hill. You'll meet Davy b'fore long." With that he gave a short wave an' ran off down the road, fearin' Clay'd rope him back on into the auto-carriage somehow.

"Alright, Abner," said Clay, watchin' Jeremiah kickin' up dust on down the road. "Stop lyin' about. We've got a fair bit o' travel ahead o' us."

Still on his side, Abner shook his head.

"Come on now, dammit," said Clay. "I don't want t' have t' throw you up here myself, now!"

Abner rolled his eyes at Clay's choice o' words an' sat up, begrudgin' every moment o' it. It took a fair an' wobbly minute, but he made it up onto the seat again.

"Onward!" cheered Clay. "To destiny!" an' with a streak o' red flame they were off.

The turn at the raccoon tail weren't much more'n a footpath, with rocks an' branches lyin' all about. Navigatin' up that, along with the dark shade o' the trees, made Clay slow the autocarriage to a crawl. He'da done it begrudgin'ly, havin' got used t' the speed the White Lightnin' afforded him, but once he saw that the red glow o' the headlights weren't no good at lightin' the road, he gave in.

Abner was plumb glad they'd slowed up a pace, an' he said so, mentionin' how they wouldn't want t' smack into a tree or a rock or somethin'. The mountain air sure seemed t' be doin' him good, an' the slow goin' meant less jostlin' about, which was doubtless just as healin'. He lifted his head an' looked 'round as they climbed into the hills, the color returnin' t' his cheeks. The trees were close an' thick an' there was a sort o' fungal scent on the breeze. 'This forest ain't never been cut nor cleared,' he thought. It felt strange t' him how old the growth was. The Crocketts had their homestead up here somewhere, an' there was supposed t' be a mine 'round the bend a ways. How the Crocketts could'a fashioned a cabin an' kept their cookfire goin' without clearin' some o' the trees n' brush he couldn't figure. 'An' then there's the mine!' he thought. 'What sort o' damn fool miner doesn't strip the forest for support beams?'

"How d'you like my land?" asked the man standin' on Petunia's runnin' board.

Both Abner n' Clay near shot out'ta their seats. Turnin' t' get a look at the feller, Clay jerked the wheel 'round, sendin' the auto-carriage lurchin' an' skiddin' t' a stop. When they'd regained their heads, the boys looked 'round again. The man weren't on the runnin' board no longer. Instead they found him standin' in front o' the headlamps, his face flickerin' red in the light.

"Well?" he asked. "How d'you like my hills?"

"There's somethin' powerful peculiar 'bout 'em," said Abner b'fore he could stop hisself.

"That there is!" said the man, with a smile. "What about you?" he asked Clay.

Clay raised an eyebrow in frustration. "Well, it sure does make for rough drivin'," he replied.

"Haha!" laughed the man in the lamplight. "I'm sure it does at that! Now what do you want with me?"

There was somethin' dangerous in the way he'd asked that question, Abner thought, as if the way they answered it might decide their fate.

"I assume you're Mr. Davy Crockett?" said Clay.

"Well, sir," said the man, restin' his hand on his hip, "that all depends."

Abner couldn't help but notice that there was a big ol' Bowie knife strapped t' the man's belt just where he'da rested his hand.

"Would you happen t' be from that there mine just 'round the bend?" asked the man.

"Nope," said Clay.

"Tax men?"

"Nope."

"Recruitin' for the cavalry or some such?"

"Nothin' quite like that, no."

"Well," said the man, "then you done found Davy Crockett, alright. Though t' be fair I go by David now. We call the boy Davy."

"I think we heard somethin' 'bout that," said Abner, "though I remember it bein' more convoluted at the time."

"God dammit!" said David, "you went an' got Jeremiah Hardy drunk didn't you? I told that sneak-thief moonshiner not t' let on t' anybody that I was up here!" He stomped 'round in the dirt a minute an' swore again. "Well there ain't no helpin' it now. I suppose you'll want 'coonskin hats or huntin' lessons or somethin' now you've found the famous Davy Crockett," he said exasperatedly. "Well, I'm retired! Closed fer business! Matter o' fact, I'm dead! Now take your infernal contraption off'a my land, an' yourselves with it, ya tourists!"

Abner was flummoxed. He hadn'a expected that sort o' reaction 'tall. Clay laughed his big barrelous laugh an' shut off the auto-carriage.

"Fact is," he said, "we weren't even lookin' for you 'til last night. I personally thought you'd been shot at the Alamo. Mr. Jenks here thought you'd been drowned crossin' the Mississippi!"

David sighed.

"I started them rumors m'self," he said. "Y'see there comes a time when a man wants t' settle down an' live the quiet life. Only, when you're so well heard of as I am there ain't no such thing as quiet 'til the grave... so I died!"

"Mighty good thinkin'," said Abner, "but why twice?"

"Too many people saw me alive while I was gettin' the family out here," said David. "I knew the local boys'd spoil my death if they knew I was alive, so I died again. Jeremiah might well be the only man alive who knows where I am, an' him only because I'm no good at makin' my own bourbon!"

"What luck that we ran into him, then," said Clay. "Some might even call it fate!"

"They might at that," said Abner.

"You're an odd couple o' fellers," said David. "What're your names an' how can you've been fated t' meet me if you didn't but start lookin' last night?"

"Where are my manners?" asked Clay. "I'm Cassius Marcellus Clay, from Lexington, Kentucky, an' this here's Abner Jenks, outt'a Arkansas. As for the rest o' it, that is a tale. Why, I'd go so far as to say that it's as good as some that I've heard about you, Mr. Crockett!"

"Maybe not quite so good as the one 'bout you tamin' that catamount," said Abner with a twinkle in his eye. "That one always was my favorite."

David smiled an easy smile at Abner. "You know I still have that lioness skin, Mr. Jenks," he said. "Come on up to the cabin an' I'll show it to ya! Then you can meet the missus an' regale us with your tale."

"Absolutely! An' you can jus' call me Abner if you like."

Abner grabbed up the pair o' haversacks from out'ta the auto-carriage quick as a wink. David smiled his easy smile again an' waved at the boys t' follow him on up the hill. Clay couldn't help but notice how much healthier Abner looked all o' a sudden.

"So you're a Crockett fan, eh?" he asked Abner under his breath, when David had got a few paces ahead.

"A fan?" asked Abner, shocked. "Well there ain't a soul alive what ain't heard o' Davy Crockett, the hero o' the Alamo. An' here he is in the flesh, an' us headin' up t' his own cabin like we was his friends!" Abner's smile was real wide an' that twinkle was still fixed in his eye. "You know how you was sayin' that you ain't yet met your match, Cassius? Well you just done so; yours an' mine an' the damn fool Borderer's t' boot!"

Clay didn't much like the sound o' that, but he kept the feelin' t' hisself on account o' how excited Abner was.

It weren't that long a walk b'fore they spied the Crockett homestead. Sure 'nough the cabin was made o' stacked-up logs, but still there weren't no sign o' where they'd been cut from. The cabin was nestled in amongst the trees an' only the little path they was walkin' along seemed cleared away 'tall.

"There's somethin' powerful peculiar 'bout these woods," said Abner, repeatin' hisself.

"That," said David, swingin' open the door t' the cabin an' usherin' the boys inside, "is the entire idea."

The light in the cabin was warm an' the color o' amber. They saw a pair o' invitin' little oil lamps sittin' on a carved round table in the middle o' the room when they entered, but not a soul was in sight. There were three little chairs 'round the table, each o' them carved just as nice as the table itself, an' a number o' cupboards lined the walls. There was a bend 'round one wall o' the room which the boys figured led t' the bedroom. It was a small cabin, but cheery an' warm. It suddenly struck the boys that it must'a turned toward evenin' already, what with how bright the lamplight shone 'round the room.

"Have a seat, boys," said David. "I'll see if there's a bit o' Jeremiah's Old Tom 'round here somewhere."

"No no, that's just fine," an' "don't put yerself out," said the boys almost in unison.

"Maybe jus' some water?" added Abner, tryin' not t' be ungrateful.

"Well, we definitely got that," said David, plunkin' three tin cups on the table an' fillin' each with a bit o' murky lookin' well water.

"What'd you mean," asked Abner, after testin' his cup an' findin' the water more'n adequate, "when you said that the peculiar nature o' this forest was 'the whole point'?"

"Well," said David, "you seem t' have heard 'bout them Northerners over the hill in their mine. Is that right?"

"Just what Jeremiah told us," said Clay. "There's a couple o' Northern boys over there who set up minin' operations, an' that they'll shoot a man on sight if you head over their way."

"That's about half true," said David. "There's more'n a couple o' 'em for starters. Maybe there used t' be less of 'em out there, but nowadays there's a right gaggle o' foremen, who you can see walkin' 'round from time t' time, an' I can't begin t' say how many slaves they got cooped up underground."

"Slaves?" asked Abner. "There ain't slaves no more, is there? Just freed men an' women."

"That may be true in the good ol' United States," said David, "but this here's Indian Territory, an' there's different rules out here. Now, truth be told I hain't seen one Indian in all the years we been out here, not a one. I seen plenty o' slaves, though. They bring 'em out t' the mine in big auto-trolleys, like the ones you see in the city, only boarded up real tight. Once them auto-trolleys get 'em t' the mines, you don't never see them folk come back out."

Abner an' Clay looked aghast. His blood poundin' in his veins, Abner stood an' slammed his fist down onto the table.

"You're tellin' me the North's workin' slaves after they done shot an' killed us for more'n four years t' free 'em in the first place? An' you..." he said, turnin' on David, "you didn't do nothin' t' stop 'em?"

"Well, now," said David, "that's two different questions. I promise I got an answer for each if you'll settle down an' hear 'em, Abner."

Abner set back down real heavy-like so as t' show his protest, but nodded his agreement just the same.

"First," said David, "I don't recall exactly when it was, but it weren't *right* after the war ended they started cartin' slave laborers into that mine. Bein' dead sometimes has its disadvantages an' not gettin' the news too quick is one of 'em. Best I can figure, though, them auto-trolleys started showin' up sometime after Lincoln got shot. Maybe the North got ornery after that. Who can say?"

"You still could'a done somethin' yerself!" said Abner. "You're

Davy Crockett, dammit!"

"Now, I was still gettin' t' that," said David, "an' you promised t' hear me out, if you recall." He said it so calm an' quiet, an' with such a steely sense about him that Abner didn't know whether t' be afeared or ashamed. "It's true that I know what's goin' on over that hill, but despite my bein' 'Davy Crockett' like you said, I remain one man an' one man only. They got dozens, all o' them armed.

"There was a time, a few months back now, that a couple o' them foremen came snoopin' 'round my cabin. They didn't look much like they were over t' borrow a cup o' sugar 'tall, so my rifle fixed 'em both up, easy enough. What d'you know but the next auto-trolley that showed up was carryin' four new foremen t' replace the two I'd shot. It was after we saw that that the missus an' I set out fixin' up the forest out here t' feel wrong t' folks too curious for their own good. We'd play a trick or two on them that still ventured on up an' we nailed hides an' meat an' bones t' the trees all 'round. Mostly that's enough t' keep out the bastards who might want t' do us harm. Now how's that explanation sit with you, Abner? What would you have done different?"

"I'da told somebody!" said Abner, still upset.

"Dead men ain't much good at that, I'm afraid," said David, sighin'. "Besides, there ain't no government out here t' tell, an' I ain't convinced that them up north don't know what's goin' on anyway."

Abner was quiet a minute, thinkin' that over.

"I got a sharecropper I ain't heard from since he went north," he said finally. "If he's one o' them that's down in that mine, I don't know what I'll do."

"I don't know what any o' us can," said Clay, pipin' up for the first time since David'd started his tale. "But now that there's more of us that know 'bout it, maybe we can figure somethin' out. If only I knew where they ran off to with my printing press!"

Another moment o' silence passed.

"I might find use for that drink after all," said Clay.

"Hear hear," said David, thumping his fist on the table in agreement. He stood from the table, pointin' absentmindedly t'ward the wall with his thumb as he headed t' the cupboard. "By the way, Abner, there's yer tamed catamount skin." Sure 'nough, nailed t' the wall hung the pelt o' a lioness, big as a man.

"Here's t' the catamount," said David, after he'da poured the drinks.

"To the catamount," repeated Abner n' Clay. It seemed a somber toast, Abner thought; but then it'd turned into a somber evenin'.

"Now," said David, "I recall askin' you boys up here t' hear your tale o' fate an' findin' me; an' far as I can tell, I've done most o' the talkin'. Now don't that just sit wrong in yer gut?"

Abner n' Clay agreed, an' began tellin' their tale, even though a bit o' the magic o' the story seemed t' have gone out in the retellin' an' on account o' their darkened moods. Abner had an especially difficult time recountin' Johnny's death. He couldn't shake the feelin' that his missin' sharecropper was down in that mine over the hill, an' that would mean that Johnny weren't the only friend he'da let down back home. They'd only got t' the point wherein the mob'd cornered 'em in the print works o' The Abolitionist, when they heard a loud set o' footsteps comin' from the bedroom.

"David Crockett!" said a woman's voice emanatin' from the corner o' the little hallway. "Why is it that I'm hearin' loud carousin' an' foul language as I'm tryin' t' put Davy t' bed?"

She appeared 'round the corner just then, an' all them boys sittin' 'round the table stopped their yammerin' an' stared. Mrs. Crockett stood there, hands on her hips, wearin nothin' but a thin, sheer nightshirt. She was a strong an' slender woman with a shock o' flaxen hair which wound in lazy twists an' curls down t'ward her breasts, which were nigh on visible through her nightshirt. She was strikin' beautiful an' Clay couldn't help hisself from oglin' her, until he saw the look o' fury in her eye. There, in them twin pools the color o' raw gold, Cassius Marcellus Clay finally did meet his match.

There was somethin' dauntless in them eyes, he reckoned: somethin' that took up mettle an' grit an' bore 'em right t'ward recklessness. The way she stood there, not carin' for the world who the men in her home were, nor botherin' t' cover herself in the slightest moved him right t' his core. All he could figure t' do was sit an' stare.

"David," she said, "you know plum well that it's Davy's bedtime, an here you are bringin' strangers over jus' the same. I trust these boys ain't from the mine?"

"Evenin' Alce!" said David. "These here are Cassius Clay an' Abner Jenks. Boys, this is my lovely wife, Alice. An' no Alce, they sure ain't from the mine, they're from Kentucky an' Arkansas respectively. I only jus' got finished tellin' 'em what the mine was all about, an' now they're tellin' me one whopper o' a tale o' their own. Pull up a chair an' hear it yerself!"

"Pleased t' meet you boys," said Alice, her tone not exactly matchin' the sentiment o' her words an' her eyes steely as ever. "We don't oft get visitors 'round these parts, 'specially 'round bedtime."

"It's the same back on my plantation," said Abner. "I beg yer pardon for the inconvenience."

"Beg yer pardon," echoed Clay numbly.

Alice's eyes softened a bit an' the unintended beginnin' o' a smile graced the corner o' her mouth.

"That's all right," she said, "but keep quiet while I..."

"Mommy?" said a small voice from behind her hip.

Alice turned 'round, revealin' a small boy 'round about the age o' five holdin' onto the corner o' her nightshirt.

"Davy, I tole you t' stay in bed!" said Alice sternly, though with a hint o' care she hadn'ta offered David an' the boys. She stooped down an' grabbed up the boy, her hair fallin' across his face as she did so. Davy giggled an' shooed her curls away as she lifted him up. "Looks like I won't be havin' the time for stories tonight, boys," she said. "The battle b'tween sleep an' wake rages on." She turned to head back toward the bedroom, every eye in the room on her as she went.

Somethin' small landed on Abner's hand. Not wishin' t' look away from Alice's figure for an instant, he brushed distracted-like at whatever it was. He got stung right quick, just between his thumb an' his trigger finger. Surprised, he yelped an' looked down at his hand. The rest o' them in the cabin looked 'round then t' see whatever it was that was the matter; all except for Clay that is, who couldn't for the life o' him take his eyes away from Alice's backside. A bee lay there dyin', its stinger still stuck in Abner's skin. He puzzled over the thing a moment.

"Isn't it a bit late for bees t' be out n' about?" asked David.

"Bees..." muttered Abner, his eyes still fixed on the dyin' insect.

"How oft d'you notice bees?"

"What's that?" asked Clay, finally wrenchin' his eyes from Alice.

"Ever since Johnny died," said Abner, "There ain't been a time I can't recall noticin' bees hangin' 'round. What's the meanin' o' a bee?"

"Maybe they think you're sweet!" said David, chucklin'.

Somethin' heavy landed with a thud in the dirt out beyond the front door. Alice's eyes went wide at the sound an' she tightened her grip 'round Davy. David an' the boys spun 'round in their seats t' face the door. The porch creaked with the weight o' somethin' big; then it creaked again. There was somethin' out beyond the door alright, somethin' with two legs. Clay stood, quiet as he could from his chair, reachin' for his gun.

"Who's there?" he bellowed.

The blade o' a tall an' wicked axe burst through the door, shatterin' the timbers t' pieces. Clay covered his face, shrinkin' back instinctively from the shards o' the door that came flyin' in at him. Abner yelled in surprise. David stood, his hand on the back o' his chair an' his eyes on the doorway. Alice took a measured step away from the door, her lip curlin' t'ward a scowl. There in the dark, the light o' the lamps fallin' across his leather hood, crouched The Borderer, big as a bear an' more. Crawlin' along the black o' his leathers was a bike o' bees o' all sorts an' sizes. He lifted his head t'ward Abner.

"Abner Jenks," he said, his dark, taut hood hummin' as he spoke, "I allowed you to keep your life when last we met. Now, my winged messengers report to me the folly of this act."

In a swift, smooth motion, The Borderer shrugged his shoulder down through the doorway an' slung his axe up from the ground in a deadly arc t'ward Abner's head. Abner flinched an' closed his eyes.

There was a crack an' a bang an' Abner's eyes popped back open. He was still livin' an' breathin' an' he didn't have a scratch on hisself, savin' o' course for the bee sting. Clay stood beside him, a smokin' gun in his hand. David stood before the two o' them, the splintered remains o' his chair in his hands an' a wild look in his eye. The Borderer was gone. Wild, bloody anger pulsed through Abner's veins; his fists shook an' he grit his teeth.

"So it's me you want?!" he yelled to the dark beyond the doorway. "Well you got me, you murderous son of a bitch!" He turned t' Clay an' put out his hand. "Gimme a gun," he said.

Clay obliged, stoopin' down t' pull a rifle from out o' a long case strapped t' his haversack. The butt o' the gun was wire-thin an' the whole o' the weapon glistened a dull green. Along the barrel were lined a spiral o' triggers, twelve in all.

"Now that there's an in-line repeater rifle," he began t' say, but Abner cut him off.

"I don't have time t' marvel at your gun collection, Clay," he said "Does it fire when I pull the trigger?"

"It does," said Clay.

"That's good enough for me," said Abner, an' at that he made for the door. A heavy hand slapped down onto his shoulder b'fore he'd gone but one step.

"Now that I've seen the feller, I figure you might like my help after all," said Clay, his gun raised in his free hand in a sort o' salute.

"Then it's decided," said David. "We're all goin' after the bastard."

Abner looked 'round, astonished at the offer, an' saw that in the time it'd taken him t' get the rifle from Clay, David had armed hisself with a tomahawk, his Bowie knife, an' a rifle o' his own. The men exchanged a smile an' a nod an' David pulled on his 'coonskin cap.

Somethin' creaked up on the roof.

"Alce," said David, turnin' t' his wife, "take Davy away an' keep him safe!" His eyes flicked over t' the catamount skin on the wall an' back t' Alice as he said it.

"But," she said, lookin' bewildered.

"No time for guesswork," said David. "I love you, an' I'll tame that wild heart all over again if I need to. Now, go!"

"But you know I can't..." she said.

"Have the boy do it!" shouted David, an' he ran out through the doorway, beckonin' the boys t' follow him.

The night was dark an' starless as Abner shot outta the cabin. Dark, dry clouds had rolled on in, makin' the forest all the more black for their presence.

"Cassius Marcellus Clay," rang The Borderer's voice from out in the night, "you have been judged a threat to the Union. For that which you would do tomorrow, you shall die today."

Clay, standin' out in the dark b'fore Abner, spun on the spot an' fired at the place where he thought the voice had come from. *Blam, blam, blam!* Three rounds went whizzin' through the air an' dug into the body o' a tree, sendin' a shower o' splintered wood fallin' t'ward the ground.

"Oh, I'm a far sight from dead yet," he shouted into the dark, "an' I'll see you along your way t' the inferno before I meet up with you there!"

A branch, weakened by Clay's gunfire, snapped an' fell t' earth. Abner spun 'round, checkin' the area where it'd fallen for signs o' The Borderer. When he looked up again, him n' Clay were alone. There weren't no sign o' The Borderer nor David neither.

"Dammit," said Clay. "Where'd Crockett run off to?"

"Shh," shushed Abner, "I can't listen for 'em through your swearin'!"

For a moment they both stood quiet as the grave, listenin' t' the dark.

"You reckon Crockett'll kill that feller like my scroll said he would?" asked Clay.

"Damn that bit o' goat's flesh if he does it without me!" said Abner. "I don't care how old an' important the fool thing is. If I don't get my vengeance, I'll have failed Johnny twice over, an' I'm not about t' do that!"

Just then, off in the forest, there was a crack o' gunfire an' a yell. It was pretty far off, further than Abner'd expected anybody t' be able t' get to so fast; but when a low bellow o' a yell followed behind the first, he knew. Him an' Clay ran for the sound like a pair o' suitors after the same sweetheart.

David pulled his tomahawk free o' the wound he'd made in The Borderer's arm, causin' the behemoth t' cry out again. It was like the sound o' a lungshot bull, cryin' inta the night. Once he had his tomahawk free, David hopped back a pace, back t'ward where he'da let drop his spent rifle. The Borderer swung his axe 'round, near catchin' David with the blade. He had a hell o' a reach, David noted, an' one swing o' that big axe was all he'd need t' kill a man.

"Davy Crockett," growled The Borderer, raisin' hisself back up t' his full ten feet. "You have removed yourself from the world of men. Your name and life need not be sacrificed to my blade. Repent and be free of this folly!"

"My name might not be on your list, Murderer," said David, "but you put your mark down on *mine* when you cut into my door. And the name's David now. If you're gonna jot it down somewhere, make sure you get it right!"

"Indeed," said The Borderer, lunging toward David with his axe.

David let the tomahawk fall from his grip an' kicked the rifle up from the dirt into his waitin' palm in one quick motion. Spinnin' 'round he brought the butt o' the gun down against The Borderer's axe, drivin' it deep into the soil. He would have t' be quick as a lark an' strong as a catamount t' keep a man like The Borderer at bay.

Secretly, David didn't quite know if he was still up t' such viscious sport, but he weren't about t' let on about it. If he was still as lucky as a jackrabbit, The Borderer'd be through before he noticed how winded David was gettin'. David had his Bowie knife in his hand the second the axe had struck ground, an' he sprang straight for The Borderer's chest with it. The giant o' a man was quicker than he looked an' landed a fist the size o' a millstone across David's hip b'fore the knife could get so close as t' scrape against his leathers. David went reelin' t' the earth, but dizzy as he was, he popped up again quick as a wink, Bowie Knife still clutched in his grip.

"You are an accomplished tracker and fighter, David Crockett," said The Borderer, "but your cause is lost this night. You cannot evade my axe forever."

"Or you minc!" shouted David, scrapin' his tomahawk up from the dirt an' loosin' it head over tail at The Borderer, catchin' him in the flank.

The Borderer bayed in pain again. He reached down an' pulled the tomahawk from his side. David was right on top o' him then, an' drove his knife into The Borderer's calf. Again the giant man called out in pain, thrashin' about so ferocious that David had t' back off a pace so as not t' get stuck.

"It is dangerous to bleed so, near as I am to the blade of my axe," The Borderer said, workin' his way up t' his feet again. "It can smell the ichor on the air and shall demand tribute soon. I assure you I am entirely unwilling to cede the cost myself."

"Shut yer damn yap!" yelled David, runnin' at The Borderer again, swingin' his rifle like a heavy club.

The blow o' David's rifle caught The Borderer off guard, glancin' off o' the side o' his head. The big man's neck wrenched to the side. He recovered right quick, though, an' swiped at David with his axe, grazin' Crockett's shoulder with the blade o' the thing.

It was the kind o' wound David'd laughed off more times in his life than he'd skinned a deer fer supper. Yet The Borderer's axe weren't no natural blade. No, not by a long shot it weren't. David's heart skipped a beat the second the blade struck, an' his lungs let out his breath in a whoosh. He recovered quick enough, but while he was forcin' the air back into his lungs an' tellin' his heart t' keep beatin' for him, David could'a swore that somethin' both impossible an' frightnin'd happened along the blade o' The Borderer's axe. The drips o' his blood that'd been carried away on the tip o' the axe'd seemed t' soak right into the blade. Not only that, but some o' the blood that should'a by all rights stayed upon his cheek'd followed along with it. None o' them droplets o' blood was visible on the blade no more. The blade itself was a different story. David would'a swore that it shone all the brighter jus' then, like the axe'd drunk up all the blood it'd sliced out'ta his cheek an grown stronger from it. He didn't like the thought o' that 'tall. Though his heart was achin' an though the wind didn't much want t' stay in his lungs, he raised up his rifle once more.

Just about then, Clay an' Abner burst out'ta the trees nearby. "There they are!" shouted Clay, an' Abner leveled his rifle at The Borderer.

David's rifle swung down toward The Borderer's head, meanin' t' deal a deadly blow, but b'fore the weapon could strike, a giant fist caught it mid-stock. The rifle snapped in two against the power o' the blow. Up swung the great big axe then, catchin' David in the gut. So powerful was the force behind that blade that it cut David near in twain, rippin' its way out though his ribcage. He fell to the ground, dead before he struck.

"No!" shouted Clay, "That can't happen!"

Abner lowered his gun, a look o' shocked disbelief on his face.

"We... we ain't got a chance against a man like that," he said. "Ain't nobody that does, not if Davy Crockett couldn't kill him."

The Borderer lowered his axe toward David's body, its blade shinin' red with his blood. Up from David's cleft belly came the red fluid. Up it ran along the blade an' along its bloodlets toward the gnarled hilt. There the blood sank an' was leeched inward t'ward the center o' the wicked thing. Somethin' akin t' a heartbeat an' concussive as a cannon blast pulsed out o' the axe an' through the trees.

"Witchcraft," said Clay. "That man ain't human, Abner. You're right, we've got no chance in this fight. Run!"

An' with that, Clay turned tail, pullin' Abner's stunned self along with him. They ran through the trees, Clay goin' full pelt. Abner, stunned an' shakin', tried his best t' keep up but lost sight o' Clay after a couple o' minutes. It didn't matter none, not really. All he knew was that he had t' keep runnin', runnin' from the man he'da tried t' kill, runnin' from his failed revenge for Johnny, runnin' from the man he'da idolized an' led t' his death.

He fell t' the ground an' lay there weepin' an' shudderin' in shame an' fear an' failure.

Clay ran fast as he could 'til he found the cabin, not believin' what he'da seen. 'How long,' he thought, 'have I held them manuscripts sacred — those bits o' goatsflesh so precious t' me as life itself? An' all for nothin'! All they amounted to was my gettin' a man killed an' widowin' the loveliest creature I ever did see. Well I'll be damned if I see her come t' any harm for my stupid sake!'

He gripped the empty doorframe an' swung hisself into the cabin. There stood Alice right where he'da seen her last. She was holdin' her son up t' the catamount skin on the wall. The boy's little hands were busy workin' at the last o' the nails that kept the skin up on the wall.

"No time!" heaved Clay, tryin' t' catch his breath. "No time for personal effects! He'll be comin' for us soon!"

Alice looked at Clay, that rough an' dangerous look in her eye again.

"Then there's no time for niceties," she said. Davy tugged hard an' the catamount skin fell t' the floor.

"Leave it!" said Clay. "Come with me. I'll pile you both into my

Petunia, my autocarriage that is, an' get us out'ta here lickety-split!"

Alice's gaze was full o' warnin' as she stooped down an' picked up the catamount skin, settin' down her son as she did so.

"You mean well, Mr. Clay," she said, "but us Crocketts can take care o' ourselves."

With that, she tugged at the knot at the shoulder o' her nightshirt an' let it fall t' the floor. Clay stood stunned. Alice was even more beautiful than he'da concieved possible. Her sleek, feminine frame stood naked before him, an' with each an' every breath she took, he found himself more drawn t' her. Her skin dimpled in the cold o' the night air.

"Alice, I don't..." he said.

"Then don't!" she said. "Run, Mr. Clay. Run while you still have a chance and don't look back!" There was somethin' dangerous in her voice again, neither threat nor command, but somethin' visceral an' wild that made him obey. He flung hisself out the door an' sped on down the path. He meant not to, but he gave the cabin one last look over his shoulder as he ran. What he saw was a great big catamount lioness springin' out'ta the cabin an' into the night. Clutched in her teeth was a child's nightshirt, an' swingin' from it was Davy Crockett.

The Borderer stood still as stone, starin' down at the ruin that had been David Crockett. His axe had drunk deep o' the man's blood an' was sated. Deep in the recesses o' his leather hood, The Borderer could not say the same. Somethin' in him had cracked an' broke right along with Crockett's ribs. His chest heaved uncontrollably. His eyes darted from his hand t' his axe an' back again. He tried t' calm his breathin' but it was no use. Slow-like somethin' long lost t' him welled up from his gut an' overcame him. From them deep, dark recesses o' his hood somethin' welled up an' fell through the air, landin' wet on David's cold cheek.

Thunder rumbled across the hills an' echoed through the trees. An' then somethin' truly remarkable happened: rain began t' fall in the South. Heavy drops o' the stuff chased each other out'ta the sky; whole herds o' 'em.

There was a flash o' light in the sky an' The Borderer was gone.

When the story was concluded, Arthur sat dumbfounded. Maggie and Morgan looked much the same. The porridge had gone cold and the fire had died, taking with it the last remnants of Kilkaenen the Unseen. One by one, they took their leave in silence, shuffling off to their waiting beds.

The first rays of daylight were creeping in under the sea-door as Arthur entered his bed chamber. The gulls were calling as he lay upon the bed, the scorch marks upon the floor a forgotten memory of the night before. Morgan tucked him in, as was her duty, and the both of them fell asleep; she under the sheepskin in her antechamber, and he in the bed of his father.

It would be many a year before Arthur would ask Merlin for another story.

Acknowledgments

The author would like to thank the following people, without who's support this book would not have been possible.

Hands of the King
Kate Chadwick
M. Patricia Chadwick
Brian Druce
Nina Druce
S. Michele McFadden

Knights of the Round
Marcia and Steve Block
Jennifer Chadwick
Zoey Holguin
Carrie O'Brien
Drew Levine
Modesta Levy-Groth
Alfonso Neavez
Scott Wallace
Richard Warren

Guests at Arthur's Table

Amparo Bernal	Gail Mangham
John Blaylock	Marion Pack
Zara Bukirin	Carlos Sanchez
Robert J Contri	Kari-Ann Skogshagen
Ric & Ellen Diesta	Sue Thomas
Molly Druce	Herb & Tamara Voss
Gil & Melinda Florano	Linda Wolf
Richard Hamel	Estelle Worden
Penny Loomer	

A NOTE ON THE AUTHOR

Colin P. Druce-McFadden currently resides in Queens, New York with his girlfriend Kate and their ridiculous cat Pigeon. He is a contributing writer for DVICE.com, the SyFy Channel's tech blog.
This is his first novel.

If you would like to follow along with Colin's creative pursuits, you can find him at:

http://themisforgottenpress.blogspot.com/

A NOTE ON THE ILLUSTRATOR

Mel Chadwick has been an artist and graphic illustrator most of his life. He has illustrated books for many different genres. After graduating college with a Bachelors Degree in fine art, he has worked both as a painter and illustrator, and continues to do so from his studio in California.

www.ingramcontent.com/pod-product-compliance
Lightning Source LLC
Chambersburg PA
CBHW020344180626
46812CB00001B/334